M000281153

Insynnium

Tim Cole

BookLocker

Copyright © 2018 Tim Cole

ISBN: 978-1-64438-358-2

All rights reserved. No part of this publication may be reproduced, stored in a retrieval system, or transmitted in any form or by any means, electronic, mechanical, recording or otherwise, without the prior written permission of the author.

Published by BookLocker.com, Inc., St. Petersburg, Florida.

Printed on acid-free paper.

The characters and events in this book are fictitious. Any similarity to real persons, living or dead, is coincidental and not intended by the author.

BookLocker.com, Inc.
2018

First Edition

For Heather

Not every truth is the better for showing its face undisguised; and often silence is the wisest thing for a man to heed.

- Pindar

Prelude

Since late autumn, 2014, the city of Brandon, Manitoba has remained puzzled by the unsolved disappearance of local businessman, Max McVista. His wife, Rachel, who claims to know nothing of her husband's whereabouts, holds out hope that Max, like the Northern Flicker, will one day return on the breeze of a changing season.

In another part of Canada, special agents assigned to Interpol flight #437 – en route from Cuba to Toronto – have never arrived at a credible explanation as to how international criminal suspect Vincent Fairentosh escaped their custody.

In popular culture, the Billboard Year-End Hot 100 Singles are still an accurate reflection of people's musical taste.

*And the mysterious substance known as **Insynnium** continues to be the sleep aid of choice for discriminating dreamers.*

Part I

Confession or Concealment

2014

-Autumn-

"It sounds like Happy, so shouldn't I be smiling?"

<10/19/14 @ 13:06>

To: r_redcalf@vmail.com
From: mmcvista73@jetmail.com
Subject: The Truth

Dear Rachel,
I don't know how to tell you what I need to tell you, so I'll just begin.

I've been keeping a secret from you; many secrets, in fact.

First of all, the root of my spontaneous skills and abilities, not to mention my overall life transformation in the past few years, have not been the result of a traumatic brain injury, but rather something much more profound and difficult to explain, like extracting light from coal, if you catch my drift.

I've been creating stories and lying to you and the boys for years now, all in an effort to avoid telling you the truth because I never thought you'd believe it.

Please don't think I'm crazy, but I've been -

"Oh shit!" said Max, as he jumped back in his chair to avoid the plummeting shower of food and beverage that was landing on him.

The girl had long toes and knocked knees, and she tripped on the back of her flip flop as she hurried past him at the crowded fast food stop. It was a pirouetting stumble that was nicely accented by the fumbling toss of her fully loaded meal tray. If he hadn't been so absorbed in his e-mail, he might have seen the mishap coming from thirty feet away.

"Oh my god! I'm so sorry; are you alright?" said the clumsy thirteen-year-old as she awkwardly dabbed at him with a napkin.

"I'm fine, it's okay, don't worry about it," he said.

In the excitement, he dropped his phone, and it was soaking up cola like a sponge. He retrieved his device from the liquid as fast as he could.

"Rhonda! What the hell? You have to watch where you're going, girl," said a visibly exasperated mother as she came to Max's aid with additional paper towels.

"I'm sorry, sir. I apologize for my daughter. I can pay for your phone if it's damaged; is it bad?"

"No, no, it's just an accident, shit happens," said Max.

But his phone was fucked, completely ruined.

He knew at a glance that nothing electronic could survive such a liberal dose of *Coke*. Salted french fries and hamburger sauce decorated the remainder of his table.

His act of contrition had been paralyzed in the wake of the girl's slip and fall. Gone was his latest attempt at the correspondence that was to set all matters straight. He felt the pride of his convictions evaporating, and his complicated explanation drifting away with his courage.

He continued to press the buttons on his phone with quiet desperation, but there was no response. The gadget and its contents had been lost to the cryogenics of corn syrup.

Suddenly, another fumbling teenager wearing the uniform of the franchise began escorting him to a clean table by a window. Soon the manager arrived and gave him complementary vouchers redeemable for hamburgers in the future; though he doubted he'd ever be back.

Fate had intervened.

His hands steadied as his panic ebbed. The cardiac restriction around his chest slowly gave way to a meager wave of euphoria.

Perhaps he had been too hasty, he told himself, or maybe 'thoughtless' was a better word for it. Had he not appreciated what was at stake? Of course he had, Rachel was his wife for god's sake, if anyone ought to believe him it should be her?

Recently, he'd been seized by a fixation to come clean with her; put all his cards on the table, so to speak. He wondered whether he could keep all the details straight in a somewhat plausible narrative.

Insynnium was at the root of everything, so naturally, he'd have to begin there.

The comas, he'd have to mention that.

And time travel; that was a big one.

He took a moment at the thought of the next person who came to mind; Duncan, he'd definitely have to tell her about Duncan, there was no way around that.

Duncan was there when it all began and he was the one who told Max to remain silent about the comas and the time travel. It was Duncan who helped Max understand that a lie could be more effective than the truth. But the truth should at least remain somewhere in sight, shouldn't it? Besides, where was his friend now?

Sometimes it occurred to Max that it was all a ridiculous joke at the hands of a capricious god.

He asked himself if he had in fact added one hundred and forty-three years to his life.

Yes, he thought, most certainly.

It was hard to believe, but it was true. By reliving his life in one-year segments - multiple times and multiple ways - he had arrived at a total existence of more than 1.8 centuries.

He also asked himself whether the very fabric of his character had been altered, and therefore his destiny?

Yes, he thought, definitely.

He'd led astonishing lives in a hundred and fifty different directions, and it was the labyrinth of the past that had landed him in the treasure of the present – the love of his wife and kids and a life with unending possibility.

It was this possibility, this promise of adding additional years to his life that led him to the West again. Not as a mountain biking aficionado or a compulsive rock climber - as he told friends and neighbors back home - but as a quiet camper... the quietest in fact; a hibernator; a narcoleptic traveler; an anomaly in the linear progression of time.

Perhaps this 'activity' he engaged in should never be revealed, not even to Rachel or the boys. The truth might be healing, but then again, it might not be, he thought. It had been ten years a lie, maybe the facts should remain locked in his skull indefinitely.

It was the third year in a row now that he'd made his anticipated trip from Manitoba to Alberta. It was a 760-mile drive across the prairies that terminated in the foothills of the Rockies, and he looked forward to every minute of it immensely.

He looked out the window toward the parking lot and saw a beat up Chevy Valiant missing a rear hubcap pull into the space next to his Land Cruiser. An overweight woman of about sixty, along with her adult son, ambled from the freshly parked car[1]. The

---

[1]#1 on the Billboard Year-End Hot 100 singles of 2014.
"Happy" by Pharrell Williams from the album Despicable Me 2: Original Motion Picture Soundtrack. Back Lot Music, 2013. The car just sat there, and Max stared at it while chewing his burger. Williams' voice was on full display. It was the song from that movie he and Rachel had seen in the summer, and basically the most unavoidable tune in the nation. He watched as the doors of the car opened and cigarette smoke billowed out. Several empty

two didn't seem to notice the peculiarity of his vehicle; and why should they, he thought. Nonetheless, he subtly resented them for their obliviousness. He studied them as they shuffled toward the entrance, and decided that their curiosity had been exchanged for a strain of malignant resignation. He wondered what it was that sometimes went wrong between mothers and sons.

The son was dressed in cargo shorts with a Pac-Man tee-shirt pulled over a middle-aged paunch, and the mother held his arm with a protective expression that informed the world no wife would ever get between her and her boy.

It would be hard to properly ask the sort of question that Max held under his breath without appearing like a meddling lunatic, but he wanted to ask this mother and son if there were years in their past they would be curious to re-live.

He wanted to know if they had a favorite age or decade, a day or a year when the tide was on their side. If they could do it all over again would they live their lives the same way or would they try something new? You know, make the same choices and eat the same

---

cans of Mountain Dew fell to the ground and rolled beneath the wheels. A small yappy dog burst to life out of nowhere and ran between the tires. Max realized the music was a product of an amplified stereo connected to a USB. The depth of the sound ricocheted to everyone in earshot, and the entire spectacle of the awkward two disembarking from the car was as captivating as any roadside attraction charging admission.

food. Would there be more love and less hate and dances with different steps? Before death, thought Max, everyone should be given a chance to explore that place in their brain where every memory became a multitude.

He recalled the journeys he'd taken back into his own life; the release from pattern and habit, the overcoming of inhibitions, the extension of experience to raw and total ends. Life was lived by the minute and the week and the year, but it was reviewed and judged in those moments that fell outside of time.

He glanced at his watch.

In an hour he'd be in Nordegg.

In two hours he'd be setting up his camp.

There was more ahead, but the drive from Brandon was almost behind him. He would continue cautiously, keeping his jeep to the right of an endless parade of yellow dashes that led like bread crumbs to the mountains. The steering column on the road weary Toyota tended to pull hard to the left, and the pull made him think of Rachel every time he grabbed a gear.

It was no longer Max's habit to get attached to things, but he definitely felt a bond to the Toyota. The first FJ he ever drove was in Margaret River during an AUE. He supposed it was his fondness for eucalyptus trees, surfboards, and *Cold Chisel* that made him partial to the particular model, an '82 diesel extended body (FJ45). He purchased the one he was driving seven years ago from an online car broker in Australia.

He had it shipped over in pieces on a freighter from Brisbane.

Those were the days when he didn't tell Rachel what he was spending his money on, how could he? The two of them had only been back together for a month, and his grocery store hadn't even turned a profit yet. But he understood her, and he knew it was easier to seek forgiveness than permission. And so one day the Toyota showed up in the driveway as nothing more than fractions of rubber and steel stuffed into a shipping container. He could read her expression the moment she laid eyes on the sea-can full of jeep parts; it was a look of bewilderment mixed with resistance, an expression that he'd come to know well.

He single-handedly assembled the delivery and gave it a beige paint job that finished it off nicely. Rachel indulged his fixation on the FJ wholeheartedly, and over the years became attached to the vehicle in her own way. Her enduring tolerance did not, however, keep her from rolling her eyes and letting out long sighs whenever he announced that he was sinking more cash into the replacement of an obsolete headlight or the repair of a worn clutch plate.

The Toyota might have been old, he told himself, but it was perfect for his protracted camping trips. He packed a ton of supplies under its canopy and secured heavier items to the roof rack. After countless miles of freeways and potholes, the FJ kept taking him places other vehicles refused to go.

A dreamcatcher hung from the rearview mirror, and the interior held the faint smell of sweetgrass and sage. It was a smoky combination that had, over time, pressed itself into the vinyl walls and penetrated the leather seats to make the spirit of his journeys more auspicious. He'd never seen Rachel smudge his truck, but he knew it was her who was caring for his soul in her quiet Cree way. The scent inside the FJ reminded him of their tipi at Indian Days.

He almost told her everything at Thanksgiving. He wanted to, but it was complicated. Although he was born in 1973, his true age wasn't on his face, it was somewhere inside, deep in the center of his being. Maybe it was his advanced internal years that accounted for it, the desire to leave certain things between the two of them unsaid.

For Max, the truth of his life had become enormous and untouchable, and it was often plagued by the nagging fear that a dark curse was on everything. At times he thought he could hear voices forbidding him from disclosing to Rachel both his use of Insynnium and its time travelling side effects; it was a voice that sounded a lot like Duncan's. But the other part of him, the part that was less superstitious, said it was only his fear whispering nonsense. He knew he owed it to Rachel to come clean with her, but where on earth would he begin? And how on earth would she understand?

Across the vigor of summer, and into the presently collapsing fall, he had ventured precipitously close to the cliff of truth; a fall from which would reveal the powerful gravity of multiple existences.

Every now and again, he would let clues slip from his tongue. Thoughts and impressions held close to his chest would drift to the floor like worn pages from a loosely bound atlas. But the unprovable subjectiveness of mind scattered maps and private dog-eared thoughts were the only evidence of the things he'd done at the edges of intoxicating places.

At a house party, just before driving west, he mentioned to a couple who'd recently returned from Machu Picchu that the most amazing thing *he* had ever witnessed was himself as an eleven-year-old child. His odd statement commenced an awkward silence, followed by the inevitable question: "McVista, what the damn hell are you going on about this time?"

Rachel and the boys, along with friends and employees, were mildly puzzled and entertained by Max's eccentric utterances. Everyone made allowances for his strange turns, however, because of his medical condition. It was a completely fictional medical condition, mind you, involving a brain injury with cognitive repercussions, but it was one he had massaged into an oddly believable truth. In any event, it was a fiction that couldn't be allowed to crumble even as random thoughts bubbled to the surface of his awareness.

His repeated experiences with Insynnium and its resultant time travel had allowed him to relive his life with enviable variation. As a result, it barely taxed his imagination to contemplate the universal appeal such an opportunity presented to the world. What person would not want to return to a time in their life - anytime of their choosing - and relive it in any way they wanted with no repercussions or consequences in the present?

Although popular but increasingly expensive, Insynnium remained the sleep aid of choice for those in need of a little magic inside the mind. It allowed its users to dream about their lives in Technicolor clarity and with chronological accuracy. And while the dreams people had under the influence of Insynnium were astounding, they were nothing, absolutely nothing, compared to what Max McVista experienced. What interested Max was not what the drug was, but what the drug could be: a substance offering an untapped portal into another dimension; a final frontier, a pseudo-immortality of sorts.

Although Max regularly experienced the full potential of Insynnium, he actually knew very little about the drug itself. He didn't know where it came from, for example, or how its infamous seeds were germinated, and he certainly had no idea how the drug was engineered to take you to different times in your life. In these respects, he knew as much or as little as anyone else.

The mechanics, the horticulture, the history of Insynnium all remained opaque to him, and it was that failure to be one hundred percent certain of the drug's immaculate design that frightened him at a fundamental level. It also accounted for the reason he hesitated to tell Rachel everything; because it tended to highlight the grim possibility that he was nothing more than irreversibly mad, a psychological evaluation that he knew Duncan had always maintained no matter what he'd said to the contrary.

The last time they spoke, Duncan was living in Riyadh and seemed apologetic and overly contrite. Perhaps it was all an act, thought Max; but what did it really matter whether Duncan believed him now? They were separate men, long gone separate ways. Still, it saddened Max to imagine Duncan clinging to life in the Middle East, having never known what lay deep in his soul.

Max had spent years plumbing the depths of Insynnium, but remained unable to share his time travel secret because of what Duncan convincingly told him about the perceptions of other people. How effective Duncan had been in his efforts to help, thought Max, not to mention his ability to harm.

Though Duncan told Max that he no longer took Insynnium, Max couldn't help but feel that Duncan was weirdly attached to the drug in some other way. He imagined Duncan's connection to Insynnium, however, to be slightly different than his own; more umbilical, more inseparable. Like a source of magic that delivered him light for the price of darkness.

It was a feeling, nothing more.

Max pushed Duncan from his mind, and his eyes came to rest on a photo of Rachel that he carried in his wallet. It was a picture taken in sepia from a vacation in the Okanogan and it looked a hundred years old. He put his wallet back in his pocket and got up to leave the restaurant.

A whirlwind of dead leaves was moving across the parking lot, and the air was dry and alive with static. The scattered gravel looked like flint, and the sky was flammable.

2014

-Autumn-

*"I can't actually say I've had lipstick on
my passport, but..."*

Duncan wore a brown fedora with black Ray-Bans. His hat and glasses were highly complimentary to the faux-beard that he glued to his chin. It was a simple but effective disguise he'd been donning variations of for the better part of two years. He stepped lightly around town and attempted to stir up minimal interest with his nocturnal movements.

He walked in from the street where he'd been peering into windows and looking down alleys with the hope of getting to know what awaited him[2]. He

---

[2]**#6** on the Billboard Year-End Hot 100 singles of 2014. **"Talk Dirty"** by Jason Derulo featuring 2 Chainz from the album *Talk Dirty*. Beluga Heights, Atlantic, 2014. The underground clubs played American stuff all night. The Cuban booty was impressive, even after months on the island. Duncan decided to leave through the back door, though. The vibe was too, how do you say, millennial; or was it millenarian? This was another generation bumping, and he was twice their age. The base and the beat predicted something was coming. Out on the avenue, in the humid licks of wind, there were uniformed boys trying to collect paychecks with their badges. He smiled and walked past

told himself it was one of two things: either the police would tighten their snare and he'd be nabbed, or their sudden interest in the backwater village would wane, and his freedom would once again return.

Manzanillo was quiet as a rule, only minor sounds; nothing like the tremendous rush of sirens and boots that moved over the roads and bridges fifty minutes earlier. There had been choppers in the air with their spotlights aimed at the ground, and bloodhounds on the trail of disappearing scents. The authorities were definitely after someone. Duncan couldn't be sure, but he swore the experience was the same one that Pierre described when French investigators closed in on him.

He unlocked the door and slowly entered his apartment. He went to the fridge and took out a premixed daiquiri and poured himself a glass. He indulgently sipped the cocktail under the dim and expiring light of the kitchen. There were a finite number of ways to encounter your fate, he thought, and be damned if he'd be taken without a drink. He felt oddly protected by the rush of rum in his veins. There was a full moon, and everything was filled with stillness, except for a distant wood chime he could faintly hear bumping in the breeze.

---

them. The real hunters were hiding in the periphery. They were identifying profiles and waiting; being clever, and piecing together clues. He felt like Robert Leon Davis, or maybe Keyser Soze, but in all truth he was probably more akin to some nameless hacker in a deserted Romanian village.

* * *

He didn't know if he had the mettle to stand up under interrogation and torture. Nor did he know, in the event that he was captured, what techniques they might use to extract the secret from his head. The only thing he knew for certain was that if they succeeded in obtaining what they were after, then Grace would perish, just as sure as the curse had predicted.

Who 'they' were, was anybody's guess: secret police, Russian mafia, big pharma henchman, the list went on. It was all because of Grace that Duncan did the things he did because, in the end, it was her that he loved more than any other. His love for her was also the reason she had no idea that he was still in Cuba. For her safety, he said that he moved to Riyadh to conduct statistical research for the Kingdom. But of course, he remained in *Manzanillo,* the same place he'd been when she visited in the winter. They met in Havana; he told her he was living there, somewhere in the San Miguel district.

Over the past decade, he had done everything he could to be free of the curse, but he knew that freedom from something so dark could only be achieved through the lightness of anonymity. The nature of what he knew required him to shroud himself in mystery and remain completely at large. After all, someone with his money and influence could've made a decision to live in regal opulence years ago. But here he was, tenaciously hiding in a solitary part of a communist-held island where no one knew his name.

For Duncan, hiding was its own way of living. His curious life had evolved special skills and talents to blend in and be immemorable. The key was to make everything spartanly plain and reliably simple, such as his appearance and his needs. The only person that ever knew his true whereabouts was Pierre. Others, including Grace and Max, were often under the impression that he was in places like Beirut or Damascus. And detectives and bounty hunters operated with the mistaken assumption that he would eventually be spotted on the streets of Bixby Knolls, Fitzroy North, or York Mills, all of which were random and completely misleading.

It wasn't exactly an accident that he landed in Cuba; it was more like bad advice. But at any rate, he soon realized he wasn't just temporarily marooned in the equatorial heat, but rather permanently fastened by some tropical weld. It could be worse, he thought, he could be fastened to Montreal or Toronto – the anti-tropics by his estimate – where he'd be forced to flee north to homes hung with icicles, suicidal Eskimos, and permafrost beaches. He had to admit, though, that at least in the cold and distinct seasons of Canada he might have found contiguous places to hide, unlike Cuba, where the inescapable water formed an infinite mote.

He wanted nothing more than to exit the island, but somewhere along the line he found himself trapped and without a soul to trust. He told himself there was nothing he could do but lay low and wait for the storm to pass. He suffered from a hurricane of thoughts as bits and pieces of his confidence blew loose.

His apartment was on the third floor of a converted hotel in a derelict part of town. The place was vented with a rum vapor breeze, and geckos covered the walls with their lizard aroma. There was a line of ants marching with weathered intention from the cramped kitchen to a mahogany bookcase with titles salvaged from a second-hand vendor. On a salty bamboo shelf between Grace's birthday card and Pierre's bottle of wine rested a manila envelope full of snapshots taken from days gone by. Duncan liked to reach into the envelope and pull out pictures at random so he could touch the exposed memories with his hands.

He looked at a photo of Max in Arcata. He decided it must have been taken in 2004 - shortly after his first coma - because he still had that weird look of obsessed panic written all over his features. As Duncan recalled, it was a look that took weeks to dissipate, if in fact it ever dissipated at all. Max's coma was so shocking it would have been impossible for anyone to forget. It rocked Duncan and Pierre back on their heels and left them dazed like punchy fighters clinging to the ropes.

And then there was the follow-up combination that nearly knocked them to the canvas as he recounted his time travel; a story that was completely outrageous, even in an outrageous world. It made Duncan uneasy to think about Max's brush with insanity. In those early days, he and Pierre had no idea what they'd unleashed or how long it would follow them.

Years had gone by, and probably more than a hundred million people, in the grip of a global fascination, had ingested Insynnium, a godsend for insomniacs and sentimentalists alike. But no one ever claimed to time travel on the shit, except Max. It was like saying that you'd witnessed the birth of India on *Ambien,* or drank tea with Genghis Khan while lounging on *Lunesta.* It was beyond improbable, and Duncan felt it called into question the stability of any mind that would entertain such a notion.

Although he and Max, in large part, had gone their separate directions, it still irritated him to know that Max maintained his obsessive ways. Max's pursuit of alternative universes was as firm and unshakable as anything Duncan had ever encountered.

It also irritated him that Max had gone back to Rachel. He tried to keep the two apart, but mistakes were made, and hearts were reunified. He wanted to soften his disdain for her, but it was a Sisyphean task. She had a history of deep subconscious awareness and a tectonic ability to psychologically fracture those of less resilient constitutions (namely Max), and Duncan resented her for it. He knew Rachel would eventually coax Max into telling her everything; it was simply a matter of time. Love did strange things to the mind, he thought. After all, it was love that led him to such an unusual existence himself.

The last time the two men spoke, Max said he was on the verge of disclosing everything to her. Duncan was certain that she was casting her extractive spells on Max's mind, pushing for a confession without appearing to be pushing for a confession. In the end, it all came down to how attached he was to his secret. For Max, giving up the goods would be like giving up an appendage. He'd held on to the fiction of his life for so many years, thought Duncan, it would be doubtful whether a confession could even set him free.

Duncan convinced Max that skeptical minds would never believe his time travel assertions. And in his heart Max knew it wasn't a believable story; he had no proof, no evidence. He knew he ran the risk of alienating Rachel and losing his boys again. Duncan told him that if he went to the media, they would paint him with an insanity brush and make him out to be a nut. If he went to the doctors there would be DSM IV categories and fuddled prescriptions for psychotropic meds that would probably lead to involuntary commitment. Duncan asked Max how easy it would be to run a business on lithium. The prospect of these many eventualities was at the core of the two men's enduring pact never to mention comas or time travel.

Duncan always held fast to Pierre's convincing diagnosis that Max's comas were the result of an allergic reaction to Insynnium. It seemed like a logical and medically competent explanation. However, in his last conversation, the professor had changed the prognosis. Pierre said that he'd anonymously posted Max the Rosetta stone to the entire time travel conundrum. But Max never mentioned receiving a delivery from Pierre, and he was definitely the sort of person who would mention such a thing. Maybe Pierre hadn't sent Max anything, thought Duncan. Maybe Pierre's words were the delusional ramblings of a man suffering under the duress of French authorities or Slovakian torturers?

The line between myth and reality had begun to blur.

The creeping bacterium of paranoia was a septic and festering issue with Duncan, and it converted every optimistic notion into a dead end of double meanings and tangled motives. He had long lived with the hard burden of keeping the secret to Insynnium hidden. It was difficult for him to imagine a time when he hadn't known such things. He tried to convince himself it was a burden that he could unyoke from by allowing the drug to recede into dormancy; however improbable that might be.

* * *

The bulb in the kitchen finally died, and he sat in the dark with another daiquiri while the moon sent a slice of light through the windowpane. A knock at the door forced him to emerge from his mildly intoxicated thoughts. He wanted the knocking to go away. He thought perhaps the callers had an incorrect address, but the pounding persisted. He decided to answer, but he knew that he should have been somewhere else, somewhere miles up a river or huddled in a mountain cabin. He remembered the revolver in his bureau and the three cartridges resting in its cylinder. He retrieved the side arm and stuffed it down the back of his trousers. He went to the door and opened it. There was a man standing in the hallway wearing khakis and a sweaty polo.

"Mr. Vincent Fairentosh?" said the man.

Duncan studied the man's unflinching features with a vexed expression. He was conscious of something, something hidden and long forgotten. The feeling was dark and vague like the rage before a murder, but soon his better senses returned, and he answered.

"I'm sorry; you must have the wrong apartment."

"Well, I'll be damned?" said the man in a not unfriendly tone, "Would you mind if we asked you a couple of questions anyway?"

The man's partner came out from among the shadows, and that's when Duncan noticed the two were wearing badges on their belts.

As he stood in the frame of the doorway, he thought of Insynnium, with its simple secret and its deadly curse; sustaining and haunting him for so long. He thought about Grace and the love that she'd given him. He thought about the great friendships of Max and Pierre, as well as the deep disappointment of Rachel. He thought of their fates intertwined through the years such as they were. Then suddenly, every thought left his head, except for the one that told him to run.

He stepped back into his apartment and slammed the door. He turned the deadbolt into the strike plate and wedged a chair under the brass knob. He climbed onto the wrought iron balcony and tossed a rope over the edge where a fire escape had once been. He slid down three floors with his hands on fire until his shoes hit the pavement; then he ran. He ran for his life through the narrow streets, and away from the cops and the dogs.

PART II

Everything Begins Somewhere

2003

-Autumn-

"What's got me looking so crazy these days?"

It had been close to a month, and she knew his voice would make her uneasy; he'd slur his words as he told her he was coming to see the boys someday soon. She found him more unsettling each time; the warped convictions of a drunkard holding onto that which should not be held onto. She knew there'd be a rough-edged argument between the two of them, doomed to end in a fight. The points at issue were both obvious and inconspicuous.

She sat on the leather sofa near the wood burner. The faint whiffs of smoke escaping its vents entered her nose and connected with a part of her that found calm in the presence of a seasonal fire. The heat from the flames was turning the cast iron a dull red and its warmth radiated to her face with a steady persistence. The '42 pot belly stove had taken the chill off the house for years, and the present night was no exception.

Hugh had been over earlier to clean the chimney and check the flue. The boys were sleeping upstairs, and she was re-reading *Selected Stories*; short fiction with titles like, *Simon's Luck* and, *The Turkey Season*.

Max's mother gave her the book when she came to visit after his father passed away. She always thought of her mother-in-law when she read Alice Munro's captivating prose; tales of Canadian woman shorn of securities and forced to be resilient, but also weak and obsequious; and oddly, she thought, there was something to that as well.

She loved Canada, and she loved living in Brandon. She often got the sense that people had trouble understanding her choice; especially friends from college who seemed to imply that it was a failure to return to your hometown after you'd had a taste of grander and more sophisticated fare. Maybe they were right. Maybe she should have gone abroad or made her life in Kitsilano or the Glebe. But the Plains were her home, and they'd been her home long before her existence was one of flesh. She could hear the wind blowing across the prairies with a sharper ear than most, and what it revealed in the rustled movements of tall grass and ripened grain was the words of the Great Spirit telling her how to breathe.

It was subtle in the blood, her attachment to Manitoba, but it lurked and coursed beneath her skin just as sure as Dauphin Lake held water. She knew Max was a person of place as well, but his fear and hopelessness had pushed him outside of their home. She was no longer sure what his commitment to her was, but she was strong in her resolve to stay put.

She thought about the fly fishing trips that she and Max once took to Atikaki Provincial Park. The two of them would lay by the bulrushes and drink from the river. It was like they were resetting their vows on those long days of sun and rain. She loved being with him among the silent eyes and nibbling preoccupations of the deer and the pheasants. It was a world the opposite of asphalt and microwaves. It was an Eden of peace and sober green.

Before the children were born, she would go cross country skiing and ice fishing, especially further north at Riding Mountain. She and Max enjoyed winter camping in those regions as well, sometimes venturing on snowmobiles to points far beyond. The hibernal elements were good for their health and vitality. It froze the noise and ambition of the modern distracted life they were supposed to be chasing. On those occasions, there was only the white reticence of nature to still the mind and keep the heart alive.

Her solitary picnic along the Assiniboine River the other day made her wonder how she and Max had gone from wild embraces in long meadow grasses or on orange speckled tundra to the sad and estranged arrangement of the present.

The cold weather was moving in, and as she had since childhood, Rachel found herself growing plump in attractive and unexpected ways; mammalian and warm. The additional layer of fat was somewhat embarrassing, but it enhanced her constitution and gave her a beautiful glow beneath every snowflake that fell. The irony of her seasonal resistance elicited hugs and compliments from folks around town who were captivated by the gravity of her wintery aura.

Her thoughts drifted to the Northern Flickers living in the old poplar behind the house, pecking out their plan to fly south. She'd watched the duo since late summer and wondered when they would finally leave. The pair seemed strained to abandon their nest in a tree soon to be bearing hard frost. She wanted the birds to go, to fly off in the final throws of fall. Someone told her that the Northern Flicker mates for life, but like so many things of late, she found it hard to believe.

She was struggling to come to terms with what Kelly told her at the hairdresser's. Kelly said she'd heard rumors that Max had been sleeping with a cheerleader over the summer. The news stung Rachel like a slap in the face. She felt her cheeks turn crimson with shame for what others in the community knew to be her life with such a philandering drunk.

She was a social worker who'd stumbled in the management of her own dismal case. Her pride made her ashamed for her weaknesses, and the weaknesses of her husband. Max had totally quit on his boys, they barely knew him at all. And he had absolutely given up on her. The boys needed their father, but his drinking made him too much of a risk for them to be left with him. She knew it broke his heart to take the boys, but sole custody was the only option. Otherwise, god only knew what would happen.

Max made attempts to see Kevin and Josh about once a fortnight, but he was notoriously unreliable because of the distance he had to cover to get there. He'd moved back to his mom's place at Nipawin. It was his choice. Rachel wanted him to remain in Brandon with her and the boys, but he wouldn't hear of it. He made it abundantly clear through his actions how tepid his valuation of her wishes were. He was lucky his mom took him in, thought Rachel; few parents would be as understanding as she. Rachel spoke with her on the phone now and again, and she sounded strong as ever, but she was certain that Max's mother had suffered much in the vortex of her son's alcoholic spiral.

Rachel could only guess what filled Max's days. Aside from visiting with his mom, fishing, and feeding the animals, she assumed that he passed listless hours imbibing tumblers of whiskey at the local tavern. When she last saw him, his skin had the hard-bitten redness of that seen among street people fighting with addictions; it was a permanent change in the living fabric that was hard to erase. He'd become malnourished and physically weak from a fundamentally alcohol diet. His once luminous blue eyes were dim as they moved with deserted interest behind prematurely gray bangs.

It was the saddest surrender of her life to watch the man she loved so intensely self-destruct. She was unable to know whether to be thankful or frustrated with her inability to see her husband's future. Although, with a little guess work she could easily surmise what was headed his way.

She knew how it started, but there was no definitive beginning, as such. From the first time she met him, he drank, but then again, so did she. They drank socially like people drink, until one day he was drinking a whole lot more. She noticed his glass of wine turn into a bottle at dinner, and he mentioned that his job was stressful. She saw his can of beer turn into three fingers of bourbon, and he said that he was worried about his brother. She tried to say something to him, but then his dad passed away and a sad comfort formed in the unending wake.

There was one event, however, more than any other, which anchored him to his unquenchable thirst: the death of Aubrey Fender.

Aubrey was a seventeen-year-old kid in his last year of high school, and he worked part time for Max at Tucker's car wash out on Veteran's Way until he was murdered in cold blood. The boy's parents told the police that their son had gone back to the car wash to retrieve a textbook he'd forgotten there the night before. He walked in on a drug deal and was shot dead.

After Aubrey died, Max became lost to the spirits.

Nobody in town, including the boy's family, ever blamed Max, but Max blamed himself. He felt he'd made a series of poor decisions that led to Aubrey's death, and Rachel could find no way to dissuade him from that position. Her brother, Darcy, was also involved in the shooting, and that, too, complicated matters in unforeseen ways.

She watched like a reluctant accomplice as Max took unbearable quantities of liquor into his already leaden soul. He was a man actively drowning himself. But sometimes it appeared to be more than guilt pulling him to the bottom of the well; he was using booze to sink other regrets as well.

Following months of inebriation and consistent unemployment, he started frequenting a run-down pub on Ninth Street that had a reputation for serving Brandon's most inveterate winos. Rachel's tolerance for her husband's behavior was near its breaking point when he unexpectedly announced that he was going to work on a drilling rig in Alberta. Though he left three sheets to the wind, she hoped he would return as the man she once knew; it was a foolish expectation. He would be gone for weeks at a time, and then arrive back in town with nothing on his mind but gambling and booze. She and the boys ended up with the remainder of his money and attention, which was bupkis.

He drank while on his way to see the boys because she could smell it on his breath. She also heard that he was driving with a suspended license. She wondered if she really needed more reasons to bring a motion before the court to have his visitations suspended. She didn't want the boys to see their father fall apart the same way she'd watched her own dad go to pieces.

And then there was Rachel's mother, Cassandra; a storm of negative influence who constantly bemoaned her daughter's domestic problems. Cassandra despised Max, and spoke so unkindly of him behind his back that her explosive vituperation often left Rachel frightened. As the responsible daughter she was forced to rub her mother's feet and give reminders about blood pressure and fragile arteries. She knew her mother would have preferred to see her married to someone like Hugh Dempsey.

The thought of Hugh made Rachel sigh.

Her good friend, Kelly, said the best way for a woman to move on was to have an affair. But Rachel rolled her eyes at her friend's suggestion. A fling, given her circumstance, was akin to going fishing in an earthquake. It was hard for her to imagine fulfilling the need for intimacy with a guy she barely knew. And although Max had made stupid choices, Rachel wasn't about to complicate matters by sleeping with a neighbor.

A few weeks back, she joined Kelly and her husband, Daryl, on a night out that featured Hugh. Was it a date? Who knew? It seemed rather ridiculous at their age, she thought. Nonetheless, the four went bowling, and Hugh was cool.[3] He was handsome like

---

[3] **#4** on the Billboard Year-End Hot 100 singles of 2003. **"Crazy in Love"** by <u>Beyoncé featuring Jay Z</u> from the album *Dangerously in Love.* Columbia, 2003. The song was infectious, thought Rachel, the R&B funk. It pushed up against the walls of the bowling alley and made everyone in the lanes want to groove; even in Brandon, where 90% of people polled were country music fans. Rachel felt the remnants of her youth swirling around inside her overweight life. Joy under layers of sadness; silk under blankets of burlap. Fugitive emotions buried by inertia. And although they were merely rolling balls at pins, Beyoncé's music made it feel like they were dancing and vibrating and playing with temptation.

a pilot crossed with a cowboy. She thought she recognized him from another time, and then suddenly she realized she did. He was no stranger. He'd grown up in Brandon and shared a seventh-grade classroom with her at P.F. Westlock Junior High. He'd studied agriculture in Winnipeg and lived there for awhile until he came back to Brandon to look after his ailing mother. He was charming and kind, but Rachel made a point to remind him that she was still a married woman.

She couldn't decide if she said something brilliant or utterly stupid on the night they got reacquainted because soon he began dropping by her house on a regular basis. She explained her situation clearly, and he told her he understood, but sometimes she wasn't so sure that he got the picture. She probably needed to be more like her mom on some occasions. Cassandra would have told him to fuck off if she didn't like his advances, no matter how innocent or mistaken they might have been. Rachel, however, seemed to feel the need to walk a socially inoffensive line. She affected a demeanor that accommodated Hugh's efforts and yet didn't lead him on, or so she liked to think.

He was mechanical and good with his hands, so the garden and the house went through some needed repairs; the sort of seasonal maintenance to which Max's neglect had brought rot. Rachel offered to pay Hugh for his work, but he wouldn't accept. She never blushed at his generosity, and she secretly enjoyed the free attention in ways she didn't care to elaborate on.

There were aspects of Hugh's patient ways that reminded her of Max at his best, and she couldn't deny that she wasn't drawn to those parts of the man that were replacing her husband's. The boys felt it too. Whenever Hugh came over, he made time for Kevin and Josh's street hockey or softball. The boys expected him to entertain their childish rules and inventions, and to those ends he did his best. Rachel appreciated the simple example that he set.

She wanted to put the brakes on her 'relationship' with him - whatever it was or might become - but the situation was strangely complicated. Soon after getting to know him again, she had a dream where he was diagnosed with Lou Gehrig's disease. She would never breathe a word about the illness that was to befall him because she never discussed with people their futures, especially if they couldn't be changed - and Hugh's clearly couldn't. So, she continued accepting his helping gestures even if they hinted at the promise of something more. Providing hope, after all, was the least she could do in light of what she'd come to know.

"So what happened between you two?" said Hugh earlier in the evening when Rachel returned to the kitchen after putting the boys to bed.

"We stopped talking, I guess," she said. "Somewhere along the way, you know, we just sort of stopped connecting with one another."

"Because of the drinking?" said Hugh.

"Yeah mostly, you can imagine how hard it is for me to see him shitfaced all the time."

"You still love him?" said Hugh.

"Wow, that's personal."

"Sorry," he said.

"I haven't given up on him if that's what you mean?" she said defensively.

She collected herself and thought about her emotions and all the strange chemical routes that they took through her system.

"Look," she said with emphasis, "I'll never not love him. I just wish I could rescue him or do something for him. I'd do anything for him if he'd just ask."

"So what are you going to do?" said Hugh. "For yourself, I mean?"

The implication of Hugh's question pointed to places that Rachel didn't care to go.

"I don't know," she replied, and then she turned her head and looked out the window and into the darkness of the coming winter.

"I'll stop by and see you when I get back from Estevan, how's that?" he said, with a big hopeful grin.

Again, she didn't care for the meaning attached to the subtext of what he was saying; she felt like she was projecting the stranded damsel persona, and she'd always hated that about women who were in situations like hers.

"That would be fine, Hugh, thanks," she replied with a gentle smile.

After he left the house, she felt like a sinner for everything she was doing, but mostly for the things that she wasn't. She distracted herself by calling Kelly to remind her of their lunch date. She made a point to thank Kelly for being kind and well intentioned. The two women made plans to go bowling again the following weekend.

Rachel braced herself against the cold emptiness that was creeping into her home and creeping into her life. She was a character in a story. A woman in a house with a stove on fire and two kiddos upstairs under the covers; she wanted to pull the blanket over her head and hide from the world, if only for an evening.

She understood the importance of who you spend your time with, because shared hours like those could never be undone or forgotten, they could only be enjoyed or regretted. Almost every other night she had a variation on the same poignant dream, a dream where she and Max were together. But not all her dreams were premonitions, and she knew this only too well. She often found herself awake in the early hours of the morning with tears on her face, mourning the loss of something that no longer existed, except as a memory.

The fire burned low as her stomach grumbled and her eyes grew heavy. She picked up the book and tried to read.

2003

-Autumn-

"I'm totally unwell, but what of it?"

It was mid-morning, and Max was at the Arrowhead Tavern with a couple of beers under his belt when the ring tone on his phone went off.

ACDC - Back in Black.

"Hello?"

The voice on the other end was instantly recognizable. The man spoke with a serpentine elegance, a velvet glove comfortably at ease with difficult conversations; unforgettable.

Six years had passed, and Duncan called Max out of nowhere.

"I have a paper to deliver for an engineering conference at the University of Saskatchewan. I don't know if you can make it over from Brandon, but if you could, I'd like to see you again."

"I'm not in Brandon anymore," said Max.

"Well, where the hell are you then? Yellowknife?" kidded Duncan.

It seemed weird, Duncan's calling. But it pleased Max in a comforting way. Listening to Duncan's voice over the phone put him in mind of their college days, and for the first time in a long time he sensed an emotion close to hope.

"I'm back at Nipawin on the farm," he said, "I'm sort of helping Mom look after the place."

"I see," said Duncan, the tone of his voice suggesting he didn't trust a word from Max's mouth, "Well, see if you can meet me in Saskatoon for the weekend," he coaxed, "They're putting me up in the Delta Bessborough on Spadina. We'll raise some hell. It'll be like old times."

There were about five seconds of silence as Max considered the offer. Rachel had sole custody of his children 350 miles from where he lived, he was currently in between jobs - to say the least - and he figured his mom could probably feed the chickens for the weekend.

"Okay, I'll be there," he said.

"Oh, and one other thing," said Duncan, "Don't tell anybody I've been in contact with you. Not Rachel, or your mom, or anyone else. I'd like to keep it just between the two of us for awhile. Is that cool?"

"Fine with me," said Max.

In college, Max told a well worn joke that Saskatchewan was so flat you could watch a dog run away for three days. He wasn't watching for stray canines, though, as he drove across the province. He was watching for the Mounties. He knew that they had an affinity for hiding their ghost cars in plain sight, and he also knew that they'd throw his ass behind bars if they caught him driving under the influence again.

He slipped into Saskatoon before dark using back roads and side streets. His precautions to avoid entanglements with the police were negated, however, when he boldly chose to park his truck downtown.

When he walked into the Delta Bessborough, he saw Duncan at the far end of the lobby charming the clothes off a curvaceous engineering student from Prince George. The ease with which he was able to spot his former college roommate irritated him in an atavistic way. It seemed a godless and unforgiving world that allowed Duncan to slip past the grapples of whatever it was that crushed the balls of lesser men.

As he approached his friend, he could almost physically observe the magnetic pull of Duncan's magical pheromones as they extracted every ounce of resistance the young lady was capable of offering. Duncan's unyielding gravitation had the woman running her hands across his shoulders and reflecting a look that shamelessly revealed the extent of her primal urges.

Fuck, he thought, as he walked up to say hello, some things never change.

Duncan turned, and a broad grin came across his face. He pulled Max close in an embrace that felt almost desperate.

"Christ, it's good to see you, man!" said Duncan, as he looked at Max with wonder. "Nancy, this is Max; Max, Nancy."

"Hey," said Max, as he was introduced to a flirtatious redhead who looked as though she were fighting to suppress an orgasm.

He couldn't remember the last time he'd spoken to a woman so physically attractive.

"We haven't seen each other in like, what, six years, eh Brother?" said Duncan.

They might have been like brothers once, thought Max, but what of it remained to be seen.

"Something like that," he said.

"Well, it's nice to meet you," said Nancy, "I imagine that the two of you have a good deal of catching up to do. Keep him out of trouble, will you, Max."

She gave Duncan a sexy pout and then bid both men adieu.

The two watched as she made her way to the elevator in a dark Versace skirt and sharp Prada heels.

Duncan turned to Max with a serious face.

"Sorry about your dad."

"Huh?" said Max.

"You called to tell me about him three years ago," said Duncan, "I just never called back. It's how I had your number in case you were wondering."

"I wasn't wondering," said Max. He needed a drink.

Duncan was candid as to why he'd tracked Max down after such a long time. He told Max that he'd had enough with the grudge and the *persona non grata*. He said he wanted Max back in his life and that he missed the connection the two men once shared. Duncan was so earnest about everything that Max feared his friend was about to tell him he'd found Jesus.

It was hard to dislike Duncan in the same way that it was hard to dislike your favorite animal. If you were a dog lover, he was a dog; if you liked cats, then he was a cat. In a manner of speaking, you could say that he carried the mark of the beast. Although logic informed you that he was the opposite of vulnerable, you still wanted to protect him in the same way you would defend a pet. You were more than yourself in his presence, as though his proximity gave you an untapped social confidence.

Initially, Max tried to resist the seductive flash of Duncan's reentry into his life. He wanted to hold onto his grievances, those simmering resentments. But it wasn't long before he was swept up in the magic of Duncan's company. The conversations were better than he expected. The slices of humor still sharp among mannerisms that could never be duplicated. The burden of bearing hard feelings began to lift and dissolve.

The two men went over the main events of their lives since they'd last seen each another. Duncan told Max that he still hadn't found Mrs. Right; which, of course, was no surprise given what Max had seen in the lobby only hours earlier. By Max's estimate though, except for women, Duncan's life had been largely consumed by academic pursuits and uninteresting vacations. It was hard for Max to fathom, but Duncan seemed to have become almost tame.

At around seven, the two went up to their room, and Duncan asked Max if he wanted to get high before they went out on the town. Max looked at Duncan with the resigned eyes of an alcoholic.

"I don't touch dope no more," he said, as he opened a can of Coors.

"That's cool," said Duncan, almost apologetically.

He put away his pipe and decided to indulge Max with a cocktail instead. After two or three rum and Coke, Duncan told Max that he looked like shit, and the two had a good laugh about that.

Max *did* inarguably look like shit.

He had a beer gut that forced him to fart whenever he pulled on his boots, and there was no doubt from outward appearances as to the maladies of his innards. There were also a number of poorly chosen tattoos that decorated his arms down to the wrists, including several he didn't remembered getting. But the worst was his wasted pasty skin so clammy to the touch. For Duncan, shaking his hand was like squeezing a fish paw. Age had not crept up on Maximilian with evasiveness; it had clobbered him over the head with its hourglass mallet.

On the other hand, Max could see that Duncan had not entirely evaded time either, as evidenced by the crow feet that were creeping at the edges of his eyes. He might have aged less dramatically than Max, but neither was immune to gravity and stress. As they sat together in Duncan's outrageously priced accommodation, something else occurred to Max: Duncan had grown heavier. Not physically heavier, but heavier in less identifiable ways, as though he'd swallowed a gold bar that now sat in his belly like a valuable ballast. It was as if Duncan had acquired stability for the price of hauling rare cargo. Max thought about this as he listened to his friend.

Later in the evening, they waded through dance clubs and half heartedly surveyed the Saskatoon night life, but the spark that once animated their youth began to wane around one, and they were asleep by two. The following morning when they emerged from the hotel, the smell of harvest was reclaiming the streets from an abuse of perfume the night before. The lifting dew left a chill, and the solid brisk air made the city sublime between sunrise and noon.

The night before, in a maze of conversations, Max had arrived at the conclusion that Duncan's visit was a catalyst of sorts; an incentive to change course. He had a focus and purpose he hadn't felt in ages – he planned to get custody of his boys back. He would approach Rachel and have her reconsider the parenting plan. Surely she would appreciate the important influence he was on Kevin and Josh. The boys needed their dad, he told himself, and he would make it a priority to support them, even if it meant going back to the greasy oil rigs for another season.

The two men were seated across from one another in a chrome plated diner. They wore the dour faces of leaders at a failed summit. Max ordered ham and eggs and smoked a cigarette while he waited for the food to arrive. Duncan had a coffee. The restaurant radio was playing Clint Black singing about becoming a better man.

Tired looking truck drivers and women accustomed to working two jobs filled the restaurant with their hot and sour sighs. Max could smell a nauseous combination of refried oil and over-used bleach products. He could not endure another minute without a drink, so he plaintively asked the waitress to pour some Bailey's into his java, and she kindly obliged.

As he sipped on his Irish-ified coffee, he studied Duncan's face. He couldn't guess exactly what it was, but there was an aspect of Duncan's presence that reminded him of the last time he'd seen Bones; a mask disguising issues that were hard to identify. Duncan's eyes suggested that he'd stared too intensely at something he wasn't fully prepared to see, and that a glimmer of whatever he'd looked at would stay with him forever.

When the waitress arrived, she leaned over and set Max's plate in front of him, but her low cleavage was obviously for Duncan's benefit as she refilled his coffee mug to overflowing. Duncan smiled and thanked her. Then he turned to Max and asked how Bones was; it felt uncanny.

Max replied that his brother was living in Colorado Springs with a wife who barely saw him. His answer floated on the air for a moment as Duncan absorbed it. But soon his countenance lightened, and for a flickering instant, he brandished a proud and mischievous look that belied a satisfaction in solving some long savored riddle. Max was at a loss.

"Your brother certainly is a piece of work," replied Duncan, as he added more cream to his coffee.

He started talking to Max about the topics they'd covered the night before. He reiterated to him the importance of psychologically distancing himself from Rachel, and attempting to get a handle on his alcohol abuse. He told Max to come down and crash with him in the Redwoods for awhile; dry out.

Max knew Duncan's offer was a good one.

He felt himself succumbing to Duncan's well-articulated suggestion that a California vacation was just what he needed. It would be more than a spa-like indulgence, he told himself; it would be an opportunity to get his life back on track. He hadn't been to the States since college when they took trips to Syracuse and Buffalo for rock concerts and hockey games. But that was years ago, and things were different now. It was a pipedream, he thought, as he steeled himself to Duncan's beguiling effort to capture his imagination.

When he mentioned to Duncan the impossibility of traveling to Arcata because of a DUI, Duncan countered, rather convincingly, that he knew a thing or two about getting around such complications. With a wink and a nod, Duncan informed him that sneaking across the border would be a cinch. Duncan liked to exert his considerable powers of persuasion and apply his charisma in ways that seemed to know no bounds.

He continued to press Max on his motives for moving back to Brandon. He asked him why on earth he would choose to freeze to death with Rachel and her icy rules when he had the opportunity to go south for acceptance and redemption. He told Max that Kevin and Josh would be fine without him, as he was of no use to them in his current condition anyway.

Max said that not everyone could be an engineering professor like Duncan, gracing former friends with their presence as they traveled to various cities delivering papers and giving scholarly lectures. He explained that, unlike Duncan, he had developed feelings for others along the way; feelings that were complicated by tragic events and tangled emotions, and that this was what compelled him to move back to Brandon.

Duncan balked at Max's pathetic rationalization for remaining drunk and said he sounded like an impaired version of Rachel. He asked Max who it was, if not her, that had pushed him into his currently unsustainable position. Max bridled at Duncan's accusations and felt reluctant to say anything about his wife's motivations.

It was no secret that Duncan disliked Rachel. Her once stubborn refusal to share prescient knowledge about his fate rendered her irredeemably selfish and emotionally disturbed in his eyes. Max never knew exactly the nature of her premonition, but whatever it was; he always felt Duncan's contempt for her was in disproportion to what she could possibly be keeping from him.

There was a time when the three of them had shared an almost sibling-like bond, but after college, it was Duncan who made the choice to leave. It now struck Max as presumptuous for Duncan to assume he could waltz back into his life and save the day. What Duncan failed to understand was that Max's deliverance lay with Rachel, and it always would[4].

Duncan could feel Max's thoughts drift to Rachel, and he abruptly decided to take a different tack.

"We had some fun trips to the farm, didn't we?" said Duncan, in a question that landed like a statement.

"Yeah, my parents loved you. Robert loved you too. Fuck, Rachel loved you. You were so goddamn funny, and you always brought the party," said Max.

"Remember when that asshole from the local garage came over while we were having that get together with your parent's friends?" said Duncan. "He called your dad a pansy yank because your dad had dodged the draft back in the day. Remember what happened next? Do you remember how funny it was? That poor bastard shit himself when he saw Bones

---

[4]**#6** on the Billboard Year-End Hot 100 singles of 2003.
"Unwell" by <u>Matchbox Twenty</u> from the album *More Than You Think You Are*. Atlantic, 2003. Another short order cook must have come on shift, thought Max, because the music suddenly changed from Country to Alt Rock over the course of the breakfast. Max put Tabasco on his eggs and listened to Rob Thomas describe his symptoms. He liked to think he could stand the high ground when it came to Rachel. He knew he'd gone out roaming but now he was ready to come home to her. He knew he was sick but it was time to get well. He'd find the appeal that would reach her heart and get him his boys back. It felt like there wasn't a longer distance in the world than the miles that stretched from where he was to the place he needed to be.

walk out from the breeze way and come down to the fire."

"Yes, I remember. That was Bones for you."

"I know your parents didn't approve of your brother's choices, but you have to admit, even they laughed hard at that one. I mean the irony. In full dress uniform, with the fucking beret and all," said Duncan, as he was overcome by a satisfying fit of laughter at recounting the memory.

"So Duncan, it's been great to see you again after so many years," redirected Max, "Your visit has been good for me. I feel like I've been able to let go of some things. It seems better between us. I hope we can stay in contact; you know what I mean? But right now I better get you over to the airport."

Max wanted to emphasize the finality of their reunion and place things back in a practical perspective, but Duncan wasn't buying it.

"You're going to see her again aren't you?" he said.

"Yeah, I am," said Max, "Your visit has reminded me about what's important."

"Which is what, exactly?" said Duncan.

"Kevin and Josh," said Max.

Duncan pressed him with a skeptical stare.

"I don't know, maybe Rachel too," he said.

"You have my email and my phone number," said Duncan, with an edge of frustration. "Think about my offer, and do something about taking your goddamn life back."

Max was looking out the window. "I know what I'm doing, Duncan, but thanks anyway," he said. His booze pickled reasoning had already moved on to other matters.

After he dropped off Duncan at the airport, he would grab a six pack and a cheese burger and head back to the farm. He'd convinced his mom he was attending a job interview for a company that had offices in Saskatoon and Red Deer. He'd tell her the interview went well and that he was hopeful.

He wouldn't mention Duncan. He'd never mention Duncan.

2004

-Spring-

"Lean back, cause this shit is bad ass."

Duncan cavalierly named it, 'the powder,' because that's what it was - powder. It had the consistency of baking flour coupled with a plutonium-like weight. Its coloring was rust, like turmeric crossed with cayenne. After the first harvest, he and Pierre marveled at the mounds of it piled high on the basement work station. Duncan thought it looked like a diorama of Tatooine. He started talking about Landspeeders and Sandpeople.

Then he thought of *Dune*.

He wanted an epic name, something suggesting the sprawl of space and the reach of stars. He thought nothing would be better than a reference to Frank Herbert's *Melange*? For a time, he was completely convinced that the powder should become known as 'the spice.' But Pierre wasn't of the same mind, he said the stuff needed a pharmaceutical sounding name, someting that would lend credibility to their discovery.

Pierre was persnickety, and he insisted on being personally in charge of reducing the seeds to powder. He employed a sturdy and venerable Cuisinart grinder to get the job done. He was painstakingly careful and scientific about each gram of powder. One afternoon, however, in distraction or haste, the lid flew off the grinder and the spice went everywhere, including all over himself.

"Fuck," he said in frustrated French.

Duncan thought it was funny. "Dude, you look like you're covered in cinnamon."

"Insinniom? What's insinniom?" The stuff was obviously in his ears.

"Not 'Insinniom,' 'in cinnamon,'" said Duncan.

They stared at each other and then began to laugh.

They tinkered with the spelling and soon the name rolled off the tongue: INSYNNIUM; aka powder or spice.

Duncan and Pierre worked on the dosage for many weeks to calibrate the stuff to an amount that would reveal its promise. It was eventually established that one capsule of powder consistently gave the user a great night's sleep. Depending on the dosage, however, the dreams would vary. One capsule, for example, would provide memorable dreams, while two capsules could push the dreamer toward more intense recollections of their past. But it was the three capsule maximum that forcefully gave the user a vivid flashback into their life.

The two men discovered that using more than three capsules within a twenty-four-hour time frame conferred no additional psychotropic benefit. They'd heard of individual's swallowing up to ten capsules in a day, but those over indulgent folks were generally found sticking a finger down their throat or pissing green, not the added effect they were searching for. It was as if the brain attained a sweet-spot with the three capsule ceiling, a sort of dream equilibrium. Users found they could easily scale back the dosage or go off the spice completely. It was commonly acknowledged that Insynnium was NOT addictive.

The powder appeared to hyper activate neurons in the frontal and occipital lobes responsible for causing extreme regression into the minutia of retained thought. It enabled users to have fantastic dreams, furnished with previously forgotten or inaccessible memories, all wrapped up in a parcel of rest and rejuvenation. A typical experience with Insynnium consisted of an individual probing, in a heightened fashion, those impressions from their past typically unavailable through ordinary mental processes. Upon ingestion of the powder, dormant areas of stored memory were reanimated in combination with all of one's accessible reflections. The whole effect produced a delicious and combustible explosion of sensory stimuli while the user slept in a deep REM state.

The only side effects from Insynnium appeared to be satisfied and chilled out individuals who were neither desperate nor dependent.

Until Max's coma, that was.

Duncan sat in Jesus' Pizza – by his reckoning, the best restaurant in Arcata[5]. He was thinking about where Insynnium might be headed, and was stumped for a clue concerning any destination at all.

The hands on the clock moved past eight.

Before Max had his coma, Duncan was only weeks away from sitting down with Mr. Enderby to discuss an intriguing business prospect. He was eager to plug his spice into Enderby's well established network of users, dealers, and promoters. It would be the distribution component of Duncan's aggressive strategy to ensure that Insynnium got expanded to the four corners of America.

Before he made another move, however, he needed to figure out why Max had reacted to the

---

[5]**#10** on the billboard Year-End Hot 100 singles of 2004. **"Lean Back"** by <u>Terror Squad featuring Fat Joe and Remy</u> from the album *True Story*. Universal Records, 2004. That was what Duncan loved about Jesus' Pizza Parlor, the Hip hop. Duncan liked it all; the soul, the R&B, the Rap, the Funk, and the What the Fuck. He was in Jesus' settled beside Monty and yelling at Jim; the typical visit. He could hear Jim exit at the back of the restaurant and go out into the night with el dente pasta and Chianti for the bums' who slept in the alley by the dumpster. Duncan's eyes were closed as he scratched at the hairball next to him. He asked himself if he'd done the right thing by bringing Max to Arcata to dry out. As soon as Terror Squad came on 105.1 Duncan suddenly thought fuck, fuck, fuck, I've lit dynamite and glued my hands to the stick. He wondered what he was thinking when he let Max try Insynnium. He decided he must have been thinking about Grace.

powder in such a bizarre fashion. Resolving Max's spice related health concerns was paramount to his ambition to push Insynnium into the mainstream. He knew that one day the spice would have its tentacles spread around the globe, and that repeat users would be users that were neither in comas nor dangling from the edge of insanity.

As he sat there in Jesus' sipping stout and eating anchovies on toast, he thought of Max, out pounding his brittle knees on a five-mile run. He couldn't help but chuckle over Max's new devotion to health and fitness. To see him so diligently improving his body was a pleasant contrast to the cringe-worthy slob who had arrived in Arcata nearly three months before.

Max started out with jogging, and then he progressed to yoga, and before long he was cooking meals for himself. Over the course of the last twenty days, however, he had intensified his health regime yet again. His additional repetitions of burpees and pull-ups - not to mention his staggering intake of kale and Quinoa - were all in an effort to precipitate another 'event.' He was under the impression that his improved conditioning and lower cholesterol would trigger another coma-like reaction to Insynnium.

Duncan frequently reminded him that a coma was no trifling matter and that the last thing he needed was a dead friend on his conscience, something Max appeared to have trouble appreciating. He informed Duncan that he would not only he wake up from his next coma - surely bound to occur - but that he would bring back evidence to prove he wasn't crazy.

What was he going to do, thought Duncan, come back in a DeLorean?

Max's story about time traveling back to his childhood seemed utterly preposterous to Duncan, and just marginally less so for Pierre. Granted, Max was in a brief and unexplained coma, but he was in Duncan's presence and under Pierre's care the entire time he was unconscious. He went nowhere. On the face of things, the claims were sad and ridiculous, but they pointed to a deeper problem that was more unsettling. Pierre mentioned to Duncan that Max was likely suffering from the delayed symptoms of a nervous breakdown; and now, perhaps due to Insynnium, a completely fractured psyche.

Duncan wondered how he would ever explain such a thing to Grace.

* * *

He had the best of intentions for Maximilian when he brought him to Arcata in the winter.

Following his visit to Saskatoon in the fall, Duncan couldn't say he was surprised when he eventually received Max's request for help. The collision course he was on seemed rather obvious to anyone who cared to notice. His naive appeal to Rachel had backfired miserably, and his last email to Duncan was nothing short of a plea for intervention.

Following the receipt of Max's existential SOS, Duncan jumped into his Gran Sport and drove all the way to Nipawin in a single sweep. Thirty-five hours after leaving Arcata he came to a coasting stop on rural Saskatchewan gravel with snowflakes collecting on the windshield. He'd explained to Max how things would go down, and Max had agreed to follow directions, no questions.

He crept the car ahead with the engine idling and the headlights beaming forward through the night. When Max came into view, he was standing at the crossroads shivering in the wind. His face had a pallor that was coterminous with death, and Duncan could see the whisper of disease sidled up beside him. Max jumped in the passenger door and immediately basked in the warmth of the Buick's heater, his only possessions were the clothes on his back along with his wallet and phone.

After a few days, they were back in Arcata.

Duncan gave Max free range around the house and showed him how to navigate the town. But it was soon apparent that Max needed to be corralled. His rye infused personality was drawing attention to Duncan and Pierre in ways the two men had trouble appreciating. It made Duncan particularly uneasy to see Max day after day in such an alcohol marooned condition. He had no self-control, and many of his social filters had simply slipped away.

Duncan also speculated that his friend's liver had to be approaching the size of a football, and likely harboring the inconspicuous yet certain probability of cirrhosis. He knew he had to get Max off the Canadian Club ASAP. So, he took him to see the only person capable of assisting in such a feat under limited time constraints; a local Nepalese hypnotist who practiced something called, 'irreversible aversion.' After two sessions of hypnosis and a touch of yak butter tea, Max's liquor consumption dwindled to a halt.

Once the addiction had been cured, Max started to reemerge, and Duncan began recognizing remnants of the guy he'd once known so well. As the days crawled into weeks, it felt like the two of them were back in Kingston again, ruminating on good weed in the ambience of a college town. Duncan brought out some old snap shots that he'd taken at a pub back in Peterborough during their second year at Queens; there was also one from a house party in Cornwall, and, of course, numerous pictures from the farm. As he reminisced with Max about road trips and missed opportunities, the topic of Insynnium came up.

The stuff was circulating freely around Humboldt County and Max had been given a handful by someone. He'd heard that the innocuous looking substance could alter everything associated with a standard dream. He'd heard that the powder stimulated memories in a fashion one could not imagine. He also heard that when users awoke they felt rested and more alive than they'd been in ages.

Max asked Duncan if this was true.

He said it was.

Max asked Duncan if he'd tried it.

He said that he had.

Duncan told Max a standard and well-fabricated story about the origins of the spice; it was imperative that Max, like everyone else, know nothing of

Duncan's involvement. It was a mercurial narrative with a shadowy cast of foreign figures involving modes of manufacturing and distribution vaguely located around the world. There were also personal intrigues and haphazard connections surrounding the drug's migration to the West Coast, or so the story went.

Duncan mentioned some truths about the drug as well. For example, he said that Insynnium became molecularly invisible when contacted by blood, therefore completely untraceable in the human system. He said that even forensic toxicologists couldn't attest to who had ingested the stuff. As the story unfolded, he and Max were as high as they could get on a rare strain of cannabis known as, 'Grand Propulsion' - a potently bred grade of marijuana that came from a basement in Chicago.

Although Max's curiosity about Insynnium had been peaked, Duncan remained ambivalent about his friend trying the stuff. In the end, it was a discussion with Pierre that convinced him to let Max give it a go. Pierre thought that Insynnium might assist Max in working out his unconscious entanglements with the past and clarifying his future. It didn't seem unreasonable or irresponsible for them to encourage Max to swallow a capsule or two. By the looks of the bags under his eyes, thought Duncan, a deep and restorative rest was something that Max, at the very least, could certainly do with.

His first encounter with Insynnium left him floored. Like others before him, Max couldn't believe what he'd seen, not to mention the mental and physical restoration he felt afterward. Following his first two ingestions of the drug, he became visibly changed. His eyes became brighter, and his hair became lighter, and he spoke enthusiastically about the clarity of his regressions and the astonishing relaxation of his sleep. Duncan smiled at his exuberance; he too, had learned long ago the value of a good nights rest.

On March 1, 2004, Max took three capsules of Insynnium and quickly went to sleep. Duncan and Pierre paid little attention to the swiftness and depth of his slumber; they simply left him to rest peacefully in Aloysius's old quarters, a spacious bedroom at the back of the house that was slowly, and by default, becoming Max's.

In the morning, when he failed to show up for breakfast, Duncan went to check on him. When he saw Max lying morbidly still under the comforter, the ghastly thought occurred that his friend was dead. He moved in close and placed the back of his hand against Max's skin; it was tacky and pasty and matte-finish white, but still warm. He grabbed Max by his shoulders and shook him, but it was like seizing the attention of an incubating jellyfish. He shouted his name, but there was no sign of response. He grabbed his wrists and listened, and that's when he felt the diminished pulse of hibernating vitality. Though Max's breath was faint to the point of extinguishing, he was still alive.

At Duncan's request, Pierre, a medical doctor by training, came back to the house from his offices at the university. Together the two men observed and languished over Max the entire day. On more than one occasion the two considered taking him to the Mad River clinic for care; but care for what, they asked themselves, overdosing on an untraceable drug they secretly planned to interface with the U.S. population?

It was medically clear to Pierre that Max had fallen into a coma, and that he was absolutely un-revivable. After twenty-four hours of indecision and nervous anxiety, Duncan finally made the choice to load Max into his car and deliver him to the hospital. The plan was to quietly dump him at the emergency entrance and let the doctors on shift worry about his prognosis.

As the two men carried him by his arms and legs over the threshold of the house, he began to groan and wrestle with their grapple. They plunked him on the sofa and watched with avid fixation as he reanimated. His face was the picture of someone in utter confusion, while at the same time pressed with a Vesuvius-like need to speak. He manically attempted to describe the nature of the dream from which he'd just awoken, but his mind was finding it spectacularly difficult to square matters of space and time.

He said that he'd been living in Nipawin for a year when he was eleven.

Not a single user of Insynnium had ever been knocked out like Max. He'd slept death-style for twenty-four hours, and then awoke groggy and confused, with a story to rival *McFly's*. He had an enormous amount of concern that every detail of his life be the same as it was when he'd fallen asleep. He looked like a man who'd been held in solitary confinement for a cruel and unusual length of time. He adamantly questioned Duncan and Pierre about the events of the past year and the health of his children and the state of the union and so on and so forth. It took almost three hours to settle him down.

"Come on Max, pull it together, you haven't altered time or changed anything here in the present. You've been in a coma for twenty-four hours, and that's significant, but you haven't gone anywhere, I can assure you of that," said Duncan.

"But I felt like I time travelled," said Max, "No, damn it, I know I time travelled. I was living on the farm just as sure as I'm sitting here right now."

His agitated and confused sensibilities were only made worse by Duncan's grinning failure to take the claims seriously. Although, in actual fairness, it was raw nerves rather than disbelieving humor that accounted for Duncan's giddy disposition - mostly the product of the relief he was experiencing at Max's physical revival.

"So nobody else has had this happen with Insynnium?" said Max.

"If they have, I've never heard of it. I mean, I don't know much about the drug," lied Duncan, "But I've spoken with a lot of people about it, you know, trying to understand it more, and no one has ever mentioned a reaction like this."

"Maybe you're confusing dream intensity with time travel, no?" said Pierre, well aware that the question was a mistake long before it breached his lips.

"Look, Professor, I know it's impossible for you to grasp, but I was in 1984 for a long fucking time," said Max in a heated voice that was running at a frenetic pace. "It was an entire year, and it was just as real as I'm talking to you two assholes right now."

Duncan knew that Max was still fragile from his bouts of dipsomania and the abandonment of his children, and so he asked himself if he should've known better than to encourage him to try Insynnium. Pierre, on the other hand, showed less responsibility. He reminded Duncan about individuals with problems far worse than Max and how the spice had undoubly helped them. There were war wounded vets, drug addicts, and hyperstressed professors trying to halt their decaying minds and they'd been eating the spice like Jolly Ranchers at a Canada Day parade. Pierre said there was no way they could have predicted Max would suffer such unforeseeable complications in relation to the spice.

Following his recuperation from the coma, it slowly became evident that Max was mulling over novel and fantastic possibilities in his head, and so it was that he informed Duncan about his desire to try the spice again.

A panic gripped Duncan's chest, and his initial inclination was to discourage Max from taking more Insynnium. The idea also floated through his head to give Max a placebo as a way of indirectly denying another coma. But who was he fooling? The spice had already been released into public circulation. If Max actively wanted to get his hands on the stuff, he would do it, regardless of Duncan's attempts to get around it. So the choice was made to let him try it again, but at the house, as it was preferable to an alley or the backseat of a junkyard car. There would also be some specific and formal controls to try and figure out what was going on.

* * *

Outside, the day was growing dim, and the street lamps were beginning to scatter their artificial light. Duncan shouted at Jim in the back of the restaurant to let him know he was leaving as he pushed through the door and walked out into the night. He knew by the time he reached the house that Pierre would have Max wired up for another attempt at a comatose state. It made him sick to his stomach to think about it.

Pierre got Max's permission to hook him up to a brainwave device, as well as other pieces of sleep assessment equipment. He told Max that the monitors were in place in case of another coma and for the purposes of learning whether he was inflicting irreparable harm on his brain. Unfortunately, the scientific atmosphere of the entire investigation gave Max the dubious impression that they were legitimizing his time travel account. Feeling vindicated, though, Max agreed to keep everything on the Q.T.

Pierre was confident that the time traveling claims were nothing more than Max's overactive imagination in combination with the mind blowing clarity of the drug's regressive sequences. Both he and Duncan were troubled, however, by Max's bizarre coma. They asked themselves what would cause such an extended period of unconsciousness. Everyone else who'd taken Insynnium was arouse-able with a good shake. Max, on the other hand, could not be retrieved from the depths of his sleep by any means.

And he wasn't reacting normally to Insynnium in other ways, either. For example, twenty days had passed, and he was still showing no susceptibility to the spice. He had been taking three capsules every night, but nothing was happening, and Duncan had no decent answers. When he grew restless and agitated, Duncan began appeasing his friend's impatience by inventing facts.

Duncan told him that he needed to prioritize exercise, particularly running, and eat plenty of leafy green vegetables, as this was a method known to enhance the effects of Insynnium. It was all lies, of course, but Duncan was banking on the chance that Max's improved blood pressure and hyper-oxygenated existence would naturally straighten out his mind and put an end to the entire affair.

He took heart in the possibility that Max might never again suffer from a coma while using Insynnium. It would be an outcome in the best interests of everyone, especially Duncan, who needed to put the unfortunate chapter behind him and refocus his entrepreneurial ambitions on the spice – a substance that seemed to have an expansion plan of its own.

1984

AUE

"I roll with the punches to feel what's real, and I jump"

It had been two hundred and forty days, and Max was still caught off guard by the sound of his voice, his diminutive hands, and the unnerving duration of the drug's effect. Every day he wanted to believe that Insynnium was diminishing in his system, molecule by molecule he imagined it evaporating from his blood stream – it was the only thought that brought him hope in a world where much else left him with a sense of dread.

He was sitting on a milking stool in the hay loft of the hip-roofed barn. He fiddled with a Rubik's Cube in the diminishing daylight, but the running colors of the three-dimensional puzzle couldn't effectively distract him, no matter how hard he tried to get his head around its logic.

When he arrived at the farm in 1984, he was startled and captivated on a scale he could never have imagined. At first, he wondered how long he could contain himself before he began blurting out random pieces of information that lied far in the future. How long until he started telling childhood friends detailed stories about the coming decades. He planned to shock everyone with ideas and explanations that used articulate sentences improbably contained within the mind of a child. But none of these things happened, exactly. In fact, he said very little about anything. He often climbed into the cavernous loft to sit among the cats and the pigeons. It was a challenge to stay calm in the face of the central question to which his existence had been distilled - the question as to whether he would ever wake up.

He found himself paralyzed between acting too radically on one hand, and fear of not acting radically enough on the other. He was convinced that his predicament was an example of any number of time travel movies he'd seen; scenarios where changing past events completely altered the future in terrible and unforeseen ways. In point of fact, he spent most of his hours anxious and paranoid about the possible damage he'd already inflicted on a future for which those around him had little conception.

* * *

Nine months ago, he awoke in the house of his childhood and became instantly aware that the flesh he embodied was no longer that of a thirty-one-year-old man, but rather that of a young boy, his previous self. His brain shorted out on several circuits from the unbelievable reality of what he was observing.

And what he observed that first morning, as he rolled out of bed with trepid anticipation, was overwhelming evidence of a former life faithfully reacquired down to the minutiae. He was instantly convinced that the effects of Insynnium had been woefully understated. He'd tried the drug before at a lower dose, but the three capsules he swallowed were obviously a threshold of sorts; and to be fair, Duncan had told him as much. But neither Duncan nor Pierre had mentioned time travel or the possibility of finding oneself at the theoretical limits of quantum mechanics.

He did not even try to achieve emotional composure as he ran to the bathroom to relieve himself. His small, nimble fingers fumbled with his tiny penis, but soon he was laughing as he whizzed, and marveling at his reacquired proportions. He was a prepubescent child still un-oppressed by the curses of the glands. He finished releasing his stream into the toilet and eyeballed the rest of his exposed flesh.

In the light of the bathroom, under the revealing incandescence of several stark bulbs, he gazed upon himself with the attention of a dermatologist. He ran his hands over the goose bumps on his arms and marveled at the quality of his skin surface, so lean and clear. He was overcome by his hairless, whiskerless, tattoo-less appearance. He smelled the palms of his hands and stuck his nose into his armpit. Not a single pore had yet been corrupted by the sourness of adolescence. He felt empty of weight and full of springing vitality. In almost every conceivable way he was reminded of the extent to which he'd forgotten himself.

When he looked into the moist and tooth particulate speckled mirror above the sink, his mind began racing down alternating tracks between dumbfounded amazement and heart arresting panic. He was totally seized by the extent and influence of the mind altering spice that he'd ingested. His eyes reflected back at him with a clear and contact-less acuity, despite the pasty glimmer of nausea he could feel flickering in his stomach.

He was startled out of his looking-glass trance when his father's voice began shouting through the bathroom door.

"For Christ sakes, Max, hurry up, you're going to miss the bus," said Glenn.

Glenn had a strident and unflappable manner, but his words were often stained at their fringes, as though his syllables were at risk of crumbling from the unpredictable weight of raising two boys.

His dad's voice, so long unheard, reverberated in Max's ears and caused him to almost unhinge the door as he tore it open. He peered deep and directly into his father's eyes with a look of fascination and disbelief.

"Jesus, Max, easy with the door," said Glenn, "Is everything okay, are you alright?"

His father's frustration morphed into puzzlement, and then into a look of mild concern.

"Yeah I'm fine, Dad," replied Max, through a wonderstruck falsetto that he momentarily confused with that of a preteen girl speaking on his behalf.

But Max was far from fine, and even a further distance from okay. He was wholly overwhelmed by his transformed existence and the reality co-opting effects of whatever he'd swallowed moments earlier.

His entire sense of linear time had collapsed and folded back on itself in ways that he couldn't competently assimilate.

The chance to see his father again was so exquisite and magical that he simply grabbed his dad around the waist and hugged him for all he was worth. His face pushed into his father's belly and he could sense paternal warmth go into his core. Max had, on occasion, half-religiously contemplated a reunion with his dad in the afterlife, but no quantity of imagination or abundance of belief could account for the present phenomenon. As he allowed his father's energy to enfold him, he felt himself become a small dependent child again. Tears welled in his eyes, and he asked himself how it was that he had entered such a destabilizing vortex.

His eyes had played tricks on him before, and he was aware that his vision could be fooled by the convincing drug. But it was his sense of smell that effectively extinguished all doubt about where in fact he was. The air he inhaled held the unmistakable sandalwood scent of his father, the caffeinated aroma of percolating Folgers, and the olfactory residue of his mom's incense that hid behind paintings and circulated under upholstery.

The McVista house was alive and irresistibly tactile. In many ways, it seemed to Max that his entire life had been a dream, and it was only now that he was finally awake. He felt the reassuring pressure of his father's hands as they rested on his back offering comfort to a rapid pulse. He thought about the weight of a parent's touch and the small unacknowledged moments of youth that evaporate from memory.

He let go of his dad in a childish squirm, and with discombobulated senses ran to his bedroom to seize hold of his faculties in a weak and dysfunctional grasp. He leaned his back against the door and wondered how long the day would last.

"Come get your eggs, Max, they're getting cold," said his mom, in a voice that was soft and fresh, and not yet injured by loss.

He bounded down the stairs wearing a miniature collared shirt and a sweater that he couldn't believe reached his wrists. His jeans were of an equally diminished size, hand-me-down raiments from neighbor families who stored their cotton and denim in closets with mothballs.

He entered the kitchen and found the place stoked with wood heat and a kettle whistling on the range. When his mother emerged from the pantry, he was unprepared for the impact of her presence. Although he'd eaten dinner with her on the night he vanished, it had been ages since he'd looked upon her in such a state of youth. Her beauty was unstressed, and her face was wide with kindness. He felt several emotions teetering precariously all at once, and his eyes began to fill with tears again.

"Your dad says you're upset, what's going on?"

"It's nothing, Mom. I'll be fine."

He could tell that she didn't believe him.

He sat at the kitchen table – aged oak under varnish with knots like bull's-eyes – and tried to mentally arrest his slide into the oblivion of yesteryear. His entire sensorium was completely tweaked by the inexorable thrust of his new dimension which came at him with the startling declivity of an avalanche.

"Max, grab your shit and let's go!" commanded Robert, as he recklessly wound through the kitchen.

"Bones, please, the language. You're brother's not feeling well," said Grace, as Robert disappeared into the boot-room.

"I'm just saying, if we don't move our asses, Jake's gonna lay on the horn and make us look like a couple of dorks," shouted Robert, as he rummaged for something in the breezeway.

He soon returned to the kitchen and approached the table. He brought his face close to Max's and gave him a silent appraisal; it was a swift assessment, but enough for him to gain assurance that whatever was bothering his brother would soon pass.

"Let's go, Bro," he said in a whispered and convincing tone.

The two boys sprinted down the driveway to the gravel road just as a mud encrusted yellow bus pulled up in the spring slush. Max's heart was pounding in his throat, but his weightless legs could have carried him across the Serengeti. He wanted to scream at the highest ranges of his breath in an attempt to wake himself up, but he intuitively knew that any outburst would be futile and that there was no easy exit from the abyss he'd fallen into.

The retro-slang banter on the school bus would have been comical for anyone, but for Max - as an adult camouflaged in the body of a child - the effect was particularly profound. He sat silently for a few moments with a stupid grin smeared across his face, afraid to open his mouth for fear of revealing his true age or speaking in a baritone grumble.

It didn't take long, however, for his childhood friend, Keith, to start pumping him for information and soliciting opinions regarding matters of which he retained only the dimmest recollection. Keith wanted to know which movie they'd recently seen together was better: *The Karate Kid* or *Ghostbusters*. What about sneaking into *Beverly Hills Cop* or maybe *A Nightmare on Elm Street*? Did he watch *The Fall Guy* last night? Had he heard about the new joystick for the *Commodore 64*? Max had no choice; he soon found himself answering with a meager supply of faded factoids. He found the courage to embrace his renewed youth and began contributing to the highs and lows of the multiple conversations seamlessly taking place as the bus made its way into town in a series of stops and starts.

It wasn't long before he found himself adrift in a sea-sickening classroom. His cramped wooden desk, defaced by generations of vandalizing sixth graders, floated underneath him like a miniature galleon encrusted with barnacles of chewing gum. The sounds and sensations of Crestview Elementary became fatally real as waves of arithmetic handouts floated through the room like flotsam and jetsam.

Mr. McFadden surveyed the class with the ridiculous absent minded gaze of a man high on his own thoughts. Max's adult mind was given to understand that the teacher was probably contemplating whether to plant barley or oats in his fallow fields, rather than the correct positioning of any particular student's decimal point.

Max wondered what the amassment of hours or the passing of time in 1984 now represented in 2004 as he continued to mull over the morning's events bouncing around in his head.

"Staring out the window will not bring recess any faster, Mr. McVista. What is it you're working on, anyway?"

McFadden walked up to Max's desk and looked down with an appalled expression at the lack of academic diligence. Max had managed to convert very few fractions into anything other than doodles. He was mostly just staring at his classmates and the budding trees at the edges of the playground.

"Very disappointing, Maximilian; you need to get through these fractions by recess, or you'll be remaining inside. Do you understand what you're doing?" prodded the one part pedagogue, two part farmer, with only a passing concern for Max's scholastic promise.

"Yes," replied Max.

He wanted to be the class smart ass and crack wise on it all. Mentally he was almost the same age as his teacher, so who was McFadden to tell him what to do? The emotional toll of the drug, however, continued to absorb every ounce of his oxygen. The situation was not unlike being trapped beneath a barbell, and he failed to exert anything other than acquiescence to the teacher's pressing authority.

His timid reticence, however, wasn't to last long. After a fortnight of adjustments to his astronomically altered circumstances, he began taking small and vane delights in his time advantaged position. He soon landed squarely in the principal's office for supplying his male classmates' with *Ludacris* gangsta talk and a hip-hop vernacular that spread like measles in the boy's room. He also took historical liberty by editorializing on a mundane lesson in current affairs class.

The social studies teacher, Mr. Kellogg, was discussing the arms buildup and the specter of nuclear annihilation in a lesson designed to help understand news coverage. Students were offering ideas and comments to spark discussion, but the opinions were tepid and mind numbingly jejune. Max attempted to enliven the situation by stating that Reagan was a war monger who would outspend the Soviet Union on medium and long range intercontinental ballistic missiles. He added that by 1989 the Berlin wall would be crumbling under the sledgehammers of bankrupt East Germans. He used the words, 'Perestroika,' 'Glasnost,' and 'Gorbachev,' all in one elaborate sentence. He also took a certain relish in belittling the fickle theory of trickle down economics.

Mr. Kellogg, a member of the Saskatchewan Progressive Conservative Party, responded that Max's contribution to the Cold War debate had been speculative at best and plain 'asinine' at worst – a word that's vague definition among his classmates precipitated resounding laughter. Max's attempt to be mentally impressive came off rather weak. His expansive rhetorical ambitions shriveled as he confronted the incomprehensible distance between himself and the other eleven-year-old children who now considered him freakishly disabled thanks to his precocious insights and over-the-top political ramblings.

He became acutely sensitive to the delicate time trap he was mired in. He changed his free wheeling stance and converted to the cautious discipline of following a behavioral pattern that was consistent with his original life script. Even innocuous references to minor events, he theorized, could place him in dire risk of altering the fragile space/ time continuum – and Robert Zemeckis hadn't even released *Back to the Future* yet.

He had no idea what dimension he'd entered, or if he'd ever escape from the hole he'd fallen into, but he knew he'd never be able to forgive himself if he re-emerged in 2004 and found it even more fucked up than the version he'd left, all on account of his unwillingness to take precaution with the words that came out of his mouth. He was convinced there had to be a Chinese proverb forbidding such a cosmic faux pas.

In addition to all this, Max began to feel distinctly uncomfortable when his adult mind concluded that there was no angle or lighting arrangement from which his mother did not look blazingly attractive. He wondered how it was that he hadn't noticed this before. He also thought about how his life might have been different had he received slightly more of his mother's genetic material. Not that his father was any slouch, but his mom was in a category separate from most others.

"What's for dinner?" said Glenn.

"Max helped me make samosas and red lentil masala with spinach," said Grace. "Isn't that impressive?"

It was a simple Indian dish, but it spoke volumes about Grace's culinary dexterity and indelible curiosity. She started making the spicy entrées after taking a cooking class focused on Central Asian cuisine.

The course was taught by a husband and wife; Sikh refugees that the Canadian government had resettled in Nipawin as part of a visa requirement to assimilate displaced persons. Apparently, the Department of Immigration thought it would be 'multicultural' to stick an Amritsar family in the middle of a town noted for its Northern Pike Festival.

The man wore a turban, and in those years, that was as memorable as anything that ever came to those parts. The couple opened a marvelous restaurant that over a short period of time ended up being frequented by most of the locals. The acquisition of the Punjabi taste proved remarkably tenacious; so much so, that a cooking class was organized at the local Knights of Columbus hall where it gained rapid popularity.

"I made the papadams and the peppermint sauce," said Max.

Grace and Glenn looked proudly at their son.

He could see that his true age and unbounded dimensions were as hidden from his parents as the concept of mitochondria from a cow.

He fumbled his way around the messy kitchen, passing his mom sifters and spatulas as she fussed over the curry leaves and the ghee. He asked her questions to which he faintly remembered the answers from years before, but each reply she offered was now magnified into a breathtaking sweep of understanding.

He was particularly captivated by the poignancy of magnificent memories grown dim, such as the rumpus room volatility of his father's almost pathological enthusiasm for the Edmonton Oilers during NHL playoffs. Goals and, more importantly, near goals, caused his father to leap off the Chesterfield with fan inspired agility as balletic as a Gretzky replay. Being a part of such relived moments made him feel that his innocence had been handed back to him and his sense of wonder restored.

Sadly, however, moments of such regressive childhood purity were rare. It was more often the case that he found his thirty-one year-old brain aching with the knowledge of events that hadn't taken place yet. It was distressing to know the lives and fates of the children that he chased around the playground, lives and fates he had been gratefully ignorant of the first time through.

There was a girl called, 'Fat Louise.' A child picked on because of her clumsy weight and poorly fitted clothes. A girl whose struggles were not illuminated by the light of facts until later in life: a cruelly abused orphan, a foster child, a victim of accidental disfigurement at the hands of a careless guardian. Her limping shuffle and early death made it difficult for Max to make eye contact when they passed in the hallway or stood next to one another by the school's rusting swing set. It pained him to understand the anguish that filled her days, while his - even on a second tour - moved ahead in a fortunate and comfortable rhythm. He wasn't a child in truth, and he hated himself for his lack of courage every time he saw her standing alone in her troubled solitude.

Knowing the present conditions and ultimate eventualities of the children that surrounded him was crippling. Some of their fates had already played out by 2004. It was less than a year ago that he attended Teddy Rigby's funeral, and he thought about that as he watched Teddy running with the others. And then there was Margaret Duchamp, who lost two of her children in a trailer fire; the list went on - divorces, brain injuries, cancer, you name it. There was also happiness for many, but that remained harder to appreciate among the tragedies.

Not only was Max emotionally unprepared for time travel, but his lagging physical development took a toll as well. He had never learned how to fight or mastered a rudimentary technique of self-defense in his life. But in spite of this, his adult mind told him that he could easily kick the ass of any little coeval he pleased. To his chagrin, though, he discovered many of them to be as tough as stevedores in a Boston Harbor brawl, and he was reluctantly forced to come to terms with an unsettling new relativity about his size and his competency in a fight.

In May, a chain link fence was erected between the high school and Crestview Elementary in a dubious attempt to keep the younger children from entering the 'sphere of influence and intimidation' that the older grades presented. It seemed to Max that the school board was trying to achieve the unachievable. And of course, he was proven correct on more occasions than staff cared to admit.

Older boys would inevitably scale the fence and torment the younger ones. Generally, this consisted of a gang of Neanderthal bullies slinging threats at the timid and the meek with the sadistic intent of scaring them out of their britches. Other times, student contact would be displayed through greater physical aggression, such as a spontaneous and lopsided sports competition in which the smaller and less hormonally endowed would be flattened. Once in a while, however, the interactions would be decidedly pugilisitc and manifest themselves in an outright fist fight. But, for this, Max had a protector.

Robert was a head banger. He wore a faded denim vest over a black leather jacket, and even in the winter he pulled on *Black Sabbath* and *Iron Maiden* t-shirts.

He tucked his acid wash jeans into his Reebok high tops and sported a mullet and a wallet chain.

During recesses and lunch hours, Robert and his buddies smoked cigarettes behind the skate shack.[6] Max knew that they toked on weed and drank Old Milwaukee out there as well. But sensitive information like that always remained encased in the walls of his skull in an attempt to be a part of Robert's dangerous and brazen fraternity.

Though Robert never made a show of it, he was always looking out for his little brother.

One day at recess, when the usual remedial suspects from Hope-La-Rouge High School came over the fence and began confronting Max and his friends with their atavistic displays, Max took exception to their threats and fired back a caustic and biting put down.

---

[6] **#6** on the Billboard Year-End Hot 100 singles of 1984. **"Jump"** by <u>Van Halen</u> from the album *1984*. Warner Bros, 1983. For Max this was Robert's song because his brother's life seemed to be in its wake. Bones was a rural cut version of Diamond Dave, especially the karate kicks and the high flair, even if his hair was all Eddie's. The song roared against the backdrop of every day, over played on ghetto blasters and radio stations from Prince Rupert to Swift Current. Robert was a boy again and Max saw his brother just as he remembered him, before the house of pain, before grenades and serrated blades, before close quarter executions, before the life of the quiet professional. His brother was still mischievous and free, and not yet the dark figure trading arms along the Somalian shore, stamped with the lasting imprint of war.

A thirty-one-year-old man could be counted on to send some pretty humiliating invective in the direction of a grade ten bully. The boys all laughed, including the ones accompanying the ringleader. But Max knew the fleeting seconds between the levity of his bold comments and the physical reply were merely a pyrrhic victory. He received a vicious blow to his solar plexus, a blow that came with such force that it dropped him to the patches on his knees.

Robert saw the punch, and ran over from the skate shack like some drill sergeant with a big can of whoop-ass. He was thirteen, and most of the bullies were at least two years his senior. The only thing Robert did better than throw a punch, however, was take one. He fought vigorously with the older boys, and he came out on top.

It wasn't pretty; it was repetitive blunt force trauma. It was bruised meat, swollen lips, and bitten knuckles. It was skeletal damage that showed up as marks on the forehead and dents under the eyes. There wasn't much blood but there were plenty of injuries lurking under shirts and in the crotches of pants, and aches that would last for days. The older boys were physically hurt, and though it went unspoken, everyone knew they wouldn't return. There might be other boys, on other days, but not these ones, they were finished, schooled.

Max felt pride, even as a man, when he and his friends, along with Robert and his, walked across the playfield and back into the school. Max entered his classroom victorious, but not before glancing across the hall to see Bones go into the boy's room to scrub congealed blood from under his fingernails and clean the scratches along his neck. Bones was strong and flexible like barbed wire, a reminder that he could be stretched but shouldn't be tangled with. He possessed precious metal properties like density and impenetrability, and these weighty qualities often rubbed hard against the resistance of others; like a Spanish American milled dollar rolling around with plastic casino poker chips. Max could see once again, in Robert's lunging movements toward teen-hood, the wild and feral tendencies that would make his brother a legend in their hometown.

Robert's friends and most everyone else eventually referred to him as, 'Bones.' The exact derivation of the moniker always eluded Max, but from the first time he saw his brother in a fist fight he realized that Robert's nickname had an association with destruction at its core. That's what Bones did; he destroyed other boys, and then later in life, men. In a scrap or a brawl, and most certainly in a battle, he reduced his opponents to bones, to ashes, to dust. Everyone respected and liked him, and not just because he was tough as fuck. He seemed to be moving towards something larger than life, and his movement created a certainty that inspired easy confidence in those that chose to follow him.

He was outstanding at creating lasting memories in the minds of those that knew him best, and as a consequence, Max had some well imprinted childhood vignettes. There was Robert's attempt to water Mr.

Bradshaw's thirsty sows with the balance of Grace's crab apple vino. Robert once said that if you'd never seen a pig drunk at high noon then you simply hadn't lived. And then there was his stunning and gymnastic freefall from the top deck of the old railroad trestle while escaping a posse of fundamentalist Bible College fanatics. Not to mention the Tom Sawyer-like raft ride down the Saskatchewan River with the bikini clad Federbach sisters, a bottle of Captain Morgan, and a quarter ounce of chronic – gradually rounded up by two good humored Mounties at the urging of concerned parents.

On his thirteenth birthday, Robert sent himself a subscription to *Soldier of Fortune* magazine.

"What's this?" asked Grace.

"It's from Granddad Jack," said Robert.

"Jesus, Glenn, look at this. What's your dad trying to do, encourage our son to join the foreign legion?" said Grace.

She would have preferred to find Robert leafing through *Playboy,* rather than reading war stories and rifle reviews in a pseudo-military publication that advocated the virtues of a mercenary lifestyle.

But that was the sort of kid Robert was, streetwise beyond his years; willing to exploit certain sensitivities in the McVista family to get what he wanted. Although the act caused a stir of distress for his parents, it was a brazen move that Max still couldn't help but admire, even after all these years.

Glenn had fled to Canada to avoid the Vietnam draft, but his father had viewed the act as nothing less than treason. As a result, Glenn had not been on speaking terms with his father for years; although the two men did, at the grandmother's behest, communicate periodically.

"I'm going to call that old bastard and tell him that if he thinks he can pull this kind of shit, he's got another thing coming. I mean, what sort of message is he sending our boys?" said Glenn.

As soon as the call was placed, Robert assumed the charade was up. While Glenn waited for an answer, Robert looked at Max with a sealed lip grin.

Much to Robert's surprise and Max's perplexed fascination; however, their Granddad told their father he was simply sending his adventurous grandson a subscription to an adventurous magazine. It was as if Robert had telepathically requested his grandfather to be an accomplice in a covert family prank.

There were long pauses between Glenn's side of the conversation and whatever was being said on the other end by the grandfather. Glenn's utterances, however, were enough to create a sketch of the tension.

"Robert's too young to be reading shit like that."

"Is that right?"

"An understanding of geopolitics?"

"Who says?"

"Oh, now Trudeau is a communist. For Christ sakes, Dad, don't lecture me."

"Yes."

"They are."

"Maybe this fall, I don't know. Why don't you guys try to come up here?"

"Turkey."

"I will."

"No, you can't."

"Bye Dad."

Grace and Glenn allowed Robert to keep the *Soldier Of Fortune* subscription despite their grave misgivings. And Bones kept it current for at least six more years. He'd long since gone to the deserts of Kuwait, even as his parents still continued receiving magazine renewal cards through the post.

In the years that followed, Robert never told Max whether he and his grandfather ever discussed the subscription, but, for Max, it seemed poetically fitting to imagine that the unspoken collusion was taken to the grave without ever being further mentioned.

* * *

So, this is what everything has come to, he thought; a hay loft, a Rubik's Cube, and nine months of an indeterminate sentence served. In general terms, he could recall his childhood with decent accuracy, but with the extraordinary details he was accumulating on his second run through, 1984 was fleshed out to the point of nausea.

He remembered Duncan telling him to have fun with the experience, not to be fearful, just to relax and enjoy. But the dreamscape before him was not the one Duncan had assured him of. It was more than an exceptional recollection; it was a life relived with a brain full of the previous one.

Insynnium, through some rare alchemy, had taken his fixed and leaden memory and transformed it into a virtual living replica of his past. He controlled his destiny as much or as little as he had in the ordinary course of events that was his life in 2004. He felt the pain of an ache, the itch of wool, and the tickle of hair. If he cut himself, he bled. Food tasted as food should, or shouldn't. Water made him wet. There was no doubt that he was a fully functioning 11-year-old boy in 1984, with the experience and knowledge of a thirty-one year-old man from 2004.

He had gained access to an alternate universe. A place both identical and independent in all respects from the one in which he'd come. Months had passed, however, and he was starting to worry that he might be trapped in the situation for the remainder of his natural life. He had dreams about a future that he'd already lived, and thought about people he knew but hadn't even met. He kept telling himself the situation would 'autocorrect'; that the drug would leave his system and he'd wake up. But sometimes the thought occurred that he might be dead, and that this was the after-life. Supposedly, death made everything pass before your eyes, but at this glacial speed, it would be a slow version of hell. Thoughts like this made it difficult for him to continue acting in the interests of chronological integrity and personal preservation, both of which might not ultimately matter.

Often things didn't seem fair when he was eleven, and now that he'd become eleven again, it was positively perverse. He couldn't drive a car legally or get into an R-rated film. Even sneaking the occasional Kokanee involved more vigor and evasiveness then he could consistently muster.

And then there was Tara, his grade six crush, who now looked like a little girl. He supposed that through some morality distorting lens he could make out with her by rationalizing their age equivalency, but it was the sort of action that would require self-deception beyond his capacity.

A converse and tempting option for a roll in the hay, however, was the regional librarian, Ms. Mayflower, who was hotter and more voluptuous than he remembered. It was a frustration of the first order to know that there was nothing he could say or do to alter her vision of him as a child.

He had selected three capsules of Insynnium dated, '1984', because he longed for a nostalgic visit to his home, a prelapsarian glimpse into his childhood. He ignorantly assumed that the drug would simply intensify his recollections in the same dreamy and vicarious way it had on other occasions. Had he known he'd be time travelling, he would have chosen the birth of Grunge or the impeachment of Bill Clinton as possible kick-off points instead; now those were years, he told himself, that he could have done something with.

2004

-Late Summer-

"That tune makes everybody wanna dance now!"

It was still warm under the Northern California sun as Max made his way on foot from the grocery store back to Pierre's. Suddenly he stopped, dropped his bags, and reached for the receipt that was tucked into the breast pocket of his shirt. He hurriedly scratched a note on the back of it with a miniature pencil he'd taken from the local food co-op:

Learn something extraordinary that can't be acquired in a short amount of time

In the winter, he'd crossed the border into North Dakota while locked in the trunk of a car. Now, three months later, he was living at a house in Humboldt County where he found himself crossing a different kind of border. His time in Arcata had given him his life back, and then some. As the illuminating summer simmered out and another fall ignited its amber fires, descriptors such as 'fantastic' and 'unbelievable' were inferior place holders for language not yet invented to describe his detachment from a linear existence.

He thought about Kevin and Josh with the negligent anguish of an irresponsible parent. He had not seen or communicated with his boys in close to ten months, and the struggle with his callous abandonment ate at him like an aggressive cancer. He wanted to touch their faces and see what changes the year had brought. He wanted to understand the day's events through their eager conversations, and know the lightness of innocence by the sound of their voices. He knew that he had to return to his children before his absence transformed him into a stranger.

He just needed a little more time, that's all.

There was an aspect of himself that he had discovered, overflowing and miraculous; a human dimension that no longer fit a standard shape or held a conventional mold. He'd passed through the crucible of a bizarre coma and into a new reality, and the journey had taken him from despair to euphoria.

As the world turned, he found himself at its axis.

* * *

Before Christmas 2003, he was pulled from the steel womb of a Buick Gran Sport and delivered into the crisp white expanse that is the American prairie in late December.

After Duncan cleared U.S. Customs at Oungre, he drove to a service station and popped the trunk. At a desolate Texaco, Max climbed from his hiding spot like a grizzly northern refugee. He walked around and stretched his legs. He breathed in the fumes of gasoline hovering in the air. He lit a cigarette and let the smoke explode inside his lungs. His life had finally collapsed, and from under the rubble he'd sent out an S.O.S. He exhaled the warm tobacco and watched it float over the bleak landscape. He heard the car horn honking and knew that Duncan wasn't fucking around.

As the two glided across the prairies and twisted through the mountains, Max sucked back cans of Pabst Blue Ribbon and ate preservatives dressed up as edible food substances. His life loomed with grotesqueness, obese and disorientated, a disagreeable situation with no possibility of resolution. He asked himself in a drunk and puzzled tone whether he was simply weak minded or a natural born fool.

Duncan wanted nothing of Max's self-loathing. He remained adamant that two or three months of clean living would give Max a fresh perspective and put him in a position to wrestle back custody of his children.

Duncan said that Max needed to release himself from Rachel's paralyzing grip; he said it would be Max's first step in achieving psychological independence. The two men drove at high speeds as Max listened to Duncan dissect Rachel with psychoanalytic precision. Some of Duncan's comments caused Max to wince, and once or twice he tried to argue with Duncan's logic, but in the end, he made queasy concessions to almost every assertion concerning her. He felt wounded in several ways. He sat silently in the passenger seat and watched the tachometer push into the red along the straight-aways and up the aggressive grades. He sipped on his beer, and as the trip neared its destination, he exhibited a complete lack of ambition in defending his life, such as it was.

When they arrived in Arcata, Duncan insisted that Max stop drinking. But he was critically inebriated ninety-five percent of the time and largely oblivious to the action and judgment of sober people. He consumed Southern Comfort in Stewart Park until he passed out on the lawn. He was often roused to consciousness by case workers from the Department of Health and Human Services. They would find him sleeping under soggy piles of newsprint and take him back to Duncan's. After two weeks of wandering and retrieval, Duncan decided that it was time to take Max to meet an acquaintance.

Duncan was a man with no shortage of connections to individuals with talents, abilities, and knowledge outside the received wisdom. His life was populated with retired cosmologists from Boston and palm readers from Charlotte with names like Thad Van Hellson and Piccolo Free-Breeze; men and women who spent summers foraging for berries and winters in yurts creating artisanal pottery and Kim-chi. Far and away the best handle was, Thricealighteningonwater, a chainsaw sculptor who dwelled in a tree house and was once a member of the Arizona bar.

It wasn't a particular stretch for Max to be introduced to a small and animated man by the name of Tenzim T. Choesom. A Nepalese hypnotist by training, Mr. Choesom had fled a Maoist uprising in the Himalayas only to find himself in the Redwoods prostituting his skills to the kids of dead hippies and West Coast wannabes from Brooklyn.

In addition to his powers of suggestion, Tenzim was also an amateur phrenologist with a fetish for foreheads. To Max's mild amusement, Tenzim held him in some esteem because of the prominent thought-lines that creased across his brow. Tenzim was particularly intrigued by the overall shape of Max's noggin. His callused Asian fingers assessed every ridge and plateau on Max's dome. He told Max he had a one-in-a-million skull; a 'skull for the ages' he called it, and smiled.

Following the cranial appraisal, the two men got down to the brass tacks of addiction recovery. At the conclusion of his first hypnosis session, Max came to associate anything from a shot of scotch to a hearty Black Russian with the inextricable need to vomit. 'Margarita-Martini' and 'Cosmo-Manhattan' were semantic combinations that caused him to retch and reach for water. And so, as they say, that was that.

But it wasn't just that, there was more.

"You have a name inside your head that greatly pains you," said Tenzim, during one of their sessions.

Max looked at Tenzim with the same hesitation of belief he often gave Rachel in moments of uncanny prescience.

"Aubrey Fender," said Max without hesitation.

Tenzim closed his eyes, and when he opened them again his gaze prefigured the words that emerged from his mouth, words that Max had been hearing for years but finally chose to listen to for the first time.

"He doesn't blame you for his death," said Tenzim. "He wants you to let him go. He needs to transition."

"Transition?" said Max.

"Yes. Each time you think of him you pull his spirit energy back into the material world," said Tenzim, "You must say goodbye so he can be reborn in another form."

The knee of regret pressing into Max's chest for so long had been lifted. He felt his diaphragm open, and the air poured into his lungs like he hadn't taken a breath for several minutes. In the eight second exhale, he released a million particles of sadness related to all things Aubrey as he watched the boy go free. As Aubrey drifted off to discover another life, Max realized the same was true for himself.

Once he achieved sobriety and was displaying appropriate social comportment, it was only a matter of time before Duncan broached the sensitive topic that occupied the air between them. He still wanted to know what Rachel knew about his death. And under his renewed questioning, Max found himself resenting his friend's suspicions in the same obstinate manner he had years before. It was a psychic fact that refused to die.

Toward the end of college, Rachel adumbrated to Max a premonition she'd had regarding Duncan, and then forever hesitated to divulge more. He always suspected it concerned Duncan's parents rather than Duncan himself, though he could never be certain. What was certain, however, was that Rachel was uncomfortable with the revelation she had received, and her attitude toward Duncan grew increasingly cold and disagreeable.

Max wanted to preserve the friendship they shared, so he asked Rachel to speak with Duncan. But she replied that she wasn't able to discuss what she'd seen because the mysterious ways of the Great Spirit were not hers to expound on or interfere with. It was always the whispering wind, the behavior of animals, and the pull of the seasons with Rachel, but Max knew better than to question her judgment when it came to understanding the vague power of things unseen.

Duncan's renewed and uncomfortable inquiry dredged up a tension that had never been resolved. Max didn't know what Rachel knew, yet Duncan still suspected Max as an accomplice, secretly sequestering facts critical to his fate. There was a standoff of sorts in the garden behind Pierre's house as they assessed the positions they'd been adhering to for years. For a moment, Max thought that his lingering vestige of loyalty to Rachel would be a deal breaker to Duncan's hospitality and assistance, and that Duncan would send him packing back to Brandon. But Duncan had changed, and remarkably he let the matter drop, or at least Max's inconsequential role in the entire affair. It struck Max as funny, and he began to laugh. After so many years, he'd finally gotten what he wanted from Duncan: something roughly related to forgiveness.

On other fronts, Max had been led to believe that Duncan was a professor of industrial engineering at Humboldt State when he came to visit him that time in Saskatoon. When Max arrived in Arcata, however, it became readily obvious that Duncan had no associate professorship; in fact, there were few scholarly credentials whatsoever.

"If you weren't up there on a conference," asked Max, "Then why all the pretext to come see me?"

"You'd been on my mind, I felt I needed to reach out for some reason," said Duncan, "I guess I thought you'd figure I was some desperate lost friend if I came up there for no reason other than to see you."

"Yeah, I know," said Max, "You're such a fag."

Duncan laughed.

"Of course, when I discovered what a mess you were," he said, "My intuition was vindicated."

Max smiled.

"So what the fuck *are* you doing down here?"

As it turned out, Duncan had not only lied about his academic success but his home-ownership as well. He was living rent free in a large furnished house provided by a professor who went by the name, Pierre Lévesque. Duncan tried to convince Max that he was assisting the professor on important statistical research that would lead to a Ph.D., but Duncan's domestic and scholastic arrangements gave Max pause.

Duncan's doctoral thesis was based on a research project far above Max's comprehension. It was hard for him to evaluate the legitimacy of Duncan's assertions, but the professor backed Duncan up, and

Max thought that was pretty important. The study sounded confusing to him, and hyper-theoretical, and quite frankly, boring. The most he was able to decipher was that Duncan was trying to validate some scale or index by demonstrating that its constituent items loaded on the same factor, whatever that meant. The project seemed to involve a lot of multivariate analysis and computational algorithms. Duncan told him that he and the professor were stalled by the dimensionality of a certain problem, but it was never clear what the problem or the dimensionality was. Apparently, Duncan and the professor were trying to get around their impasse by using surrogate models, another idea that completely flummoxed Max. Though most of Duncan's days were spent at an office evaluating equations, Max was never able to completely let go of the sense that Duncan and the Professor were sharing more than a love of probability distributions.

Max explored the town in a state of sober clarity, but it wasn't long before he realized that Arcata wasn't the sort of place he could live for very long. The contrast between reality and the projected vibe often left him ill at ease. The area tended to attract the kind of pseudo-intellectual posers and Birkenstock vegan class that invariably congregated around academic bonfires. He kept meeting privileged people intensely dissatisfied with their lives, and he thought quite a bit about the frayed social logic that led to such a problem. In his opinion there was a lot of form over content; where brand-names amounted to a synecdoche for character; rendered hypocritical by the non-material mindset many aspired to exude. The only folks in town smiling from their hearts were the starving artists and broke entrepreneurs because they seemed to cling to a more modest expectation of happiness, and that was an important distinction as well, thought Max. And finally, there was the weather that never seemed to reach those high temperatures he associated with California. He usually felt chilled in his extremities on most days and just plain cold at night.

Duncan, in his social astuteness, picked up on Max's restless frustration. He suggested that a job opportunity might alleviate Max's soggy attitude, and so he found him a part-time gig at 'Jesus' Pizza.' The owner was an atheist ex-lumberjack known about town for having been shot in the shoulder by a disgruntled sophomore over the freshness of a topping. Jim Kimparis, the bearded, plaid wearing proprietor, insisted on acting as a culinary mentor and taught Max how to bake a fine capriccioso.

Working with his hands in the dough and tomatoes got Max thinking about his future, and the scattered aspirations of his past started congealing into a fixed constellation. He knew at some point he'd return to Canada an emancipated man, and it was this notion of freedom that he turned over in his head for several cycles. Each time his thoughts resurfaced they focused on an old business ambition from Queens. When he got back to Brandon he would open an organic grocery store and sell whole foods and supplements to everyone in the city and the country.

It was a good plan.

But he was smoking pot again.

Though his romance with the green intoxicant fell on the rocks back in Brandon, his eventual acquiescence to toke up again was like giving in to an old flame for one final fuck. Duncan introduced him to a strain of Mary Jane with a high beyond the usual and accustomed areas, and a bowl of its smoke seemed to set everything straight.

His first lung full of *Grand Propulsion* was the high water mark of his cannabis experience. When he asked Duncan where the weed came from, Duncan smiled and told him it was grown in a basement in Southside Chicago.

They were stoned, but the conversation continued.

"I was talking with Frank yesterday over at Penny Lane Books," said Max. "He gave me these and said they'd help me sleep. He also said they'd give me crazy ass dreams."

He showed Duncan four or five rust colored capsules in his hand. "I think he said it's called Insyllium or Insichium or something like that."

"Insynnium," said Duncan.

"What is it," asked Max.

"It works like a sleeping pill, except much stronger," said Duncan. "It super-intensifies your dreams. Think of the best dream you've ever had and times it by like a hundred."

"How does it work?"

"I have no idea," said Duncan, "I just know that it hyper-inflates the memories attached to certain periods of your life."

"Look, see this," he said, as he showed Max a date stamped into one of the capsules he was holding. "This is the year you'll dream about if you take this one."

"You're shitting me?" said Max.

"No, you'll be totally blown away, Dude."

"What if something terrible happened that year, will I be completely depressed?"

"There's no such thing as a bad trip on this stuff," said Duncan, "I've never heard of anybody having a nightmare, it tends to regress to the best memories, it's pretty fantastic shit."

"So, you've tried it?" said Max.

"Oh yeah, lots of times," said Duncan.

"So why didn't you mention this before?"

"I don't know. I just figured you'd find it on your own if it was meant to be."

What a fucking Duncan thing to say, thought Max.

"What is it," he said, "some sort of intense pharmaceutical or something?"

"No. Nobody knows what it is, exactly."

"What do you mean, nobody knows? Obviously, it's made from something that comes from somewhere," said Max, as he coughed his way through an overly ambitious toke.

"Okay, well, listen to this then," said Duncan.

"The stuff is rumored to be derived from seeds that were supposedly smuggled out of Alexandria following the opening of the tombs in the early Twenties. The renegade archeologist who appeared to be responsible for the theft claimed that the seeds were not seeds at all, but rather small insoluble particles from another galaxy. The space origin theory was rooted in the archeologist's inability to germinate the seeds. He claimed that the cellular composition didn't match anything in the annals of known horticulture at the time.

"Well anyway, the archeologist in question turned up dead in Germany some years later on the precipice of the Nuremberg night. The story I heard, was that a motley crew of unfortunates from outside the Aryan caste, who were fleeing the Third Reich, took the seeds to the Levant where they figured out how to sprout them and promulgate the drug."

"If this stuff is so great," said Max, "And it's been around since the Forties, why haven't I heard of it until now?"

"Because the Soviets got their hands it and were planning to weaponize it," said Duncan, "But a dissident Russian scientist stole all the documentation along with the remaining seeds and hid them away for the duration of the Cold War. Nobody knows what happened to the scientist, but four years ago a European contractor demolishing a tract of rundown houses in Warsaw came across a safe in one of the basements. Supposedly, a Dutch engineer working on the project cracked the safe and got his hands on everything. I guess he took the contents back to Amsterdam and the rest is history."

"Who told you this?" said Max.

"The guy at the service station on Chestnut Avenue where I buy my weed," said Duncan, as he took another hit off the pipe.

"Do you believe it?" said Max.

"I've heard several versions," said Duncan, "But this one's the best. As it gets more popular the real story will emerge, no doubt. It probably won't be half as interesting."

"But it works?" said Max, credulous, and gullibly stoned.

"Yeah, it's a fuckin' trip, man, you can't even imagine," said Duncan.

"And if I try this shit, I'm not going to develop some kind of goddamn habit am I?"

"You'll be totally fine," said Duncan. "This shit isn't addictive. I mean, it's not like heroin or even *Oxycontin*. It's just an intense sleeping pill, that's all."

The following night Duncan told Max to consider the dates stamped onto the capsules and then decide which year he wanted to visit. Duncan said that the capsules would stimulate his memories the way shaking soda pop stimulates soda pop. He said that once you pulled the tab, you saw everything at once.

Max selected 1991 - the year he met Duncan - for his first trip on Insynnium. He ingested a single pill and felt his limbs fill with lead. The pace of his heart slowed as though he'd been sedated for a bypass. His eye lids drew down like the overhead door of a street-side shop closing for the weekend. The dendritic synopses of his past started stirring like the floor of an undisturbed ocean trench probed by the motors of a submarine.

In Max's dream it was late August '91, and he'd just arrived at Ban Righ Hall with his entourage of luggage. Humidity anchored his shirt to his sticky back as he fumbled to find his dorm. There was a surge of mixed emotions coursing through his recollections as he felt the promise of youth reassert itself in his mind. The dream was outrageously vivid, and there was pattern and sequence. In some ways it wasn't like a dream at all because it was logical and followed a chronology that imparted a feeling of motion or advancement. He noticed bits and pieces of past perceptions ordinarily unrecallable from a standard thought.

From among the university's thick stone buildings and decorative old-world architecture, an absolutely stunning young brunette emerged in sharp relief to everyone around her. She was helping with orientation, and she approached Max to ask him if he knew where he was going. *Max had forgotten how blindingly attractive Rachel was the first time he saw her*. She pointed out where he'd gone wrong on the campus map, and she explained that if he carried on straight ahead he would reach his destination. She was beautiful, and he wished their interaction had been longer.

He lugged his backpack and a trunk up several flights of stairs to a fifth floor landing. Once he located his room, he immediately seized upon the fact that his roommate had already laid claim to the sturdier of the two beds, upon which sat a rucksack, a sleeping bag, and a pillow; completely unpacked and invigilated by no one. He had difficulty accepting that anyone could survive a year at college with such a meager amount of possessions. He unbuckled, unlatched, hoisted, and moved his belongings around the conservatively shared space, half expecting the roommate to return, but it never happened.

His room was one of four off a main suite that had two bathrooms, a TV, and a couple of sofas punctuated with a coffee table of un-discernable origin. Students were drifting in and out, and though he introduced himself to several people, he remained mystified as to who he would be sharing his quarters with.

A ruckus barbecue was taking place in the residential courtyard, and he was encouraged by others to make his way over for a hotdog and a beer. He mingled in the sun with several other students and attempted to leave a memorable impression with a humid group of girls sipping wine coolers through straws.[7] As afternoon sunk to dusk, players from the

---

[7] #3 on the Billboard Year-End Hot 100 singles of 1991. **"Gonna Make You Sweat (Everybody Dance Now)"** by <u>C+C Music Factory featuring Freedom Williams</u> from the album *Gonna Make You Sweat*. Columbia, 1990. Clinton wasn't President yet, and Arsineo Hall was dictating fashion. The Eighties were so pernicious that they attached to the bottom of the Nineties like a fungus. MC Hammer and Young MC were shoving their baggy pants in the faces of hair bands from Houston to New Haven, and

lacrosse team began handing out tickets for a concert taking place across the harbor. They kept re-enforcing with enthusiasm that the band was screaming to be seen live.

That night, the grass at Fort Henry was slick with spilled refreshments, and the coed Max was dancing with had her eyes closed and her major undeclared. He basked in the music and travelled with the lyrics. His arms were in the air, and he was mesmerized by the lead singer who moved on the stage like rats were nibbling at his toes. He looked up and saw the stars between his fingers and imagined himself to be hanging off the earth; dangling like a Jedi among stalactites. He knew it was only a matter of time before the empire of gravity released its grip on his ankles. He was totally ready to dive off the pale blue dot and into the vacuum of space until he was solidly bumped by a guy who looked like Lennie Kravitz.

The guy shouted in Max's ear, "Do you follow 'The Dead'?"

In the surreal atmosphere of the evening, Max wasn't certain of the question or the tone in which it was asked, but he assumed it had to do with the fact he was milling about the concert grounds in a Grateful

---

making room for an explosion of Nirvana in Seattle. Max felt as though he'd gone back to the top of the rock that the world had just jumped off of. The future was Grunge, and it was coming fast in plaid and there wasn't a fucking thing Axl Rose or Vanilla Ice could do to stop it.

Dead t-shirt that Robert once gave him from a show he attended near Angel's Camp in '87.

"No, my brother got it for me at a concert in California," shouted Max.

The guy smiled and passed him a joint. "I'm Duncan by the way," he said.

He told Max that his last name was Wisegerber, from the infamous Haitian Wisegerber family, and he winked as if in jest.

Through a rapid cataract of question and answer the two young men deduced that they were roommates.

After The Tragically Hip played their last set in the humid dim, everyone looked at one another like they'd found their next band. Max and Duncan decided the best way to christen such a discovery, as well as their life together in res, was to survey the bars of Kingston for drink specials and reefer deals. Max found it heady and intoxicating to be hanging with a guy who attracted female attention like a Labrador puppy. It was obvious that Duncan could've had his cock stroked by anyone that night, but he was bent on staying high and dragging Max through the streets in a two man parade.

Max noticed that every girl they encountered felt compelled to rest her hands on Duncan in some way or another and that most of the men were not immune either; many tried to rub shoulders on the dance floor or brush up beside him in the drink line. Duncan's charm split the air like a bolt of magic and Max stepped through the gap like a parted curtain onto center stage. They discussed waste management with

Scotch drinking sanitation engineers and talked about
Freedom 55 with martini swilling financial advisors.
Every tavern on Princess Street shook as they poured
out their pints of lager and ale, and no one
remembered going home.

Max was beside himself when he woke up.
He told Duncan that the dream was like being
there.
"Wait until you swallow two," said Duncan with a
grin.
Max began snooping around town to see what else
he could dig up on the drug. He didn't distrust Duncan,
but he wanted to learn more about the primary dealer
and the extent of the market. No matter where he
turned, however, he received only shrugs of
uncertainty and ballpark estimates. Rumors abounded,
but every person he spoke with agreed on one point:
that Insynnium was the brainchild of a shadowy
conglomerate operated from the Netherlands. When it
came to the spice, everybody knew something, but
nobody knew everything. When he told Duncan about
the information he was attempting to uncover, he
seemed largely dismissive. Max could see that he was
distracted by his Ph.D. research, and that second-hand
news about a sleep aid wasn't high on his list of
priorities.
Or at least that's how it appeared until the evening
of March 1, 2004, when Max took three capsules of
Insynnium and fell into a coma.

When he awoke, a year of his life had elapsed, or so it seemed. He remembered opening his eyes and stumbling backward onto the sofa and fumbling with the cushions in a vertigo-like fashion. He remembered his brain being clouded with a monstrous confusion. And of course, he recalled the strained faces of Duncan and Pierre as they stared at him with astonishment. They informed him that he'd just come out of a twenty-four-hour coma. An issue of unconsciousness that, by all accounts, was rather alarming.

In the wake of the coma, it took several minutes to grasp where he was, and it was embarrassing and awkward to start asking the sort of questions that needed asking because they made him sound totally un-tethered. His sole concern was for the time/ space arrangement. He wanted to know if his boys and his mom were okay; if everything was the same as when he'd left. Who was the president and who was at war and where was Russia? Naturally, Duncan informed him that he hadn't gone anywhere, much less altered global politics. But each reassurance was opposite in its effect.

He couldn't even begin to explain it, of course, but somehow 1984 had parenthetically inserted itself in the present, leaving a chasm in the fabric of reality that was spectacular and vast. He soon realized it was naive to expect Duncan or Pierre to believe such a story; he would have scarcely believed it himself were the shoe on the other foot. It just wasn't the sort of thing that happened every day.

Unlike rain

Pebble sized droplets pelted the sidewalk as Max looked forlornly from the dining room window.

The Professor was sipping a cappuccino.

"I've tried it several times myself, you know," said Pierre, "its powerful stuff. I don't think it's unreasonable to suspect that there might be other dimensions to it. In fact, there's probably a good bit more to this drug than anybody realizes. You'll try it again, no?"

"Yeah, maybe," said Max, "but no more childhood visits, its way too fucked up. I think I'll to go back to '93 or '94 next time."

"I once worked in a sleep lab at McGill," said Pierre. "Would you be bothered if I monitored your vitals the next time you take Insynnium; assuming, of course, that you experience another coma?"

"Yeah, okay with me. What do you expect to find?"

"I'm not sure. It's mostly just for show," said Pierre. "It's Duncan; he's bothered by the coma. He feels responsible for your health, thinks we can figure it out."

"It's not his fault that I chose to take the stuff. I just want...-"

Max stopped mid-sentence and looked at the professor. It suddenly occurred to him what was going on.

"He thinks I'm nuts, doesn't he?" said Max, "He thinks I've lost my marbles, crippled my mind with that shit."

"Duncan's under some stress with his dissertation," said Pierre.

"I fucking time travelled," said Max. "Be straight with me, Professor, do I sound crazy?"

"I want to believe you," said Pierre, "but you *do* sound a little crazy."

"Okay then," said Max, "let's do this thing."

The following evening, he was attached to sensors with small colorful wires running to complex looking machines that measured galvanic skin responses and minuscule bio-secretions. He girded his system and swallowed a dose of spice that was calibrated to place him somewhere in his third year at Queens.

But nothing happened.

For the next three weeks, he took the capsules with a religious fervor, but it was like sucking vitamin C to attain a cocaine high, and the results were consistently nil. He thought Duncan and Pierre were screwing with the dosage or giving him a placebo so he secretly purchased capsules from other sources and consumed them in a halfway house on the west side of town, but still nothing occurred.

He was told to exercise with vigor and consume a vegan diet, and though it reduced his frustration and lowered his cholesterol, it did nothing to stimulate the Insynnium.

Time has a way of solving everything, however, and eventually the drug's seismic punch knocked him unconscious again. And like the first time, there were no words.

* * *

When Max got back to the house with his groceries, he placed the perishables in the fridge and took the other items to the pantry. He went to his room and transferred what he'd jotted on the back of the receipt into a scribbler that contained notes on Insynnium. He wasn't a gifted documentarian, but he had a good sense of the rules that were at play:

He called his sleep induced realities: **A**lternative **U**niverse **E**xperiences, or **AUE**'s for short.

- *The twenty-four-hour coma was equal to one year of his past, but he only had the capacity for a coma once every thirty days.*

- *He suffered no memory loss, and what memories he did have travelled in both directions. He estimated that in the six months the professor had been monitoring his comas, he'd gained six years of life experience.*

- *His **AUE**'s were independent of the space/ time continuum, which meant that he could avail himself of a 360-day consequence-free existence each month.*

He embraced the uncharted boundaries of inner space with zeal. He thought about the first monkey's that were shot into orbit. Simian pioneers without words to explain where they'd been or what they'd seen. And now here he was, like a wide eyed chimp, rocketing toward the unknown ends of a splintering universe.

2004

-Autumn-

"What have I got if I ain't got you?"

No matter what Rachel told herself, she'd never wanted Max this gone. The status of her husband's life was the source of a lonesome anxiety that followed her through her days and survived the restless hours of darkness that should've been given to sleep. He had vanished like a vapor and never returned, and his year long disappearance reminded her of every difficult choice she'd ever made. The last thing she told the boys was that their father was working on a drilling platform in the North Sea, and they thought that was pretty cool.

She sat outside on the porch so that Kevin, who was minding his younger brother, couldn't see her crying through the frosted window pane. She was bundled in a wool pullover with the weighty weave of a Hudson's Bay blanket over her shoulders. It was November, and a low-pressure system had pushed its way west from Ontario. She looked at the snow, blue beneath the yard light. The birds had gone south. She felt the wind begin to still.

She held the weathered beauty of a Calumet in her fingerless gloves. Traditionally, a ceremonial pipe was kept with the tribe, but this one was different. It was given to her by her mother's cousin who once lived south of Kenora near the Eagle Dogtooth Provincial Park. She recalled the Chippewa elder as a smoky crone who drove a rusty Datsun on the two occasions that she visited.

Rachel was seven years old the first time, and she remembered the old woman using pliers to pull porcupine quills from the nose of a neighbor's Sheltie. She also remembered sage grass burning in the family trailer and a conversation about the necessity of clearing spirits.

She was nine the second time, when the old woman gave her a quartzite artifact wrapped in rawhide. The elder had intuited that Rachel's connection to the Great Spirit was tangled, and she knew that Rachel would need guidance to make sense of what had awakened inside her. She called Rachel, 'Crowchild,' and taught her how to listen to the wind.

Heavy tears pushed tracks down her face as she massaged the pipestone in her palm. She would ask the wild tobacco and the willow bark to carry her prayers to the attention of the creator. She wouldn't inhale because the smoke was not for her. But she hoped that someday it would find her again by returning with an answer that she could locate in the nature of things.

She dabbed at her eyes with the back of her sleeve and thought about the voice of the Great Spirit with its Omni-modal dialect. She also thought of her friend Kelly, her reliable cousin Marilyn, and of course

Hugh, the man whose DNA was tragically flawed but whose strength as a neighbor remained unimpaired.

Hugh no longer stopped in as often as he once did, but he still called to remind her about things that she tended to forget, such as insulating the outdoor faucets before a frost or regular maintenance on the gas fired furnace.

A few months ago, Hugh met someone who loved him the way he deserved. When Rachel saw them together, however, it made her stomach hurt, because the sight of a couple so plainly happy made her nauseous for everything she'd lost.

It's odd what comes to mind, she thought, as she recalled the warm summer she and Max moved back to Brandon. The two of them would get high on Friday nights along the banks of the river down at Dinsdale Park, and then peddle their bicycles back into town for Chow Mein at the Empress Gardens. After eating, they'd walk to the Paramount Theater for a movie, their heads thick on love and herb. College had finished, and Kingston was gone, and their 'Freedom Fridays,' as they called them, were a tingling reminder of what remained the best part of their lives, namely each other.

She still got high once in a while, usually with Marilyn, her cousin smoked to help with an arthritic hip. It was a strain of cannabis that relieved every pain and worry. Marilyn told her she got it from a dealer in Lambton Shores. Marilyn's husband, Chad, had grown up on Lake Huron, and when they visited his family in the summer Marilyn purchased three ounces.

It was known as, 'Grand Propulsion,' and it was rumored to have been grown in a basement in Chicago. The pot was remarkable in its effects, but even it couldn't put her at ease with Max's disappearance.

How could she explain what happened to her husband? Did he run away? Was he abducted on a desolate stretch of road? Maybe he'd killed himself? Or had he become, like her father once had, a faceless drunk wandering lost and unrecognized among the homeless and hungry on Yonge Street.

Cassandra was Rachel's mother, and the one person who should have been able to empathize with her daughter's plight, but in point of fact, she was completely incapable of helping. She offered Rachel reassuring words and sympathetic solicitations, but her heart was empty of those things to which it should have been full. She could play the role of the doting mother and vigilant grandmother, but Rachel understood her true sentiments from the beginning: Cassandra was glad that Max was gone, and she hoped that he would remain gone, immured in a state of permanent disappearance.

She tried to make her mother understand how stuck she was, and how much Max's unexplained absence pulled on her heart. Cassandra, however, cared little for the state of the heart, and told her daughter that an ounce of emotional unraveling would become a gram with time, whatever that was intended to mean. Rachel, on the other hand, felt as though everything was crumbling, and that her life would soon unravel irreparably.

* * *

Max was drunk when he showed up at the house. He arrived earlier than expected so Hugh was still there. Hugh looked at Rachel with concern as Max slammed the door of his truck and walked through the backyard kicking toys out of his way. She smiled in an effort to put her male friend at ease. She'd never been scared of Max in her life, and she knew he'd never lay a hand on her in violence.

This did nothing to reassure Hugh, however, as he made an expedient and awkward exit past Max at the door and went out into the night.

"Who the fuck was that?" said Max.

"Hugh," replied Rachel.

"Hugh? Who the fuck is Hugh?"

"He's a friend of mine. We went to school together when we were children."

"Oh yeah, well good for you, Rach."

Max was the worst she'd ever seen him. Not himself at all. He was bleary faced and hadn't shaved in a couple of weeks. He came at her with the same hangdog expression and apologetic excuses he'd been dragging to their conversations for the last six months. He couldn't emphasize enough how his drinking was the product of the guilt he felt over Aubrey Fender's death, Darcy's criminality, and his dad's untimely passing. He stressed how vital it was for them to remain a family. He asked Rachel to help him find work. He told her that Josh and Kevin would give him a reason to stay sober. The promises were empty and went on and on; yadda, yadda, yadda.

She didn't want to be callous, but she'd heard it all before, and now here he was falling apart in front of her again. She let him know that he wouldn't be allowed to see the boys in his inebriated state. He replied with a flippant gesture that indicated, 'whatever'. But Rachel stood her ground. She informed him that he wasn't getting custody back, and that his visitations had been revoked by court order until he could get his drinking under control.

After hearing what she had to say, he sat down at the kitchen table and placed his head on his forearm as though he were about to start sobbing, another exasperating ploy he liked to leverage against her.

He spoke into the table with an uncomfortable baritone grumble that caused her to step away. He told her to stop fucking around and bring the boys downstairs. But she refused. When he told her to get the whiskey from the cabinet above the sink, she told him that she'd poured it down the drain.

"Well, you certainly are a damn fool," he said.

"Have you listened to yourself lately," she replied.

"You're starting to get pretty fat there, Babe."

"Gee, thanks, Max."

"No, really, you've let yourself go, Rach. Shouldn't you join *Weight Watchers* or something to get that under control?" he said, as he snickered to himself.

"What the hell's wrong with you? Why have you become like this?"

"Like what, Rach, honest?"

"You don't fucking care about anything anymore, do you?" she said.

The release of her words recoiled against her. It was a statement that was never truer than at the moment it was uttered. It sucked the breath from her chest and her pulse clenched on its beat. She was reminded that sometimes words are more than words, they're bare knuckles, and she felt her eyes fill with tears.

She told him to get out of the house, and that if he had any sense left he would wean himself off the Seagram's and do something about raising his children. After all, if anyone ought to know about raising boys it should be Max, she thought, he had the best role models in the world.

They stared into each other's eyes for a brief and captured second. In the tension of their emotions she glimpsed a sad desperation on his face. He was a man lost to the most precious pieces of his life, and it was an image of him that would stay etched with her through every day that followed.

"With any luck, I'll end up as a drunken traffic fatality on my way back to Mom's," he said.

"Look, if you can be nice you can sleep it off here," she said with calm resignation and a small touch of hope.

"Can't I see my boys before I leave? I just want to give them a hug. I drove *all* this way, Rach," begged Max.

"Well, they're not here. They're over at Mom's."

"Why the hell are my boys at your mom's?"

Rachel saw an unexpected rage cloud Max's face, and for the first time in her life she was frightened of him.

"You're fucking that guy," he said, "that prick that was here earlier. You wanted the boys out of the house. Fuck me, Rachel, for real?"

"Max, the boys are at Mom's because I knew you'd be drunk. I didn't want them to see you this way. Was I wrong?"

"Thanks Rachel. My life is so fucked. Thank you very much."

"Your life isn't fucked," she said, "Just sober up for Christ's sake."

"It just hasn't gone the way I wanted it to, Rach," he said, as though he'd decided something of fundamental importance.

"What hasn't, Max?"

"Life," he said, "I should've gone travelling after college. I should have lived in different places and done different things. Instead, I came back here and…"

Even in his distressed state, she couldn't help but smile at the limited scope of his life summation.

"And what Max?" she said. "You have two boys who miss you and a wife that still loves you, come back to us. Surely your life has been more than what happened with Aubrey, and besides, it was never your fault."

"It *was* my fault Rachel, he was my responsibility," said Max. "And that fucking psychotic brother of yours, where's he at these days?"

"You have to put it behind you, Max. You have to find closure."

"Closure? I don't even know what that means. Jesus Christ, think about it."

"What?"

"A young man died because of something I should have been aware of, or at least had the fucking wherewithal to see, and now I'm stuck with that for the rest of my life."

There was a deeply embedded guilt in Max's being, and in combination with the alcohol, it gave Rachel an unsettling thought about suicidal tendencies.

Before she could reply or throw her arms around him, he spun on his heels and marched out the door, stumbling across the dead lawn on his way to the truck. She went after him but he climbed inside the cab and slammed the door. A cloud of fumes billowed up from the exhaust and almost coagulated in the cold air. She watched him open a can of beer over the steering wheel and put the vehicle into gear. He left her standing by the trash bins next to the fence as he pulled away on bald tires and drove into the icy night.

* * *

Rachel had a habit of feeling sorry for herself from time to time.[8] She was constantly trying to spot the flaw on the track that led to the derailment, but it was entirely futile. And wishing for a guiding premonition was equally hopeless. She'd never had a clairvoyant moment about Max in her life, and there was no reason to believe that his disappearance should occasion one.

So, she turned to Grace.

She'd been in regular contact with Max's mother since his disappearance. The two women reached out to those that might know of his whereabouts, but nobody knew a thing. His pickup had been abandoned at the Arrow Head Tavern in Nipawin. As far as Grace could tell, all of her son's belongings, except for his wallet and his cell phone, were still at the

---

[8]#3 on the Billboard Year-End Hot 100 singles of 2004. **"If I Ain't Got You"** by <u>Alicia Keys</u> from the album *The Diary of Alicia Keys*. J, 2004. Rachel noticed how often Ms. Keys R&B melody brushed her with its pleading vocals as though moved by her own loss. Max had fallen into an abyss, and Rachel was powerless to see the bottom of it. In her blindness she felt panic at the dysfunction in her heart. She didn't want her boys to grow up thinking they had to avoid looking into her cheerless Cree face. When she heard the song in March she cried, but when she heard it in September she smiled, something was moving in the fog of loss. Perhaps the sadness had migrated to a different part of her mind, like whales moving through the sea or geese flying in the sky. Every time she looked into the mirror she saw herself faltering and improving, faltering and improving, until the day when one would eventually overtake the other.

house. The RCMP conducted an investigation, or so they claimed. But they, too, came up empty-handed. According to them, the probability of foul play was remote.

Rachel commiserated with Grace over the phone. They talked and talked, and that was somehow supposed to make it easier, but it didn't. What Rachel really needed was Grace's gentle touch and calming presence. She was temped to move up to Nipawin and stay with her for awhile, but it was impossible with her job and the boys. So, she invited Grace to come to Brandon instead, and the offer was accepted. But it never came to pass because Cassandra wouldn't hear of it. Rachel's mother dug in like a badger and defended her turf by tooth and nail and promised to make life miserable if Grace ever came to town.

Grace was a hippie formed from the combustion of the Sixties who never lost her youthful exuberance or forthright opinions concerning issues larger than herself. And in spite of everything that had taken place, she remained remarkably centered. Her secrets were much deeper than they appeared, and Rachel knew the mysteries swirling inside her would never be known, but that was okay, because Rachel loved her just the same.

Max had been missing for three months when Rachel finally made up her mind to confront Grace about a topic that had carried tension between the two women for years. She wanted to know if Grace had heard from, or had any means of contacting, Duncan Wisegerber.

Duncan was a remarkable character by many accounts. And Rachel remembered him as a stunningly handsome polymath who excelled in situations of every description. He made you feel like laughing at the most inopportune moments, and you loved him for all the ways he caused your heart explode inside your chest. He had a knack for setting you free, and when you were with him, you wanted nothing more than to ride the wave. He was careless and reckless and insanely likeable. Being around him was like eating chocolate; you knew a little was good, but the taste and texture were too appealing to keep it from becoming anything but a habit.

The first time she met him, she wanted nothing more than to touch him, and it wasn't just her. His presence compelled people to grab him by his hand or place their fingers on his shoulder, whatever gave them the physical contact they craved. If you were a woman, your sexual energy went through the ceiling. Rachel recalled her heightened arousal and the formidable animal lust that accompanied her initial interaction with Duncan; so intense that it felt wrong to resist. She was a freshman from the sticks with no sexual past, and his libidinous magic was almost overwhelming. In that first fall of college, she, and every other ardent ingénue, was pining for the chance to jump his bones.

As it was, nothing came of her attraction to Duncan because she was already in love with Maximilian, even if she didn't fully comprehend it at the time. That's not to say she was excused from

Duncan's gravitational pull, it's only to say that had the conditions of love been otherwise, it's hard to tell where her feverish infatuation might have led.

There was no doubt that Duncan was a force of nature in ways large and small, just as there was no doubt that he slept with many women because of his irresistible magnetism. But Rachel always maintained a suspicion, re-enforced by telepathic abilities, that he would never find the love he sought because of an unconscious obstacle of which he was unaware.

Her ominous hunches were validated when she had a disturbing nightmare that revealed a powerful repression operating at the center of his being. Because of the magnitude of the disturbance illuminated, she was never able to look at Duncan in the same light again. At first, she wanted to help him, but the voice of the Great Spirit roaming in the wind told her to leave him alone; it was the guiding voice of her life, and she lived with its instruction. And so it was that the friendship between them became strained and then torn.

She could be stubborn, and Duncan came to hate her for that. It was hard for someone like him, so accustomed to knowing so much, to concede to not knowing everything. He made a choice that if he couldn't get what he wanted from her then he'd spend the rest of his life running from it. Everything ended in bitter words and hard goodbyes and regrets that clung close to the bone.

Grace told Rachel that she hadn't heard from Duncan in years, and her eyes were exceptionally sad when she said this. Rachel was gripped by a heavy guilt as she recalled how things ended up. Maybe she should have ignored the Great Spirit and been more generous with her friend, but things came like a flood in those days, and Duncan got swept away; they all did.

Rachel imagined Duncan climbing mountains or going on safaris, or perhaps pacing around a boardroom on the 45th floor; alive in whatever form he'd taken but forever undiscoverable. She remembered how he had received high honors in engineering, so maybe that was what he was doing; calculating the designs for a world dominating creation; travelling regularly from MIT to Geneva. Maybe there was a wife and a child, she thought; but then again, maybe there wasn't. The one thing she knew for sure, however, was that no matter where on earth Duncan was he probably knew nothing about the location of her husband. And with that simple epiphany, she let him recede to the back of her mind, and went back to worrying about the father of her children.

2005

-Summer-

"It ended, that loco life I was living"

Duncan was staying at the Hilton in Chicago, in a room down the hall from Eric Enderby and Moe Bringa. He'd flown in from Missoula, Montana, where he'd reluctantly seen Max off to Canada.

He told himself that Max was better in one way, and worse in another. He was clean and sober, and exceptionally healthy in the physical sense. Mentally, though, Duncan worried; Max had become obsessed with ingesting the spice once per month, consistently leaving him in a deep and serious coma.

Pierre told Duncan it was almost a certainty that Max's comas were the result of an allergy to the powder. Pierre suspected that Max was irreversibly compromising his hypothalamus, as well as other higher cortical functions, but the hard data supporting this hypothesis was meager and weak in the face of Max's entrenched psychic experiences.

If one were to consider the psychiatric adage that the difference between a neurotic and a psychotic was that neurotics build castles in the sky while psychotics live in them, then by that reckoning, Max was well beyond the construction phase of his edifice in the firmament, and the movers were coming any day.

Pierre's suspicion was that Max's neurons were firing with an aggressive dopamine obsession that found comfort in the Nineties. This theory was given traction after several false starts using dates past the millennium. Max fell into a coma for any time prior to 1999, but he wouldn't so much as dose off if given a pill after 2000. Though he wasn't inventing the comas, Duncan was convinced that he was using his imagination to invent the rest.

He attempted to provide evidence of his time travels by displaying examples of knowledge and skills he had acquired while in an unconscious state. Though he undoubtedly accumulated a fair amount of material, it was hard for Duncan to genuinely concede that the changes in his friend were the product of time travel and not just simply a sober grasp of everything he had been exposed to during his stay at Humboldt.

One emergent talent, however, did give Duncan pause. He noticed that Max had learned an impressive number of songs on the guitar. It was somewhat unusual, since Duncan had never known Max to be musically inclined whatsoever. He told himself it was attributable to Max's lessons with Maurice, and his jam sessions at the garage with Gerry and Andre. But the musicians all told him the same thing: they'd never seen anyone improve so rapidly, and not one of them ever believed Max was a beginner.

Eventually, Duncan stopped resisting Max's claims, and it wasn't solely because of the guitar playing; he decided it would be easier to feign acceptance than continue running at odds with his friend. What else could he do? Max had convinced himself that he was time traveling, and there was no reversing that. Besides, the moment had arrived for all of them to move on with their lives.

Pierre thought it would be a good idea for them to gift Max a substantial supply of Insynnium as a parting gesture. Ironically, he reasoned that despite the risky comas, Max's other twenty-nine days of the month were models of focus and balance. He said that Insynnium amounted to a form of medication, something that, perversely enough, might help Max remain strong; supposing, of course, he didn't fall into a prolonged vegetative state or simply die in his sleep, two rather obvious and daunting side-effects of such a gamble.

Max accepted the generous offer, but he insisted that each capsule of Insynnium be destined for a date in the Nineteen-Nineties. He told Duncan that he wanted to consistently travel back to those days when Stump Merrill replaced Bucky Dent at the Yankee's or when the Earth Liberation Front set fire to Vail Mountain. He mentioned that a dependable date in the center of the decade – such as Fisher Price's merger with Mattel - would be the most satisfying. Max's crazy chronological needs and the undoubting confidence with which he asserted them irritated Duncan in a fundamental way.

While he honored Max's requests by assembling a collection of capsules for a variety of dates in the decade controlled by Clinton and understood by Seinfeld, he took the liberty of surreptitiously altering the stamps on nine of them. He took spice from '74 and '86 and disguised it with a '93 marking. He didn't know what made him do it, but there was a part of him that found justice imaging Max, so sanguine in his delusions of time travel, being confronted with the breast milk of his mother or the awkward onset of puberty.

When they parted in Missoula, Duncan gave him two directives: keep your mouth shut about time traveling, and stay away from Rachel Redcalf.

Max agreed to do both.

Moe picked up Duncan at Midway, and the two men drove to a house in West Englewood where Moe was still conducting business with a green thumb.

"Over there is some *Afghan Kush* and some *Sour Diesels*," said Moe, as he began showing Duncan the specialty operation that was still pulling in cash.

"This one's gaining some weight and get'n nice and chunky. See the heaviness on top, it's got some nice formations, the colas are super developed," said Moe, "And look at the sugar on that one, we'll definitely get finger hash from that."

"There it is, baby, there's *Grand Propulsion*; still look'n good, Moe," said Duncan.

"No, my friend, that's a *TGA Chernobyl*. The *Grand Propulsion* has finished its cycle. I'm cutting up the last of it in about an hour, thought you might wanna help?"

Duncan grinned slyly as he reached into his coat and pulled out a Ziploc of rust colored capsules.

"I assume Eric has a place we can all get comfortable for the evening?" said Duncan, as he waved a bag of Insynnium in front of Moe.

"He has a suite at the Hilton," said Moe. "After what you told him on the phone he thinks his ship has finally arrived."

"Well, it has, Moe, it most certainly has," said Duncan.

* * *

In 1996 Duncan started working for a company called, Brushworthe Capacity - an engineering firm headquartered in Chicago. Brushworthe hired Duncan on a Trade NAFTA visa after he submitted a brilliant and innovative application that was immediately followed by a successful panel interview. After the prompt and enjoyable seduction of one of the panelists, Duncan received the offer of a position.

He found it invigorating to be living in Chicago, and he accepted the job primarily because of the city. The Bulls and the Bears and the Blackhawks kept him occupied through every season. The first six months were a party; but the second six, not so much. He soon found himself drifting, and his illicit assortment of indulgences was the opposite of an anchor in the cities churning social sea.

He'd been working in the city for a year when he received Max and Rachel's invitation to come to Nipawin for their nuptials. He'd been in touch with

Max off and on since they'd all parted ways in Kingston. And although he replied that he was unable to attend their union, he purchased a set of steak knives and some classic cutlery on their registry. He believed that his absence would send a message about the permanence of grudges, or something like that.

The wedding came and went, and he received updates from Max for a time, but after a while he stopped responding, and his silence eventually created a reciprocal attitude. As he drifted free of Max and Rachel, he discovered snippets of meaninglessness creeping into his life. He thought he had all but exhausted his interest for remaining in The United States until a chance meeting with an obsessive compulsive Floridian named, Eric Enderby.

Enderby worked for Brushworthe in mergers and acquisitions, and he told Duncan that he thought the company was a dead end. He said a guy like Duncan would only be frustrated professionally in the long run working at a place like Brushworthe. Eric said that he had an eye for aggressive talent, and he invited Duncan over for dinner to discuss career options and possibilities for advancement.

Following an Indonesian supper provocatively catered by Filipino call girls, Eric described to Duncan the multi-million dollar 'grow' operation he was conducting in South Side Chicago. Eric suggested that Duncan consider making some changes to his life; opportunities that would lead him to appreciate substantially more of the U.S. than just the Carbide & Carbon Building on Michigan Avenue.

Through great labor and secrecy, Eric had established a loyal and reliable network of cannabis retailers and consumers throughout the lower 48. Most of his clients were professionals and artists who were extremely partial to the quality of the product they were buying, and no one balked at forking over the premium that the high of all highs demanded. Eric told Duncan that he was in need of a regional courier who could be professional and discreet. Someone who clients could feel comfortable with, and as Eric once put it, 'talk sensible about shit.'

Duncan listened carefully to the job pitch and the tone with which Eric waxed enthusiastic about his business model. He had an intricate and effective distribution chain staffed with inconspicuous company drones and disenfranchised interns from Brushworthe. The unsuspecting and tight-lipped bunch led double lives as assistant growers, trimmers, packers, and delivery drivers. Though Duncan wasn't clear on every detail of the enterprise, he decided to accept Eric's offer nonetheless.

He soon discovered, however, that *Direct to You Inc.* was not the multi-million dollar bonanza Eric had gushed over, but that there was, in any event, a solid and considerable revenue stream. He also learned that Eric had a highly competent and inventive grower named Moe Bringa; a brilliant but cagey Bosniak who'd fled the former Yugoslavia as its constituent parts were free falling into darkness. He was often reminded of Max's brother whenever he listened to Moe's bitter thoughts on Baltic politics.

Moe had abandoned everything, including his language, to seek refuge in America, and what he discovered in the time since he'd walked off the plane at LaGuardia was an enormous talent for growing cannabis. Moe began by producing wicked strains of weed in a basement in Archer Heights that was fucking up the local neighborhoods, and word soon got to Eric, who was in search of a talented grower. It wasn't long before Moe's god given proclivities were producing flowering plants in the basements of several condemned houses along West Marquette.

Moe emphasized to Duncan the importance of adopting a 'road identity.' He said that before Duncan started making deliveries, he needed to assume a physical presence that would simultaneously alert people to both promise and menace. He mentioned, almost with envy, that Duncan's skin tone was an asset. He schooled Duncan in the nuances of instilling an Eastern European sense of dread into the American middle class.

"These soft people," said Moe, "For them, you need to be nice, and scary."

Duncan sold his BMW to Moe and used the money to buy a chestnut brown, 1971 Buick Gran Sport with gold anodized Centre Lines. He also purchased a hand gun and a switch blade. He grew his sideburns with a mustache and started wearing a black leather sport coat. Moe said that he looked perfect, like a chilled out version of that infamous Congolese arms dealer whose name he couldn't remember.

Duncan was being propelled into an existence that encouraged him to tap into aspects of his personality that were often discouraged by those who had chosen to live their lives above ground. He returned to the neon caverns and dark tunnels that had once lured him in as a teenager. Urges that had been set aside and never spoke of were beginning to re-emerge. The lethargy of his anathematizing job at Brushworthe began to disappear in spasms of primordial electricity that flow through the veins of someone transforming back into a morally and legally oppositional entity.

His life started feeling like he thought it ought to, like one illicit thrill. He did the bare minimum required at Brushworthe and ran state lines the rest of the time. He was hauling Moe Bringa's herb in duffle bags to Cincinnati, Milwaukee, and Cleveland. Asphalt and gravel led him to smaller centers such as Terre Haute, Champaign, and Rockford. It never crossed his mind that he'd ever get caught; it wasn't even part of the equation.

At one point, he even went so far as to make a few brave forays into Canada. He delivered the bud to small communities along the eastern flanks of Lake Huron; places like Lambton Shores, Bayfield, and Goderich. In one small community known as Grand Bend, there was an amorous widow with cats and an itch that couldn't be scratched, and she made Duncan hard for miles. But at the end of one long and predominantly naked weekend the lovely widow spied her resurrected husband marching up the walk. Duncan escaped with his balls before the burly tugboat operator could catch him with his lying missus *flagrante delicto*.

His road trips to Canada were subversive and addictive, and a bit of a thrill went off in the primitive part of his brain every time he was able to get a load of 'Grand Propulsion' across the border. But the border and its concomitant risks eventually came to an end. In late fall, the Hell's Angels got careless at the Sarnia crossing and were relieved of thousands in drugs by U.S. Customs and Immigration. The border got tight, Eric got paranoid, and Duncan's smuggling into Canada ceased.

The decision to cool trafficking along the 49th ultimately led Duncan to Los Angles just before Christmas. Eric had a client in the Hollywood Hills who was flush with cash, but stingy on likeability. Eric explained to Duncan that the previous courier had been beaten senseless by body guards for some unmemorable indiscretion.

It seemed odd to Duncan. There was plenty of weed in California. It was hard for him to imagine that anybody who lived among the sun and the palms couldn't find a superior grade of smoke then the shit Moe was blowing from a basement in Englewood. But when he voiced his skepticism, Eric simply re-emphasized the importance of maintaining the commercial flow of Mr. Bringa's plant based enlightenment; horticulturally complex arrangements of bliss that evidently no other botanical Mozart could rival.

On the eve of his departure to California, Eric and Moe suggested that the three of them burn a bolt of Grand Propulsion as a send off of sorts.

What the hell, thought Duncan.

Prior to his impending shuffle to the Pacific, Duncan had never smoked any of Moe's magic. In fact, he'd entirely abstained from marijuana since beginning his stint as Mary Jane's chauffeur, due to the misplaced and naïve principle that one should never partake in ones own supply.

The high that he received from Grand Propulsion was singular in its effect. Moe's divine molecular talents placed Duncan in a 'rethink your thinking' dimension; it was like pot on pot. The hybridized combination involved traits of *Burmese Kush* and *Blue Rhino*, as well as something additional, an extra touch of breeding that set it apart; a trade secret that Moe remained adamantly taciturn about.

Grand Propulsion floated Duncan on a blanket of confidence and inspiration. He said that 'calm' was the highest achievement of 'self.' He told himself to live light, travel light, spread the light, and be the light. His bliss wasn't even interrupted when his two closest associates reminded him that California, and especially L.A., was chockablock with crazies.

Eric and Moe told him to watch his ass.

He simply smiled and told his friends he'd return with a story to rival all others.

Charger Astkount was a pornographic film producer who had a studio somewhere in the San

Fernando Valley. Duncan never set foot on Charger's sound stage, but he did visit his home on two occasions. Charger's mansion along Mulholland was a rambling fortress with a hyperactive security system backed up by a couple of Doberman Pinchers.

Charger was quick tempered and sulphurous and afflicted with a bad case of halitosis. He was also a narcissist with a bad sense of humor. Duncan could see the man was a screwball the first time he set eyes on him, but it was equally obvious that the nut-bar had business acumen coming out of his wazzu. He made specialty smut for what he liked to term 'the sexually petit bourgeois.' He made no sense when he spoke, especially when he told Duncan how he catered to a 'penile and clitorically challenged middle-class whose sole ambition was to masturbate to the pulse of a high-class beat.' Duncan laughed when he tried to envision someone like Marx hopped up on crack and Das Kapital and a dose of Viagra.

As a weed courier, Duncan's experiences had brought him into contact with a veritable pastiche of dipshits and deviants searching for the summit of stoned mountain, but with Charger he knew he was nearing the top of the range. He wanted nothing more than to take his leave of the man from the moment he walked into his presence with a payload of dope in a satchel under his arm.

The lecherous abomination told Duncan he didn't have the cash to pay until the following day.

Duncan returned to the estate twelve hours later and found a party underway in the ballroom involving several deplorable fetishes and a mountain of cocaine. Charger gave him an awkward fist bump under the portico at the entrance and tried to make like they were soul brothers who'd just performed an alleyoop or cut a rap single. White folk, thought Duncan, fuck me.

Charger handed him a duffle bag of cash in exchange for the weed, and then vanished into the fleshy crowd made up of partier's dressed in leather and spandex. It occurred to Duncan that probably the only thing that sated Charger's greedy appetites was zoning out on Moe Bringa's green symphony. The dragon had gone back to his lair.

As Duncan escaped out the back of the phallically decorated castle and into the freedom of daylight, his eyes came to rest on Candie Wayne. She was oddly alone and sunbathing topless by the edge of a shimmering infinity pool. The sexual magnetism was immediate and he soon found himself in the midst of her reckless flirting. It seemed remarkably clear to him that while visiting the valley of decadence it would be both darkly logical and vaguely appropriate to have a fling with an adult film star.

Candie Wayne was part of Charger's myopic and hedonistic empire of sex. She was one of the star attractions in the ocular carnival of lust known as, 'Sensation Productions.' She was also Charger's common law wife.

Ms. Wayne didn't shoot a scene every day, and when she did it only took a take or two, so Duncan was privy to an abundance of carnal hook-ups off set.

Although conducted on the low-down, he sometimes asked himself if he fully appreciated the risks he was taking in seeking Candie for his own selfish gratification. He certainly couldn't argue about being blinded by the physical intensity of the sex; Candie was so good in bed that it almost made him hurt. He told himself that he only needed her shapely ways and pretty face a few more times, in a few more positions, and then he would go back to the regular and proportional arrangement of natures plan.

During an afternoon visit to Disneyland, he took a picture of Candie standing in the shadow of Magic Mountain. Through the lens of his camera, she appeared like a girl lost in anomie and sadness. She'd grown up in Rosemead as a typical suburban kid with a mom and a dad. He was momentarily distressed by the thought of everything the aspiring young actress had likely given up to become the queen of cock. She was groping for some kind of light, but blinded by the bling. She treated him to painfully kitsch purchases at Knott's Berry Farm and Universal Studios, things he knew he'd later be forced to throw away in the interests of good taste.

They took walks together along Manhattan Beach, but their emotions were superficial, and their feet seldom sank into the sand. The two of them would amble through tacky stores along Hollywood Boulevard or snoop through outrageously priced boutiques on Rodeo Drive.

With Candie, everything was a search for distraction. She was a woman who had been socially coerced into monetizing her body in the lucrative campaign to sell ass to man's untiring libido. Charger might have wielded his wife like a trophy, thought Duncan, but it was still preferable to his own unsavory acts, which amounted to nothing more than indulgences in someone else's silicone wet dream.

One afternoon while savoring a post coital, post Christmas Reuben at a delicatessen in Reseda, not far from the Ventura Freeway, Duncan let Candie know that their fling was over and it was time he got on back to the windy city. She told him that she understood. She said a lot of guys had trouble being with a porn star. He attempted to explain that that wasn't exactly the issue, but Candie merely replied with a sultry smile as she wrapped her lips around his straw and sucked on his frozen coffee.

They hadn't walked ten paces from the sandwich shop when Charger drove up in a metallic red Cadillac – you could almost taste iron in the air. He looked like a man on mescaline as he jumped from his car waving a pistol. He marched up to Candie and looked deep into the ascendancy of her eyes. Then he took the musty Colt revolver and shot his cheating wife in the head. It happened so fast, and with such freakish abandon, that Duncan found himself paralyzed under the splatter of her blood.

Before he could find a semblance of locomotion, he too, was in the sights of Charger's .45. The psychopath told him to reach for the sky like a highway marauder relieving him of valuables. As soon as his hands were in the air, he heard the weapon discharge twice, and then everything below his waist went cold. One of the bullets partially amputated his penis before grazing his rectum and exiting through his ass. The other missed his privates completely but went a mile deep into his femoral artery.

In three flashes of a gun barrel, Duncan saw daylight and darkness merge into senselessness. As Candie's life was absorbed into the pores of warm pavement, he bled out rapidly next to Charger's Caddy. Seconds had the time-value of minutes as brave patrons from nearby stores tackled Charger to the ground and subdued him. Someone also had the good sense to apply direct pressure to Duncan's femoral wound which miraculously saved him.

It didn't, however, save him from the residual shock and trauma of being fundamentally altered. Nor did it spare him from the slow ticking of time that accompanies such fundamental alterations. The hours and days and weeks were linked together in a series of painful realizations that turned on themes of loss and distress and placed him for the first time in his life at odds with himself.

He managed to say a few words at Candie's graveside service, but there was something missing in the city of sensation and he appeared thin and shriveled in his urine-scented wheelchair. Charger was sent to prison, where Duncan's imagination took revenge by envisioning the vile monster being eaten alive by the other inmates; though in reality nothing of the sort happened. In fact, Charger was eventually transferred to a minimum security playground in

Florida to serve out the remainder of his sentence. After his release, though, he was never seen or heard from again.

Despite everything, Duncan was eternally grateful to the emergency team at UCLA Medical Center who managed to spare life, leg, and shlong; and before long he was transferred to the care of chief urologist, Dr. Solomon Finkelbinder, who focused with the highest level of professionalism on the nearly severed shaft.

For Duncan, the early hideous months following the shooting seemed to pass like catatonic eons, but eventually those sluggish months evolved into a year. After eight surgeries and a surfeit of referrals, Dr. Finkelbinder stated with assuredness that Duncan had recovered as much as one could hope, given such an unordinary wound. The doctor threw around the phrase, 'healthy and generally normal urological functioning,' which was true, so long as one didn't count an erection as part of the penile equation.

When it became medically obvious that no more surgeries were going to pump life into his limp extremity, and that no more support groups were going to bestow a hug with enough reassurance to carry him through his crisis, he plummeted into despair. He became seriously - one might say clinically - depressed. His profound disillusionment with the state of his pecker was only aggravated by the irony of his continued and remarkable magnetism to women. Los Angeles, with all its futile stimulation, was more than he could bear.

It was only a glitch with the safety on his Beretta, combined with Eric and Moe's indefatigable concern that kept Duncan from topping himself in the spring of 1999. At least twice a month either Eric or Moe flew out West for a visit. Eric's alternative gardening business paid for the enormous hospital bills, and Moe Bringa's potent herb elevated the spirits to the extent that any herb could. But even *Grand Propulsion* had its limits, and if there was a ceiling on feeling good then Duncan had reached it. He felt hunched and pushed up against himself as if the air and the earth were compressing into one.

In the end, it was a routine follow-up with Dr. Finkelbinder that changed Duncan's trajectory. The doctor said that he had a niece; a 'specialist,' who recently moved her office from Palm Springs to Culver City. The doctor insisted that Duncan pay her a visit. He told Duncan that she was the best in the business and that if anyone could help him, it would likely be her. Though Duncan initially balked at the suggestion, he eventually yielded to the doctor's persistence.

The niece, Dr. Sarah Samuels, had a niche psychiatric practice working with men and couples who were dealing with prolonged and largely incurable impotency issues. Duncan didn't like the prospect of accepting whatever it was he was accepting by attending a session with a sex therapist specializing in such dilemmas, but his options for a satisfactory recovery had dwindled significantly.

He liked Sarah from the beginning. She was like nobody he'd ever met, except perhaps Grace. Yet unlike Grace, Sarah was less complicated emotionally and more available sexually. He became convinced that she was his savior – though he would never tell her such a thing - and that she would restore meaning to his life. He attended regular sessions with her and even did his homework. For her part, she did not indulge his self-pity nor entertain his eccentric appetites, which was something of a miracle in itself.

Although Sarah, like every other woman that entered Duncan's vortex, found him sexually attractive, her lust for him was formed by something deeper, something closer to his core; subtle and beautiful; and for that he remained secretly grateful. He attended therapy with her for close to a month before their professional relationship evaporated in the heat of summer and the dry predictions of Y2K.

One morning as they stretched naked on the sheets with a shellac of sweat on their flesh, a soft breeze came gently whispering through a window left ajar. Duncan was reminded of the Santa Ana winds blowing what wind blows. Sarah whispered in his ear that the coffee roaster down the street was selling lemon meringue pie and cappuccinos for three dollars. She thought they should hurry before the morning sun became too hot and they could no longer linger in the refreshing shade of the Elm trees on the corner.[9]

While she had a multitude of exquisite features to attract the eye, Duncan always found himself staring at her marvelous ass when she pulled on her skirt – a perfect peach. Sometimes she'd catch him watching and wiggle her bum. She revealed herself to him in pieces that were unscripted and intimate, and he peeked around every corner with the hope of glimpsing more.

"You know," he said, as he pulled on his pants, "When you say you don't care about me having a working member, I think I actually believe you."

"Trust me, Baby, I want you hard, but what's a girl gonna do?" she replied, with her tongue in the corner of her mouth.

"What *is* a girl gonna do?" said Duncan.

---

[9] **#10** on the Billboard year-end hot 100 singles of 1999. **"Livin' la Vida Loca"** by Ricky Martin from the album *Ricky Martin*. Columbia, 1999. Duncan knew that he'd soon be eating pie down at the cobblestone intersection under the protection of a thick and sturdy elm. He'd watch Sarah lick her lips with satisfaction. In an instant he realized that he'd come to the end of his history and that he was lying on a bed at the terminus of his first life. Everything had arrived at this moment, and now everything would be moments-plus. The song on the radio was so outrageously captivating that it made him wonder about the magic bouncing around inside the skull from which it sprang. The roller coaster that he'd spent his first incarnation reaching the top of was about to go into freefall, and the sky was the color of mocha.

"How would you like to come with me to Israel?" she said.

"Israel?" said Duncan, "What's in Israel?"

"Well, some relatives for starters," said Sarah. "I have a cousin on my Mom's side who lives north of Tel Aviv; we could stay with her. But more importantly for you, I have some information on an old Middle Eastern cure for erectile dysfunction."

She delivered her statement with a teasing grin. She was having a moment of girlish insouciance that Duncan had come to understand as a harbinger of truth. And in that instant, he became more or less convinced that she did, in fact, possess such information.

"You're hoping a trip to Israel will give me a hard on?" he said.

"I'm hoping a trip to Israel will expand your horizons and give you an international flare."

"You know I've been abroad before," he said.

"Not like this you haven't," she replied.

* * *

Eric and Moe were already gone for breakfast by the time Duncan rolled out of bed. The night before, they'd each taken a dose of Insynnium. But it was Duncan who felt like he'd swallowed more memories than he could digest. There was a message scrawled on a memo pad that had been slid beneath the door, the message made it plain that the other two had seen plenty as well. The note said they wanted to discuss their dreams ASAP.

It was 9:30 when Duncan wandered out from the lobby of the Hilton; its tumbling steps falling onto a street that was transforming with a steady accretion of heat and noise. He discovered Eric and Moe slurping coffee and devouring pancakes in a restaurant along East Grand Avenue. They tried to appear discrete when they saw him, but as he walked up he could tell the two men were on fire. As soon as he took a seat, Eric leaned across the table and spoke in a barely modulated tone.

"Last night was fucking awesome!"

Duncan never ceased to enjoy the look on people's faces after they'd tried Insynnium for the first time. It was consistently the same; like nothing anyone could imagine. He could tell the two were still swimming in their memories, but he went ahead and told them about the drug's other attributes as well. Eric nearly choked on his maple syrup when Duncan mentioned the drug's untraceable solubility in the blood.

"We're gonna make like a kazillion fucking dollars, Dude," said Eric. "How much of this shit do you have?"

"I don't have any," said Duncan, "I mean, other than what I gave you guys last night."

"What?"

"I have a name, though," said Duncan, "'Szhmeets'."

He handed Eric a slip of paper containing all the information Eric would ever need to make all the money he'd ever wanted.

"Szhmeets? Who? What is this? Are you joking?" said Eric.

"You bastards have been the best friends a guy could ever ask for," said Duncan. "I want to see you both get stinking rich. Call that number, and you'll never need another cent."

"And you?" said Moe.

"I'm good. I'm going straight," said Duncan. "I've almost finished my Ph.D., and I've got a lead on a job in D.C.; working for a think tank."

"No shit? Well, we'll keep you flush with cash, Bro," said Eric.

"No, I think this is it," said Duncan. "From what I've heard Insynnium is pretty secret shit. The guy who gave me the information you're holding in your hands told me the whole operation is run by a temperamental tech czar who orchestrates everything from Amsterdam. If you follow up with that number, I believe the two of you will soon find yourselves moving in very different circles."

"What about us, man, the three fucking amigos?" said Moe, aghast that Duncan would abandon them.

"Hey, what can I say, we had some great times. Seriously though, the biggest favor you can do for me is to never mention where you got that number."

2005

-Autumn-

"Don't hold your breath, he said; breathe,
just breathe"

Rachel was cooking the turkey and potatoes, everyone else would bring a dish of their choice. It seemed that the second Monday in October was the perfect time to be grateful for what life had bestowed. So, naturally, when the Great Spirit told her that the time for a healing feast was at hand she chose to make the extra effort. After all, she had a lot to be thankful for this year: everyone's continued good health, the support of family and friends, two beautiful boys, and, of course, Maximilian's return.

From the street-side window, she could see Max approaching the house on the leaf covered walkway. Kevin was leading him by one hand, and he carried a colorful yam salad in the other. The boys were overjoyed with the presence of their father. For the last three months, Max had been taking care of his two little men in touching and practical ways that made Rachel's heart come alive. He had become a better man, she thought; there was no denying such an obvious fact.

On July 16th, she opened her door and saw him standing there. She started to shake. Not a shake he could see, but one that she could certainly feel, like an invisible tremor passing through her cells at a microscopic level.

She was flooded with unspeakable relief at the sight of her long missing husband, followed by a cascade of confusion and anger. She had too many questions and too much heartbreak to begin thinking about what his return might mean.

She hugged him hard in spite of everything.

He looked good, she thought, he looked younger. His wavy and darting hair was trimmed spruce, and his face was clean shaven. He appeared sharp and confident in a worn denim jacket and brown corduroy trousers.

When she found the words to ask him where he'd been, he told her that he'd walked out of the Arrow Head Tavern one morning and hitchhiked to Vancouver for no apparent reason. He said he'd been living in a shelter on Hastings Street courtesy of an outreach organization that found him near death in an alley one night. He said that he'd saved up some money working construction on the coast. He also told her that he'd been sober for over a year after completing an outpatient program for alcohol addiction.

In her haste to assign culpability, she informed him that she had been single-handedly raising their children, saving money, and fretting day and night over his whereabouts. Although she could see that he was sympathetic to her grievances, she could also see that he had changed and become largely impervious to her guilt trip. The man in front of her was long past self-condemnation and loathing, but his new confidence irritated her. She wanted him to feel emotionally compromised by what he'd done to her and the boys, and then she hated herself for such retributive desires. She swallowed and told herself to breathe, lest she become like her mom with the coronary palpitations and bedeviling migraines.

According to Max, the year and a half in Vancouver got him square; though, for Rachel, it was not easy to understand how this was so. He said that contacting her and the boys would have made his recovery impossible and compromised his treatment goals. She could tell he was lying, and she wanted to scream, but she refused to let her anger control her. Instead, she chose to focus on the man rather than his obviously fabricated tale.

In many ways, Max appeared to be as he was before he started drinking. But it was the ways in which he was different that fascinated Rachel. He was more than just sober, she thought; he appeared to be almost enlightened. He had a contented presence, and all the unhappy and restless impulses once hiding in his soul seemed to have dissipated, especially whatever feelings he harbored about his role in the death of Aubrey Fender. There was something else, too, something that she couldn't quite put her finger on. He managed to hide it well, but there was a part of him that had become aged and indifferent, like what you might expect from the self-contained nature of an old barn cat.

When she told him how her hair had turned gray from the stress of his long and unexplained absence, he took her in his arms and looked into her eyes with every ounce of care she'd ever known, and for a moment she believed that he needed her.

"Sorry, Rach," he said.

His apology was like a grave marker on the final resting place of a past that could never be changed. Through the sincerity and weight of his expression, she could see that he'd eaten bitterness. He'd struggled with himself and come out alive on the other side; she knew there was no lie in that.

Shortly after he returned, she decided to let him move back in with her and the boys, but he chose not to. In fact, despite her willingness, she and Max didn't even make the occasional effort to share a bed. She soon discovered that he pretty much lived at the construction site of his new building. And when he wasn't there, he was doing something with the boys. She often saw him around town, and the light in his face told her that those things that once drove him to drink were finally buried and decomposing into the elements required for growing a new life.

There was something in the way of his return, however, that made her feel as though there were more to his vanishing act than merely living for eighteen months in a flop house between Hastings and Pender. She often got the sense that there was another woman in his life; someone satisfying his needs in ways that she couldn't. But who was it? And why had she never seen her? She knew it had to be more than a phantom that was feeding her husband's appetites and polishing his attitude.

She greeted Max at the door and Kevin took the salad into the kitchen. He was the first to arrive, and somehow that seemed appropriate.

"Smells good Rach."

"Just like old times, eh?"

"Almost," he said, as he looked across the street.

"It's still vacant," she said.

It was the Fender house.

For a moment, both their gazes were fixed under the unified thought that time had healed something previously considered incurable. Their shared memories, so inextricably linked, weaved and meandered in the deciduous colors of autumn. She thought that perhaps their time apart had brought something very valuable back into their lives.

* * *

In 1997, they purchased the house on Glass Avenue. It sat directly across from a rental bungalow that was consistently vacant. Various tenants occupied it from time to time but none with the devotion and permanency of the Fender family when they eventually moved in.

Oscar Fender was a farm implement salesman struggling with a bad back, and his wife, Bev, worked as a house cleaner. The two had a teenage son, Aubrey, who was friends with some of the kids at the Native youth center were Rachel worked. Aubrey was a pretty regular teen; he did okay in school, played some sports, sort of had a girlfriend, and engaged in the kind of mischief expected of boys his age.

When Aubrey asked Max if he could get a summer job at the car wash, Rachel encouraged Max to hire him. In fact, Aubrey worked out so well that Max had him stay on part-time during the school year. Max, like Rachel, developed a fondness for Aubrey. They encouraged the young man to save money and think about his future.

One day Max came home from work and told Rachel, with satisfaction, that Aubrey had been accepted into the Southern Alberta Institute of Technology to learn auto mechanics.

"Good job," she said. "You really worked with him on that application, and it paid off."

"It feels great," said Max, "Oscar and Bev are totally stoked. I think he's going to do really well."

Baby Kevin came toddling over while Max was giving Rachel the scoop. He picked up his son and held him. She had a clear memory of the expression on his face that day; it was a solid combination of love and hope.

It was shortly after that that the phone started ringing at three in the morning on a regular basis and interrupting everyone's sleep.

Tucker's Carwash and Garage was suffering from a rash of break-ins and random prowling. The RCMP would show up and make a report, but nothing was ever missing or stolen. Max would drive over to

Tucker's and have a look around and return by five. It was happening once a week and becoming a pain in the ass.

"Do you think its Darcy?" said Rachel.

"Maybe," said Max, "He's using again, you know?"

"Mom says he's not."

"Your mom is protecting him like she always does. Besides, isn't he supposed to be doing random UA's for Corrections or something? It's like a probation violation for him to be smoking that shit, you know?"

"If you want to report him, you have my permission."

"He needs treatment, not jail," said Max.

"Good luck with that."

Rachel had little sympathy for her brother. He was a mean-hearted bastard, and had been so for as long as she could remember. He treated her badly when they were kids; punched her, kicked her, trespassed against her. When he grew up and got married and had kids of his own he punched and kicked them as well. Then he went to jail for a while after beating the shit out of his second wife.

When he got released, Max hired him as a shop janitor at the car wash. It was a favor to Rachel's mother who still referred to her son as a, 'good boy.' To Rachel's surprise, the arrangement actually worked out. Darcy checked in regularly with his parole officer, attended Narcotic's Anonymous, and showed up for work almost every day. But there were things that weren't right as well, things harder to put your finger on, and Rachel knew that Darcy was sliding back into his old criminal habits; he was a liar and a cheat and a fiend, but they all kept avoiding that conversation.

The city of Brandon had seen a spike in Methamphetamine use over the past year, and Rachel was worried that her brother was a part of the scene. She suspected that he might be involved with whoever was bringing the stuff into town. By the time Max finally made up his mind to confront him, however, it was too late.

She had a bad feeling when the phone rang to report another break-in. She told Max to be careful. He went over as he always did, but what he discovered when he got there was horrifying. The place was a crime scene, and the news was tragic.

Aubrey Fender had been shot.

Rachel and Max rushed to the hospital, but when they arrived the doctor was in the midst of informing Aubrey's parents that their son had not survived. Bev Fender went to pieces in the waiting room, and her wailing cut Rachel like glass. When Oscar asked Max how something like this could have happened to his son, there were no words.

A small ring of drug dealers in Brandon had been using the back office at Tucker's as a hand-off point for shipments of meth brought in by a criminal syndicate from Hamilton. Darcy Redcalf had been receiving weekly 'transactional' fees for making the office at Tucker's available. The RCMP attempted to untangle how a young man from a solid working class home wound up murdered by out of town thugs at two in the morning on a school night. Crimes like that weren't supposed to happen in Brandon.

In the midst of the investigation, Rachel and Max received sudden and crushing news that his father had passed away. Everyone was completely stunned. Not even Rachel had the slightest psychic warning. With his careful diet and regular exercise, she imagined her father-in-law living past ninety. But the autopsy revealed that Glenn had a faulty valve in his heart, and always had; congenital, unavoidable.

It was the third week in June when they drove up to the farm for the funeral.[10] If a more beautiful place on earth existed, Rachel couldn't imagine where it might be. It had been raining during the service, but when they emerged from the church, the sun made God's creation a wonder to behold.

Beyond the graveyard, at the edge of the woods, the light of long days stretched on forever, and she saw spring's startling beauty collide with the approach of summer. Beneath the hovering swarms of insects

---

[10]**#1** on the Billboard Year-End Hot 100 singles of 2000. **"Breathe"** by Faith Hill from the album *Breathe*. Warner Bros Nashville, 1999. Rachel didn't know it at the time, but she was in the calm before the storm. The car got a flat in Yorkton and Kevin wouldn't stop crying, so her and Max rented a motel for the night. There was thunder and lightening and the rain bounced off the pavement like a million tiny racket balls. It was the last time Max really held her before things started to slide. She must have heard Ms. Hill sing her song thirty times on the drive, but it was in the motel room where the memory cemented itself.

caught between the poplars and the bulrushes, she could feel the heart of a deer beating. The steady rhythm of nature was such that she could lose herself in the slipstream of racing senses and instincts for things on the invisible plane.

Later, at the house, by the rail on the porch, she saw the ghost of Glenn McVista take a farewell assessment of his small rural creation, and then transition eastward into the timeless eternity that surrounded them all with its day to day elegance.

She was six months pregnant and thinking about the new life she carried inside her when the name, "Joshua", came whispering in her ear. At that moment, she knew Max's father had given her the name for his unborn grandson. She placed her hands on her belly as if christening in the sanctity of a life passing.

Following Glenn's wake at the Knights of Columbus hall, Rachel took a walk with Grace across the pasture behind the aging hip-roof barn. As the two women stood in the dew-resisting grass, Rachel took hold of her mother-in-law's arm. Grace was holding a picture of Glenn taken in sepia that could've belonged to the nineteenth century. Rachel saw the tears that had dried to Grace's face; both the ones at present and the ones that were to come.

"You still love it up here, don't you?" said Grace, "I can see it in your eyes."

"Yeah, I've always loved this place; from the very first time I set foot here it seemed to capture me," replied Rachel.

"Glenn and I fell in love with it right away too," said Grace. "As soon as we saw it, we knew."

Rachel watched as Grace searched for the words that could do justice to her thoughts.

"I was with him in the summer of love, you know; '67 and all the protests, it was quite a time," said Grace. "The boys had him through the best years of his life, the ones where he shared all his love. And he got to meet Kevin. He left on a high note; unaware, unanswerable, working on his outboard, getting ready for another fishing season."

"What about you; what now?" said Rachel.

"I'll stay. This is home. My sisters want me in Connecticut shuffling antiques in that ancient parlor they wish they could sell. They winter on those terrible cruise ships, you know, haunted by Viagra fed men. But not me, I'm inured to the North," she said, "You might have the blood, girl, but I'm the real Cree. I'm the one who knows the land and can persevere through the darkness and the blizzards. I can't imagine not canoeing on the rivers or growing sweet peas and carrots in the loam."

Rachel thought about Grace's words, and the power and the accuracy of her intentions.

"I'd have been a different person if you were my mother," she said, "In fact, I wish you were my mom. God, I can't believe I just said that. It feels good though; it's the truth. I love you. I love you so much. You should know that. This is where I should've grown up. Nowhere else has ever felt so much like home."

"Oh, Honey, my beautiful and precious Rachel, you *are* my daughter, the daughter I always wanted. Come now," she said through tears.

They embraced in the twilight of natures rustling amphitheater. An Eden filled with unconscious and nocturnal conversations taking place in more or less the same cadence since before man was a twinkle in the Almighty's eyes.

When they got back to the house, Rachel found Max and Robert in the basement asleep in front of the TV. They'd been watching their dad's favorite movie, *Slap Shot*. It was funny to her that a comedy about hockey was the eulogy that connected the boys to their father. Old laces, sweaty elbow pads, puck bruises, and the pain of lost teeth. She stood in the presence of the two sleeping men as she watched the scene where Paul Newman finally discovers who has controlling interest in his team. After that, she woke Max and they went up to bed.

Before they fell asleep Max told her that he was worried about Robert. He said that his brother had post traumatic stress from his time in the Balkans. It had been bad business in the Balkans, and Robert was struggling to digest the horrors. From a pile of rubble in Sarajevo, he peered across a land of atrocities. With ghastly disbelief, he witnessed a holocaust and a triumph of fears galloping its way through Eastern Europe.

He was still active-duty, being sent to hot spots around the globe. He said he could handle it; that he'd been trained to assimilate such things. But Max

wasn't convinced. Bones was fracturing from the
rushing impact of combat adrenalin. The evil intent
encased in bullets and bayonets was painfully
murdering him. Max said his brother was becoming
lost. But 'Bones lost' was a phrase Rachel found
impossible to imagine.

Following a period of mourning that would always
be woefully insufficient, they made their way back to
Brandon. In a dust covered hamlet along the highway
home, she saw the motel where they'd spent a rainy
night on the drive up. She and Max had made love
behind its poorly locked doors. In the morning there
had been a wakeup call that was far too early and a
hair dryer that wouldn't work. She also thought about
the Russian woman at the front desk who asked her
what tribe she was from.

Aubrey's shooting dominating the news that
summer, and Max was questioned by the police, as
were many, including the Fenders. But it was a drug
dealer named Beaver McLennan who ultimately
handed over the details to the crime. In an agreement
with the Crown to reduce charges, Beaver told the
jury everything they needed to hear to reach a guilty
verdict. Several of the defendants received lengthy
sentences, including Darcy Redcalf who got ten years
in a maximum pen.

The court found that Darcy threatened Aubrey
with bodily harm to induce the kid to give up the
master key to Tucker's. Due to Darcy's intimidation
and coercion, Aubrey was present on the night in

question. According to testimony, Aubrey was singled out as a snitch and the gangsters from Hamilton shot him where he stood. The whole city was unified in the feeling that ten years in Millhaven went nowhere near making things right.

The Fenders moved back to Western Ontario to live with Bev's sister; they said that they could no longer stay in a town where such terrible things had occurred. Each day that the house across the street sat empty, Max was reminded of everything he should've done. Rachel had played no less of a role in all that had gone down, and it was her who lugged around the stigma of a murderous brother, but it was Max who did the drinking. When men start drinking to escape the inescapable, she thought, it never comes to any good.

* * *

She averted her gaze from across the street and brought her focus back to Max; he was still staring at the former Fender residence with an indefinable expression. She wanted to touch his profile, both sturdy and bleak, like those pictures of Chief Poundmaker she'd seen as a child. She kept looking at him; she'd been observing odd occurrences since his return.

On one occasion, while downtown having lunch with Kelly, she saw him walk by with a bunch of men in suits. She wasn't certain what to make of it, but she assumed they were investors in his new business. Later the same week, she noticed him again in a very different situation. He was playing *Rocket Man* on the community piano by Buckley's Drug Store. Several people had stopped to listen and were totally impressed as they cheered and clapped. She was amazed. Then, six weeks later in a pub, she saw him playing guitar with a local band. He saw her as well, but she left before he finished the set.

Rachel knew Max better than anyone, and she'd never known him to have a musical bone in his body. When she made a remark about his impressive new ability, he told her that he'd learned to play while living in Vancouver. She wasn't fooled by his answer or the nonchalance with which it was given. She knew there was no way in hell that he could've learned the guitar and piano in one year, especially while working as a day laborer and attending treatment.

His answers didn't add up.

Like the construction project for GROWERS taking place on the corner of Rosser Street across from the Chamber of Commerce. She could see that he was running the show there. He appeared to know an improbable amount about carpentry, welding, and general contracting. It was the sort of stuff he had passing familiarity with from being raised on a farm. But she was unwilling to concede that he'd expanded his knowledge base to the extent she was witnessing due to one year of trade work on the Coast. And it was more than just simple tasks; he had the traits of a professional and skills that took years to acquire.

She was mesmerized by his tendency to behave as though he'd been remodeling commercial real estate, playing music, and speaking French for years. She was more than certain he was hiding something. It wasn't criminal or sinister, she thought, it was something that he couldn't quite explain yet or bring himself to share.

Sometimes she sat across the street at lunch and watched him and the other tradesmen transform the skeleton of the former IGA into the new centerpiece in town: GROWERS. Once in awhile, he would see her sitting there and walk over to say hi.

"What do you think," he asked.

"I can't wait to shop there," she said, "When will it open?"

"Easter," said Max.

The tone in his voice had been tempered by self-application and a clear strain of expertise. She didn't like to admit it to herself, but the added depth of his new dimensions resonated with her. He wasn't arrogant or overly self-assured; he was simply doing what he loved, and she found his diligence charming. He was a man transformed.

"Come in; I'll show you around," he said.

They walked through the open beams and took a wide and prolonged survey of the emerging isles, the produce section, and the deli.

"What are you living on?" she said, not quite sure how he managed to make ends meet, and concerned that he might be pushing his venture imprudently.

"Savings and a business loan," said Max, as though it should have been plainly obvious to her.

His answer wasn't totally implausible, but it seemed like a stretch. A project like GROWERS took significant capital, and not the sort that he had any practice at amassing. But it wasn't like he was flashy or driving a fancy sports car. In fact, it could be argued that his personal situation was just the opposite. His commercial ambitions might have been grand, but his physical existence was humble. He was focused on nutrition and strength training, and he told Rachel that he wanted to get the people of Brandon living healthier. In her strangest days, she could've never imagined such a pronounced metamorphosis.

He turned his attention from the place across the street and brought his eyes to rest on hers.

"How many are coming over today?" he said, as he took a breath of fall air.

"There'll be about ten of us."

"Nice," he said, as he handed her a check, "Thanks for inviting me."

"What's this?" she said.

"Back child support," said Max.

When he returned to Brandon, he petitioned the court for shared custody of the boys, and Rachel wasn't adverse to such an arrangement once she realized that he'd cleaned up his act. His candor before the magistrate was matter of fact. He admitted that his disappearance and delayed return was inexcusable. He made no secret that his absence had been a travesty for his family.

"I'm sorry," he said, "I know the last two years have been skint for you and the boys. You deserve better."

"It's just good to see you alive and healthy," she said, "I'm glad you're back."

She touched his face.

"You know the pine in the backyard is almost dead," he said to sober the conversation. "If you want, I could come by with the chainsaw and knock it down. I'm sure Daryl would give me a hand if I asked him."

"No, there's still a couple of yellow-shafted flickers living inside it," she said. "I'm not sure they're flying south this winter."

"You know those goddamn woodpeckers probably killed that tree in the first place," said Max.

"No, I think it's the bark beetle everyone keeps talking about," she said.

"Ok, it's your call," said Max as he smiled gently at her. "I know you love those birds, I just don't want to see a tree falling on the house."

"Don't worry about it," she said.

She put the check in her pocket and kissed him on the cheek. They went into the house and started helping the boys set the table for Thanksgiving.

2005

-Winter-

"Babe, you were meant for me, she said"

Value Village had marked down the price on their chairs, so Max bought three. They went nicely with the chrome arborite table he'd recently purchased. The rest of his furniture had been salvaged from garage sales and curbside giveaways. He couldn't be certain, but it felt as though some of the items were still wierdly attached to the prior owners by some supernatural combination of electrons.

His rental house near Errol Black Park was hopelessly dilapidated but relatively inexpensive. He looked at the chipped dishes in the sink and the flaking bits of drywall above the baseboard heaters. The bitter wind was almost coming through the walls. There was a small black and white T.V for watching the news, and a stack of overdue Lonely Planets resting on top of an overturned milk crate. He was thinking about his next trip to Winnipeg, his AUE's, and the twenty-one years of life that he'd managed to squeeze into less than two.

He walked thirteen blocks to work every morning and used an expired Saskatchewan driver's license for identification. He'd spent every last dime of his money to start GROWERS, and besides his comas, it was the single biggest gamble he'd ever taken in his life. When he thought about his situation and the risks involved with failure he wasn't fazed though; in fact, he felt expansive, as though he'd been reborn as multitudes. He also thought that he might be a little crazy, like the way some folks get during a full moon or a planetary retrograde.

The moon had definitely changed since he came back to Canada, or at least it appeared that way to new eyes. He was in a condition much different from the one in which he'd left. There was no squeezing into car trunks or stopping for six packs and cigarettes every two hours on the way home. Instead, he drove with Duncan from California to Montana. They camped and fished along the way, and discussed what they might do with the rest of their lives.

Both agreed it would be best if Max kept his reactions to Insynnium a secret. It seemed reasonable, at least until there was evidence of other people having similar episodes. Besides, he had all the spice he needed to keep him time travelling for years, it was the prize of an amplified sobriety, and that should have been enough for anyone, he thought.

"So, this is it," said Duncan, "you're finally going back?"

They were standing like two cowboys on a street in Missoula.

"Yeah," said Max. "Thanks for everything, man. What is my life, hey?"

"It's all good," said Duncan. "Remember to stay in touch. Pierre and I will let you know if we hear about anyone else…, well, you know."

"Sure," said Max.

"Just be careful with the comas, okay?" said Duncan.

"I will," said Max. "And good luck with your dissertation. I suppose the next time we see each other you'll be in D.C. or lecturing in Montreal or some damn thing?"

"Maybe," said Duncan, "We'll see. Keep your head about you; especially with Rachel. You don't need to stay in Brandon with her anymore; you can move on, you understand that, right?"

"I know, but the boys are there," he said. "It'll work out. I'm in a different place now."

"You sure as hell are," said Duncan with a smile.

Max gave his friend a hug. It always felt good to hug Duncan.

"Well, here comes the posse, bro. These guys will get you where you need to go," said Duncan, as he eyed two approaching men.

Max walked over to a black suburban idling by the curb. He took one last look at Duncan before he climbed inside. It would be years, and he would never again see him as he saw him that day. It was goodbye.

The SUV was driven by two beefy linebackers who worked for god-knows-who. They drove Max from Missoula to a ranch on the outskirts of Cut Bank. There, he was introduced to a human smuggler named Bibb Poteet. He was told by Duncan that if he followed Mr. Poteet's advice, everything would go smoothly.

Bibb was a wryly old raison of a rancher who kept horses and chickens and not much besides. He escorted Max along a range road just south of the Canadian border. When they reached the departure point, Bibb instructed Max to ride due north until he hit Highway 501, make a left onto the asphalt, and follow it to Cardston. Bibb said that people had been crossing into Canada this way for years and that Max would be back in Brandon before two switches of a mule's tail.

Max kick started the dirt bike; a four stroke escape hatch that was part of a pre-arranged deal. He tore up the prairie hard grass as he sped away. He looked in the bike's rearview mirror and saw Bibb leaning into the wind with a lenten expression and a dry strand of timothy clutched in his teeth. The sky was as big as a sky could get.

There was no Greyhound service when he reached Cardston, so he took his chances and rode on to Fort Macleod. He ended up selling the Yamaha for cash to a Piikani kid from Pincher Creek. The ponytailed denim clad youth put him in mind of Rachel's brother Gary. He thought about Gary's lugubrious stories of living and working on the Res at Shoal River, and then he thought about Kevin and Joshua.

Two days later, he stepped off the bus in Brandon. He walked down the street with only a backpack and a vague plan. He dusted off his jeans as he entered the Imperial Bank of Commerce and proceeded to deposit an enormous cashier's check – the thing had been taped to his hide for a thousand miles and some of his flesh came off with the adhesive. Pierre referred to the hefty check he'd written as 'compensation' for Max's willingness to allow him to scientifically investigate his comas. Max was thankful for Pierre's French Canadian generosity, and understood that the lion's share of the money was really largesse to get him started again.

It wasn't long before he found his boys at a playground under the supervision of a demanding and moody caretaker whom he immediately identified as his mother-in-law. It felt like years had elapsed. He and Cassandra had never made amends. There might have been a million miles between them, but in her eyes he was still a derelict dad and absentee husband.

He was thin with a reddish beard, and wore faded Wrangler's that needed a wash. His green t-shirt had a hole in the shoulder, and his shoes were losing their tread. He spent several days lurking behind juniper shrubs and jack pines spying on his family with hope and regret. He felt like some sort of unregenerate exhibitionist waiting to pounce on display as he secretly observed his kids dashing and rolling in the freshly mowed grass.

After two weeks of relative invisibility, the time was ripe to act. He went to a barbershop and then to the Goodwill before paying a visit to Rachel. When she answered the door, he was disarmed by how graciously she accepted his return. When her hands touched his face, and her eyes looked into his, he almost lapsed in his promise to Duncan.

* * *

Rachel Redcalf was from Brandon, Manitoba, but her blood flowed all the way from the pre-confederation tribes that once drifted with the buffalo. Max knew that even her Baccalaureate could not attenuate her attachment to the Plains.

After college, he and Rachel could've easily stayed in Kingston or travelled to Paris, but they moved back to Brandon instead. She had his heart, and he wanted to make sure that his life remained with her. In those days the world was a diamond, and she was the glitter at its core.

Rachel used her talents in social work to change the lives of Brandon's most vulnerable citizens. She volunteered at the food bank and blended in at the farmers market. She drank coffee with truckers in diners and ate donuts with teachers at town hall. She was natural; she fit, yet she didn't; like a wild rose at the edge of a summer fallow field.

Max's adjustment wasn't as seamless as hers. After attempting to work his way into the grocery business, he gave up and accepted a management position at a car wash out on Veteran's Way. The job wasn't exactly what he had in mind when he reflected on his collegiate aspirations, but Rachel was happy, and he found her enthusiasm rubbing off on him. They took for granted the rare nature of their bond and assumed their love for one another was a given.

But it wasn't all apple pie.

Rachel's two brothers and her sister struggled with a history of marginalization and substance abuse. They all had children, they all had continuous money problems, and they all had issues before the courts in some fashion or another.

And then there was Rachel's mother who was overly meddlesome and practically unavoidable. Cassandra was gloomy and negative and relentless with a grudge. Max discovered the woman harboring so many resentments and long smoldering slights that even a statistician would struggle to make sense of her score board.

Over time, however, he became inured to Cassandra's long winded bitching about sales people and the price of sugar. He got used to Gary and Darcy's money requests, and he took Rachel's half-sister, Jennifer, pretty much any place she needed to go after she wrecked her car. All of these demands, no matter how prickly or frustrating, were ultimately minor to him, and never came close to eclipsing his devotion to Rachel.

It could be argued that the pitfalls and difficulties confronting the Redcalf family caused Max and Rachel to soften against each other's edges in ways other couples couldn't. Their connection seemed stronger for what they wrestled with, including Rachel's reluctance to get married. They lived in sin until a whimsical trip to Winnipeg when he asked her to tie the knot and she surprisingly said, yes.

Naturally, she wanted the wedding to take place at the farm. She wanted to wear white among the viridescent vines and sprawling flowers of the wild McVista garden. She told Max that she wanted to gaze into his eyes under a canopy of violet clouds. The entire array of what she wanted included the fulfillment of amorous urges on starlit summer nights and warm promising mornings.

Except for Duncan Wisegerber, everyone made the effort to attend Max and Rachel's union. All were consociative and gracious in the Arcadian atmosphere, even Rachel's family. Robert also managed to make it, which astonished and delighted everyone in the extended community. The celebration was momentous and grand.

The days between their honeymoon and their first anniversary were a mere evanescence; a life swallowed by the time eclipsing attributes of love. The two spoke intimately about their dreams for the future as they screwed and sanded their way through the constant renovations demanded by the 'fixer-upper' they'd purchased.

Max said he wanted to start an organic grocery store. He pledged that he would tap into the whole foods movement and get the people of Brandon eating healthier. Rachel encouraged him in his goals, but other things intervened. Such as the extraordinary arrival of Kevin who distracted Max in a manner that made him wonder if any ambition could match the thrill of raising a child. There was also the unfathomable guilt over what happened to Aubrey

Fender, and the devastating shock of his father's passing.

And, of course, there was Bones.

In June of 2000, as good rolled with bad, Max found himself sitting with Robert in the basement of the farmhouse in front of a TV, much as they'd done as kids. It was post funeral and their dad was in the ground. Rachel had taken a walk with Grace, and the two were alone. They hadn't seen one another in close to three years. Robert had a coffee and Max held a martini.

The television was spewing news: *Vladimir Putin recently selected president of Russia; a follow up investigative piece on the damage from a tornado in Fort Worth; the fallout from Microsoft's violation of antitrust laws; the massive earthquake in southwestern Sumantra; and the shooting death of a high school student in Brandon, Manitoba.*

"Christ, can we turn this shit off?" said Max.

"You don't want to see if you get mentioned?" said Robert.

Max looked at his brother with pleading eyes.

"Let's put in *Slap Shot*?" said Bones, "Dad loved that one."

"Alright," said Max. He knew that the film would fill the gaps in the conversation they were trying to have.

"Why do you think Dad liked this movie so much?" said Robert, as he slid the DVD into the player.

Max thought about his dad.

His earliest memories of his father were of him smoking Player's and holding a drink containing ice cubes. He told stories that made the men around him laugh and some of the women blush – Max couldn't have been more than three or four at the time. He remembered his dad having sideburns and longish hair and shirts with large collars.

"I think it was the age, you know, the Seventies," he said. "I think the movie just represented his time. Besides, he always thought Newman was a great actor, and he loved hockey, so there you go."

"You know Dad used to bring joints to parties?" said Bones.

"No way," said Max, smiling a little.

"Way," said Robert. "And he was super cool about it too. Why do you think those things always ended up so mellow? He would bust out the weed around midnight, and everyone would take a toke. The smell was very distinct."

"I guess I was too young," said Max, "I just thought it was cigarettes?"

"Pretty funny, eh?" said Robert.

"I don't remember him smoking pot when we were growing up?" said Max.

"That's because Mom made him stop. I used to hear them fight about it," said Robert. "She told him word travelled fast in a small community, and that if they became known as potheads, it would make it hard for her at school. You know how this place was back then. People were fucking backward compared to them. It seemed like they were from another planet sometimes."

"They had friends, though," said Max.

"Hell yeah, people thought they were far out, they had all these fucking stories, these crazy hippies that fled to Canada," said Robert. "They were great entertainers. Remember when Dad got that new stereo for the living room along with all those albums from Zeppelin and the Eagles? I mean, how many times did we listen to, '*One of These Nights*' or zone out on '*No Quarter*'? And let's be honest, Mom was quite a looker back then; out shakin' it with the ladies."

Max thought about his mom.

"Yeah, Dad was pretty lucky, huh? What do you think made her love him so much?" he said.

"He could dance," said Robert, "I mean, he wasn't Fred Astaire, but he wasn't afraid to get out there and let it go. It made him cool, you know, not giving a fuck."

"He was pretty smart, too" continued Robert, "he always knew what to say to her, and he knew how to listen."

"I'm going to miss him," said Max.

"Me too," said Robert, as he looked at his younger brother like a parent might. "Is that why you're drinking so bloody much?"

"What do you mean?" said Max.

"I mean you've been knocking back high balls since you got here," said Robert.

"It's the shit going on back in Brandon, it's killing me," said Max. "I feel like I caused it. I should have fired that fucking asshole before anything went down. I knew something bad was about to happen and I just stood by and did nothing. I mean, you should have seen the parents; he was their only fucking kid. It was heartbreaking."

"Well, I'm not going to sit here and tell you war stories, but I've seen alcohol rip through the lives of more than a few men and I don't want to see it happen to you."

"Come on Robert; don't patronize me with that bullshit. You telling me you've never taken a drink or two to get through a rough patch."

"This isn't about me. You've got a beautiful family with another kid on the way, and Mom counts on you, especially now."

"Yeah, because we all know you're going back to the dark ends of the earth," said Max. "You know you're not right, man. You're running from your demons; you need help. As far as I'm concerned, there isn't any difference between what you're doing and what I'm doing."

"It's a little different," said Robert, with a note of resignation in his voice.

"Why don't you quit," said Max, "It's already cost you a marriage and your mental health."

"You're one to talk about goddamn mental health," said Robert.

"How many times do you think you've seen Mom in the last five years?" said Max. "It stresses her out. She never knows where you're at on those long deployments or what kind of shit you're mixed up in."

"Don't put a bunch of guilt on me for the life I've chosen," said Robert, "I'm keeping The West free. Besides, I'm not the one turning into a piss-head."

"Yeah, you're doing great; a fucking war junky, good on ya," said Max.

Robert looked at him and began to chuckle.

"What?" said Max un-amused.

"You're right, Bro, I am a goddamn war junky, what can I say. You know, if Dad were sitting here he'd probably roll a joint and tell us to chill out; 'live and let die'."

Robert smiled.

But Max failed to see the humor in his brother's synopsis, he went off to take a piss and make himself another martini.

Slap Shot continued playing.

The next thing he remembered was Rachel waking him up to come to bed.

After the funeral, Max kept drinking, and part of it had to do with the fact that he felt largely functional, even as the amount of booze he consumed continued to climb. Though he was becoming pathetic to Rachel and antagonistic to her family, there was a sad and despondent part of him that relished such a slide. The drinking allowed him to avoid seeing himself in the bright light of sobriety. Alcohol fully captured him in its numbing comforts; it was the crutch upon which his courage rested, and the emotional Kevlar of his existence. Once everything had slipped about as far as things could slip, the winds of self-destruction blew him completely out of town.

One day with rain falling in two directions and a succession of hail showers tormenting the crops, he found himself sitting on a barstool pissing away the last of his wife's money.

The whiskey tasted good as he eavesdropped on a conversation taking place at the far end of the counter. A big ornery bear of a man was whinging to the bartender about the price of oil and the origins of the petrodollar. The man worked on a drilling rig in Alberta, and he'd come home to visit his kids and brag to whoever would listen about all the money he was making.

"Are you lookin' for guys?" said Max.

"I don't know. Am I lookin' for guys, Bill?" said the man to the bartender, and they both laughed.

Max took another drink of whiskey and decided they could go fuck themselves.

"Hey, buddy, I'm just messin' with you," said the man, "Of course I'm lookin' for guys, I'm always lookin' for guys. If you can stay sober and don't mind living in a camp, you can start Friday."

The man was Stan, and he was a former toolpush who'd gone back to the brake handle for personal reasons and tax exemptions, and he told Max that his rig was drilling for gas; up to six weeks on directional bores. He said he was headed to Drayton Valley and that Max could catch a ride. When Max told Rachel he was leaving town for awhile; she seemed halfway hopeful about his prospects.

By Canada Day, he was mixing mud and racking back drill pipe in the derrick like somebody who knew what they were doing. The term 'dry camp' didn't carry much weight, and he easily found other crew members willing to partake in a cocktail hour. They drank bourbon and vodka near the river behind the generator, and sometimes mangy brown bears would wander out onto the banks and sniff at the air. Max would growl and throw empty bottles at them. He remembered the scruffy cinnamon colored animals having the saddest eyes he'd ever seen.

When the crew moved back to Calgary to work in the rig yard, Stan told Max he could live with him at his place in the city. The driller had a split-level off Shaganappi Trail that he rented to University students and foreigners doing post-doctoral research. But as it was the middle of summer, the only other person in the house besides Max and Stan was a dancer named Tracy.

Tracy claimed to be an aspiring cheerleader, and she seemed to get off scampering around the house in revealing outfits and tanning naked in the backyard. She said she was saving money to move back to Burnaby and study accounting at Simon Fraser. She had one of those tiny delicate dogs that wear sweaters and a Subaru with a bad ignition.

Stan's house was cool with a nice directional breeze that blew gently out of the Bow Valley. On days off, and with little ambition to go back to Brandon, Max would kick it in the comfortable lounge chairs on the deck drinking gin and tonics with Tracy.

To exist in a state of unrelenting inebriation his faculties had undergone a recalibration to accommodate the bottles of distilled grain product floating around on his hemoglobin. On rare occasions when he found himself accidentally sober, he would be forced to look deep into the pit of a dipsomaniac's recollection in order to conjure up what the fuck he'd done while completely blotto.

What he'd done, Stan intently told him, was sleep with Tracy. Stan also told him that if he continued to keep his dick wet with the house dancer, he'd probably catch the clap. He told him to go home and see his kids.

Max knew Stan was right on all counts. He knew that each time he trespassed against Rachel or neglected to visit the boys, he slipped further into a cocktail of despair.

In September there was a work accident while the guys were cutting a length of drill cable. One of the roughnecks lost part of his hand. It may or may not have been Max's fault, but Stan fired him regardless, and that was the catalyst that drove him back to Brandon.

When he arrived in the Wheat City, he found it intolerable. Rachel didn't exactly kick him out of the house, but her rules were impossible. So, he decided to move up to Nipawin where his mom agreed to take him in. As autumn gave way to winter, he gathered his nuts ahead of the approaching frost, an activity which mostly involved squirreling away spirits.

* * *

Max felt like his past was two decades back, rather than merely the year before last. Rachel was showing him the audacity of forgiveness, and for that he was grateful. But everything between them looked like the vestiges of a relationship extinguished twenty years ago. The past and the future had all been reshaped, and he'd experienced too many things in his AUE's for anything to stay the same. In another twelve months he'd have new eyes again; a completely different man, changed by another decade. For him, the present had become but a weigh station for voyages into accelerated learning and extra-sensory indulgence never known by another person.

He had no illusions about the extent to which he'd damaged Rachel's heart. Her large hazel eyes, of which he'd seen few that could compare, still stared uncompromisingly into his soul. He tried not to look too deeply into her questioning glances because they begged for a truth he simply could not deliver.

It was the great irony of time travel, he thought: the more you did it, the more convinced you became that no one would ever believe you.

Rachel was always dropping by his construction site with the boys. She told him that Kevin and Josh were fascinated by the tools and the machinery. But he was fairly certain it was Rachel who was fascinated. She showed up unexpectedly and often in the strangest places. He could tell that she was looking for something, and he figured it was for signs of another woman. But she wouldn't glimpse a soul, he told himself, not in this world.

On three-dollar Wednesdays, he played guitar for a band called, '*Pink Pants and the Woo*,' at the Ralston County Road House along the Trans-Canada. At one point in the evening the lead singer, a woman, covered a favorite by request.[11] Max caught sight of Rachel standing at the back of the room. She had tears in her eyes, and for a moment he felt the need to run to her. But his urge surfed over the crowd and passed as fast as it arrived. The next thing he knew he was smiling at a hungry cougar dancing close to the stage. When he looked up again, Rachel was gone, and he saw the bouncer pull the door shut as snow from the street blew in around its edges.

---

[11] **#2** on the Billboard Year-End Hot 100 singles of 1997. **"You Were Meant for Me"** by <u>Jewel</u> from the album *Pieces of You.* Atlantic, 1996. Max and Rachel had gone to Winnipeg to get away from Brandon for the weekend. They'd bought new clothes and a blender and were hungry for steaks and beer. The restaurant they selected was fancy with a dance floor in the middle. A group of intoxicated Nova Scotians were dominating the jukebox, but when Jewel's song came through its speakers Max grabbed Rachel and they danced. At the end of the song he held her close and asked her to marry him. She kissed him on the lips with her sensuous reply.

Part III

The Sound
Of
Germination

2007

-Winter-

*"It would be impossible to forget
something so supernatural"*

The late afternoon air had a way of forcing a chill beneath the street-side door. A heater with its coils aglow hummed in the corner, repelling the invading cold that roamed through the restaurant.

Duncan asked himself how many hours he'd spent sitting in Jim's culinary establishment munching on olives and reviewing calculations. Two fingers of Cutty Sark sat before him in a glass with ice. Monty was next to him sleeping on the bench. They were waiting for Pierre.

He knew everyone wanted more. He told himself that if the enterprise went beyond America, then he and Pierre would have to put serious thought into relocation. So far, however, their role was still unknown, and hiding in plain sight continued to be their greatest asset.

When he passed the spice to Eric and Moe, he knew that the armature had been set in motion to spread the substance from New Jersey to Albuquerque. What he hadn't fully appreciated was the almost rabid demand that followed. Although Insynnium wasn't physically addictive, the psychological implications of dreaming with historical and personal clarity made folks mad with need. He and Pierre had to ramp up production to stay ahead of the curve. That, of course, introduced a perplexing set of challenges to the secret exchange methods feeding Eric's networks and alliances. Duncan didn't care to court risk of exposure. It was readily apparent that Insynnium was not containable, and he and Pierre had to decide whether to reel it in or take the brakes off completely. Either way, their creation seemed bent on swallowing the world whole.

He rarely consumed the stuff anymore, but he'd taken some capsules the night before last to remind himself why people were so drawn to its qualities. The powder gave him a dose of his past that he wouldn't have forgotten with or without enhancement.

* * *

On their first day in Tel Aviv sand was in the air and biting hard under a red sun. The pre-noon streets stirred with an impatient faux-dawn fever, as though war had been declared, or perhaps Saturnalia.

Sarah was on the phone trying to reach her cousin so the three of them could meet up for a drink at a bistro along Allenby. The tonic of the Middle East was not for the faint of heart, but Duncan's emerging fascination with Israel's omnibus of adaptations was a distraction from the country's existential unease.

Sarah said that her cousin, Barbara, was a Sabra from Galilee. But when Duncan met her, he found

Barbara's English to have a dominant Spanish accent sprinkled with only traces of Hebrew. She was alluring, no doubt, and though he suspected her to be linked to espionage activities, this did nothing to stop her tongue from caressing his ear with its lilting inflections; a not-so-subtle reminder of the reason he'd come to Israel in the first place.

"This city is full on," he said to her, as the evening revelry escalated along the avenue.

"Yeah, I know, it's like Marti Gras. Visitors always expect it to be like before when everybody was marching with Dayan through the Negev. But it's not like that anymore. It's all about Ecstasy. There're pills, and it's open and sexy and totally free," she said.

Someone suggested they get high.

That night the three danced through the clubs and the bacchanal forests of house music amplified by strobe lights and pelvic beats aggressively ushering in a new century of freedom and ambition. At four in the morning they crashed from exhaustion near the waves along the Shlomo Lahat Promenade.

After sunrise, they located Barbara's car and drove north. She was a kibbutznik from the Haifa district, and she insisted that Duncan and Sarah stay with her. After all, she was mishpocha, and that was one prong of the couple's trip; as for the prime objective, Barbara said she required more time to finish tracking down contacts and arranging for introductions.

Duncan and Sarah did not expect to work physically on the land during their visit to Palestine, but it was hard to correctly anticipate such a place.

After a month, however, the sun and the earth made an oven of the desert, and its baking effect fixed a golden shine to Sarah's skin while Duncan became positively charcoal. Over the course of five weeks, the couple morphed into tough and agile farmers who worked outdoors and laughed from their bellies at the startling state of the human condition. Duncan hadn't felt so alive or at peace since his summer visits to Nipawin. He'd also fallen in love with Sarah, and that helped a bit too.

Eventually, there came an evening on which the two were driven to Timrat to visit with an eminently old but shockingly well-preserved woman named, Leah. Duncan noted that the woman had the presence of an oracle when she entered the candle lit and corner-less adobe kitchen. Her eyes informed everyone present that she'd witnessed suffering on a catastrophic scale; what happens when human compassion is eclipsed across continents?

Leah brought her arms up from her lap and they rested on a circular walnut table. Her meticulous fingers interlaced as she studied Barbara's expression before moving her eyes to Sarah, and then on to Duncan, where they ambitiously settled. She told him that she knew of a man, still living, who possessed the remedy he was in search of.

Outside, a Blackhawk helo ripped through the overhead air in the direction of Nazareth; a dark pursuit taking shape according to covert plans. The concussion of its rotating blades punctuated Leah's movements as she rolled up her sleeve. There was a number inked onto an otherwise flawless forearm. She said she'd known a man in Bergen Belsen who'd been a survivor like herself - a fellow prisoner in the devil's paradise who'd gone by the name of Felix.

He had been a well-respected scientist working in Leipzig among a small and secretive avant-garde investigating the nascent discipline of molecular biology. He was also the son of a Jewish mother and a notorious seducer of men. He had the radical misfortune of being captured by the German army just when his passage to America seemed assured. In the concentration camp, he gained a reputation for being a 'mixer of herbs.' And by way of his unique talent, he managed to stay alive in the Nazi grasp.

"He gave that psychopath, Mengele, the ability to sleep at night," said Leah, with a wry expression that stressed the brilliance of an inner light. "Apparently when you run too far afoul of your humanness the darkness makes you an insomniac."

"What exactly did Felix do?" said Barbara in a manner that sounded marginally interrogative of the old woman.

"He fed his potions and concoctions to the Nazi brass, and to the guards, and even to the dogs once in awhile," she said. "Admittedly, he gave comfort to the enemy, but they respected his ability and took mercy on those he favored."

"And he favored you, did he?" said Barbara skeptically.

"Yes," said Leah. "He once told me that I reminded him of his sister who died in a flu epidemic before the war."

Duncan could see that Barbara was unconvinced, and her eyes held an intense Mossad-ish gleam as she looked at Leah with the expectation, or perhaps insinuation, that there should have been more to her answer.

"It was war, and worse than war," said Leah in defiance of Barbara's unspoken accusations. "It was hunger and cruelty and babies too weak to cry out; it was extermination. Moments of peace were like hen's teeth in the brutality. The world wasn't even aware of what was happening to us yet. Everyone wanted to dream about the life they'd had before everything was stolen."

There was a silent pause as those at the table thought about occult spells, Third Reich captors, and skeptical minds.

"Young man," said Leah, as she looked at Duncan. "Felix lives in a town called, Sinop; a place that rests its gaze on the Black Sea. When you get off the bus near the main square, you will see a large bazaar. Walk to the prominent spice stand at the center and he will find you there."

She continued to look at Duncan and then said, "Give him my best will you, it's been years since I've seen him."

Following his meeting with Leah, Duncan became slightly unsettled about locating Felix in Turkey. He reviewed in his mind what Leah had reported, and began to wonder what kind of a man created such veiled and insoluble elixirs; products, that by the looks of Leah, could reach well beyond what modern pharmaceutical science was capable of achieving.

"She was amazing," said Duncan, "Her posture and her skin, for a ninety-three-year-old woman?"

"She told Barbara that it's all about coconut oil and yoga," said Sarah, half in jest. "But, yeah, it's true, she looks good considering her past."

"This Felix guy sounds like more of a magician than a scientist," said Duncan.

"Are you alright?" said Sarah.

"Yeah, I'm fine, it just feels a little odd, you know? Going to meet this guy," said Duncan.

"Mr. Wisegerber, are you getting cold feet?" she teased.

"I might feel better if you went with me," he said.

"Call it female intuition," she said, "but I think it's best if you meet him on your own."

"Do you think he can restore me?"

"Look at you," she said, "You've already been restored. This is just the physical stage."

"You know what I mean."

"Relax, no matter what happens we'll always have Israel."

"Yeah, sure," he said as he raised a glass of Slivovitz. "L'chiam."

Sinop was a tiled roofed city eight hours by bus from Istanbul, and it reminded Duncan of a place he once visited in Cypress. He disembarked on Batur

Road and made his way into the heart of the market. It was crowded and dusty with groups of Turkish and Arab men smoking shishas and playing Backgammon and women feeding chickens in pothole infected alleys. The entire sight was a living cliché.

It wasn't long before Duncan was spotted and intercepted by a gentleman who told him, using a translation device, that he was Felix's neighbor. Duncan considered the machinations that had created such a rendezvous. He thought about the maze of messages that must have passed lips and charted cell phones to occasion such a well timed moment. He climbed into the back of a dark sedan of European vintage and made his way to the house of god only knew who.

Felix was a hundred on the day Duncan met him, and he could tell at an instant that the old man knew secrets well beyond the ken of your average secret keeper. Felix's voice was undiminished, and he spoke English with a continental accent that was hard to pinpoint but seemed to move on a sliding scale between Hamburg and Bucharest. His mobility was mesmerizing in its agile and unaided fluidity. Like Leah, the man was a marvel, considering his age.

He understood why Duncan had come to see him, and he exhibited a certain amount of feisty and slightly racist resistance to a young black man in search of an erection. He eyed Duncan suspiciously as though Duncan might be feigning impotence to get at other information; facts buried much deeper. He informed Duncan that all his secrets would go with him to the grave, and that he hadn't taught a single soul his ancient craft nor did he intend to. He said that not even Leah could begin to guess what was inside his century savoring skull.

Though he had neighbors who checked in on him, he was largely solitary and found solace in meditation. He told Duncan he was financially independent because of money sent from overseas; mostly former lovers whom he amusingly referred to as 'spellbound.' Although there were moments of cultural awkwardness, the men strolled through town together and visited with assorted locals. Duncan was undoubtedly under Felix's scrutiny as the old man evaluated the young man's capacity to assimilate and hold confidences – pieces of himself he would not ordinarily share. As he began disclosing more and more, Duncan got the disquieting sense that the enchanting archimage was about to unburden himself of some heavy and long held piece of information not meant to be known by others.

At the conclusion of a captivating fortnight, Felix handed Duncan a small twig of White Saxaul and asked him to chew it thoroughly. It was covered in a strange ointment that tasted vaguely of horse radish. Duncan washed the masticated wood down with a goblet of water. Next, he was instructed by Felix to enjoy a glass of port, on the heels of which he was to take a nap with erotic thoughts on his mind.

Duncan retired to a cot at the back of the dwelling and fell into the grips of a siesta that contained tropical beaches rousingly occupied by sparsely clad woman.

When he awoke, he had the most wonderful sensation of being whole again. He felt a sturdy banana-like protuberance rising between his legs. He pulled down his boxers and allowed a springing erection to reach full attention. At the very moment he suspected he was hallucinating, Felix appeared beside him.

"It'll be hard like that for another ten minutes or so," said Felix in a matter-of-fact tone. "It's just the initial effect of what I gave you. How does it feel?"

Duncan was startled by the old man's materialization, so silent in the shadows of the house. He had come to expect the scratch of a shuffling step or the rasp of a cough as semaphores of the elderly. But not with Felix, he was as quiet as a lizard in the cool reprieve of the den-like anteroom.

"It feels awesome," said Duncan, gradually unabashed by the old wizard's presence as he smiled broadly without the slightest detumescence.

"Enjoy it, my boy, and try not to get shot again," said Felix.

"What do I owe you for this, how can I repay you?" said Duncan, staring at his miraculously resurrected penis.

"It's been so long since I've had the opportunity to help a gentleman with his cock that I've sort of forgotten what the fee is, though I suspect it was something ludicrous. Maybe you can do me a favor, and we can call it even?"

"Anything," said Duncan, "you've restored me." He pulled on a pair of khakis along with a thread strained polo shirt.

Later, after the potency of the marinated wood had subsided, the two men took tea, with cream and sugar, at a table under a date palm in a courtyard surveilled by a Siamese cat.

"I need you to deliver a personal message to an old friend," said Felix, "His name is Aloysius Smyth, and he'd be about ninety by now. I received a letter from him last month, and he told me that he hasn't got long. He wants my forgiveness before he dies."

"Where does he live?" said Duncan.

"That's a good question. There hasn't been a return address on his letters for years. But I believe that he's somewhere in Oregon or Northern California."

"That's pretty vague, but I'll see what I can do," said Duncan. "What would you like me to say when I find him?"

"Tell him that it's over. Tell him that I forgive him. He'll know that you've spoken with me when you mention the seeds."

"I'm sorry, I think I've lost you," said Duncan. "I don't quite follow, what was that about seeds?"

Felix chuckled at Duncan's perplexed expression. "I once gave Aloysius a bag of seeds along with some notes on their history and properties. It was a farewell gesture when our relationship ended. I told him that his duplicity would be forgiven when he sprouted them."

There was a thoughtful pause between the two as they studied each other.

"Alex is convinced that the seeds are completely un-sprout-able, but they're not," said Felix, "they're most certainly not."

"So, what's the story?" said Duncan.

Felix took a deep breath and proceeded to tell him a lengthy and unbelievable story about the seeds and the secret to their germination. When he finished, he wrapped things up with a dire warning.

"Because the seeds are Egyptian, they're also surrounded by a pernicious curse."

"Naturally," said Duncan, certifiably intrigued but slightly the smart ass.

Felix looked at Duncan in a very unusual way, and the old man's expression wizened and turned grim.

"I'm quite serious, kid," he said, "Don't underestimate this one."

He leaned in close to Duncan's ear for added effect.

"Only three can ever know, so never tell a soul, lest the one you love the most be devoured by a ghost."

Duncan was silent.

"This means that after you tell Aloysius the secret to germination, you can never mention it to another living soul, otherwise those you cherish most will be swiftly and unexpectedly gathered up by the reaper. I've seen it happen."

This time, the thoughtful pause between the two stretched for days.

On the afternoon of his departure, Felix fixed a worn kaffiyeh around Duncan's neck and ran his hands over his face. "This brought me luck when I wandered with the Bedouins," said Felix.

Duncan swore he saw Felix perform a mummified shape shift, if only for a second. There was something dark and unavoidable that had been passed to him like a virus; the stains - was it blood? - and the smell - was it camel? - on the kaffiyeh were a visceral reminder not to fuck with the curse.

"Walk in the way of the light," said Felix.

As Duncan took his leave, he realized that he'd consented to a not insignificant burden in tracking down Aloysius. But everything had its cost, he told himself, and Felix's fee for services rendered appeared a meager price in the face of such a robust Fisher King cure.

He had a mild case of butterflies as the plane touched down at Ben Gurion International. His reawakened potency was accentuated by the fact that within hours he'd be in Sarah's arms. He wanted to get to the kibbutz and plunge his hands into the rehabilitated land. He wanted to continue growing food and breathing air in a co-habitable arrangement that finally felt sustainable. There was a moment on the tarmac when he positively envisioned settling in Israel with Sarah, or perhaps Canada, if it came to that. He might even look up Max.

The airport was more crowded and chaotic than usual, and travelers were encountering the confusion and frustration of added security as they made their way to the baggage claim. When he hailed a cab, the driver informed him that it would take awhile to reach his destination because of a blockage on one of the main thoroughfares out of the city.

According to news reports, a bus travelling south on the Ayalon Highway north of Hadera was destroyed by a bomb. It was a suicide attack that always came as a cold surprise no matter how inured everyone seemed to such inevitabilities. The bus and its riders had been annihilated by ball bearings, nails, and fire. The police and military were attempting to piece it together.

The cab driver took keen notice of arterial options to steer them around the carnage, but no level of fancy driving would allow anyone to avoid the social reverberations set off by those dead set on blowing themselves up. It was a whole other category of the human stain, far beyond the reach of the poet, that caused minds, so deprived of freedom and crippled by despair, to migrate into the nihilistic vortex. Duncan knew that he'd never understand the struggle because he didn't have enough flesh invested. Maybe it was like Bones once said: politics doesn't become real until you debate it through the sights of a rifle.

When the cab reached the Kibbutz, Duncan went to the house where he and Sarah were shacked up. He let himself in through the side door and immediately saw her in the garden tending some flowers in a raised bed. She was facing away from him, and her dark locks were blowing in the breeze as he approached her from behind. He was about to seize her by the waist when he noticed that she'd cut her hair.

She turned to face him, and she was crying.

That's when he realized he was looking at Barbara; the Sabra, the huntress, the spy.

"What's going on?" he said with puzzlement set on edge.

"Oh Duncan," she said, with loss and anguish in her voice, "Sarah was killed in a terrorist attack."

"The bus outside Hadera?"

"Yes."

"What was she doing on the bus?"

"She was going to meet you. She wanted to surprise you."

They held each other in a heart crippled embrace and wept devastated inconsolable tears.

Duncan didn't know where to go, so he stayed at the kibbutz in a semi-paralyzed state.

There were no reasons for the attack, it was random and senseless. There were many reasons for the attach it was planned and purposeful. It was something and nothing at the same time.

There were no answers and there was no justice.

Sarah's remains were repatriated to California.

Barbara disappeared for several weeks.

Duncan discovered she was back when he bumped into her at Café that the three of them used to frequent.

Her lips were full, and her eyes were eager and piercing. Her voice made his rejuvenated loins come to life. She sat close, and he could smell coffee and tobacco on her breath; ordinarily a nauseating effrontery that would've completely turned him off, but from her lungs it was like breathing the aroma of revolution and plowed earth. His thoughts regressed and wandered.[12]

"I'm leaving for good next week," she said, "and I think you should do the same."

He was suddenly alerted to the now.

"Where are you going?" he said.

"Chile. My dad helps organize farm workers north of Santiago."

"So, you're not really from here then, are you?"

"It's complicated."

"Tell me about it."

"Maybe another time," she said.

But Duncan knew there would never be another time.

"We had plans, you know," he said.

---

[12]**#2** on the Billboard Year-End hot 100 singles of 2000. **"Smooth"** by <u>Santana featuring Rob Thomas</u> from the album *Supernatural*. Matt Serletic, 1999. The heroes of Israel weren't the ones that came to mind when Duncan rocked up on the scene. Nobody seemed to give a shit about the commandos and the fighter pilots anymore. Everyone was gushing over actors he'd never heard of, and singers that he couldn't imitate; and all the fucking DJ's with their Chicago House and Detroit Techno. And the women, who were all so hot that it was like travelling through Cosmo. But it was Santana's infectious Latin number sung by Thomas that ruled the airwaves and remained in Duncan's head as he heard it again and again. It was even playing at the café as Barbara explained to him how it had to be, just before she became a memory.

"I know," said Barbara, "You loved her, and so did I. You'll need time, but not here, and not with me. Look after yourself, and find out what it is that you need to do; what comforts you need to sacrifice so that you can move on."

"I could go with you to Chile, I speak pretty decent Spanish," said Duncan. He'd never sounded so pathetic in his life as he sipped at a macchiato.

"It would take more than Spanish," she said.

She kissed Duncan, and placed her hands on top of his; her way of letting him know that she was totally impervious to his charms and his magnetism.

When she got up to leave, he knew that she was beyond him.

"Thanks for the coffee," she said as she walked away.

"Don't mention it," he replied.

* * *

Pierre entered Jesus' carrying a post card and threw it on the table in front of Duncan. Monty stirred with a muffled growl as Pierre took a seat across from them.

"Hey, Kimparis, can we get two more whiskeys over here," hollered Pierre. "Maybe something in a single malt variety."

"Hold on to your balls," shouted Jim from a nether region of the kitchen, "I'm trying to make a goddamn calzone here."

"I thought you hired college kids to bake those for you?" yelled Pierre toward the rear of the empty parlor as he winked at Duncan.

"Good help is hard to find, you want a job?" said Jim sarcastically, as he disappeared through the back door to have a smoke.

Pierre looked at Duncan in a confiding manner and began speaking in a tone that was barely more than a whisper.

"I think we need to talk about the risks of expanding. You know, there's nothing wrong with keeping the supply fixed and allowing the price to continue to climb if you catch my drift?"

"Eric wants to expand the spice into Europe, he senses a huge opportunity there," said Duncan.

"Yeah, and I want a bigger cock," said Pierre. "Look, it doesn't matter what Eric does or does not want. We call the shots. Eric is not running the show despite what he believes. None of us is hurting for cash. You and I are still completely anonymous, and the interest of the FBI, the pharmaceuticals, and the mob is still relatively low."

"You know Eric and his ambitious commercial designs," said Duncan, "we're the ones who gave him that freedom. We knew this when we set it free, Pierre."

"Well, perhaps we need to have our 'Dutch associates' exert a little force on his ass to remind him that this thing is bigger than him."

"Only if it comes to that; Eric's my friend and he's our front man to the world. He's the face of Insynnium, and for that we should be thankful."

"Yeah, well, he's starting to piss me off," said Pierre. "And speaking of friends, I got that in the mail today." He pointed to the post card resting on the table.

The card had been sent to Pierre from Niagara Falls and was signed by Max. The correspondence revealed nothing of a psychosis or the ramblings of time travel, and both men sort of half smiled at one another as they wondered what Max could be doing at Niagara Falls. The simple message on the back mentioned that he was enjoying the company of his boys and running his grocery business.

Duncan stared at the postcard; it was a beautifully captured photo of one of the world's largest waterfalls tumbling with spectacular quantity from its crest to the river below. He pictured Max going over the rim in a barrel, and then he tossed the card on the table and looked up at Pierre.

"Seems like Max is doing well," said Pierre.

"Yes, it seems that way," said Duncan, as he took another sip of Scotch.

1994

-AUE-

"There's never one sign, it's many; and the road forks often"

In general, Max would take a monthly dose of Insynnium and wake up in Kingston; either in his old dorm room or in the aging Victorian on Peel Street where he shared a bed with Rachel. Less frequently he would wake up in Brandon, and on rare occasions, back at the farm in Nipawin.

In any case, it was never long, after returning to his past, that he informed Duncan or Rachel (invariably his roommate or bedmate in the consistently executed AUE's) that he had no intention to continue studying commerce at Queens.

Duncan's blasé and unalterable refrain was to look at Max quizzically and ask, "So dude, what are you gonna do then?" To which Max, over the course of successive AUE's, formulated a variety of interesting responses, or simply shrugged and changed the subject.

Rachel, on the other hand, was more consoling and process orientated regarding his academic goals and life decisions, but the net result was always the same: he would leave the university, abandon Rachel, part ways with Duncan, and basically sever all ties to his former existence.

The actual physical departure, however, was as subtle as walking out the door as if he were on his way to a movie or the library, but instead of returning he just disappeared into the world.

When he awoke on April 5, 1994, it seemed to be courtesy of Kurt Cobain. *Smells Like Teen Spirit* was on the radio alarm, and it blasted into his ear with its grungy concussion. He sat up with a start. Rachel merely stirred and continued to sleep.

In the kitchen, while still dressed in his pajamas, he was informed by Duncan that he had an economics final at Kenny Hall in thirty-seven minutes. It took him a moment, as it always did, to realize exactly where he was. But soon confusion gave way to gratitude for the additional year of life he was about to receive.

He viewed copious amounts of *Seinfeld*, *The Fresh Prince of Bel-Air*, and *Kids in the Hall* to mentally prepare for the shock of the Nineties, but his preparation was never sufficient enough to effectively fortify him against the abrupt bump of an internet-less reality.

He went to the front room and flipped on the television: *discussion of the ceasefire in Croatia, interview with Elvis Stojko, something about Netscape Communications, and Tony Curtis's heart.* He switched off the TV and returned to his room. He realized that he was the only person on earth who knew what would happen the following day: *Chuck Jones would be found guilty of breaking into Marla Maples home, the Rwandan Genocide would begin, and the world would learn that the lead singer of Nirvana was gone.*

He packed a duffle bag, grabbed a durable coat, and kissed Rachel on a sleeping cheek. Then he walked to the bus depot and bought a ticket to Montreal.

That was ten months ago.

Since then, he'd used his AUE to become an Albanian carpenter working in central Spain.

Sebastian handed him a freshly cut 2x4, and he used it to support the small lean-to that he'd constructed off the back of the house. Sebastian was the nine-year-old boy who lived in the house with his mother, Sarita, in the town of Constantina. He was a cute kid who had endless patience for Max and his unnatural Spanish.

Children were super-effective teachers of language, thought Max. Kids could be counted on to be persistent in their attempts to understand and be understood. And that's how it was with Seb; there was frankness about the clarity of Max's pronunciation that would have been difficult to accept from an adult. The boy was linguistically ruthless, and Max loved that about him.

On the weekends, Seb had no school, so he would help Max make repairs around the house. They operated like a father and son team, fixing plumbing, changing light bulbs, and eating cold cut sandwiches beneath the penetrating rays of the spring sun. Sebastian's real father lived in Madrid and seemed to have scant interest in visiting his son. Max thought about his own boys, and, of course, the day he would be forced to leave Seb.

But Seb would always have his mother.

Sarita was sultry and contagious, and Max had capitalized on her status as an amorous divorcee to live out an intricate romantic sex fantasy. In the psychological jumble of his multi-life existence he had developed an attraction to desperate and beautiful woman with one or two children, so the arrangement was perfect.

He'd travelled to Spain several times. He would settle into various domestic patterns in different towns with different women. The way he figured it, spending his days breathing the mountain air of a small village or his nights playing music in a local band was far more meaningful than visiting every tourist site in Western Europe.

He competed with no one in his AUE's, nor did he strive for the fleeting and commercialized allure of youth and virility, since his AUE's handed him these attributes in perpetuity. Your imagination and ambitions change, he told himself, when your life becomes less finite. The simple pleasures of living in the backwaters of Andalusia or Catalonia were by far the best way to spend a year. The only way such a self-contained and pastoral adventure could be enhanced, he discovered, was through the remarkable existential twist of becoming another person.

When it came to adopting a new identity, he looked for obscurity, not popularity; and that's how he fell upon Albania. He learned that to become an Albanian – or any other nationality for that matter - it was necessary to become acquainted with a man named, Jean-Luc, who sold used cars in Saint Hubert. Jean-Luc knew a guy who knew a guy who could get his hands on falsified travel documents smuggled through Jacque Cartier Pier in the heart of Old Montreal.

For Max, the time and trouble expended to procure a false passport from a small misunderstood country was far outweighed by the thrill of playing a non-existent person in an inconsequential universe. Besides, a regular vacation from living as a Canadian tended to be liberating. Every time he erased his nationality, the currency and trappings of the English language moved away from him, along with the expectations and privileges that went with it.

As soon as he boarded the cargo ship docked at the mouth of the Saint Laurence, he ceased to be a man from a wealthy G7 nation with a maple leaf sewn onto his backpack; instead, he became Fatmir Gashi from Tirana, who framed houses and installed kitchen cabinets with his hands.

He switched vessels in Portsmouth[13] and made his way to the entrance of the Alboran Sea on a British oil tanker. The freighter anchored in Gibraltar where the Royal Navy still maintained a significant presence. Although he had travelled the same route in prior AUE's, it never ceased making him feel timeless and invincible to have the ocean churning in his guts as he strode off the gangway onto the dock. It was as though he were a part of some eternal maritime canvas with the cruisers and corvettes of a former empire coloring the seascape behind him.

In a small town west of Cordoba in the Sierra Morena Mountains, he found work as a carpenter. He had a decent grasp of Spanish because of previous AUE's in Costa Rica and Paraguay, not to mention Spain itself. The people in the village were kind and hospitable to a fault, but they all wanted to know what an Albanian was doing living in Constantina.

---

[13]#1 on the Billboard Year-End Hot 100 singles of 1994. **"The Sign"** by Ace of Base from the album *Happy Nation*. Arista, 1993. Max was in a pub near Gunwharf Quay playing darts with an Tanzanian national, a Welshmen, and some guy who said he was Lebanese but Max remained convinced was Iranian. There was a group of sailors from Southampton fiddling with a shortwave radio that was picking up a Portuguese signal out of Lisbon, and everyone in the pub laughed when the sailors tuned into the dance number by Ace of Base. They'd all been drinking vodka and orange juice to a man, and as Max looked into the handsome Tanzanian's eyes he was gripped by the thought of how much the man resembled Duncan.

He told the community his fictional truth; after all, he'd become a proficient liar. He said that he'd come from Turkey on a Russian vessel bound for Western Sahara. He said that while on shore leave, he decided to abandon post and explore Spain. He told the town folk how much he loved the country and how much he wanted to stay. They accepted his fabricated status, which upon repetition sounded less like a lie every time.

He couldn't get enough of his twenty-one-year-old age; it was physically addictive. His spleen was strong, and his blood vessels were engorged with clarity. Even after a night of wine, the learning and working offered no resistance to his thirty-something ambitions. He could only imagine how good time traveling would feel when he was eighty-five. To the end of his days, he'd be young and handsome enough to appeal to the likes of women such as Sarita, who consistently made his vigorous treks into the Latin regions of the world so conquistadorial.

During the week, he worked with several brick layers and a masonry apprentice. They were the ones who told him about Sarita; a single mom who lived outside of town on a spur road off *Blas Infante*. The men said she was a free spirit unconfined by expectations. They said that her ex left town one day with all her cash and her car. She was known, according to these men who worked in plaster and cement, to be a splendid dancer immensely intrigued by foreigners – especially Eastern Europeans and Southern Russians with big cocks they said as they laughed. The tradesmen told Max to be wary, though; they said Sarita would attract him with her guileless charm and that by sunrise he'd be in shackles. Of course, they added conversely, that perhaps an Albanian like himself would be the perfect match for such an alluring temptress.

When he was introduced to her at a local cabaret, he did not find her attractive in the way that he had expected. She couldn't dance the Paso-doble worth a damn, nor could she do any better with the Fandango, but she was beautiful in a way that eclipsed any technical skill. She worked in a pastry shop and painted landscapes in her free time. In the nine months that Max had known her, his Spanish had improved toward native fluency, and he had grown very fond of her son, Sebastian.

His carpentry was piecemeal and sporadic, so in the gaps between jobs he and Sarita would take Sebastian and go on road trips around the Iberian Peninsula. He didn't make a lot of money, but he earned enough to allow the three of them to enjoy a few unexpected vacations.

Recently, however, the fun had begun to ebb. He could sense her becoming serious about whatever it was that was developing between them. He could feel the weight of her hopes and the drive of her domestic ambition start to grab him. It was just a matter of time, he told himself, before she began prioritizing the security of money over the joy of seizing the moment; by that time, however, he knew that he'd be long gone, completely vanished from the universe they shared.

* * *

Max's determination to convince Duncan and Pierre that he was re-living years of his past while slumbering under the influence of Insynnium propelled him to focus on acquiring a skill for which he had absolutely no inclination or talent. He figured that if Duncan were to witness him mastering something intricate and complex that ordinarily took years to acquire, it would surely prove that he had access to a well of time. It was for this reason that he picked up the guitar without hesitation.

His focus on learning the stringed instrument consumed five entire AUE's, not to mention the hours of practice that took place when he wasn't in a coma. He would wake up from 365 days of picking and strumming, and immediately walk over to Vince's to jam with Gary and Andre for days on end. He lived in a world of fret boards and whammy bars and finger calluses. He memorized Clapton and Knopfler and reflected on the power of practice and Gladwell's theory of ten thousand hours.

He would consistently drop out of college in every single AUE. He would telephone his parents from places like Cape Breton and Moncton to tell them that he'd quit school to focus on his new passion for music. His father was speechless as he described learning the guitar while hitchhiking around the Maritimes. His mother, on the other hand, was overjoyed with her son's choice to live feral as a minstrel rather than chasing a career in business or economics.

Later on, in subsequent and bolder AUE's, he would call collect from cities such as Antwerp and Bastia and Limerick. Grace would ask him if he was travelling with Gypsies and marginal characters in search of day jobs and festivals, and each time he replied to his mother in the affirmative he could see her smiling with delight on the other end of the line.

He travelled around Canada - and later the rest of the world - on student loans and summer savings intended for college. He realized that these funds, originally for tuition and books, could spearhead a year of interesting pursuits with more important educational results. Occasionally he'd run out of money, but he never starved. He learned to stretch a dollar by living on Ichiban noodles and the wilted produce found in dumpsters behind grocery stores.

In terms of health, he knew that he'd wake up in a year, so he didn't need to be obsessive about looking after himself. After all, he thought, what amount of sugar, sodium, or nicotine could jeopardize the beat of his heart or the chemistry of his blood in a twelve-month span? Besides, he wasn't planning his life in decades, and youth was on his side.

It was about practice abundant months and ingrained procedural recall as he busked his way from Fredericton to Prince Rupert. He grew more or less inseparable from his guitar as the muscle memory of his fingers became reflexive and imprinted on his mind like a tattoo. Whenever he camped in deserted parks or slept on lonely streets, he never failed to feel eternally consoled by the sound of the reverberating strings as they echoed through his veins with their meditative sensations.

In the real world - whatever that was - the world outside AUE's, Max could feel his diligence boring into Duncan's skepticism, and that was the true measure of his efforts; each time he played *Eruption* on the Stratocaster or *Saltons of Swing* on the Les Paul, Max could see Duncan giving in, inch by inch.

But still, there was resistance to accept what appeared impossible.

"You've obviously got an aptitude," said Duncan.

"I have *no* aptitude Dipshit; I have a tin ear, that's what makes what I'm demonstrating so amazing. I now have a skill that should have taken me years instead of months to acquire because I'm learning it in my comas, can't you see?"

Duncan gave Max an exasperated look.

"Anyway…," said Duncan, as he tried to change the subject.

But Max was a dog with a bone, and three months later his ever improving talents finally forced Duncan to begrudgingly cede a passing acceptance of his multi-verse contentions.

Following Duncan's reluctant acquiescence, however, Max was left without focus or direction. The whole guitar obsession had been a pyrrhic victory; so much time had been spent to prove so little, he thought.

Now what? He asked himself.

The obvious answer was anything; he didn't need a plan or a goal or a purpose. He loved playing music and traveling and learning, so why not continue with that? When it came to AUE's he was his own counsel.

At the next opportunity, he went to Amsterdam, but soon found himself moving across the continent on a curious cultural trek. He became impressed with the languages that everyone around him could speak, especially French - which irritated him in high school. For six consecutive AUE's (six years), he played guitar from Cologne to Bordeaux while sounding out French verbs and perfecting German grammar.

In Europe, he occasionally discovered that his diverted college funds failed to last the duration of an entire AUE. In Munich, he became involved in a petty theft ring and was placed behind bars for six months. It was an excessive sentence that illustrated not only the surprising harshness of the German correctional system but also the wasteful loss that crime conferred on AUE's. It was a bit of a no-brainer to realize that the addition of legally viable skills was the key to more fulfilling experiences over time.

So, when he wasn't travelling the roads between Lyon and Marseille with a musical troupe, he apprenticed as a chef in the Rhone valley. In other AUE's he apprenticed as a brick layer in Genoa, a car mechanic in Hanover, a plumber in Athens, as well as an electrician in Zurich. The intrinsic value of his pursuits proved to be as inexorable as Jovian gravity, and he was repeatedly drawn toward the palpable and concrete nature of trades and crafts.

In spite of his burgeoning abilities and first-hand knowledge of life between the Alps and the Adriatic, he was not immune to certain vices, the first of which was gambling. He became sidetracked for a time by the seductive possibility of monetizing his AUE's. He postulated that through his knowledge of the future he could simply identify the numbers to a winning lotto ticket, and then, with the correct time shot, return and claim a massive jackpot.

He entertained grandiose notions of bags filled with pearls in a world that would become his oyster. But his pursuit of riches became a grinding and Sisyphean task. He discovered how brief a year could be, and how monotonously slow and imprecise the gears of society move when you're waiting for something as fickle as money.

As initial matters, there was the planning and the timing of his AUE's, not always certain. He could land on the wrong day or forget a number through some slip of memory. Subsequent stoning along the gauntlet to his winnings could come in the form of an overlooked tax commitment or an unforeseen legal constraint, both of which stopped him dead in his tracks.

The cash that was supposed to confer a mega spending AUE ended up rendering him exhausted and over extended. He had to honestly ask himself what it was that he wanted to buy with such purchasing power; planes, boats, women? And where did he plan to go with such bling? How many times could he travel around the world on the backs of other people?

Besides, he could never keep a cent of it anyway. Each time he jumped back into a new AUE everything would be erased, and he'd be at the mercy of going through the entire ordeal again: the winning of the lottery, the parsing of the winnings, the feel good gratuities, the exceptional explaining.

Following many considered attempts, Max eventually foreclosed on any hope that he would ever triumphantly capture the promise of the lotto. Instead of spending his winnings, his pursuit of money was spending him, along with his precious AUE's. It didn't take long for him to resent squandering his time gift on such a pointless chase.

But it wasn't only the glitter of diamonds that distracted him. Sometimes he got caught up in things that drifted beyond his control. Like the time he was flat out on cocaine with Thai prostitutes, pirates, and an arms shipment in the hull of a stolen yacht between Sumatra and Malaysia. Although he could neither confirm nor deny whether he'd stolen the yacht, hired the whores, or barred the doors, he could definitely attest to the fact that it was the shock of shocks to wake up from buccaneers and high seas debauchery contorted and disorientated in a motel on the outskirts of Moose Jaw.

In spite of his uncanny adeptness at avoiding payment for bad behavior with life, liberty or money, he never felt the corruptive urge to devolve into a criminal, or use excessive amounts of illicit drugs, or unduly risk his life within the reality of an AUE.[14] Though Max knew he could escape the consequences of any action upon emergence from his coma - no matter how deplorable the act - he would own the memory of it for the rest of his days; all rationalizations notwithstanding. Whether he was consciously aware of it or not, some part of him was forever captured by the other dimensions he visited. He was routinely left with the sense that he had deposited a ghostly residue on each possibility that he touched, and it began to make him wonder just how thin his soul could be spread.

If there lingered any ultimate meaning behind his AUE's, it eluded him. He had undergone years of sustained effort to make him a practiced hand in many fields, and yet there were growing moments where his time travelling seemed nothing more than grotesque temporal fistulas mangling the progression of his life; useless and greedy abominations, like a stack of gold that could only be spent on piercings or egg rolls.

---

[14] Dying inside an AUE was not remarkable. Max simply woke up with no memory of the AUE whatsoever. But it was also by this token that he avoided taking unacceptable risks with his life as much or as little as he would in the real world. After all, every time he died he was losing the opportunity to acquire additional memory and experience. When he thought about the effort involved in learning the things he'd learned, it seemed like the height of ungratefulness to risk such fortune on a turn of pitch and toss.

While browsing in a bookstore on the corner of Blakeheart Drive, Max discovered a hard bound version of a series of essays called, *Blowing up Your House*, by Patricia Eldon Morris. The essayist suggested that life's true beauty was to be found in the lush and expansive valleys that exist between what we falsely assume to be the pinnacle events of human existence. Morris said that most people forgot to breathe, watched too much TV, and ate far too much sugar. She also said that before we knew it our lives were over with much of its purpose lost in the pursuit of manufactured distractions created by a system that rewarded conformity.

Morris asserted that freedom was a practical fiction largely because our social logic kept us chained to deeply flawed notions of what it means to be human. People tended to be unconsciously frustrated by religion or seductively mollified by consumerism, or both. But Morris was an optimist at heart, and she felt that the collective unconscious was slowly correcting societal shortcomings by moving humanity into a co-operative and matriarchal arrangement. Morris didn't think that women were particularly better than men, but she did imagine that the people of the future would understand four things: first of all, that men and women searching for clarity and substance would strike a better balance between their over-stimulated waking lives and the quiet pleasure of sleep, where the restorative juices of dreams answer our most fundamental questions; second, that the most beautiful sight in the world is tears because it is evidence of having received the greatest gift, which is the salty and abrasive treasure of letting go; third, that one should never ask a hypothetical question and expect a satisfying answer because the possibilities are infinite, and trying to see them all will only make you crazy; and fourth, that when life ceases to be a competition there will no longer be losers, no matter how hard anyone tries.

After reading Morris's book, Max began taking opportunities in his AUE's to discover the subtleties of life. Although learning and mastery remained at the front of his time trips, his ego moved into the background. He found himself roaming across prefectures and annexed regions of countries no longer on maps or recognized on continents. Wandering penniless through outposts and villages in worn lungis and camel hair coats with self-shorn locks and eyes like jewels, relying on languages learned and skills slowly mastered, he received experiences on earth not purchasable or accessible to an individual of a single time or identity.

Through seemingly implausible reincarnations, Max undertook great journey's with no destination, movements with no purpose other than the joy of the movement at the moment; he became almost monk-like and something of an 'existence connoisseur.' In both his surface life and in his AUE's he grappled with Morris's challenge not to hold his breath or close his eyes. He ran through streets naked and rolled in clover fields. And when he listened to Kevin and Josh with renewed acuity they sounded like Shakespeare when they spoke; and naturally, as it would be, Rachel was totally forgiven in his heart. His comas were like successive chrysalises, and each time he emerged, he became increasingly woke to the true nature of things.

The last time he saw the Manitoban sun it was turning wheat kings the color of amber rum; and he knew, not like a human anymore, but like a deity hidden within the instincts of an animal, that the seasons had changed.

* * *

He'd wake up in a month, but for now, he'd enjoy. He followed Seb down off the roof they'd been fixing and kissed Sarita gently to the side of her lips as she handed him a glass of sangria. The three of them took a seat in the shade and gazed at her car in the sunshine – a glittering lime sports coupe.

Sarita was pleased to be in possession of her car once again. She and Max had taken a train to Madrid to retrieve the thing from her ex-husband in a string of misadventures that resulted in Max bribing a garage owner in Barcelona to have the vehicle repainted.

Max speculated that Sarita's new plan was to sell the car and use the money to buy a faster one or pay rent or something to those ends.

When Sebastian went into the house, Sarita turned to Max and asked, "Do you love me, Fatmir."

"Yes," replied Max.

"How do you know?"

"I just do, that's all, how can I explain something like love," he said.

"You've experienced it before, then?" she said.

"Of course, haven't you?"

"No, you're the first man I have ever truly loved. Sometimes it hurts me to think what I would do if something were to happen to you."

"Nothing will happen to me," he said.

"Maybe we can visit your family in Albania. Will you take me sometime?"

"Sure, just as soon as we save up enough money, how's that?"

"Good," she said, as her eyes rested on the horizon with a hopeful gaze.

2008

-Spring-

*"It's outrageous to think you can rule the world, but
of course, everybody wants to"*

It was April, and windy.

The cemetery had been inconveniently littered
with the latest addition to generations of human
throughput. The weightless and pulpy fragments of
trash blew around like ill smelling confetti and
streamed hauntingly from the headstones of persons
no longer animated by flesh.

Rachel's mother, Cassandra, had passed away, and
Rachel sat silently with the other mourners as the
squawk of seagulls – circling in the sky above -
rivaled the audibility of the sermon. The preacher
raised his voice sentence by sentence to compete with
the aggressive birds and salvage the grave side service.
But Rachel wasn't listening to the Methodist reverend;
she was listening to the seagulls, for they were the
ones The Great Spirit was speaking through.

Cassandra would be mildly pleased with the avian
send off, thought Rachel, although slightly miffed that
the birds were drawn by the smell of refuse and not
the eminence of the deceased. The temporary and

relative aspects of garbage flickered with signs of permanence that were distressing.

She was introduced to say a few words about her mother. Her modest eulogy felt glib and rehearsed, but it was the only way she could deliver it, otherwise she would be reduced to tears as she spoke.

She waxed somewhat unauthentic about her mother's generosity and kindness. She told deceptive and euphemistic stories that attempted to tickle and remind others of the memorable quirks and funny mannerisms that had made Cassandra such a notorious personality.

Her mother had a vindictive side, though, much maligned and disliked, and fully operational nine-tenths of the time. But Rachel wanted to use her moment standing before the others to shoulder Cassandra's uncomfortable pathology into the grave permanently. As she looked upon the familiar faces that had gathered, she saw tears and stoic acceptance for Cassandra's passing. She felt that it should have been easier than it was to let death be a parting reminder of the light each of them shared, rather than the darkness they seemed resigned to quietly carry. But when she looked toward the man she loved, seated next to the boys she adored, there was relief and the promise of better days.

Her mother had voiced several misgivings when Max returned to Brandon in 2005, and she let her daughter know her displeasure when Rachel accepted Max back into the family house. Cassandra made a point, whenever she could, to tell Rachel that Max would only cause her pain. She even went so far as to petition the court not to allow him custody of his boys.

Everything backfired on her, however, because Max was a different man, and the way in which he defused the entire situation dampened Cassandra's powder. It never completely erased her desire to fire shots at him, but it became a grudge without teeth. Besides, everyone knew that not even Chief Big Bear had the capacity to stay in Cassandra's good books for long.

Rachel cast her eyes over the cemetery as she spoke. She could see that much of the grounds had emerged from the cover of winter, and she could imagine the place in summertime with a thick lawn and manicured hedges. At present, though, the brownish landscape, with archipelagos of melting snow, was unattractively strewn with plastic bags and Tampex wrappers diverted from a landfill destiny.

The Route 47 garbage truck had had a major mishap beside the graveyard.

Rachel saw the accident in a dream.

She witnessed the cab-over blow a front tire and swerve to the curb where it bounced over the nature strip and tipped over. Its great guts of unwanted ugly spilled forth as if it were some kind of manufactured vomit. She saw the whole thing unfold just as plain as she stood watching torn receipts and silver gum foil blow over shoes and underneath chairs.

The ability to see things that would eventually come to pass were a part of her psychic makeup. It was also the reason she knew in advance of her mother's impending death. Three months earlier, in a deep and eventful sleep, she saw her mom succumb to an aneurysm while washing dishes; it was an end that could not be averted.

Rachel had spent the last twenty-four years of her life coming to terms with how she handled knowledge about the random and unexpected fates of people, pets, and property. And it never got easier, deciding when to act on an insight or when to let it play out uninterrupted. She possessed no crystal ball, nor was her prescience on the scale of Nostradamus, although on occasion she had the sneaking suspicion that her and the great fourteenth century seer shared a similar intuition.

Some people sold their gifts, and others lamented their afflictions. But for Rachel, her clairvoyant endowment was neither a blessing nor a curse; it was just something that happened, like blinking or remembering.

* * *

Growing up, Rachel felt like an ugly duckling because of certain exaggerated features that were too large for her small body to aesthetically accommodate; and, of course, a lasting layer of childhood fat that refused to melt away. Her mother told her to be patient and said that she would eventually shed the unwanted pounds and grow into her ears and hands. But there was a restless and creative appetite to overcome such visible incongruities. While reading an animated version of *The Clan of the Cave Bear*, she chose to willfully exude the internal picture the book had fastened her to; that of a resilient and beautiful girl-child running on lichen covered tundra through a mammoth and sabertooth past. Her intentions made her appear as intentions will; a brilliant flower emerging from the crevices of a glacially fractured landscape.

There was no doubt she felt unusual in her physical body. Her early and inchoate thoughts were fantasies about the preferability of having no actual corporeal presence whatsoever. She wanted to be a light breeze drifting among the hard versions of others. People seemed so unpleasantly immured in the weight and inertia of their bodies; life should be buoyant and soft. She would always envy birds and reject the gilded cage.

As time passed, her mother was proven correct as the young woman became symmetrical and proportional and very beautiful over the course of several seasons; but that was well after she found the wings to fly.

Not long after her seventh birthday – likely in the foliage of '81 - Rachel was running by herself in an abandoned lot behind the distressed apartment complex where she lived. Her right shoe snagged on a root, and she stumbled over her feet onto the ground. It would have been an otherwise minor accident, save for the fact that she was unable to arrest her fall, her arms simply failed to come to her rescue. Her forehead struck a rock and she was knocked unconscious. Following an unknown lapse of time, she recovered awareness, and in a confused and disorientated state made her way home. Her brothers told her she'd fallen because of her chubby and clumsy nature. She received a couple of stitches on her brow below the hairline, the scar of which would always remain.

Two weeks after her accident she experienced the first of what would be a lifetime of portents and premonitions. In her first truly memorable vision, she saw her father lying by the side of the road on a snowy birch covered stretch of the Canadian Shield. There was spring sleet, and a strong presence of alcohol in the air. The vision was tangibly real, and she was like a ghost passing over the land with every sensatory faculty at her disposal. Her emotions were solid and neutral like bricks in a wall.

She was told by her mother not to mention the dream to others, as Cassandra claimed few people could sensibly accept and understand such a puzzling omen. Cassandra was a shrewd manipulator of people, especially her own children, and her insistence upon silence was allegedly designed to spare her daughter the 'misunderstandings' of the community.

Six months following Rachel's vision, her father was found dead at the edge of a highway on the outskirts of a small town in Ontario. He had been living in a halfway house and working as a dish washer. Alcoholism had driven him from the Redcalf home two years prior. Rachel had heard from time to time that her father was drifting around places like

Wabigoon and English River performing odd jobs for pocket jingle, but mostly just drinking. Her mother said that her father was a disaster, and that he had made his decision about the significance of Rachel and her brothers when he took up with the bottle. It was the first she understood how cold and unforgiving her mother could be, like stone under ice.

One August morning, after the landlord tacked a 'pay or vacate' notice to the door of their rental unit, Cassandra loaded the children into a dented station wagon and left Winnipeg. They drove to Brandon, where Cassandra had a sister. Rachel was given to understand that they were going for a visit, but after a month she discovered the move was permanent.

Her Aunt Joyce - whose ramrod posture and Cree features reminded Rachel of her mom – was kind and caring, and made the penurious welfare strapped family feel safe in her small three bedroom house full of kids and pets.

Cassandra ended up finding employment as a receptionist at a travel agency, and the wages from her job soon allowed the family to move out from Joyce's and relocate to a trailer park on the fringe of town. Cassandra would bring home colorful brochures and picturesque flyers from work; places one could visit if they possessed a passport and a ticket. Rachel would read out loud to her mother from the living room about island countries and marvelous cities and places with cool sounding names like Phuket, Katmandu, and Phoenix. Her mom would listen from the kitchen while unclogging drains and rolling cigarettes and telling someone, anyone, to vacuum the wilted shag carpet.

The mobile home was cold in the winter and outrageously stuffy in the summer, and the plumbing and wiring always malfunctioned in ways that eluded repair. Other than the furniture and practical necessities contained within its vinyl on gypsum walls, there was nothing much of value the family possessed, unless you counted intangibles like thrift, perseverance, and a number of programs on the CBC.

Hockey Night in Canada, of course, was one of them, and *Seeing Things* was another - Rachel's two favorite shows[15]. She loved the fact that Lafleur never wore a helmet and that Howie Meeker and Dave Hodge were always fighting over the Habs or the Leafs. She also felt a certain sodality with Louis Ciccone; a character not only seeing things, but using his visions to solve crimes, and it made her want to be a sleuth in the worst way.

---

[15]**#7** on the Billboard Year-End Hot 100 singles of 1985. **"Everybody Wants to Rule the World"** by <u>Tears for Fears</u> from the album *Songs from the Big Chair*. Vertigo, 1985. Rachel liked to watch *Video Hits* when she got home from school. She fantasized that she'd find a dreamy Englishman like Roland Orzabal, with his new wave style and curly Basque hair. She easily lost herself in the sway of rhythm. She'd sit in front of the *Panasonic* tube eating *Hawkins Cheezies* as Samantha Taylor introduced everybody from Madonna to John Cougar. When her brothers got home, they would force her outside to play goalie or catcher or some other neglected position in their ad hoc approach to sport.

Her mother, however, applied an innate comprehension of child psychology to keep her daughter from saying anything to anyone about the premonitions she was having, never mind solving them in a Hercule Poirot way. She convinced Rachel to keep her secrets about the future within their confidence of two.

She claimed to have her daughter's best interest at heart, but her deceitful effort to discourage Rachel from trusting her psychic gifts sowed the seeds of doubt very deep in her child's mind. As seasons passed, Rachel asked herself whether it was a character flaw or some freakish affliction that allowed her mendacious mother to control her abilities. The power imbalance that held the deformity of their relationship in place reversed itself, however, when Rachel reached grade eleven. Without her mother's knowledge, she took the bold initiative to act on an insight that was too powerful to ignore.

During an afternoon nap, she dreamt that a car load of teenagers burned to death in a fiery car crash that shook the community to its foundations. She knew who the victims were, and where the car that would consume them was parked. Given her clairvoyance, an omission of action seemed criminal, so she located the vehicle and tore the distributor cap off the engine. No one drove the disabled car for five days, including the drunken teenagers who'd been scheduled by the reaper to be carbonized. The tragedy was averted, and Rachel's courageous role had been determinative.

Something awoke inside her following the proactive interference, and from that day forward she came out from behind the clouding control of her mother. She told Cassandra that her dreams were diminishing, which was a lie. And though she mentioned glimpses of minor things, she was able to convince her mother that her psychic life was slowly disappearing. Cassandra said it was a blessing that she'd finally outgrown such an ignoble curse.

At the end of high school, Rachel took a midnight walk into a neighboring part of town. With solitary confidence and fixated defiance, she entered an abandoned graveyard and dug up a tribal calumet she'd buried there years before. The pipestone – once gifted by an elderly relative - had been hidden in the ground out of shame and frustration when her mother chastised her for smoking it. As she held its ancestral weight with her palm in a field of tombstones, she asked the Great Spirit for a sign she could understand.

In the shadows of the cemetery she saw the ghosts of two wandering caribou and a Red-tail hawk.

She began volunteering at the Indian reservation south of town where her gifts and her heritage had a place in the service of others. Her acne cleared up and she began to lose weight. Despite headaches from math and a biology teacher with a veiled contempt for Natives, she studied with purpose and was accepted to university.

She had enough Cree blood coursing through her veins to claim First Nations status; a heritage her mother had always encouraged her to be mindful of, but not actively proud about. The Manitoba government was aware of her lineage too; and they sent her to Kingston with a scholarship and the possibility of a job upon return.

At Queens, she was freed from the shackles of her questionably intentioned mother and became independent and broadly aware of many things. Her interactions with Cassandra, once so mentally incestuous and omnivicarious receded to whispers in a past that, at times, could still feel strangely present.

* * *

The eulogy dwindled to its lachrymose conclusion, and Rachel closed with a Native prayer. She was not entirely sure of everything she'd said, but she felt as though her obligations to her mother were complete. She looked bravely toward Max and the boys and reflected on what a difference four seasons make.

A year ago, she had all but given up on Maximilian. Not on him as a person, but on the two of them as a couple. It was evident that his primary interest was with his grocery business, and while their paths crossed with regularity because of the boys, there was nothing in his soul that said he needed her. Time, it seemed, had healed *his* wounds, but not hers.

Inflicted with sadness, she let the decision to file for divorce roll ahead.

But then something happened.

She stopped by his grocery store one afternoon to grab a head of lettuce and some breakfast cereal, and before she knew it, the magic that once defined their relationship reinserted itself back into her life with startling force.

She generally made efforts to avoid patronizing the isles in GROWERS because the success of the place along with Max's popularity had a way of making her feel atrociously hopeless and somewhat of a failure. He had quietly become one of the most enterprising and eligible men in Brandon. She had not seen women, young and mature alike, advertising their availability in such unabashed candor since college and the days of Duncan Wisegerber. It was obvious that he enjoyed the attention, and she reluctantly had to accept that her estranged husband was capitalizing on a portion of the feminine interest that surrounded him.

"He's hot isn't he?" said a youngish looking woman who was roughly Rachel's age, "and mysterious."

The two of them were peering at Max from behind a fruit cart piled high with organic tangerines.

"What do you mean?" said Rachel.

"I mean, there's something about him, something captivating and intriguing," said the woman. "I can see by the way he carries himself that he's a man with many secrets. Do you know him?"

"Yes," said Rachel, "as a matter of fact I do."

At that point, he spotted the two women chatting and came over to be introduced.

"Hello," said Rachel.

"Hey," he said.

"Max, this is... I'm sorry I didn't catch your name?"

"Natalie," said the woman.

"New in town," he asked.

"No," said the woman in a smooth Spanish accent, "I'm visiting from Chile. I purchased one of those round the world tickets. I'm taking the train across Canada. I have family in Vancouver."

"Where you headed next," asked Max.

"Singapore, Jakarta, Israel - I have relatives on a Kibbutz."

"Quite a trip," said Max, as they all smiled easily at one another.

He was looking at Rachel in a way she hadn't seen in ages. It reminded her of the first time they met; hungry, vulnerable, and free.

Another shopper approached to ask where the baking soda was.

"It was nice to meet you, Natalie, and I hope you enjoy the rest of your holiday," said Max, as his eyes moved back to Rachel for a final look.

"It's good to see you Rach," he said.

As he walked away to go do what store owners do, Natalie reached down and took hold of Rachel's hand.

Rachel was seized by her magnetically warm touch, it reminded her of something pleasurable that sits at the border of sinfulness, but she couldn't bring herself to pull away. She could feel her entire body heat up in the pulsating grip. She noticed a sensuous tickle run down her spine and subtly terminate in her toes.

Natalie grinned at her dilated pupils.

Rachel was confused.

"What's he like in bed," she asked.

Rachel let out an embarrassed laugh. "Excuse me?" she said.

"I'm just saying, you obviously have some kind of history between you, even a stranger can see it."

Rachel thought about Natalie's statement and felt the seed of pain in her stomach grow heavy like a stone.

"He's my husband, but we're divorcing," she said, as she turned her head and tried to make her eyes look for something that wasn't there. She felt like a mess in front of this beautiful woman she'd just met.

Natalie gave her a sympathetic look.

"I wouldn't give up on things so fast, Hun," she said. "There's still a spark there. The way he was looking at you just now. He's seen something new inside your soul; something special and unexpected."

"Well if he has, he's not telling me," said Rachel.

"He will," said Natalie, "I know men, and I'm certain about that."

She squeezed Rachel's hand suggestively and then let go and walked away. Heads turned in the store as the attractive brunette sashayed her way past the checkouts and waltzed through the exit into the breeze that was calling her name. An old farmer fell over his dog and knocked his wife into the peach bin as she brushed past them.

Rachel was left standing in the cereal aisle with a head of lettuce in her hands and a bunch of unanswered questions.

That night, as she slept, she experienced the profound tremors of a sexual earthquake. In her dreams, she and Max were lovers again with an amorous aggression she'd never known. She was astonished by her physical need for him; so much so, that her moaning woke her in the middle of a sensation more satisfying than anything she'd thought possible. It was an outrageous all night organism as she eagerly connected with Max in repeated climax.

For the first time in her life, she had no idea whether she'd had a dream or a premonition.

She called in sick for work the following morning and walked to Charity Park with a blanket, a book, and a bottle of Zinfandel. And so it was that she spent the day savoring the lay of lays. She also thought about Natalie, the Chilean traveler with the charming demeanor and lilting delivery who handed her such an unexpected and tantalizing promise.

Two days later, on his way over with the divorce papers, Max absentmindedly showed up without them. He asked Rachel out for dinner instead. She realized then that the wild tobacco she'd once sent off in a cloud of smoke had returned with an answer.

And the answer was yes.

Their date took place on a typical summer Saturday, with long lingering light warming the prairie stillness. They ate what Max had prepared, a tasty assortment of Greek dishes that leapt straight from the Aegean. It was probably better than most fare on offer at restaurants in Toronto and Montreal. She studied him as they ate. She thought about her dreams, and her fears, and all this new attention.

Full and flushed, they went out onto the back deck of the weatherboard rental and shared a joint, something they hadn't done in almost eight years. As they got high, she watched as a Black-billed Magpie alighted on a power line across the street; there was also a couple of Northern Flickers rapping on a tree somewhere in the neighborhood.

They sat there with each other in equal parts sativa and indica.

"Be honest with me," she said, "What's the deal with the skills and talents? You're like a one man variety show. Is there anything you can't do? I mean, that meal we just ate was amazing."

"I don't exactly know how to explain it to you," he said, "so, bear with me.

"When I was living in Vancouver, I was beaten up by skinheads who robbed me. I got kicked really hard and ended up with a fractured skull."

He hesitated slightly before continuing.

"Due to a prior concussion that I probably wasn't aware of, I was really fucked up. I had all these stress blackouts and minor states of fugue. One day I just fainted at work. When I awoke, I was in the hospital. The doctor told me to take a week off and rest.

"During my convalescence, I grabbed a couple of books to read, and found myself remembering more details than usual. When one of the guys in my recovery group left his guitar at my apartment, I started messing around with it and realized I could play by ear. I was totally blown away. But it wasn't just music; it was anything I put my mind to. Like cooking – with a little practice I felt like Julia Child was hiding inside me."

"What did the doctor say? This isn't normal, is it?" said Rachel.

"No, not at all," said Max. "It's not typical for a head injury to enhance your mental functioning. But honestly, I didn't exactly go into a lot of detail about my cognitive situation. They said my brain seemed healthy, and that was good enough for me. The only thing the specialist told me was to watch out for headaches or blurred vision."

"Who else knows about this?"

"No one," said Max, "I mean, it's pretty hard to believe, right? I just try to avoid explanations. People don't really notice."

"Yes, they do notice," said Rachel, as she grew agitated with his weird and unverifiable story that sounded disturbingly fictitious. "People notice more than you realize. Besides, why are you telling *me* all this shit, what did you think I would say?"

"I don't know, Rach, it just seemed like I should tell you. I wanted you to know."

"So, that's what this is, a chance to get things off your chest? You want me to believe your story about skinheads and a brain injury and a weird metamorphosis; and then tell you that everything's going to be okay, is that it?"

"Come on, Rachel."

"No, you come on, Max! You've been back here for two years, and you won't even touch me; you treat me like I'm some sort of leper. And now you tell me you have this bizarre affliction, but it happens to make you the most interesting person in town. Quite frankly, it's all a bit much."

"Look," he said, almost pleading for her to make a move, "I just want to make sure there isn't anything we need to say to one another before the divorce is final, that's all."

She was caught flat footed by his unguarded invitation. She wanted to pretend that her feelings for him at that moment came from the effects of the weed, or the merlot, or perhaps the remnants of a recent dream. But in reality, it was nothing other than an inextinguishable attraction that pushed her into his arms; a long and constant craving. She grabbed his collar and pulled him close, and he accepted her lips onto his for a deep and satisfying kiss.

"You mean *that*?" she said.

He was attractively vulnerable, like the eighteen-year-old she remembered meeting at Queens so long ago. The emotional wall he'd been maintaining crumbled before her and his openness to her advances answered the only real question that existed in the breath between them.

"Yeah, like that," he said, and pulled her close once more.

The sex began like it ended, in the missionary position. But their passion could be electric at times, and every once in awhile it approached the crescendo of her dream. She knew he was the only man who would ever have her heart, and although she knew it was slightly wrong and possibly dysfunctional, it made her feel whole again to be wanted by him. There were rules of attraction that even the feminists couldn't explain, she thought, as her reawakened libido made her glow from the inside like a vigorously burnished gem.

It wasn't long after they started sleeping together again that she began running, an activity she hadn't done since college. Soon she was losing weight and gaining lightness and ambition. Although she was open to Max's advice on health and diet, it seemed to be more than just eating right and exercising that accounted for her mind and body revolution. She felt herself inching toward a tantric muscularity teased out by a vibrant and healing magic. She began to feel more than just fit; she began to feel young.

Once Max had settled back in with her and the boys, she noticed a flower of enjoyment replacing the stone of pain in her belly. She wanted to study the things he was studying; the old college contagion and the pursuit of learning started to burn. There were collections of manuals on woodworking and plumbing; a guitar tuner; an accordion; CD's on Chinese history; and a biography about Camus. Though Max has gone to college, it always seemed his degree had been merely a means to an end. Now, his runaway curiosity and hyper-autodidacticism was something altogether new; an inspiring side of her husband she was only beginning to grasp.

His cognitive realignment gave him eccentricities and quirks, to be sure; the genesis of which only the two of them understood, but she liked it like that. Sharing such a secret seemed to increase their cohesion and bond them in ways that could not easily be undone.

2008

-Summer-

"How will I know if she's dreaming of me?"

Max was teaching Kevin a few chords on the guitar when the restless ten-year-old asked his dad to play something country.

Max strummed the first thing that came to mind. It didn't sound exactly the way he wanted it to, but still, it was pretty damn good by most standards.

"That's more like rock than country," said Kevin.

"Yeah, I know," said Max, "But that's how country was when I was your age, at least some of it anyhow."

"I used to love those guys," shouted Rachel from the kitchen.

"Hey, Kev," said Max in a low voice, "watch this."

Kevin looked at his dad as though he were a magician pulling a rabbit from a hat as he turned up the amp and began generating a remarkable tune on the Gibson. Once the rhythm of the song impacted the house, Rachel materialized under the archway of the living room. Kevin watched as his mother came across the hard wood floor with a 'how did you know' look on her face. He saw her throw her arms around his dad's neck and kiss him on the lips like it was a gift.

"Oh god," said Kevin, as he rolled his eyes and pretended to look away.

"You play real good cowboy, have you been practicing lately," teased Rachel, as she looked into Max's eyes with a feigned and gooey embellishment.

Max glanced at Kevin who grinned sheepishly back at his dad as though he'd assisted in making something appear out of thin air.

"Dad can play anything," he said.

"It certainly seems so, doesn't it?" said Rachel with not a little bewilderment.

"I'm out of tune," said Max.

The recent expansion of GROWERS had taken much of his time, and despite what he'd told his family, he knew Rachel and the boys suffered from an inordinate amount of puzzlement at his adeptness in cranking new tunes from a guitar they hadn't seen him practice in months.

But several years of comas had transformed him into Max 2.0.

"You know, Kev, I think your dad is a better musician than he was last month," said Rachel, as the two of them listened to him cover *The Closer You Get* by Alabama.

"Yeah, yeah, I know, Mom. Just like the carpentry, the cooking, and the languages," said Kevin, "Have you thought about going on a talk show, Dad, I bet you could get on Letterman."

Max paid no attention, he was deep in song.

* * *

"Two things," said Duncan, "Don't tell a soul about time travelling if you expect to keep your kids. And don't let Rachel back into your heart if you expect to keep your life."

Max agreed that he wouldn't breathe a word about time travel, who in the fuck would believe him anyway, he thought. And his word got easier to keep as his life evolved into an envious reality – a blessing that he decided was not worth risking on people's incapacity to handle uncomfortable truths.

As for maintaining his distance from Rachel, it was a promise that appeared easy to keep. After all, Insynnium had given him no end to romantic partners, of which Rachel had become but one of many. As his memories of her became murky and altered by years of interceding AUE events, she ceased to be his sole companion, his rock, his only past. She became a faded jewel; a dusty portrait in a vast and eccentric gallery of lovers.

He was only two days away from taking the divorce papers for her signature; legally finishing what the heart had ended long ago. He never imagined that when he bolted the doors and closed the blinds for his monthly AUE, he would awake twenty-four hours later with the irresistible urge to ask her on a date.

Before he went under, Max had contrived an AUE that would take him trekking across the Asian Steppes. His plan was to busk and hike his way from the mouth of the Danube to the plains of Mongolia. There would be dromedaries and ox drawn carts and bitter cold nights under thin blankets bartered for in Russian. He checked everything and some things twice, including the numerals 1-9-9-4 that were stamped onto each of the three capsules of Insynnium that he swallowed.

It would be an understatement to say that he was disappointed when he woke up on Sunday, April 13, 1986, rather than May 1994. Much to his chagrin, he once again found his adult urges and sentiments confined to the limited and claustrophobic state of an adolescent. It was hard for him to establish what might have precipitated such a time error. He told himself that it must have been a labeling mistake, a manufacturing defect, or some other snafu at a rundown warehouse on the outskirts of a dilapidated post-industrial town where he imagined all shipments of Insynnium to have originated. In any event, the dates on his capsules were completely fucking erroneous.

Ever since his first unexpected coma, he had developed an aversion to going too far back in his life. He dreaded the existential status of being a man caged in the body of a child. So much unnatural precociousness felt evil and untenable in the viscera of a human pupa. But, nonetheless, here he was, an emerging thirteen-year-old with a grotesque abundance of life, completely incongruous to those around him. He knew that he couldn't leave Canada, much less go stumbling over the Eurasian Steppes in the physical form he was captured in. But he needed

some purpose, some higher goal than merely
tormenting Nipawin with his prescience and awkward
knowledge.

Gradually, a method of exploiting his
chronological predicament took root in his higher
cortical functions. He asked himself: what if he
travelled to Brandon and looked up Rachel. He started
to think the idea through, and as he made plans to find
her in a time before he'd ever actually known her, his
curiosity turned into an unstoppable quest.

One day, in a fit of focus, he stuffed a week's
worth of garments into an aging knapsack and snuck
himself onto a sulfur train bound for Winnipeg in the
middle of the night. When the locomotive and its
yellow powdered cars pulled into Brandon, he bailed
off in the rail yard. He stole a BMX that was lying in
the driveway of a suburban home and went riding
around in decrepit neighborhoods looking for a place
to live. He discovered an abandoned house on a
neglected street and made his home in its semi-
developed basement.

In the backyard next to the one he was squatting in,
there was a pitbull chained to a clothes line that
someone fed and cared for but whom Max never saw.
And though the dog barked at him every morning,
nobody questioned or investigated his presence on the
property. He often stayed out until after dark and ate
at the homes of classmates whose mothers were
generous with food. He also noticed a lot of children
playing in the streets and somehow that seemed
refreshing; his latch key status evidently carried little

concern among the adults in the various and contiguous residential blocks.

On his second day in town, he approached a middle aged burn-out loitering outside Brandon's provincial employment offices. He bribed the man to pose as his step-father in exchange for a dime bag that he'd taken from Robert before leaving Nipawin. Once the deal was sealed, he and the willing transient entered P.F. Westlock Jr. High (the school he knew to be Rachel's), and without much ado - along with a fabricated address - Max officially became grade eight student, Trevor Hillberg, Drumheller transplant.

Following his afternoon registration, he lingered by the flagpole in front of the schoolyard for a while. Then he jumped on his illegally appropriated Kuwahara Laserlite and rode into the diminishing heat of a late day sun. He knew exactly where Rachel should be living as he peddled his way from the McDonald's on Dearborn to her double wide trailer on Fawn Crescent Close.

It wasn't long before he spotted a sweaty platoon of kids playing road hockey in hand-me-down jerseys. They were running around on a 'rink' comprised of snow-boot goal posts that bookended a piece of asphalt in a struggling section of town.

He was entranced by the entire sporting spectacle unfolding in front of his eyes; it included, but was not limited to, the screech of sneakers, jeans with missing knees, and the accelerated bashing of hockey sticks competing for a worn green tennis ball that bounced off ankles and curbs and random dog mines. The kids who came from the nearby homes were scraping to get by. He considered their situation and reflected on his advantaged position. He might have been freezing his ass off in the basement of a condemned split-level, but unlike these kids, he had a choice.

Watching the miniature and immature versions of people he'd only ever known as adults was mesmerizing in a way that a photo album couldn't even begin to approximate. The first person he recognized was Darcy; fast and strong with a mean streak. Darcy barked plays to the other kids who obeyed him submissively, except for the goalie at the opposite end of the street; a girl who Max soon realized was Rachel.

As he rolled his way down to her end of the pavement, he could see that she'd been coerced into wearing a Calgary Flames jersey that appeared restrictive and uncomfortable pulled over her young chunky frame. One of only two girls in the game, and not the favorite on odds for MVP, she did her best to stop several vicious slap shots from going between what only children could construe to be goal posts.

When he asked her if he could play, she silently pointed to an extra stick at the edge of the sidewalk. She was keeping her focus on the game. She was a little overweight and a bit clumsy, but there was a steadiness to her efforts, like a ballerina trapped inside a panda. Her slightly malnourished and denture challenged coeval's, some of whom teased her, seemed reluctantly content with her ball stopping ability. He saw a couple of young show-offs blush after she re-enforced their moves with a vivacious cheer.

There was an interruption in play, and most of the boys congregated around Darcy at the far end of the pavement and set upon making farting sounds and punching one another in the nuts. Max receded to the other end of the pavement where he found himself hypnotized in Rachel's presence.

"What's your name?"

"Rachel."

She was mesmerizing to him with her young voice and laconic disposition. She was understated, like tarnished silver with inlaid gold. The iridescent luster of her incredible good looks had not yet reached the brilliant glow that he would encounter at college. She was in the starting blocks of life, and the polish of events that would transform her into a stunning coed was the sort of thing that only he and God could know.

To see her in a state of pre-emancipation from her mother's restraining psychology left him increasingly enamored through each surviving beat of his heart. She was young and fragile and beautiful, and he suddenly felt compelled to protect her from all the semi-rural bogans who slashed and charged at her stance.

"Rachel's a cool name," he said.

"It is?" she replied.

"I mean, nice to meet you." He suddenly felt creepy, like a man in a trench coat luring in minors with sweets.

"Do you live around here?" she said, "because I haven't seen you before."

"No, I live over on Van Horne. I just moved here from Drumheller. But I'm like starting at Westlock tomorrow."

"Cool," she said, and shyly glanced away.

He could see that her eyes, even at thirteen, were every bit as gentle and captivating as the ones she looked into his with on the day of their wedding.

"And where do you live?" he said. He didn't really have to ask; it was a place he knew well.

"Right over there," she said, pointing toward a dumpy trailer park situated kiddy corner to where they were standing.

"Hey new guy, are you gonna like play hockey or just chat with my fat sister all day?" said Darcy, as the other boys giggled an awkward and uncertain assent.

Though he looked to be just another feisty and hard scrabble Cree Nation brother, Max could already see Darcy's misanthropic attitude emerging. He realized that he was being addressed by nothing more than a smaller version of what Darcy would ultimately become; primarily an asshole, but also a criminal, a cripple, and a violent *felo de se*.

"Hell yeah, let's play," shouted Max as he ran down the street for a faceoff.

In a less boisterous tone he called back to Rachel, "Hey, I'll see you tomorrow in class, okay?"

"Yeah, okay," she replied.

Tim Cole

P.F. Westlock Junior High allowed him to enroll in classes and start attending straight away. He took a seat in Ms. Osborne's eighth grade homeroom. He was in a desk with a clear view of Rachel. She was wearing legwarmers over tights with a stretched neck sweater and her hair was one of those teased-out Cindy Lauper affairs. He himself was going for more of a Brian Adams look, but it came off like WHAM! entangled with Springsteen. Over the course of the lesson, though, an aspiring Madonna got a note passed to her friends pointing out that Max resembled Corey Hart. By recess, this teenage appraisal had set off a round of, "yeah totallys," from every single group of girls.

By three o'clock on his first afternoon, Max's new persona, Trevor Hillberg, had suddenly become the focus of giggling schoolgirl interest, and Rachel proved herself to be no exception. Max was captured by the bashful attention of the beguiling young version of his future wife. Of course, he knew about her struggles. He knew about her difficult mother, her dead father, and her haywire brothers. He also knew the secrets that she kept, and the woman that she would become.

He watched her as he basked in his popularity.

A popularity that disappeared as fast as it arrived due to awkward and inflated comments he felt compelled to make on virtually every topic, arcane or otherwise. He couldn't help himself with all the information he had at his fingertips, and naturally, the other kids just didn't get it. Blending in at Westlock

266

might have gone better had he kept his mouth shut and observed more. Had he known he was headed back to 1986, he would have reviewed old episodes from *The Kids of Degrassi Street* before presuming that he could deliver a passable middle school performance. His time in war torn countries and on topless beaches had not prepared him for a return to the crucible of junior high.

"It's weird that you like my sister, fag," said Darcy, as he stepped out of an alley one afternoon to confront Max and Rachel as they walked home from school.

Darcy was two years their senior, but one grade behind, and the embarrassment of this educational injustice was crystallized in his rheumy eyes. He gave Max a long sociopathic stare, and Max got the uneasy feeling that Darcy could tell he was from the future, a place where he knew things were not going to turn out well for him.

"Darce, come on, leave him alone," interjected Rachel.

"What'd you want him to feel you up, Pork chop? Fuck off," said Darcy, as he made a face at his sister while the other members of his loosely allied gang pushed Max.

"You and your future prison bitches should be careful," said Max to Darcy, as he motioned his head toward the collection of small pissants whose oily body tarter was converting them into rancid teenagers.

"What'd you say, fuck-stick?" said Darcy.

"I said, make sure you limp wristed cocksuckers don't get tennis elbow jerking each other off."

"I'm gonna kick your ass right up between your ears, numb-nuts," said Darcy, as his friends made exaggerated efforts to hold him back while he bared his teeth and growled.

The impending fight appeared inherently unfair. Darcy was Indian tough from a rough part of town with the Clubber Lang knuckles and bruises to prove it. Max was dressed preppy with spiked hair, and he beamed with an almost retarded, 'please punch my lights out,' expression.

Max hadn't anticipated a fist fight with Darcy, but he also hadn't tried to prevent such a thing either. The entire situation had escalated as part of an ill-conceived and poorly executed plan to get closer to Rachel. In the ordinary course of events, this would have been an ideal occasion for Max to have his ass handed to him in front of his peers. But this was no ordinary occasion. The difference in their age and the disparity in their size were not large advantages for Darcy when compared to the chained wrath that Max intended to unleash.

Don't be fooled by the package, someone once said.

To everyone who knew him at school, Max was an uncommonly knowledgeable class clown from the badlands of Alberta. What no one, including Darcy, could see was that the smart ass about to be thrashed was in fact a thirty-four-year-old man; and not just any man, but a boundless entity of outrageous temporal magnitude well acquainted with Judo and Krav Maga.

He was more like an accumulation of men all camouflaged within the skin of a kid. Only to the juvenile ignoramuses standing in his presence could he fairly be called a boy. There was a chilling atavistic urge lurking deep in his core that neither law nor consequence could deter. He'd lived through muggings in Harlem and body slams in the dojos of Tokyo. He had survived alcoholism and car crashes. He was a Don Juan knower of women the globe over. He spoke several languages, played music, and owned a thriving business. But to the kids standing where the alley met the street in 1986, he was nothing more than a thirteen-year-old about to receive a deviated septum.

When he looked over at Rachel, though, the young girl's expression informed him that it was not his strength that would win her heart but his vulnerability. And so, as Darcy swung hard with awkward abandon, Max allowed the blows to land. There were a couple of haymakers and a well-thrown crossover combination; two lefts and a right, with a hook to the guts and a kick to the nuts. Max trickled blood into the street and moaned in pain, but Rachel came to his aid. She held his split nose and examined his chipped teeth. The gentle energy of her fingers went into him like liniment, and his defeat felt like a total victory.

After the student onlookers and the bullies had dissipated, he was left sitting beside her under a yield sign at the intersection of Glen-Ross and Sixth Street. They walked to a 7/11 and shared a Slurpee. She wore an expression of compassion; a comforting emotion that those of less judging natures are able to conjure so as to spare fools a loss of confidence.

He asked her if she was going to the school dance the following Friday.

She said she planned to attend with friends and then go to a sleepover afterward.

The school put up a disco ball and decorated the gymnasium. Under its rotating glitter, Max gyrated with Rachel and the other eighth graders to '*Sledgehammer*' and '*West End Girls.*' He was able to get his hands on her hips during '*Holding Back the Years*' and she rested her head on his shoulder when the DJ played '*Take My Breath Away.*' She was eager and pliable, and Darcy was nowhere to be seen, on those accounts alone the evening was a major success. But the night didn't take off until he convinced her to steal away to a rodeo cabaret.

The two minors snuck into a beer garden on the fair grounds and proceeded to waltz among the inebriated cowboys who were largely oblivious to their underage presence. Max and Rachel consented to two-step on one another's feet in the drink sodden sand while an imported Nashville act covered the best country music ever recorded by the likes of Alabama, George Strait, and The Nitty Gritty Dirt Band.

At midnight they escaped from the Stetsons and the firm fitting Wranglers and found themselves a spot in the straw next to a vacant livestock bay. They sat with each other unnoticed and warm. He kissed her, and she kissed him back. Her plump dimpled flesh was soft and virgin. He was completely taken in, and she was doing the taking. There was a truth emerging that he had not experienced before, nor would ever again. He felt something deep and remarkable being revealed to him. The concentration of purpose and the elusive pursuit of the ever present, gleaned over years of AUE's, had allowed him to finally glimpse the un-seeable pieces of Rachel's soul. In a Western Star bale shed on the edge of the prairies, the timeless and alluring magic of everything she was and would ever be, touched his soul as though the future depended on it; and in that moment she became his greatest love in all possible universes.[16]

He couldn't bring himself to invite her over to his basement, so he walked her to her friend's house on Champion Street where the other girls were still awake, feverishly fawning over Rob Lowe and Emilio Estevez and lesser members of the Brat Pack in a VHS marathon.

As it turned out, the rodeo dance was as serious as Max and Rachel got in the time they had remaining.

---

[16]**#6** on the Billboard Year-End Hot 100 singles of 1986. **"How Will I Know"** by <u>Whitney Houston</u> from the album *Whitney Houston.* Arista, 1985. There was a Sony transistor radio sitting on a two-by-four next to the straw they were rolling in. Someone had placed it there to listen to during the day and then forgot about it at night. Max watched as Rachel turned it on and tuned it in to a station other than country. He swore that the song was the first thing he heard when he awoke in 1986, and it proved to be an omen as he watched her lip synch to it while falling all over herself to hold his heart and taste his mouth.

They continued to see one another at school, and without appearing overly ambitious about it, he attempted to select her on his teams during gym class and tapped his creativity to find pretexts for conversing with her in the hallways. They flirted subtly and traded grins and continued to play hockey in the streets by the trailer park.

For him, it was enough to know that she was there and that she'd always be there.

One day, the RCMP showed up at school and took him away. He was returned to his family in Nipawin; marked by psychologists and community social workers as a precocious and unusual runaway. Grace cried when he was brought home, and Glenn tried to understand such unusual adolescent motivations. Even in an alternative universe where things weren't real – in whatever sense that meant - it was never easy to deal with actions that resulted in heartbreak and anguish, especially where family and friends were concerned.

Following his emergence from the unexpected AUE, Max went to the window and drew back the blinds. Outside, there was a crescent moon gliding through the heavens with Venus hung below it like a medallion, reddish orange at its perihelion. He thought about his unpredictable orbit around Rachel as he went into the backyard and stood in the cool grass, not cut in weeks. The breeze had lost all its speed and dew worms were rising. He told himself that she was a comet streaking across the sky and that if he didn't grab hold of her his multitudinous existences would come to nothing more than star dust; a wasted supernova floating to the edges of unknown places.

* * *

He turned off the amplifier and placed the guitar back on its stand. He heard Rachel's Honda pull out of the driveway, taking Kevin to lacrosse practice. He sat still for a moment and looked around the house; it was a mess, but no one cared. Later, they'd eat dinner together and the boys would tell stories that made him laugh. Rachel would whisper in his ear the things they could do after they finished dishes. He was a lucky man.

When he moved back in with her and the boys, he purposely skipped a month of Insynnium to accommodate the new living arrangement. The tight quarters presented a challenge to privacy. After missing a couple months, he thought perhaps he might give up the stuff altogether. But as time wore on, he discovered how addicted he was; how inevitable the relapse; how ingrained the craving; how much Insynnium had changed his DNA.

His desire for time travel made him creative. He told Rachel about the need to visit other parts of Canada in promotional campaigns for GROWERS. He began taking 'business trips' once a month to cities like Sudbury and Medicine Hat. His real purpose for the self-funded junkets, however, was to get Insynnium inside him.

He got the trips down to an art form: hotel check-in around five; light dinner at six; comatose by seven. Twenty-four hours would pass as he absorbed and explored his alternative year. The following evening he would awake at seven; shower at eight, and have a late snack with a movie at nine. He would leave the following morning before noon; no questions, no problems, fail safe, as he headed back to Brandon with a caffeinated Tim Horton's buzz. His dual lives were completely compatible and yet totally irreconcilable, like two worlds running oddly in parallel.

Once, on a trip to Kamloops, he called Duncan.

Duncan swore up and down that Max was a fool to have moved back in with Rachel, but he also emphasized that no matter what, Max would remain a friend, even if his judgment was far from perfect.

"I've never mentioned anything about time travel; not even to her," said Max.

"Well that's certainly something," said Duncan, who was both troubled and astonished that Max went to the lengths he did to continue his comas.

"What about you, where are you at now?" said Max.

"Working for a tech startup in Virginia Beach, but I've got an opportunity to go abroad, so we'll see."

"And Pierre?" said Max.

"Still at Humboldt, but only for another six months or so," said Duncan, "he's moving back to France."

"I think about you guys all the time, and what you did for me."

"Don't mention it," said Duncan.

But Max had to mention it; he had to keep Duncan on the line; had to keep him talking. His phone conversations with Duncan were becoming so rare that he feared they might cease altogether. Duncan and Pierre were the only people who understood his situation. Who besides them could indulge him in discussing such elaborate and outrageous things?

Though it appeared that nobody, aside from Rachel and the boys, seemed *that* impressed by what he was acquiring in his time travels, there was, nonetheless, some interest around town; and questions naturally got asked now and again.

He made a concerted effort to be careful about what he said, but on occasion, he would carelessly and honestly answer the following questions to generalized puzzlement, fascinated stares, and blatant disbelief:

What's your secret to be such a successful businessman? Who are you hiring to re-roof your house? What mechanic do you go to? Who are you getting to wire your garage? Was it expensive to have the plumbing redone? When do you find the time to practice the piano? How do you grow such an amazing garden? You're such a faithful and attentive husband, have you ever been tempted by an affair? Did you take a mountaineering course before you and the boys went rock climbing at Dorian Tower? When did you learn karate? Were you born with a knack for languages, how many can you speak? Are those paintings yours? I didn't know you could crochet? You mix such a great drink, are you sure you can't have one? Seven card high/ low, right? Tell me, Max, how do you maintain such an impeccable poker face?

2010

-Autumn-

*"There's people and things you'll never see again,
and some that you hope to"*

Insynnium was officially everywhere.

But Duncan Wisegerber, posing down-dog at an ashram in Dharmasala, was unofficially nowhere. He removed himself to the city of exile to acquire a breath of health in the high Himalayan air. He wore a loosely tied turban and clothes made from hemp which made him look like some far-flung Nigerian yogi. Walking among the prayer flags and temples dusted with turmeric, however, he stood out no more or no less than any other tourist as he ate his way around town with a wealthy Western gusto.

He contemplated the sky, like his navel, with a mournful appraisal, and tried to decide who should replace Eric as the front-man for Insynnium. He knew it wouldn't be Moe Bringa, as Moe was gone too, although to a decidedly different end than Eric. Moe understood, as did Duncan, that there were no walls or guards that could match the sustained protection of anonymity.

When Duncan handed Eric the keys to Insynnium, he and Moe unlocked every door they could find, and it proved very lucrative. It was a profitable run, and they all made hundreds of millions. Like a puppeteer from within the shadows, Duncan used Eric's salesmanship and connections to hook America on Insynnium. He also allowed Eric to build spice routes through Europe and Asia, despite Pierre's strong misgivings.

Eric became notorious to those in the criminal underworld, and an ongoing person of interest to law enforcement communities everywhere. His persona was that of a fugitive, and he attracted the undying attention of those determined to find the secret to Insynnium. For someone who had no actual material knowledge about the true nature and origin of the spice, Eric parlayed his ignorance into the reigning myth that he knew everything. There was a general acceptance that he was the heart of Insynnium, and the most wanted man alive. Unfortunately, his most wanted status resulted in his untimely death, and Duncan knew that those who killed him would eventually – given enough time and resources – trace all roads back to Arcata.

Pierre thought it was the Bratski Krug or maybe the Gambinos, but Duncan was convinced it was a ruthless pharmaceutical that was the culprit behind Eric's murder. Big pharma hired henchmen that took teeth and snipped off digits in their cancerous and unmerciful hunt for the secret. It was this corporate group of sunless thugs that had made Duncan and Pierre recluses to the point of rumor, patiently hiding inside a transparent carapace.

Two times a year, however, they would emerge from the safety of their shells to stimulate new germinations in Pierre's Humboldt County home. Despite the risks that their activity presented, the drive of the plant was relentless, and it bent the two men to its will. Once the tiny sprouts left Duncan's hands, they entered a colossal world of avarice and greed that manhandled them to maturity, and then sold their finely ground powder to millions of eager users. Duncan knew that most of his seedlings still achieved adulthood in locations throughout the lower forty-eight, but he'd recently heard that vast fields were being cultivated in the Ukraine, and among the rolling pastoral landscapes the Etruscans once wandered. Significant and fertile ground, he thought, for a seed that no one could germinate.

He kept dummy trusts in the Cook Islands and off shore accounts in the Grand Caymans and Nevis. Although his finances were well insulated by personal asset protection strategies, it did little to relieve the uncomfortable reality that his fundamental problems could never be solved by anything as simple as money. He threw bags of Ben Franklins at intrepid and malleable operatives who only managed to tell him fewer and fewer facts as the weeks went past. These former soldiers and spies, who he had selected for their discretion and powers of observation, had no idea who he really was. He remained the unidentifiable controller, the bipedal chameleon deftly staying abreast of his unknown unknowns while the walls of anonymity slowly crumbled.

* * *

Eric picked him up at LAX; in the Gran Sport, no less.

He could feel Eric's eyes assessing him for damage – looking for the un-see-able yet conspicuous injuries of the heart. He had an enormous amount of directionless energy, and it oozed from his pores like sweat.

"Sorry about Sarah," said Eric.

"I know," said Duncan. He didn't want to talk about it. Neither of them did.

"Look, I gotta get back to Chicago tomorrow," said Eric, "but you can stay at the house for as long as you need."

"How's business?" said Duncan, not wanting to know.

"Can't complain," said Eric, not wanting to elaborate.

Eric had been halfway hopeful that Duncan's trip to Israel would turn him around. When he took up with Sarah, Eric became convinced that his friend's life was on the mend. His early return and the unpleasant news that surrounded it, however, was a deflating reminder of the random and fragile nature of everything. Eric told Duncan he should start a business and make himself stratospherically rich. It sounded stupid but he didn't know what else to say. Duncan laughed at the level of optimism Eric held and told him to say hi to Moe when he got back to Chicago.

He moved back into the rental bungalow on 16th in Santa Monica. He was sharing the flat with a couple of housemates; a smoldering and leggy pair of cougars who'd recently migrated to the sapphic side of the forest. The structural irony of the home's recent renovations weren't lost on him either; he soon discovered there wasn't a single stud beneath the interior drywall and that the entire floor had been relayed in tongue and groove. The place was alive with creeks and moans that even the craftiest carpenter would have been hard pressed to improve with wood.

He drove the Gran Sport down palm lined boulevards and saw nothing but the taillights in front of him; what could he see in streets so filled with fire? He revved up the engine on the straightaways hoping to outpace his ghosts. The dormancy of his positive emotions notwithstanding, he moved through the city of angels with his typical hormonal verve, now backed up with a rebooted Middle Eastern mojo. Even the lesbians at his domicile indicated a willingness to give dick a chance. But he couldn't bring himself to go back to the hedonistic ways of his life before Sarah. His only friends remained Eric and Moe, and they treated him more like a sacred cow than a pal. He thought about reaching out to Grace, but something told him not to – it had been too many years, and he needed a better pretext for a visit of that sort.

So, he went to visit Dr. Finkelbinder instead.

Solomon gripped him in a firm and forgiving hug. The doctor spoke gently and reminded him to be grateful for the many special memories he'd shared with his niece. He was moved to no longer be Finkelbinder's patient, but instead the thankful recipient of an avuncular solicitude.

Sol spoke of Sarah: a child that once played beneath Sugar Maples in Missouri and rode horses east of Lebanon in the Fort Leonard Wood; a kid that got good grades and moved to the city to study; a hard worker with a fine mind.

"She hiked on the Appalachian Trail, you know?" said Sol.

"I miss her."

"And you always will," he said. He gave Duncan a stern and intentional look and then continued, "Sarah would want you to do more with your life than hang out in So Cal and feel bad. You probably know that."

"Yeah," replied Duncan. But he had nothing. Other than a message for a dying man, he had nothing.

He looked at Sol.

"How did your brother end up in Chile?" he said, almost unintentionally.

"I don't have a brother."

"Then I suppose you don't have a niece named Barbara, either?"

"Nope."

"Then who's this," said Duncan, as he showed Sol a picture of Barbara taken on his phone.

"Damned if I know. She's pretty, though."

Sol looked at Duncan.

"You can't believe everything people tell you, kid. Sarah had some interesting friends, they must have been messing with your head," he said, as he chucked without malice at Duncan's perplexed expression.

"Don't think too much, just move on," he said.

"I better get going then," said Duncan.

The doctor walked him to his car.

As they parted ways, he gave his former vascular surgeon a sober and lasting look. "Thanks," he said, as he opened the door of the Buick and climbed inside.

"Good luck," said the doctor.

He swallowed all his questions regarding Barbara and decided that she was what he had surmised: a Mossad or Shin Bet agent ferreting out intel on terrorist cells. Of course, that raised a whole specter of unanswerable questions related to Sarah, Leah, and possibly Felix, as well.

It was slippery and elusive, and had a John le Carre quality.

He shifted his attention to something he felt more capable of figuring out: the whereabouts of Aloysius. There were several listings for 'Alex Smith' in Oregon and Northern California. He made telephone inquiries until he stumbled onto a listing for a gentleman named, Alec Smyth, in San Francisco.

A woman with a thick Hungarian accent answered his call, but there was no ambiguity in her pronunciation of 'ninety-five' when queried about Alec's age. The woman told Duncan that Alec had relocated to Redding several years earlier. She provided no forwarding number, but she disclosed a possible address. A note of suspicion arose in her voice after she fronted Duncan the information, as though she'd committed some egregious solecism that gave away more than she intended. She turned accusatorial and asked him how he got her number. When he told her he'd found it buried in the White Pages, she abruptly hung up; it was then that he knew he was onto something.

When he reached Grove Crescent Loop in Shasta County, he made an appraisal of the gingerbread real estate long before approaching the entrance to knock the knocker. Everything before his eyes re-enforced the nagging hunch that his search might be over before it began; the polished Volvo parked out front, the trimmed hedges, the clean neighborhood, it didn't add up. It looked like his investigation might be dead on a gentrified cul-de-sac.

A child of six or seven answered the door and then hollered at her mom, who plodded down the stairs with a heavy steel-healed foreboding. It wasn't looking promising, he thought.

"Can I help you?" said the woman.

"I'm looking for an Alec Smyth," he said.

"I'm sorry; I don't know an Alec Smyth," she replied, "Is your address correct?"

Duncan handed her a note with the address on it.

The woman looked at the address and then asked in kind regard, "Is he a friend or family?"

"He's neither. He's an old man I've been asked to deliver a message to, that's all," said Duncan, in a not unfriendly tone.

The woman's face took on a recalcitrant expression subtlety seeded with racism. But in a brilliant stroke of timing the child chimed in:

"Mommy, Mommy, what about the old man in the wheel chair who they push around here on Saturdays?"

"Oh, Sweetie, he's just a landlord checking on his properties," said the woman to her daughter, as they stood within the limited safety of the door frame.

"The old man, do you know his name by chance?" asked Duncan.

"I'm sorry, I don't. But another gentleman brings him here maybe twice a month and pushes him up and down the sidewalks. From what I've been told the older gentleman is the owner of all that property," she said, as she pointed at the houses next to hers and the four around the bend where the road made a curve to the right.

The child smiled at Duncan.

"He lives in Arcata, I think," the woman continued, "he seems pretty decrepit, though, and he hasn't come by for a while. The renters over there might have an address for him."

As it turned out, the renters did, in fact, have an address, and it lead Duncan directly to the business offices of a property management company next to a pizzeria in downtown Arcata. The property management company collected rents and trimmed hedges for a client that went by the name of Smith Holdings Ltd. The receptionist at the front desk, a meek and preoccupied gal with well manicured nails and three-inch eyelashes, was instantly susceptible to Duncan's smooth questioning, and she only wavered slightly as she handed over the address on record.

Soon he was back in the Gran Sport staring across the street at a dry porch somewhat occluded by a veil of late day rain. The car radio was on 93.1 KSLG.[17] The sky had opened up and was landing hard in the mud between him and the porch that he needed to reach.

As he jumped over puddles of uncertain depth while holding a newspaper above his head, he noticed a miled-out Westy parked in the lane missing a front tire and a section of panel, and a hard driven Chevette in front of a slope roofed garage with a pizza delivery sign attached to the top.

"If you're selling vacuums you can leave now, or steak knives, or encyclopedias, just go," said the man who answered the door.

---

[17]**#9** on the Billboard Year-End Hot 100 singles of 2001.
"Again" by Lenny Kravitz from the album *Greatest Hits.* Virgin America, 2000. Duncan had purposely shaved his head to avoid looking like Lenny. He had to take these kinds of measures because he hated the doppelganger comments and stupid ass questions about whether he was a singer as well. He saw only a fleeting resemblance between himself and Mr. Kravitz; but still, there was something about him that called to mind such comparisons. The song reminded him of Sarah and her tender mercies and all the other women that had been a part of his past but were unlikely to be in his future; a future celibate and unfathomable from where he stood.

Duncan was dripping wet. "Who sells encyclopedias door to door anymore?" he said with insouciance.

"OK, smart ass, get lost," said the man.

"Wait," said Duncan, "I'm looking for someone, his name is Aloysius Smyth."

The man filled the entire doorway and looked like someone who would be comfortable using a chainsaw or an industrial shop press. He gave Duncan a circumspect once over.

"I know an Alex Smith up on Roach Haven Lane," said the man. "That's who I bought this house from... but unless you're looking for an old faggot with a bad attitude, he's not likely your guy."

The man continued to evaluate Duncan with a fiery expression, and Duncan began to feel like a sharecropper in a small Kentucky town.

"Say, that's a nice looking Gran Sport you pulled up in," said the man, "You interested in selling her? I've been looking for a ride like that for some time."

"No, I'm not looking to sell it," said Duncan.

"Okay, well good luck with your search there, Denzel," said the man in a racially slurred tone as he started to push the door shut in Duncan's face.

He wasn't fast enough, though, because a small and determined terrier came darting through the opening and bit Duncan on the pant leg with the growling intention of dragging him off to dine.

"Quite a watch dog you got there," he said in a way that was intended to lighten the atmosphere but failed miserably.

The man leveled Duncan with his eyes and said, "Monty has never become accustomed to strangers, and honestly, I like him that way."

There was an awkward pause between the two men that eventually broke in Duncan's favor.

"How old is this Alex guy you mentioned?" said Duncan.

"Early to mid-nineties, I would guess," said the man, "he's old as fuck."

"He could be the guy I'm looking for," said Duncan, "can you give me his address?"

"Yeah sure, but I don't know why anyone would have any interest in tracking down that miserable old cocksucker," said the man. "And I can tell just by lookin' at you that you ain't no relative."

"No, obviously not," said Duncan. "I've been asked to deliver him a message."

"What? Like a singing telegram or some sort of shit?" said the man as his attitude began to lighten up.

For the first time in their conversation the man appeared as though he might smile.

"Alex moved here a few years back," said the man, "He came from San Francisco. He acquired some parcels of land and eventually sold one to me. He also rents commercial real estate downtown.

"But Alex is in no condition to handle his affairs anymore. The old queer's man friend, Pierre Leveque, manages everything for him, more of a diaper changer if you ask me. I don't need to know what interest a middle age professor of botany and mathematics has with some old Irish queen. It's always been very hush, hush. But, of course, speculation has abounded."

Duncan was taken aback by the nature of the information so candidly shared. "What sort of speculation," he asked.

"Well, the most prominent rumor in town is that Aloysius, owing to his terrible disposition and increasing frailty, put out adverts, North America wide, to find someone to come look after him so he wouldn't be moved into an aged care facility. The allure of the offer being that he would confer a large portion of his estate on the person that took up the challenge. I imagine random acts of fellatio were part of the deal as well," joked the man, as he entertained the limp possibility of such a scenario.

"Interesting," said Duncan, as he wondered what he'd gotten himself into. "Look, I'd better get going, thank you for your time."

"Yeah, well, we'll see, won't we?" said the man. "I own Jesus' Pizza Pallor downtown. Stop in for a slice before you leave these parts if you like that sort of thing."

"Thanks, man. I'm Duncan, by the way."

"Jim, Jim Kimparis," said the man. "Good luck in delivering your message 'Duncan by the Way'," he said and smiled ever so slightly to emphasize both his suspicion and curiosity at the young colored man's presence in his neck of the woods.

Jim watched Duncan walk back to his car. Duncan waved, but Jim didn't bother returning the courtesy.

Duncan was positive that Monty was still barking as he drove off to meet the rest of his life.

He stared at the address on the mailbox as though it were a prank: 420, Roach Haven Lane.

He got out of the Buick and made his way up the lichen covered steps. There was no lawn, only wild grass and flowers that once started out as bulbs. The heavy front door of the six-bedroom Tutor was wide and ajar behind a gossamer screen version of itself. Under a penumbra of Fir and Cedar, the place pulsated with potential. It felt like a destination, and it put him in mind of Charles Ryder rocking up at Brideshead (his bloody fondness for English writers was unshakable). Stone work with California moss and creeping ivy on anything vertical; the semi-clean windows lurking in the dimness of half swung shudders along with butterflies and bumble bees.

In the inconspicuous seconds of the doorbell's ringing, a crack in the order of fate emerged, and destiny began to swallow him. But then suddenly, as the door was pushed open, the ominous sensation evaporated before he could decide whether he'd claimed it or whether it had claimed him.

"Can I help you?" said the man who emerged from home's fragrant bosom.

"I hope so," he said. "My name is Duncan Wisegerber, and I'm looking for an Alex Smith. Jim Kimparis over on Claremont told me that Alex lived here."

"I see," said the man. "Jim told you that, did he?"

Duncan nodded.

"My name is Pierre," said the man in a tenor smooth Francophone accent, "Please come inside, won't you?"

As Duncan edged his way into the house, he was absorbed by its lepidopterous state and the eucalyptus scent of its interior. It was a home full of orchids and books. The broad walls and vaulted ceilings felt encyclopedic in their adornments. The atmosphere inside seemed both germinal and decaying in the distance of a single breath; it was a place quiet but alive; dark but not sinister; light but not bright. Duncan noticed striking abstract art pieces calling his attention from their perches, as well as various sculptures that had found resting places on antique tables, bureaus, and shelves. There were multitudes of details to be missed at first inspection.

"Tell me about the man that you're looking for," said Pierre.

"Well," said Duncan, "I understand that his real name is Aloysius Smyth. He should be in his mid-nineties. He lived in France during the late Seventies and early Eighties. In Paris, he knew a man named, Felix, who now resides in Turkey, he was -"

"And what is your reason for needing to see this man?" interrupted Pierre. He sensed Duncan to be much more than he appeared.

"I have a message concerning forgiveness that I need to deliver to him."

"Well, you've come to the right place," said Pierre, "The gentleman you're looking for lives here.

But you need to be aware that Aloysius is dying. He's in a bedroom at the back, and he doesn't have much time left. This will be a death bed message, can you handle that?"

"Yeah, I think so," said Duncan.

As the two made their way down the hallway and into the rear of the home, Duncan felt as though he were entering a sealed chamber were some eccentric miser had hidden Krugerrands or diamonds long ago.

When he finally cast his gaze on the terminal case, Duncan was immediately struck by the feeling that Aloysius had been waiting for him. He couldn't know it for certain as it seemed completely unexplainable, but it was as if he'd been counted on to turn up on this day at this hour all along.

Aloysius peered up at him with sad pleading eyes. "What is it, son," he said, "Is it my real estate or my finances or what? Go on, spit it out."

"It's about Felix," said Duncan, "Do you know who I'm talking about?"

The mere mention of Felix's name was like placing a heavy cinder block onto the old man's chest in an effort to force the final breaths from his life. Aloysius wheezed and coughed, but he managed to ask, "Is he okay? Is he alive? My god, it's been so long since I've seen him."

"Yes, of course," said Duncan, "He's fine. He's an amazing man, still very healthy."

"And…?" said Aloysius.

"He told me that he forgives you," said Duncan.

Tears pooled in the corners of Alex's grey and fading eyes, and then he turned his watery orbits toward Pierre. His myopia was temporarily reversed, and his vision converged on a far and distant fixation. He sucked into his lungs several urgent and struggling heaves, and then his eyes returned to him with the zeal of eternity fixed into the irises.

Pierre knelt beside him and placed a hand on the old man's brow.

"Oh, this is a great sunset for the poets," said Alex, "This is the best one yet. Can you see it, boy? Can you see the brilliant colors?"

The old man closed his eyes and went deathly quiet.

Duncan felt something brush past him; a soul escaping from its cellular prison; a spirit drifting toward heaven? The remainder of all else was nothing but a sack of desiccated flesh on the mattress.

"He's gone," said Pierre, breaking silence in the reaper's wake.

"I'm sorry," said Duncan.

"Although it surprises me to say this," said Pierre, "I am too."

There were aspects of Aloysius best left to death. But there were pieces that would live on and that's how life was.

The two men went to the kitchen.

Duncan sat with a glass of water while Pierre called the mortuary to have the body collected. Pierre was a study in equanimity and poise. His beard gave him a dignified appearance, and he wore spectacles perched on a dominant nose that made a direct slope from the top of his bald dome. His French accent did no disservice to his command of English, and Duncan found him pleasing to listen to.

Pierre made them espresso with such concentration of purpose that it was as though he were creating a distraction from death itself. Duncan watched as he ground the coffee and pressed it into a puck and placed it under pressure - the result was aromatic and robust.

There was a copy of *The Arcata Eye* resting in the center of the table. The three o'clock sun beamed white light into the kitchen, and the cupboards and walls became illuminated.

"I can't believe how fast he went once I told him the message," said Duncan.

"Alex was tired, he was barely hanging on," said Pierre, "he was ready to let go."

"I guess it was fortunate that I got here when I did?"

Pierre nodded slowly with preoccupation.

Tell me, Duncan," he said, in a slight change of tone, "Did you really meet Felix in person?"

Pierre's brow exhibited the same crenellated features of interest that one might expect to observe on the face of a physicist learning of someone's personal encounter with Einstein.

"Yeah, I met him in person," said Duncan, "You've never met him?"

"No, I've only heard stories," said Pierre. "But I have a file cabinet containing an assortment of correspondence and information on potions and elixirs sent from him over the years. Some of the stuff is unbelievably effective, you can't imagine."

Duncan thought very carefully about the next thing he shared.

"There was more to Felix's message than just forgiveness," he said, "There was also a secret that I was sworn to tell only Alex. But since he's dead, I suppose I could tell you."

"What is it?" said Pierre, somewhat caught off guard.

"It has to do with some seeds that were given to Alex back in the day. Felix told me how to make them sprout. I don't know if this means anything to you, but he said Alex would understand."

It was as if Pierre had been given an infusion of vitamin B fortified with intrigue or a massive dose of ozone laced with attention. His face gained color, and he acquired an unusual intensity in his stare. Duncan could see a thousand thoughts converging on his focused intellect.

"Well, what is it," he said, almost frantically. "What makes them sprout?"

"Music, music makes the seeds sprout" said Duncan whimsically and without gravity.

"Music!" said Pierre, "Well I'll be goddamned." His breath left his lungs like he'd been holding it for years.

Before Duncan could elaborate further, there was a knock at the door. Two young funeral home attendants stood ready to escort the remains of Mr. Smyth to the ash creator.

* * *

Duncan was reviving from shavasana with a lung full of oxygen that had rolled off some stratospheric peak in the Hindu Kush when his phone rang.

"I received confirmation," said Pierre, "You were right, it was the Russian mafia. They were working for Fyzzor. They tortured Eric to death; he couldn't tell them what he didn't know, so they chopped off his…"

"I don't want to hear it," said Duncan as he cut Pierre off. "Is your life in danger?"

"No."

"Good. How long can you stay where you're at?"

"Indefinitely, if need be," said Pierre.

"Alright, fortunately we're still in good shape. We'll lay low for awhile and let things cool off."

"Did you hear about Max?" said Pierre.

"Yes, yes I did."

"What do you think?"

"I don't know, I try not to," said Duncan, as he was consigned to contemplate Max's contortions of truth and reality in a recent media piece.

A year ago, Max had told him that he wanted to come see him. He was under the impression that Duncan was living in Raleigh working as a systems analyst for Carolina Tech, which of course was a lie. His crazy-ass comas were the last thing Duncan needed at that point. So, Duncan told Max that he'd moved overseas on a high-security assignment with the State Department to botch any incentive he had in trying to find him.

Duncan now kicked himself for underestimating the persistence of Max's imaginative disorder, or whatever it was that fastened him to such outlandish fantasies. Seven days ago, Pierre sent him U-Tube footage of Max on the CBC News. He was in a Q&A session with a reporter from the Fifth Estate trying to explain unexplainable things like brain chemistry, serendipity, and the pressure of being a hero. It was all front page stuff and pretty much entirely made up as far as Duncan could tell. His first thought was that somewhere behind it all was Rachel. He was certain that her ambitions and manipulations were responsible for most of Max's talking points, many of which were overexposed and graphically unnecessary.

2011

-Winter-

*"They said you got the moves like Jagger, but man I
don't even dance"*

The ambulance was speeding away, and the
diminishing whine of its siren held everyone silent in
the gathering snow as it faded into the distance.
People were approaching Max and offering gratitude;
some were more composed than others, but everyone
was in shock. The mayor's blood was still sticking to
the back of his hands along with other sanguine
reminders dried to his hockey sweater.

He'd never seen anything like it, and Max was a
man who'd seen things. It was a late night game of
shinny gone wrong. The mayor, playing defense, was
back-checking an opposing forward when his skate
was suddenly grabbed by an imperfection in the
outdoor rink. The Mayor tripped and fell throat first
onto the well-honed edge of another player's skate
blade. The slicing fall lacerated his jugular. Freakish
and improbable were words used by those present.

Max was on the ice when the injury occurred, and
he immediately leapt on top of the mayor and pressed
his hands onto the wound until paramedics arrived. He
was informed that his quick attention and first

responder knowledge gave the mayor a fighting chance. There had been critical blood loss, but it was predicted that the mayor would survive.

It wasn't the first time that Max had been auspiciously placed into a position to save or assist people over the last two and a half years. Whether running a business errand for GROWERS, grabbing a last minute item for Rachel, or getting the boys to sports practice, unknown forces seemed to be guiding his arrivals and overseeing his departures.

He hadn't played hockey all winter, then at the last minute he was asked to show up and fill in for a farmer who'd pulled a hamstring shoveling grain. And so, just like that, he found himself wearing shin pads and a mouth guard and intervening in a life and death situation he should never have known about until the following morning while listening to the radio. The public attention made him uncomfortable because it necessitated the retelling of a flimsy lie that had never been intended for an audience greater than that of his wife and kids.

"Oh my god, Dad, that was so cool. You just like saved Mayor Bob with your bare hands," said Josh.

Several people from the local neighborhood encircled Max and began taking pictures on their phones; he would be tweeted and posted all over Canada.[18]

---

[18] **#9** on the Billboard Year-End Hot 100 singles of 2011.
"Moves Like Jagger" by <u>Maroon 5 featuring Christina Aguilera</u> from the album *Hands All Over*. A&M/Octone, 2011. There was

"Come on guys, give him a little space," said Daryl, as he threw a wool blanket over Max's shoulders and handed him a pair of mitts.

"What would this town do without you, buddy?" he said.

Max's skates were still laced to his feet. Beyond the voices and the music and the sensation of decelerating adrenalin he looked up and saw the snow falling silently, almost reluctantly, in the dim yellow ambiance of the steel light standards illuminating the rink.

* * *

He hadn't wanted to, but Rachel and the boys insisted. They thought it would be cool if he was interviewed by Candice Risdal from the Brandon Evening News, a local affiliate of CBC Winnipeg. The station was keen for a frank interview on the record. The request stemmed from an incident where

---

a large winter fire burning behind the skate shake and some of the guys were passing around a bottle of Crown Royal to help them recover from the accident. Levine and Aguilera come at Max through a cold speaker sitting on the tailgate of a pickup truck, and he knew he had the moves like Jagger. There was a lot of nervous laughter and 'fuck yeah's' as the incident was relived and calcified like a layer of frost on the minds of everyone present. Max had almost become yesterday's story, but with the hockey accident he'd be as popular as Santa Claus by Christmas – the community would need a long thaw of forgetfulness to move on from this one, he told himself.

he had heroically and miraculously saved the life of a local farmer and his school age children.

A year and a half ago, he pulled a drowning family from their motor boat after it capsized on Pelican Lake. The father needed resuscitation and appeared to be DOA by the time Max got him on shore; where, much to his chagrin, an audience had congregated. The fishing farmer survived, along with his kids, because of the moxie and finesse that Max was able to bring to the life-saving endeavor that day – the source of which no one in town could even begin to fathom.

He performed water borne rescue techniques that only an accomplished life saver would know how to execute, and he bandaged the arm of one of the children who had received a nasty cut from the prop. There were other contusions and skin abrasions as well; all attended to in a fashion that left the real medics completely satisfied when they finally showed up.

On the day of the Pelican Lake boating incident, he was informally interviewed by the *Brandon Sun,* and questions were asked: was he an off duty fireman or perhaps a doctor or a first aid instructor? He, of course, was none of these things, he was a grocer. He shrugged off the audacious act as nothing more than a combination of luck and well-timed execution.

Not everyone was buying his nonchalant explanation, however. Locals questioned in a follow-up article said it wasn't the first time they'd noticed him exhibiting abilities and talents that surprised them.

Some said it was rumored that he spoke six languages and played several instruments. Those who had known him from before said that he was a changed man, and that it wasn't just his sobriety or his competence in baking a soufflé, it was more like a fundamental alteration in the very fabric of his being.

There were murmurings around Brandon that the eighteen months in which he had gone missing back in 2004 were actually the result of an alien abduction. It was speculated by some that he had floated with Marians on an intergalactic space odyssey that had somehow enhanced his human potential. The fact that any of this bullshit could be delivered with a straight face caused him to wonder why he chose to remain silent about time travel, since people appeared willing to believe almost anything.

The *Brandon News at Six* wanted the exclusive story on his personal transformation. People wanted to understand what sort of a fountainhead he was drinking from. They wanted to know what allowed him to grasp so many skills with such ease and adroitness.

Rachel encouraged him to be candid about his head trauma, and to describe how the injury had stimulated cortically improbable, yet amazingly absorptive, learning channels throughout his brain. And so it was that he took a deep breath and accepted the invitation to formally foist his flimsy lie onto the Canadian public with convincing enthusiasm.

Candice Risdal (CBC News Winnipeg): *Can you tell us a little about yourself, Max; who you are, where you're from, what you've done?*

Maximilian McVista (local hero): *I grew up on a farm in Saskatchewan, and I'm the owner of an organic grocery store here in Brandon. I have a degree in commerce from Queens University. I have two wonderful boys and a beautiful wife.*

CR: *I'm correct in stating that your business consumes most of your time, right? So how is it that you're able to learn all these different things? Do you not sleep at night?*

MM: *Actually, I sleep quite a bit. Probably more than most people realize [A statement wholly underappreciated in both its gravity and meaning by everyone except Max].*

CR: *So when do you learn all this stuff. It seems as though you have extra lifetimes of ability at your disposal. For example, the family on Pelican Lake, how did you know what to do?*

MM: *Common sense I suppose, and confidence.*

He remembered with clarity the lives that he had saved while dozing in the catatonic trenches of Insynnium. He wanted to tell Ms. Risdal about two similar life-saving incidents: one, off the coast of Taiwan, and another, in Nevada, but he couldn't speak to either because they'd taken place in an alternative universe – even though boats and people all sank the same rate no matter where you were.

In Taiwan, while mastering ping pong and indulging the culinary pleasures of hot pot, he was invited to an indigenous island to be an extra in a Taipei Film Board production. He was on a small commuter vessel en route to location when they were overcome by a king wave in a stretch of unpredictable sea. The boat capsized, and everyone was flushed into the open water. Along with two other strong swimmers, he saved many lives that day, but it was also the first time in an AUE when he came close to losing his own.

In the Las Vegas incident, he was working as a card dealer at the Bellagio. He had escaped the artificial and endless evenings of casino life for a day of sunbathing and swimming at Lake Mead. Two other dealers, who he knew from places along the Strip, together with three exotic dancers and a couple of jazz musicians, had rented a boat and were ripping around the lake. When they asked him to come aboard, he should have turned them down.

Too drunk to be out on a boat, and positively too drunk to be skiing on water, the lifejacket-less saxophone player wiped out and was knocked unconscious by his water ski. Almost instinctually, Max leapt into the water and swam out to recover the victim of stupidity. Once back on board and assured of the jazzman's survival, the rest of the anxious group reacquired normal heart rates. As the craft slowly motored its way back to the dock, a joint was passed around chased with a shot of bourbon. Max felt the warmth of the desert blowing over the stern of the boat as the show girls warmed up for the evening by dancing to Marvin Gaye with an absence of tan lines.

Most of his '*Baywatch*' talents were acquired through work as a life guard in places like the French Riviera, the Greeks Isles, and of course, Southern California where the contiguous proximity to bikinis made the breast stroke a must have.

But it wasn't until he reached the West Coast of Australia that lifeguarding became more than binoculars and celebrity exposures. In small towns like Exmouth and Broome, he swam in tempting thermals with manta rays and sapphire devils. His dives on the Nigaloo Reef revealed an ocean floor surging with an atmospheric pulse. And then there was Margaret River with its surf culture and undertows and delicious crab feasts; there were long boards with giant shark bites and fierce offshore storms. He grew intimately familiar with the power of the Indian Ocean as he traced his way along its powdery white sands.

In those days it was rare that an AUE could take him away from his addiction to the sea, but on occasion it occurred. One time he enrolled in a paramedic course at the University of Guelph. When he finished his first responder modules he thought that he'd seen it all; riding around in ambulances picking up body parts from traffic accidents and defibrillating old folks and overdose victims. At least that was until he decided to accompany a Croatian aid group to the former Yugoslavia. They were putting together a report for Human Rights Watch. He wasn't sure what he was thinking when he chose to go, but part of him secretly hoped to run across his brother somewhere in the midst of the genocide to which he was headed.

In the Balkans, he assisted souls suffering through the death of all comforts, including protection and security against injustice and insanity. The wounds and afflictions he treated in Omarska, and later in Keraterm, were never again matched in his hands or exorcised from his mind. From behind wire fences and through cold stucco walls, he witnessed the beautiful host of the '84 Winter Olympics dissolve into the blood purging chaos of another European Holocaust.

Although he never located Bones, he was certain that he spotted some of his brother's demolition work in the rubble and the carnage. Search and destroy missions that baffled the Serbians and led them on obsessive hunts for the American team of Green Berets hiding in the hills overlooking Mostar or in the fortified farm villages outside Zagreb.

CR: *[Smiling into the camera] But it's more than just common sense and plain confidence, right, Max? There's more you would like to tell the people of Brandon, is there not?*

MM: *Yes, Candice, there is. I suffered a concussion a few years back and following my head injury I discovered I could easily acquire certain skills and knowledge that would have otherwise taken me years to master. It seemed odd because suddenly I was able to perform tasks that should have required practice before attempting.*

    <u>CR</u>: *You're referring to your spontaneous aptitude for different sports, correct? As well as trades such as carpentry and mechanics, as I understand? Do you in some way feel like you have inexplicably triggered a photographic memory function in your brain?*

    <u>MM</u>: *It's not so much about academics and book learning as it is about long term procedural skills. It's not like I can memorize long passages from text books and novels or speak intellectually about theater and world events. In fact, you might say that the abilities I have couldn't be learned from a book at all.*

    <u>CR</u>: *I think I get it, Max. Take for instance an electrician. It would be difficult to know how to wire a commercial building from just reading a book, correct? Learning as a tradesman comes through an apprenticeship that deals with hands-on skills. But what you're trying to explain to us, is that all those years of experience and skill acquisition can be yours within in a matter of days or weeks, isn't that correct?*

    <u>MM</u>: *Yes, I suppose, to a varying degree. I don't know how else to say it, Candice, other than I just intuitively know my way around a lot of stuff. I guess I've become super-inclined in many different areas, way beyond peoples expectations, and my own for that matter.*

    <u>CR</u>: *It's almost like you've gained some sort of unlimited access to the collective experience. It's as though multiple lifetimes are living at your fingertips and bumping around inside that head of yours. What*

do you think of the far fetched theories that say you were abducted by aliens?

MM: What people choose to believe is of great interest to me. But just for the record, Candice, I've never been abducted by aliens.

CR: How much of a role do you think your imagination plays in all this? Visualizing yourself doing something before actively attempting it?

MM: Perhaps the imaginative process is at play, but when push comes to shove and I feel the need to act, the ability just unconsciously springs from my memory with little or no role on the part of my imagination. I don't think about it or plan for it, it's just there. It's like being able to tie your shoes or button your shirt.

CR: There you have it folks: Maximilian McVista, 'jack of all trades' and master of most as well, it seems. If you need your truck fixed or a cake baked, or your life saved, chances are Max is your man, just hope that he's in your neighborhood. Thank you Max, and good night everyone. I'll see you next week when I'll be speaking with Canadian R&B vocalist Janelle Wright, and her band, *Pink Pants and the Woo.*

Following the CBC interview, Max received calls from quacks and specialists alike who wanted to study his condition; sleep monitoring, circadian rhythms, non-invasive biopsies, investigations of his head and its many neuro-dendritic contents. He volunteered for a battery of tests, but no sign of brain injury or abnormality was detected. The doctors who evaluated his IQ found him to be as average as average is.

For a time, his life became a curiosity circus. The media frenzy and medical prodding related to his self-invented syndrome began to arouse the disquieting notion that he might fall prey to his own ramblings. He feared he might leak some incoherent truth about Insynnium or comas or time travel or a confused combination thereof. He felt as though his life had stalled out on a lie and he began to develop anxiety symptoms that included a persistent nervous tick at the edge of his right eye.

Fortunately, before he could be overcome by a Tourette-like oral breach or some other off-putting anti-social disorder, he received a call from the one doctor whose voice he desperately needed to hear.

"Hey, McVista, I saw the Candice Risdal interview," said Pierre, "You're becoming quite a celebrity."

"Such is life, Doc, what can I say," said Max, "I'm glad you called. What's new in France?"

"Well, actually I'm back in Arcata," said Pierre. "I still own the house here you know; had to return to check up on the place you see."

"How long will you be there?"

"September and October, then back to France. Why, you want to come down for a visit?" kidded Pierre.

"I'd love to," said Max.

"Fuck," said Pierre under his breath. He thought he'd made an improbable offer and now here he was having to make good on it.

"I'll see you at the end of next week," said Max, and hung up.

Shit, thought Pierre.

Max told Rachel he had to perform an emergency substitution for an ailing member of a business delegation going to Mexico to promote sustainable farm and manufacturing practices. She understood his emphatic need to fill in on the agricultural panel and so she gave him her blessing to go. She was good that way. He gave her no definitive time for his return.

He caught the red eye to San Francisco and rented a car to drive up the coast. When he arrived at Roach Haven Lane, he found Pierre in the backyard sitting on a wrought-iron bench beneath the tranquility of a cedar tree. Wearing a scarf and a pensive gaze, he was a classic caricature of all things French as he stubbed out his *Gauloises* on the sole of his shoe and let the remainder of smoke ease through his nostrils like some redwood bon vivant.

"You look good, Max," he said, "I mean, quite good. But it had to have been more than good looks that allowed you to get on an international flight?"

"I have my license and passport back," said Max, "so no more hiding in trunks. My good deeds haven't gone unnoticed; I was given a pardon by the Manitoba legislature *and* Ottawa, as well."

"Wow. How long sober now, eight years?" said Pierre.

"Yeah, about that," replied Max.

"You still hear from Duncan?"

"I got an email a couple weeks back. I think he's in Dubai."

Pierre nodded.

"And you, what about you? You're living in Marseille now?"

"Toulon," said Pierre.

The two sat in silence contemplating the many days that had passed between them.

"You're still taking Insynnium, no? Still time travelling, yes?" said Pierre.

"Yeah, of course," answered Max.

"How's your supply holding up?" said Pierre. "According to the news, sleep and dreams are going for a premium these days."

"I'm okay," said Max, "I only take the stuff once a month. I probably have three more years' worth."

"Really?" said Pierre, visibly impressed. "With the way prices are climbing you'll be able to sell what you have and buy a new house."

Max smiled and changed the subject. "Who do you think killed Eric Enderby?" he said. "Do you think it was a pharmaceutical company like the media claims?"

"Definitely," said Pierre.

"They say he was the mastermind, the one with the secret," said Max, "Do you think anybody else knows?"

"How to sprout the seeds?" said Pierre, "I doubt it. You can sort of tell by the way the supply has dwindled, and how the product has become expensive as hell."

"What do you think will happen?" said Max.

"The spice will eventually run out, just like oil," said Pierre. "People will have to go back to accepting a regular night's rest again."

Max listened as Pierre discussed his plan to resettle in France. He told Max that sooner or later he would list the property at Roach Haven, but that he just wasn't quite there yet. The two men laughed as they recounted Max's first visit to Arcata, and how he got sober so quickly; and how Duncan worried he was going psychotic, and of course the comas.

Pierre listened to Max with strained credulity as he described several of his AUE's in mind bending detail. At times, he appeared child-like recalling the wonders he'd encountered, and then other times almost exhausted by his recollection of events, like an old man ruminating on the world before the clock ticked past midnight.

"So, you never miss a month then, eh?" said Pierre.

"Actually, I think I'm slipping," said Max, "because I've missed the last three months. I've been so busy with the boys and my store and, you know, living life, that I sort of forget, I guess."

"And don't forget your bloody interview on *The Fifth Estate*," said Pierre with a skeptical grin.

"Yeah, that too," said Max, as he rolled his eyes. "I'm pretty topped up."

"How would you feel about a coma tonight, for old time's sake?" said Pierre. "I could dig out the monitoring devices and see if we can spot anything new going on inside that head of yours."

As Max thought about Pierre's offer, he also thought about his entire supply of Insynnium hidden behind a cinder block in a root cellar in Brandon.

"How does 1992 sound?" said Pierre, as he handed Max a Ziploc of rust colored capsules worth about $4500.

"Where did you get these?" said Max.

"Don't worry," said Pierre, "I have a dealer who gives discounts. And besides, I don't have the heart to take it anymore; I think I've seen enough."

"Whatever," said Max, "I can't accept it; this is worth thousands. Besides, I have my own, they're just not with me."

"Take twelve," said Pierre, "three for this month, and nine for the three you've missed."

"I can't do it," said Max, "You know as well as me that taking more than three at a time is a total waste. This stuff is too expensive to-"

"Just do it for Christ's sake," interrupted Pierre, "and don't worry about the goddamn price. This is for science."

He was looking over the top of the gold rimmed spectacles riding low on his Roman nose; a Caesar commanding obedience.

Max gave up the argument and went ahead with the experiment. He took all twelve capsules and entered the radical interiority of another uncharted dimension.

When the AUE began, he was gazing out a window from the farm house in Nipawin. He'd come home from college for a visit or something, but the uninspiring sight of leafless trees soaking up spring slush was gray and unaffecting. When he realized that Brian Mulroney was still prime minister the situation became depressing. So, instead of heading back to Kingston, he hitched-hiked to Saskatoon, and from there caught VIA rail to the Salish Sea. He crewed on a yacht around Horseshoe Bay for awhile, until the wind carried him to Hawaii. From the beaches of Kauai to the shores of South Africa he learned about knots and rum and the value of calluses. Twelve months rolled by quickly, but he failed to wake up.

One year turned into two as he became a mariner. He watched the changing tides from starboard to portside as their ebb and flow capsized his past. The trade winds put the curvature of the earth and the reach of the continents in an old world perspective that felt vaguely eighteenth century. If the wind blew steady it was good, but sometimes it blew in ferocious gusts, and then sometimes not at all, leaving him to float silently on the open water above the majesty of laminar cetaceans and ominous leviathans.

After dropping anchor in Willemstad following a languid and trolling search for marlin in the Leeward Antilles, he met Manisha, the daughter of a Sri Lankan tea merchant. She was a skin-diver and a surfer and a soon-to-be capable first mate.

Manisha was soft in the water and hard on deck; she ducked the boom and handled the rudder like a pro. In among the jib and the mast and the main sail and the hard fucks on the surging hull above the daggerboard, Manisha was able to convince Max to run his spinnaker all the way to the East China Sea. Her dad worked in Shanghai, and they paid him a visit at his office in the commerce of the Old World Bund. Max spoke Mandarin with a Taiwanese accent and took to the vigor of the Middle Kingdom with relish. Manisha wore chop sticks in her hair and displayed impressive seamanship as the two navigated their yacht up the crowded Yangtze.

Another year came and went as Max hibernated in the abyss.

On a slow and noodle encrusted train voyage to the ceramic necropolis at Xian, he and Manisha passed through Henan province. There, in a mountain temple surrounded by a pagoda forest, Max became lost in the kicks and fists of a group of young Kung Fu Padawans. He overlooked the tawdry-kitsch-faux-dragon façade and willingly joined the capable monks living behind its walls.

He began punishing his body through the application of inhuman and alien martial arts methods. It was a place of discipline and celibacy regrettably oppositional to the magical labial pleasures of his Ceylon princess. In the year that followed, Manisha absconded with the last of his Renminbi and returned to Colombo and into the arms of an old love. All Max could do was endure hard bamboo and build core strength until he finally opened his eyes in the amber dimness of the Arcata home where he'd fallen asleep four days earlier.

He observed a line of fluid going into his arm and felt something uncomfortable in his penis. There were gadgets pasted across his scalp, which, incidentally, had been shaved smooth to a follicle. He could hear a radio somewhere in the distance playing Frank Sinatra.

"Max; Max, can you hear me," said Pierre.

"Yeah, I can hear you, what's going on?"

He felt groggy, and his words ran into one other on his tongue.

"You've been in a coma for ninety-six hours," said Pierre.

"What is all this shit?"

"Don't worry, it's just a catheter and an IV drip," said Pierre. "I had to take some precautions. I didn't know how long you'd be under."

"What about my hair?" said Max, as his tongue fumbling with his teeth.

"Sorry," said Pierre, "It'll grow back. It was the only way I could get an accurate moisture reading off the top of your head. It actually looks pretty cool."

"Four years, Pierre. I had four years," he said, as drool ran down his chin.

"When you didn't wake up after the first twenty-four hours I kinda knew… well, you know, I did the math," said Pierre.

As Max began to move he felt achy and hung-over. Joint pain and muscle tension nagged his reawakened awareness. Initially, he had no thoughts that were not contaminated by the four years of additional life that he'd just tacked onto his existence. As usual, he knew where he'd been and what he'd done, but this time the AUE left him gasping at its vast and phenomenal expanse. And there were noticeable side effects, as well. He found himself suffering from moments of linguistic inability and blank monumental spatial stares. In the days that followed, he led a quiet recovery as his hair began to sprout along with his capacity for full sentences.

"Your reaction to Insynnium gets more bizarre every time we meet," said Pierre. "You're positive that we haven't overlooked something from your childhood, like an injury, or a disease or some chemical you might have been exposed to?"

"I can't think of anything," said Max, "I was raised on prairie air, fresh garden peas, and homemade pumpkin pie."

"You have to be careful now," said Pierre, "and you know what I'm talking about, right? You can't start doing this by yourself. I know what you're thinking, I can see it in your eyes, but you need to understand that by letting months accrue and then taking extra long AUE's you're putting yourself at great risk for other complications. Don't attempt this sort of extended coma on your own, capeesh?"

"Yeah, yeah, I get it," he said. "Look, if I decide to go for five years, I'll come find you in France, how's that?"

"Don't be a smart ass, Max. You have to promise me?"

"I promise," he said, as he held up a three finger salute like an insouciant scout.

* * *

Rachel walked up to him and put her arms around him. She was warm and the fire was hot, and the snow was melting into mud at the edge of the pit where radiant fingers of flame scorched the ground. She told him she'd received news from the hospital that the mayor was still in serious condition but the doctors had him stabilized.

She looked at him with a look he knew well.

"Let's go camping next month over the long weekend," she said, "We'll leave the boys with Daryl and Kelly and get away, just the two of us. We'll catch some fish."

He nodded agreement at her suggestion and took a seat beside her at the fire. She unlaced his skates and pulled them from his feet. He pushed his cold toes into his snow-boots and let the felt liners perform the work of pulling frost from flesh.

Rachel had been looking superb lately, he thought, and he couldn't help wondering if she was taking Insynnium. She said that she'd never touched it, but then again, he told her the same thing. It was hard to know who was taking it and who wasn't. He thought of his mom, now the remainder of two, sitting to the North, and he wondered if she'd ever tried the stuff; or maybe Kevin or even Joshua for that matter.

He and Rachel listened quietly to the lingering conversations of those still mentally digesting the grizzly hockey mishap. Everyone was embracing a primitive form of comfort as they looked into the glowing embers of the fire and watched the sparks rise in the night sky. The red hot wood popped and crackled and faded to ash as deep breaths of frosty oxygen were taken in and then exhaled again.

2011

-Winter-

*"I want you to know that I saved
the best for last"*

She snuggled in close to him with her heavy
goose-down bag; beneath them was an old buffalo rug;
a wedding gift from Gary when he worked in Mouse
Jaw. She saw her breath ascend to the ceiling of the
tent, and then watched it diminish in the weak beam
of her fading headlamp.

She and Max had taken the snowmobiles to Birch
Island on Lake Winnipegosis where they'd encamped
on the shore near the edge of the woods.

Five hundred meters out on the ice, through a
chainsaw hole, the nets had been set. They would pull
their catch at first light; a bunch of Walleye and
Sauger that would feed them through the winter.
Although Max was the avid promoter of a leafy green
diet, he never quite managed to resist Rachel's pan
seared fish on his bean and grain plate. Her delicious
Goldeye recipes would forever block his way to
complete vegetarianism.

But Max was being blocked from other things as
well, thought Rachel, such as peace of mind, and for
that she felt guilty and terribly uneasy.

To the people of Brandon, Max was a strong community member known to be generous with his time and kind to those around him; qualities that were self-evident and required no explaining. It should have remained that simple, thought Rachel, except the media always got hold of a good story and stretched it too far. She disliked the way journalists had sensationalized Max's abnormalities; trying to make her husband more sexy and mysterious than he was; rubbing his statements too thin and rendering them hard for the public to reasonably comprehend.

But what did she expect?

What did she think would happen when she took it upon herself to engineer events to play out in a particular way? Now he was explaining himself on television, and it was all very odd. It was a mistake from the beginning and she needed to make it stop.

It began with the dream of a farmer drowning.

Next came a series of intricate manipulations.

She wasn't even certain how she did it, but she managed to get him to Ninette, a fishing town obsequiously perched at the end of Pelican Lake. He'd driven there under the impression that he needed to make a delivery of raw honey to the small organic bakery on the waterfront. He arrived at the exact hour of the accident and in so doing was on hand to perform a remarkable water rescue that got his name into the newspaper.

At first, she thought she could stop with a single maneuvering of her husband's remarkable abilities, or at least be judicious with her ambition and insights. But the thrill was irresistible, and it wasn't long before he became a powerful extension of her psychic capacity.

She surreptitiously began using him to avert tragedy and skirt disaster in and around the greater Brandon area. It seemed both natural and necessary that if she were to foresee an avertable misfortune, then it fell on her to control it. Through anonymous phone calls and word-of-mouth messages, she ensured that Max arrived in certain places at specific times. Of course, she missed the mark on some occasions, but nine times out of ten she was able to guarantee that he was on hand to save the day.

She successfully finagled him into conducting some extraordinary feats. Ironically, however, it was the small courtesies and kind conveniences that went the furthest in cementing his reputation in town. Acts as random and unplanned as a roadside carburetor adjustment for a stranded farm wife, or musical accompaniment for a shorthanded band, or Spanish translation for Mexican Mennonites lost downtown. All these gestures and thoughtful indulgences garnered Max the keys to the city and made him a minor celebrity in Brandon.

But it came with a price.

Her do-gooder objectives were extinguishing his spleen fire, and she could see that his reservoir of vitality was ebbing away. The interviews and explaining were never satisfactory, and most of his answers seemed constantly inadequate. He was suffering in both hidden and obvious ways for her indulgences, and she'd never wanted it to be like that.

When a cognitive researcher from the University of Manitoba attached himself to her husband following a CBC interview, she realized that he was getting stretched beyond his breaking point. Although he remained clueless about her commandeering of his free will, she knew she'd gone too far. Her appropriation of him as a moonlighting lifesaver was negatively impacting his life, not to mention his adeptness in selling bean sprouts and tempeh in the land of wheat and cattle.

When he took a last minute trip to Mexico with an ecumenical organization promoting food sustainability, she was thrilled. She thought the small adventure would re-invigorate his dwindling reserves. But when he returned from the conspicuous poverty of Chiapas it was evident the trip had not done him any favors. He'd overtaxed his body and saturated his mind with worry. He had lost the fat from his waist, and his cheeks were gaunt and sunken. The edges of his eyes had a watery fatigue and his hair had been shaved off, apparently the result of a lice infestation at a rundown hacienda.

She propped herself up on an elbow and looked at him sleeping next to her in the tent. She noticed how much his hair had grown back, and except for the strands of gray at his temples, its tangles were still as crazy and unpredictable as the life they continued to share. Outside, she heard the howl of the cold pushing sand sized bits of ice against the flapping nylon; a snow storm.

* * *

The first time she laid eyes on Maximilian, he was lost in the commons. He appeared bewildered and looked as though he'd hitched his way to Ontario on a flatbed from Saskatoon. He had an assortment of suitcases and duffle bags like he was moving for three people. He was wearing a sun-faded Edmonton Oilers T-shirt that brought out the blue in his eyes, and his curly brown hair looked as though you could lose a comb in its complications.

As he stood among the other freshman in the moist Great Lake air, he had the relaxed appreciation for stillness that you might expect from someone raised leaning into the wind. She didn't want to admit it, but she fell in love at first sight.

She'd been at Queens for a week helping new students get sorted. She was good at spotting confused and disorientated arrivals caught up in the monstrous tangle of frosh week. As a matter of routine, she approached Max to see if he required assistance. But suddenly, in a precise moment of cosmic timing, she was gripped by the overwhelming sense that she was about to come face to face with her soul mate. No sooner had the thought occurred when he turned and took hold of her welcoming hand.

"Hello," he said.

"Hi," she replied.

In a simple act of introduction, the two unwittingly shared more of themselves than they ever intended. The entire exchange was less than thirty seconds, and soon he was walking away. She wanted to run after him, but she froze there beside herself instead.

One week later, she spotted him again. But this time everyone was noticing him; primarily because of his roommate, Duncan, who seemed to almost elude description. Duncan was the sort of person who melted people in their tracks. He reminded students and professors of someone they'd once known but couldn't quite place. He had the allure of familiarity as well as the capacity to be intriguingly strange.

Considering how well Max and Duncan got along, one would think that they'd grown up together in a suburb of Windsor or Calgary, but in fact, the two were geographic and social opposites. Max was from a small town in Saskatchewan. Duncan was from Rosedale, in Toronto. Max had attended a struggling public school. Duncan had gone to Trinity. Max's parents were forever the children of Aquarius. Duncan was raised by upwardly mobile professionals. Max was feral. Duncan was surreal. Max was white. Duncan was black.

In those early days, Rachel hunted for ways to fasten herself to Max's eyes, but it wasn't long before she realized that in order to reach him she had to forge a connection with Duncan. So, she searched for a pretext to penetrate the group of friends to which Max and Duncan belonged.

In the midst of her calculated pursuit, her brother, Gary, came to visit. She was surprised when he unexpectedly showed up at Queens. When she saw him, it occurred to her that he was finally pulling his life together, and she was pleased to have him in Kingston for a day or two. She toured him around campus, and they hung out and talked about Cassandra and Darcy, and all the years spent making something from nothing. They smoked a couple of joints and he told her that he was starting a carpentry business.

On the morning that he left to go back, he took her out for pancakes and told her that he loved her. No one in her family ever said stuff like that, and she got embarrassed and had tears in her eyes. He told her she could cry, but she laughed instead at his unexpected permission. He told her that everyone in the family knew she was the strongest and the smartest and that he was proud she was in college. He dropped her off at the dorm and gave her a hug and then handed her an ounce of Northern Lights. When he got back into his pickup to drive up to Timmins the goodbye look they gave one another stretched for many miles.

She wasn't much of a pot smoker, so she rolled up three joints and stashed the remainder of Gary's weed at the top of her closet underneath a sweater she no longer wore. She carried those bolts of Northern Light in her hoodie until the opportunity to smoke them arose.

"You know what we need right now is a joint," said Richie.

"Yeah, that would be pretty sweet, especially just before the movie," said Emily.

"I've heard that its better when you're high," said Richie, "that's what the review in the *Journal* said."

"We could call Bill and see if he's got some at his dorm," said Don.

"Smith probably has some over at Chown Hall," said Duncan.

"What about Shorty?" said Max.

"Yeah, that's true, there's always Shorty," said Duncan.

"How about this one, guys?" said Rachel, trying to sound cool as she casually produced a blunt.

"Well, what's this?" said Duncan, "I didn't know you were such a stoner."

Rachel looked at Max and smiled.

"Let's light'er up," said Don.

The group passed around the cone until it was reduced to a roach.

"This is good shit," said Duncan, and he gave Rachel a look of freshly discovered appreciation.

"Yeah, this stuff hits hard, I'm completely baked," said Richie, smiling absently at Emily.

The six of them were walking through dead leaves and windfall on their way to the Mayfair Theater to watch *Delicatessen* double billed with *Barton Fink*. Emily was a friend of Rachel's from the Native Student Association, and she was dating Richie who was a friend of Duncan's from astronomy club. At the movie, Rachel sat beside Max and voraciously shared a tub of popcorn in the dark. Whenever their buttery fingers touched, she felt their circles converging and wiggled a little closer in the narrow lumpy seating.

In the weeks that followed, she and Max hung out on several occasions; a coffee here, a lunch there, a cold beer in front of a hockey game. Sometimes the others would join them, sometimes they wouldn't. She wanted him to take her in his arms with unreserved passion. She wanted to hold his hand and walk through City Park like she'd seen other couples do. But for whatever reason the love potential between them wouldn't budge; things were static when they should have been kinetic; lust held at bay by the complications of friendship and bad timing. She started to despair because she knew that moments not seized generally passed and never came round again.

At the end of a cold and somewhat socially vacant January, Duncan unexpectedly invited her to join him and Max on a short and assuredly fun filled trip to Parliament Hill. He had a friend from Windsor who was working as a dancer in a topless bar in Vanier. He was adamant that the three of them get their asses to the nation's capital and take the lonely stripper down the frozen Rideau Canal. He told Rachel how much fun they'd all have skating through the city while sipping whiskey and eating beaver tails.

The trip to Ottawa turned out to be a maiden voyage of sorts, and it wasn't long before she, Duncan, and Max were collaborating on all sorts of interconnected mischief. The three of them got a dangerous and consistent thrill driving Duncan's Beemer at a hundred miles an hour down the 401. They partied regularly from Mississauga to Cornwall. They even went to Detroit for a Stanley Cup playoff game and to Cleveland for a Phish concert. They smoked up the rest of the pot that Gary left her, and then some. Her grades began to slip, and Max's GPA fell into academic peril. Duncan's scholastic performance, however, continued to hover on the cusp of the dean's list without the least amount of effort. Rachel wasn't blind to the risks, but it was fun, and they were riding a wave. Sometimes, in the concussive beat of an amphetaminic rave, Max would look at her with an uncharted expression, as though they were aboard a decrepit whaler in rough seas and Duncan was their mad captain.

In the early spring of '92, the three of them, along with Monique (a Francophone classmate of Duncan's) drove up to Montreal to cheer on the Habs. The Bruins were in town, and it was like being inside a volcano at the Forum. The place rioted with every goal. When the fans spilled into the streets following an overtime victory, the four friends made their way to a bar on Saint Catherine's where Monique's Québécois *amis* were waiting. They all went hard into the night.

The following morning, in a walkup brownstone along Saint Urbain, Rachel awoke hung-over and foggy. She and the others ate crepes and drank mud-thick coffee. Monique convinced everyone sitting around the table that they should depart the narrow and bilingual *rues* of *Le Plateau* and take a drive north to *Parc des Falaises.* She said that in a town at the edge of the park was a modest all season cabin owned by the McGill Outing Club. The plan was to drink wine, smoke hashish, and go cross country skiing.

By the time Sunday arrived, Rachel had been high for so long that the accumulated hours seemed to run into one. She was anxious and excited as the group waxed their skis and ventured out on the snow. She was struck by the ease with which Max moved in the outdoors; he seemed to have an innate understanding of the gentle hills and frozen rivers in the area. She followed him as the group made its way around snow covered creeks and leafless valleys as though they were part of some lost Canadian reality. She felt as Cree as she ever had while sliding along icy tracks as the group crept through narrow trails and out over open fields. Their world that day was an Algonquin hunting ground as far as the eyes could see; their history and inheritance carved together across the landscape. She took comfort in the ancestral voices that were lending peace to the choice she was arriving at, and she sensed the Great Spirit moving under the tatters of birch bark.

Before they knew it, she and Max had become distracted by the beauty of the late afternoon light, and it slowed their bones to the speed of a porcupine. They had to make an attempt to catch up. As they passed with free heals and open minds through a stand of barren Aspen she told herself to stay alert. But her athleticism began to fail as she plowed through a heavy Quebec drift. In a combination of exhaustion and impatience, she took a pirouetting fall down a short steep bank.

Max peeked over the cornice she'd broken through and let out a laugh. He reached his pole out and she grabbed hold of it. As she was righting herself, he lost his balance and went over on his head beside her. The two had snow down their necks and all around their wrists, but they laid there and stared at the sky. Max pulled a flask from his jacket and proposed a toast to the moment; the schnapps formed a brief sensatory resistance to the wet slush melting through their coats and leaking into their boots.

Indians know good stuff happens in the snow.

And suddenly Rachel was kissing Max with every ounce of passion she could muster from her buried and improbable position. She wanted to push herself into his body without the inconvenient barrier of ski pants and thermal wear, but she was too cold to even imagine taking off her gloves as she pawed at his chest. She closed her eyes and tried to let the warm condition of their lips circulate to her extremities, but it was impossible to argue with the weather and all her thoughts ended in shivers. Dusk was approaching the distant and cozy cabin faster than they were, and she could picture the others standing in dry fleece and holding pink fingers to the warmth of a fireplace.

"We need to get back," said Max, as though he could read her thoughts in their cloud of shared breath.

"Yeah, I'm starting to get wet," she said.

He looked at her and smiled.

"This summer we should drive to the farm, you'd love it up there," he said.

"How long would it take to get there from Kingston?"

"Probably two days if we took turns behind the wheel."

"Your parents wouldn't mind?"

"My parents would love it. And Robert might even be home."

"Let's do it," she said to Max, "Let's really do it."

They struggled to the top of the cornice only to be met by a winter landscape completely abandoned by a set and heatless sun. In each other's faces they recognized the naked need to return to the cabin, and they rushed in the twilight to meet love's urgency. They soon found themselves beneath the zenith of a full moon as they zipped their sleeping bags into one. Later, while the others stirred and snored, Rachel and Max aggressively shared themselves with one another. Their connection was cellular, and their bond was covalent.[19]

---

[19]**#4** on the Billboard Year-End Hot 100 singles of 1992. **"Save the Best for Last"** by <u>Vanessa Williams</u> from the album *The Comfort Zone.* 1992. As soon as they left Kingston for Montreal, Rachel told herself it was going to happen between her and Max or it would never come to pass; she would either sleep with him or that would be the end of it. She couldn't possibly have been more obvious with her signals. Max wasn't wild, but he wasn't tame either, and Rachel felt as though she had him almost all the way with her coaxing gestures. She and Max were waiting for something to consume them, to spark the chemistry between

After Quebec, it was hard for things to go back to the way they'd been. Although Max and Duncan held on as inseparable friends, Rachel commanded the lion's share of Max's attention. The changed dynamic among the three of them was difficult to define and took effort to accommodate. Rachel was sometimes left feeling like she'd committed a theft. When school recessed for summer, Duncan returned to Toronto to spend time with an old music teacher who had contracted meningitis, and Richie and Emily went tree planting in the mountains north of Chetwynd, B.C.

Rachel and Max remained in Kingston and found work. They rented a small studio apartment near Confederation Basin for two months until Duncan returned and informed them that he'd leased a rambling purple Victorian on Peel Street by the university. He said they could all live together, including Ritchie and Emily - the mosquito beleaguered couple who were making a poor living climbing over spruce limbs and root wads on the Peace Reach west of Hudson's Hope.

* * *

Rachel was awakened by the blizzard buffeting the tent. She wasn't scared, but she was definitely uneasy. She imagined Kelly and Daryl back in Brandon sleeping soundly in the gripping embrace of

---

them, to blow the top off their lives. When their need for one another finally resolved itself in Quebec, she was so excited that she bit her lip.

a stellar dream. They both took Insynnium; Kelly said she swore by it, and Rachel had to admit that her friend certainly looked good. Kelly said the spice also intensified her sex life. But Rachel had long since resolved to remain a virgin to the charms of Insynnium.

Like everyone, she followed the news.

Nobody knew where it came from, although there was no shortage of speculation. The drug emerged on the scene in 2007, and suddenly everybody was taking it, at least those who could afford it. Investigative reports said that it spawned from California, but others claimed that it came from Siberia or maybe Mesopotamia.

Researchers had their hands all over the tiny seeds from which the powder was ground. Producing the drug was relatively simple: the seeds were milled into a powder and placed into a gelatin capsule that the user simply swallowed. Rachel heard that the highest quality stuff had the date stamped right into the capsule so the user could be precise in selecting the year in which they dreamt.

The supply of Insynnium was tightly finite, and the black market price remained high because no one, including the world's elite scientists, could figure out how to germinate the damn thing. A couple of drug companies tried to synthetically manufacture it, but their efforts were an utter failure and ended up causing debilitating insomnia.

Rachel remembered reading in the Brandon Sun that the hunt for the secret was so intense that several suspects were placed into protective custody. It wasn't long after that that Fyzzor - the world's largest pharmaceutical company - was being criminally linked to the Russian mafia and the torturous death of Eric Enderby, the rumored brainchild behind the drug. Following Enderby's gruesome and sensational homicide, the price per capsule soared.

International authorities claimed that the germination secret died along with Enderby in the Dubrovnik jail where they found his remains. But six months ago, Insynnium underwent a resurgence of sorts and conspiracy theorists were at it again.

No one could've ever imagined, thought Rachel, that the most electrifying and mysterious drug of the twenty-first century would be a sleep aid that helped you dream better.

When she asked Max if he'd ever sampled the rust colored pill, he said that he hadn't. He told her that he was concerned that some unknown side-effect might eradicate his cognitive acquisition gifts. It seemed like a reasonable concern. After all, she, like her husband, also avoided Insynnium. At first, she thought the powder might compromise her ability to see the future. Then she worried that she might, like so many others, develop a voyeuristic attachment to her dreams. But in the end, what kept her from reaching for the spice was a series of strange and intense nightmares.

In these cold and foreboding dreams, she could see hordes of corpse-like people moving in mass. They were placid and affectless with minds no longer present. The towns and cities were overflowing with the wandering, the dying, and the dead; crowds of staggering and mind-caved-in persons shuffling their way to senseless oblivion. It reminded her of the British movie that won the Academy Award in 2004 called, *Ester's Hermitage;* about a doctor who discovered a contagious variant of Alzheimer's, and how the entire Shetland village where he lived became pandemically infected. The closing sequence of the film was a haunting image: villagers crawling across a beach toward frothy surf. Each time she awoke she was left with an apocalyptic sensation; a vague and uneasy sense that some large calamity was on its way.

Inside the tent, Max groaned and shifted beside her in the shared warmth.

"Having a dream?" she said, unsure if her husband was even awake enough to comprehend.

"No dreams, too tired to dream," he said in something that sounded like sleep talk.

"It's still snowing out," she said.

"I hope we don't suffocate in our tent," he replied, as he released a deep breath, rolled onto his back, and sank into the sleep from which he'd half-way emerged.

Yes, indeed, she thought, claimed by the elements.

She laid her head on the rise and fall of Max's slumbering chest and felt his body subtly twitch to the rhythm of another universe. She listened to his heart thumping out its blood under bone and muscle. It sounded dense, like it had been striking the same beat for a hundred years, and would go on for a hundred more.

A coyote began to howl at the edge of the forest, silhouetted in a clearing where snow covered buffalo grass and frost laden spruce trees formed a stoic audience for the canine octave. She closed her eyes so the winter night could take her into its revealing embrace.

2012

-Autumn-

"There's nothing quite like a new drug"

Duncan agreed that they should meet one more time in Arcata. He told Pierre they'd germinate the final batch together, and so they had.

The last shipment had shipped.

The two men were in the basement dismantling the whole operation for good. They were ripping out the sound system and tearing down the false walls – floor to ceiling sprouting chambers in the form of an elaborate Chinese medicine chest, if one could imagine such an intricate electronic and wood contraption packed with seeds and filled with music.

Duncan looked at the creation coming down before him, such a product of necessity, and he thought about all the dreams that had had their genesis beneath 420 Roach Haven Lane. The funny thing was that nobody, including Max, ever suspected a basement below the house. The entrance was hidden behind a book case that looked as permanent as the Sphinx, but if you pulled out *One Hundred Years of Solitude*, the whole thing rolled aside, and you could walk on down into the well of Insynnium. It was a

Czech edition of Marquez's novel, and no one was ever tempted to read it.

Duncan took a deep breath.

He removed a germinating tray from the cabinet and contemplated the simple elegance of their once safe and anonymous operation.

When filled with tiny starts, the tray was worth six million dollars, and sometimes he was able to sell as many as 150 trays per year – especially after Max moved back to Canada and the operation didn't have to be curtailed. Just before it shipped, the tray looked not unlike a flat of alfalfa sprouts bound for a local farmer's market. A healthy tray of germinated seeds, however, when properly spaced and grown to maturity, could cover up to 25 acres with their long voracious vines and slow creeping runners. A single crop could amass a fortune for its owner. Of course, most of the buyers were wealthy to begin with, since most of the purchases were made by persons otherwise known as blue chip corporations and mafia dons.

The sprouts were treated with a special saline formula designed to keep them preserved for 48hrs because of the chance that they could change hands as many as ten times before landing in the end purchaser's possession. Exchange was initiated through darknet markets, and payment was routed and rerouted to various accounts and then used to buy real estate that was subsequently auctioned. Eventually, the laundered and untraceable dough made its way into a Grand Cayman account for Duncan to withdraw at his leisure; a state never fully realized.

In effect, Pierre's basement in Arcata was the undiscoverable seed bank for the ambitious interests that chose to grow Insynnium - America's most lucrative and non-regenerative crop. The sprouted specimens were usually planted in a heavily guarded field or in a fortified green house until they reached maturity at ninety days, the point at which the seeds could, technically, be harvested. But soon it was discovered that rather than harvesting, the plants could be given more water and grown for an additional forty-five days into a state of post-maturity. Given the extra time, the plants got thirty times larger and could yield enough seeds to fill a seventyfive-pound sack. The seeds were ground into powder, encapsulated, and sold for ridiculous sums of money. But sooner or later the seller's stock pile would dwindle. Unable to germinate more plants, the 'buyers,' 'owners,' and 'businessmen' would willingly relinquish another six million in exchange for a new crop of sprouts, and the life cycle of Insynnium would begin again.

Duncan devised a beautiful system that made Eric Enderby and Moe Bringa the sole brokers of the sprouts without ever knowing or even imagining it could be him for whom they were working. For a long time the operation went swimmingly and everyone got abundantly wealthy. But after Eric was abducted and murdered, Duncan and Pierre decided to get out of the spice trade altogether. The two men figured they could simply leave everything buried beneath the house and walk away. They thought they could go free and live on in obscurity.

The spice was powerful, though, and had an omnipotent yearning. In a silent but forceful way, it continued to compel the men to produce more. Without Eric to buffer the source or insulate the transactions, the supply chain became easier to trace. Duncan knew they were pushing unacceptable risks by sprouting more seeds. He knew they'd be revealed to the world for who they were if they didn't begin actively defying the impulses of the plant.

He set the tray down on the work bench and looked around the augmented basement. He watched as Pierre meticulously deconstructed each and every sound box. The two worked in silence. Their resistance to the expansionary force of the spice seemed almost futile, as though the demolition effort of their hands would stall, and they would begin to reassemble everything again.

* * *

In 1994 Pierre Leveque left Quebec and its brewing sovereignty referendum to move to an address that was a stoner's joke. And at the foot of the address was Aloysius, an octogenarian enigma in need of a caregiver. Pierre was interviewed and hired for the atypical position after answering a help wanted ad in the *Globe and Mail*.

Duncan once asked him, "What made you, a tenured professor from Canada, consider and accept such an unusual geriatric bargain?"

"That bombast Parizeau and his separatists, that's who, that's what," replied Pierre. "Look, don't get me wrong, I love *Ville de Quebec*, but with all the secessionist wind making people delusional between the ears, the offer from Aloysius was just too intriguing and lucrative to pass up. Maybe I needed out; I don't know. Maybe it was a whim, eh."

In spite of what he said, it was not a whim that brought him to Arcata. It was a calculated and deliberate life change, and Duncan admired the professor for being such a bold risk taker. Pierre was no fool, and he obviously had other reasons for doing what he did, more than he ever shared with Duncan, that was for sure. Before his move to the West, he'd secured himself a teaching position at Humboldt. With his impressive curriculum vitae from Lavelle - full of botanical research and professorial credentials - the university in the Redwoods was only too eager to add him to their faculty.

He taught statistics and conducted academic research for close to five years while looking after Aloysius. But as the old man's health began failing at an increased rate, he suspended his contract with the university and became a full-time palliative physician. In his final year of life, Alex required a substantial amount of care, and Pierre's training as a medical doctor was useful to the end.

"So what's the deal," said Duncan, "now that Alex is gone does all his property go to you?"

"Yes," said Pierre. "Everything was transferred to me the day he died. That was the arrangement between us. It was never any secret. It was the deal. It was payment for doing what I did."

"Was it worth it?"

"Too soon to tell," said Pierre, "everything's always leading to something else, no? If you hadn't shown up here, I'd have sold everything and moved on. I'd probably be speaking Antillean Creole in Martinique or slicing bread in Bardou. But now, well, what can I say, you and I are on the horizon of something magnificent."

Soon after his arrival, Duncan learned that Pierre was in possession of more than just seeds, he was also the beneficiary of a file cabinet full of recipes for elixirs and potions courtesy of shipments made from Felix over the years. He said he'd used the compounds and admixtures on both himself and Aloysius to remove itching from the scalp, lines from the face, and tension from the prostate. As he described the salubrious effects of the tonics he'd created, Duncan thought of Leah with her impeccable hair and wondrous skin.

Buried among all the stuff that Pierre had accumulated, Duncan found a hefty ledger full of handwritten entries describing various vaccinations that had been given to people, including infants, between 1948 and 1978. The names of the patients had been recorded by their initials and the country in which they received their vaccine. For example: J.B./ Moscow/ 1961/ adult; or: M.M./Cuba/ 1974/ infant. The list went on for pages, and the entries could all be cross referenced to find the exact formula administered to each person. Duncan found it mind boggling to consider the number of lives Felix had altered with his remedies and vaccinations, almost exclusively in communist countries.

"I only wish he had been as meticulous in describing how to sprout the seeds," said Pierre, when he noticed Duncan leafing through the ledger.

"Yeah, well, be thankful that we still have seeds left to work with," said Duncan.

Pierre smiled sheepishly.

He had ground up half the seeds long before Duncan ever showed up at Roach Haven. The original cryptic instructions stated that if the seeds could be converted into a powder and swallowed, the result would be a spectacular and vivid dream sequence of marvelous proportion. So, Pierre ground some up and consumed them with water. But he instantly discovered the drink to be denatonium benzoate bitter and impossible to swallow.

In a follow-up attempt, he ground a few more and put their powder into capsules to avoid contact with his palate. When nothing happened in time or mind, he became convinced that the seed was a riddle. He resisted the urge to tamper with the remainder of the supply until he could grow more.

He discovered, however, that no solution or formula could cause a sprout to emerge from the seed's formidable husk. He was scientifically stymied at every intellectual junction. His reason and methods crashed into the opposite of his expectations. With professional cramping failure, he hid the seeds in a deep layaway with hopes that their physical absence would erase their horticultural perversity from his thoughts.

The missing clue, provided upon Duncan's arrival, of course, was the ingredient of music. It was elegant and melodic and outside the light world. It was the perfect factor to burst such a singularity; so obvious that no one would ever see it in a thousand years. A seismic orchestra locked in dormancy waiting for an able minded team to conduct its magnum opus.

Initially, the two men constructed twenty-five small ambient-noise-proof chambers fitted with observation windows, not unlike the vitrine of the periodic table rumored to be inside Bill Gates' home. They placed the seeds on trays that were designed to slide into the sound chambers. Then they piped various selections of music into each chamber via miniature speakers. It felt like an absurd test of patience as the tunes played 24/7 for days and days.

They hadn't the vaguest notion as to which music would stimulate the transformation. They hedged their bets from classical to hip hop. There was a chamber that had the *Goldberg Variations* on a continuous loop, and another that had *Madonna* singing uninterrupted to the virgin specimen.

The two checked on the seeds every day, and for twenty-nine days they suspected they might be the punchline in an elaborate joke. On day thirty, however, their decision to abort the experiment was halted when they found themselves face to face with twenty-five emerging sprouts. One month of music had caused all the seeds to grow, with complete indifference to rhythm, tone, or tenor.

The pale seedlings showed an aggressive yearning to survive. They demanded to be taken from the basement and into the sun. The men potted and labeled the botanical infants and then placed them in Pierre's anteroom greenhouse, a giant glass-sheeted gazebo that stretched off the backside of Roach Haven.

The developing plants grew to resemble sweet peas to a degree that was superficially indistinguishable to the uninitiated observer. Beneath their mimicking chloroplasts, however, Pierre was certain that there was nothing on the planet remotely related to their confounding cellular composition.

Owing to a dearth in horticultural techniques for raising such a plant, they resorted to methods that were largely ad-hoc and in loose combination with some of Felix's old hand scribbled thoughts. After three guarded months, pods began developing where once there'd been a silky inflorescence. After ripening, the pods became dry and could be rubbed in your hands to reveal a multitude of seeds; the heirloom progenitors of every single dream that would emerge from Insynnium.

The men took seeds from each plant and ground them into a rust colored powder. They carefully labeled each batch to indicate the music from which the mother plant had sprouted. The powder - consistent like flour and heavy like iridium - was compressed into a range of capsules.

Establishing a powder dram that would invigorate the mind to produce the sort of reaction Felix had alluded to in his finger-smudged notes took weeks for Pierre to finesse. Using empiricism that was the antonym of sensible and safe, he began methodically, though recklessly, ingesting the powder in various doses with the intention of stimulating an observable effect.

He put Bach, Beethoven, and Mozart into capsules and ate them, but nothing occurred. So he put Scott Joplin, Cab Calloway, and Glenn Miller into capsules and ate them as well, and still, nothing happened. But then one day he swallowed The Beatles in a mid-sized amount and immediately dozed off to sleep. He wasn't totally certain, but when he awoke, he told Duncan that he'd dreamt with a nuanced edge. As he increased the milligrams of his Beatle derived powder, John, Paul, George, and Ringo started handing him dreams that were exceptionally vivid.

The spice was the light, and the dose was the focus, it was an aperture perfecting memory, and as he adjusted and readjusted his powdery lens, he eventually experienced the *piece de resistance* of his dream world. He felt like the first man on the moon as he described a somnolent voyage that took him back in his memories to the week he purchased *Sgt. Pepper* at a record store on *Saint Denis*. The experience was a colorful and vivid recollection of his life in Montreal's *Latin Quarter* in September, 1967.

He described a sleeping state in which several intense images moved him through successive scenes as though he were watching a film about his life. He said that he heard birds and smelled flowers and had conversations on roof tops. He said the spice boosted his dream capacity by a factor of perspicuity and a large percentage of tangibility.

As he listened to him, Duncan felt the need to see his own life up close again in the same retro dazzling way that jolted the Frenchman into rapture. He needed to seize a dream sequence of his own and watch the powder arc in his direction, an arc that would eventually propel itself into the minds of others.

At the beginning, when the two were consisdering which music to sprout the seeds to, Duncan insisted on something by Huey Lewis. Pierre couldn't understand why a black kid from Toronto would have any affinity to Huey Lewis. But Duncan explained that he once had a friend whose older brother was a waiter at the famous Retondo-Redondo night club in the alley next to the Royal York. They were just kids, of course, but the brother snuck them in for an evening with *D Train*. And who else was in the audience? None other than *Huey Lewis and the News* – the whole bloody group sitting right there in the front row. But that's not the crazy part. The crazy part is that James D-Train Williams himself came down with laregitis moments before the show; and so Huey says, 'hey fuck it, we'll do a show if you all want us to?' And everybody was kinda like, 'okay'. The place was way too small for their tunes, although they made it work in a weird kind of way. It was the first time Duncan heard, *I want a new drug*. And though Huey might have been on drugs himself that night, he was talking to everyone and telling jokes and buying drinks and leaving the unforgetable impression of a man within reach of his highest aspirations. Duncan thought about this, especially later when Ray Parker ripped off the melody; *Ghostbusters* should have been Huey's.

When Duncan swallowed his powder (in roughly the same dosage as Pierre), he came into contact with parts of his unconscious of which he was completely unaware. His dreams were a viewfinder clicking in overdrive, and they placed him beneath the iron girders of a Toronto bridge sometime in 1984. He was an eleven-year-old delinquent among thirteen-year-old accomplices. They were a loosely knit gang of truants using a rainbow of spray bombs to tag whatever city structure they found themselves loitering under. In his dream he possessed the freedom of a rule-less child. [20]

---

[20] **#55** on the Billboard Year-End Hot 100 singles of 1984. **"I Want a New Drug"** by <u>Huey Lewis and the News</u> from the album *Sports*. Chrysalis, 1984. It was hard for Duncan not to know where he was in such an impeccable back-bite of time. He was a precocious and influential child who sometimes suspected that his demanding parents might disappear and never come back. There was a powerful dark urge that moved through his veins, but he couldn't identify the specifics. He and his friends had cigarettes, slingshots, and Kuwaharas. His entire future was there before him in his tiny manly status. Though he had disliked his youth in large part, there was a curious aspect to tripping on the powder that made him feel soothed and comforted with what his life had been. The substance he ingested had somehow sanitized

He awoke intoxicated by the drug's possibilities, its estuary of exertions and rejuvenations. The discovery was streaking across the horizon to be named; it was molten and falling fast with a trail of music stretching behind it like Mercury. He and Pierre began to compile the songs they would use for germination. It was zero hour in the ambitious plan to catch America in a net of memories, dreams, and reflections.

The cortical mechanics were distilled down to two contingencies. *First,* the spice had to be derived from a plant sprouted to music written or created in the user's lifetime - this is why Chopin and Straus had no effect on either man's dreams. *Second,* the user must have actually heard the song at some point in their life, even just once. As long as the two contingencies were met, one could dream with relative precision. Essentially, the powder was sparking memories to within a year of when the song at the heart of the regression was released. It was more than just weird science; it was an alchemy that used music to turn sleep into solid gold.

Duncan, ever the entrepreneur, considered the monetary potential in producing the spice for mass consumption. He reasoned that the drug's two contingencies could most consistently be met by using chart topping singles as the impetus for germination. It was with this thought that he and Pierre began to

the turmoil and frustration of growing up black in a wealthy white section of Toronto.

sprout seeds using the top ten songs on the Billboard Year-End Hot 100 singles from 1958 up to the present.

They gave out the rust-colored pills for free to the tired and the poor and the sick and the homeless; marginalized souls willing to experiment with far fetched and untested substances in the hope that they would find what they were looking for. Many reacted to the spice in enviable and life changing ways. Most notably they slept like they hadn't slept in ages and they saw their lives reflected back to them with a satisfaction and resolution that put them at peace in a way doctors and money couldn't.

The public had no clue how Insynnium worked, only that it did. They selected a year, swallowed a pill, and started dreaming without effort; completely unaware that the spark inside their minds had been ignited by *The Champs* or *Destiny's Child* or the hundreds of other artists who'd been horticulturally commandeered to act as germinators and stimulators.

For most people, getting enough of a good thing proved almost impossible. The specter of the drug morphed like a mushroom cloud over America, and the fact that no one could germinate the seeds only added to the specter. Questions got asked, theories developed, and answers were demanded.

But those answers would never come from Duncan or Pierre.

The prohibition against revealing the secret carried a cold certainty, and so they kept their lips sealed and their identities unknown. If the secret to Insynnium were ever to breach Duncan's lips, he knew that it would be Grace – by the terms of the curse - who would perish. As for Pierre, perhaps his silence was the result of an old flame from *Trois-Rivieres.* But no matter the motivation, both understood that it all needed to remain locked in the vaults of their skulls. The curse would never stop promising a pain deeper than either man cared to contemplate.

Duncan became the puppet master of Insynnium, the silent manipulator of a planet spanning enterprise. But he completely underestimated the weight of people's dreams and the sinister depths to which greed can reach. When Eric became the world's most wanted man, he watched night after night as the walls around Eric's empire crumbled like Pablo Escobar's. Following Eric's murder, he wanted to democratize the spice and get out from under its curse. He wanted to explain it on *U-tube* and show the world how to sprout it.

In a Hail-Mary attempt to re-negotiate his promise, he travelled back to Turkey to find Felix. He reasoned that if anyone should know how to break a decidedly bad bargain, it would be the conjurer that got him into the deal in the first place.

He buried himself in a disguise and flew to the Middle East to convince the centenarian to set him free. When he arrived in Sinop, he discovered Felix's home to be virtually unchanged in the decade since he'd been there. When he knocked on Felix's door, though, it swung open with ease. When he walked inside he knew all bets were off. There was a man and a woman drinking Ouzo through a straw and taking hits off a hookah. The couple was living in a semi-robed state without any comprehension as to who Felix was.

Duncan left the old man's former residence and wandered aimlessly into the marketplace. Near a spice vendor by a butcher shop a child emerged from among mustaches and chain smokers to hand him an epistolary message. He grasped at the child's clothing, but the kid squirmed away and dissolved into the indistinguishable sea of others. He opened the note and read the words of a man fifteen years past the century:

The curse can not be lifted or revoked. One other could know, but first I'd have to go. Not ready yet, though. You'll just have to hang in there, mate. Take it from me, find a tropical place off the beaten path and wait for the storm to pass. Whatever you do, don't let the bastards catch you or your partner from Shawinigan. Hope your cock still works. – Felix

Duncan cast his eyes around the chaotic market with sweeping vigilance, but saw no sign of the old man.

Fuck, he thought.

He folded the letter and put it in his cargo pocket. As he stood there in a breeze of complicated feelings, he made the decision to go see Grace again.

Though they communicated regularly by email and phone, he hadn't seen her in the flesh since 2009. When he turned up in Nipawin she hugged him with the intense embrace of a mother long separated from child. She listened to him with the same maternal concern she would have given to Robert or Max.

He updated her on his fictional job at a think tank in Brussels, and he mentioned the possibility of being reassigned to the Caribbean. She nodded and smiled in appreciation of his many opportunities. Her presence had a softening effect on his brooding and restless soul; she was unconditional with him, she'd always been. He stayed at the farm for several days. He exercised his body with yard work and fixed a couple fences, and she made him delicious meals with her fine lined hands. They reminisced about Glenn and spoke fondly of Max and Robert, and Rachel as well. When he departed, she wished him the best and thanked him for visiting. She said she would see him again soon, but he had to wonder about that.

* * *

There were armfuls of wires and assorted electronics that had been carried to the top of the stairs. He threw everything into a trash bin that was headed for incineration. He walked out onto the back deck and looked across the garden where he and Pierre had once spread Alex's ashes. He cast his eyes on autumn's assortment of dying vegetation. The rhubarb had wilted and shriveled, the raspberries were moving toward dormancy, and the sweet peas were…

flowering again? At least he thought they were sweat peas; but at a casual glance one could never be certain. He decided to take a closer look; after all, it might matter.

Once the basement was cleared out and the windows were boarded up, he was fairly certain he'd never see 420 Roach Haven again. As Felix's note had suggested, Duncan was moving to the tropics, somewhere in the Caribbean where he could put his feet up for a spell. Pierre, on the other hand, was returning to an undisclosed piece of property in the French country side south of Lyon.

"Can you believe we're finally done with this place?" said Duncan.

"Yeah, but it's not like I'm selling it. We might have to come back again, you never know."

"Are you out of your mind?" said Duncan, "This is over, man."

Pierre looked at Duncan in an unsettled way.

"Are you sure you're alright?"

"Yeah, I'm fine," said Pierre with weak conviction. "How long do you think before it's all gone?"

"What, Insynnium?" said Duncan, "Probably two or three years."

"Do you think they'll ever stop looking for us?"

"Yes, someday."

"What about Max," asked Pierre, "Should we send him more to tide him over?"

"I don't know, should we?" said Duncan skeptically, "What about this bullshit with the extended comas that you mentioned? Do you think he'll try it on his own?"

"Fuck," said Pierre, "It's Max we're talking about, of course he will."

The two men assessed one another silently.

"Look, if Max kills himself fucking around with this stuff, that's on him," said Pierre, "That's not on you. He's made choices, just like the rest of us. He knows the risks. You have to let him go."

Duncan knew that Pierre was right, but it was more than just letting go of Max. Duncan felt as though he were letting go of Grace, as well, in a painful and indefinable way.

Part IV

Cuba

1974

-AUE-

"Hey kids, now that's a mohair suit!"

They climbed into a retired military jeep along with a comrade he'd never seen before and drove into the park. Except for the absence of a charcoal haze and the diesel industrial bustle of migratory workers, *Valle de Vinales* reminded Max of *Yangshuo* - perched along the *Li* River in Guangxi - with its odd geologic formations and spelunk-able caverns. Even in a drought, the tropical viridescence was striking. He saw deeply tanned farmers, perspiring and grimy, working their tobacco plants in the red soil at the side of the road.

He dangled from his mom like a chimpanzee suckling. He was a baby, a mere infant with *mucho* trepidation. For a while, he suspected that his parents were double agents in a clandestine affair of international importance. Whether he liked it or not, he was wholly immersed in the process of discovering the deeper mystery of his parents, and he anticipated that his evolving picture of them was far from complete. After all, he'd been to rallies for Castro, and crowded parades that echoed calls of, '*Patria o Muerte, Vanceremos!*'

Dust billowed up from the bald tires of the jeep and settled on the hood as the vehicle rolled to a stop. They parked in front of a large shed sided with corrugated tin. Max imagined the inside of the structure to be hot like a sauna, with old men rolling cigars and picking at their teeth.

Outside, the surroundings were surreal. They floated among mogates as though they were icebergs on some land version of the sea. Once they entered the shed, however, it was like being swallowed by an autoclave, and the outer world was erased by the sterile laboratory of the interior.

It wasn't what Max was expecting.

He was placed on his back atop an operating table. He was completely naked, and his parents were there beside him, smiling. His mom rubbed his head and patted his chest as she whispered something not quite language into his ear. In addition to the three of them, there were two gentlemen who appeared to be in their early sixties. Max had no personal recollection of either man, but there was something decidedly terrifying about them, nonetheless.

He was particularly horrified by the one wielding a large hypodermic, a device that had its pointy intentions aimed directly at him. The needle was attached to a chrome syringe not dissimilar to the sort used on sheep and cows in feedlots and cattle stations. It was a bovine vaccination gun that made ratchet sounds as herd focused 'eight way' got pumped under hides.

He understood there was a plan afoot to inject him with something. He felt his heart rate increase. He wanted to cry out, but his courage had been asphyxiated by a blanket of dread heavier than anything he'd ever experienced. As the needle bearer came closer, he could see that the man had a preserved and ageless appearance, with thin immaculate lips that had whispered sympathy to the devil.

The room was blindingly bright, and he couldn't distinguish anything beyond the hazy edges of those present. He was clueless as to why he'd been brought to this undisclosed location. What was he being inoculated against? And why hadn't he been informed of these events later in life? My god, he thought, what sort of cultish practices were his parents involved with?

The man with the syringe walked around behind him. Max tried to turn his head, but his mom held him still. He'd never felt so weak and ineffectual in all his life. He struggled with every ounce of his physical ability to resist what was coming. He didn't want it to happen, but he was powerless to stop its inevitability. The shouting that finally emerged from his lungs sounded not unlike the shrieks of a hungry infant. He felt the needle slide under his skin and go up into his brain with surprisingly little pain.

It was a cold and paralyzing icicle driven deep into his hippocampus with surgical steel precision. His frontal lobe began to throb when the instrument was withdrawn from the base of his skull. A hot cloth was immediately applied to his meager atlas and it felt splendidly warm. He accepted the care of his mother's touch as her fingers pressed his flesh and brought comfort to his racing senses.

Once his fussing abated, he was laid on the table again; a bug under a microscope. Moments passed, and then smiles began to branch from the mouths of those looking down on him. His parents suddenly appeared delighted at the sight of him. He'd obviously been transformed for the better in some irreversible fashion; though he still had no conception of any pre-existing abnormality or condition.

As he lay beneath the lamps of the light infused room, a single thought pulsed in his mind: the injection he'd just received was at the root of his ability to time travel, and he knew it.

The man who pushed the needle into his cranium was a doctor of some description, and he picked up Max like a veterinarian lifting a piglet or a lamb and gave the child a tentative weigh, and then handed him over to his mother.

"Thank you, Felix," said Grace.

"Don't mention it, this is what I do, this is what comrades are for," said the man with a Continental accent that sounded slightly German.

"He looks better already, doesn't he?" said Grace, as she held Max in her arms while Glenn smiled with approval.

"I have success because no single formula is identical," said Felix. "Your son will be the only person to ever receive this particular injection because it is uniquely calibrated to his condition and constitution. He will remain healthy for many years. Now, if you will excuse us, Aloysius and I must take our leave. We have a comrade in Saint Petersburg who is ill and needs our attention."

Grace carried Max outside into the subdued brilliance of earth color and shade. He listened to the bouncing inflections of Cuban Spanish as he and his parents made their way back to the workers camp where they were staying. They passed along busy streets where no one gave a second glance or even a side eyed observation. He was alive and grateful that whatever had taken place was over and done with.

* * *

Several months earlier:

Max was lying in his crib musing on the events that led to his infancy, a comedy of errors one might say.

It all started when he told Rachel he was going camping north of Flin Flon to get his mind square with the world, when in actual fact what he was doing was driving to the foothills of Alberta and placing his life in jeopardy. Although he'd promised Pierre that he wouldn't do it, he'd taken it upon himself to navigate a five-day coma.

Five years was different than one, or even four, it was half a decade. He felt he needed to do something significant with such a stretch of time, even if it wouldn't be recognized or remembered by anyone besides himself. When he looked at his life and realized how many hours he'd spent selling health food, saving lives, and puzzling over his biochemical entanglements with Insynnium, it seemed natural and normal that he should choose to attend medical school.

He began planning his approach.

He spent March and April's AUE's studying for the MCAT. Then he skipped every AUE from May through September to save up the necessary time.

He didn't need to drive out to Alberta to undergo the radically long sleep, but he knew that camping in the shadow of the Rockies would fill him with peace and give him the profound privacy he required. He fashioned a crude campsite far up an elk trail in the ass-end of nowhere and covered everything with a camouflage net. He swallowed fifteen capsules of Insynnium and placed his head on his pillow for two and a half million minutes.

In his AUE, he was accepted into the McMaster medical program and went to Hamilton to become an MD. He worked harder intellectually than he ever thought possible, and was impressed on occasion with his ability to recall obscure anatomical names and unpronounceable pharmaceuticals. He was one year into his psychiatry residency – writing prescriptions for *Zoloft* and *Wellbutrin* - when he awoke to the howling of wolves beyond the walls of his tent.

He had a burning fever and a spastic colon, and his cot resembled an unenviable study in scatology. He stumbled in circles, confused and massively dehydrated. Though he'd brought an excess of supplies with him, he realized upon waking that they were not the correct and necessary ones. He felt like an unprepared pioneer on a heedless push through uncharted territory, lucky not to have killed himself by lack of preparation or overabundance of hubris.

When he crawled home to Rachel, she said he was a damn fool to think he could rough it for so long up in Flin Flon. She wanted to know why in hell he hadn't come back after he contracted food poisoning.

He found it hard to explain.

After recuperating for a month, he felt like a new man, and in some ways he was; viz., Dr. McVista. When a conference on the future of organic beets sprang up in Winnipeg, he took the invitation as an opportunity to visit the windy city for a good old one year AUE.

Following a borsch and vegan pierogi dinner at the Saint Regis, he went up to his room and turned out the 'do not disturb' sign. In his full and fatigued state, he failed to notice that his Insynnium had been tampered with. He swore he inspected the dates, but it mattered not, as the evidence dissolved in his blood.

And so it was that he landed on his back in a crib in a farm house outside Nipawin, circa 1974.

He bridled at his compromised position.

During his obstetrics rotation at med school, he'd delivered several babies, but this by no means prepared him to be one himself. He panicked when he realized he'd re-entered his existence as a six-month-old infant. He had a great deal of distress finding adequate oxygen with his limited lung capacity, and there was nothing to alleviate his claustrophobic anxiety.

When he opened his eyes, he wanted to speak, but he could do nothing more than squawk and choke on saliva. His most basic attempt at a simple request came out as an incomprehensible wail. The inside of his mouth was gum smooth and numb to his tongue. It felt frozen, as though a dentist were contemplating the extraction of several teeth and possibly his tonsils.

He wanted to move, but his tiny body – for all practical purposes – was totally unconnected to the commands of his fathomless brain. His limbs were short and soft with the ineffectual strength of noodles in the rain. He found himself toasty and tightly confined in a swaddle of blankets like a grilled cheese sandwich melting into its wrapper.

In the first months following his arrival, he had the near constant sensation of urine trickling down the inside of his thigh; warm, uncomfortable, enuretic effluvia leaking from un-closable valves. He grew attached to the dry attributes of Talcum powder that his mother liberally sprinkled around his nut sack.

Also, there was constantly somebody standing around his crib. It was rare when he wasn't the center of attention.

"When will he start talking?" said the girl.

"Probably the same time Robert did, close to two," said Grace.

Initially, the girl was unrecognizable through Max's under-developed and un-focus-able eyes until he realized that it was Jill Gaffney, his former baby sitter from over on Densmore Avenue. She was young and abundantly pretty. He desperately wanted to warn her about the pig farmer and the fire and the mole behind her knee. But he blah blahed, and he ba ba-ed when he spoke, and she just stood there and smiled with her Highland fair features that 1978 would render tragically lifeless.

"He's so cute; he's really growing, isn't he?" she said.

"Yes he is," said Grace, but her face showed concern, "There shouldn't be a problem, but if there is, you have the number where we can be reached. We'll be back in a few hours."

"Keep a close eye on that one," said Glenn as he pointed to Robert, "he has a way of getting into stuff if you know what I mean."

Max looked at his father with the sideburns and the butterfly collar.

"No problem, Mr. McVista, you guys have a nice time tonight," said Jill.

After the parents departed, the house went quiet, and Robert came over to investigate Max. He walked up and looked into the crib with his hands around the wooden doweling. He stood there and stared, like an inmate behind bars, attempting to move Max with a strong intention.

Ordinarily, an infant would take little notice of a gawking sibling, but then again, Max was no ordinary infant, and Robert was driving him crazy with his staring. After several minutes, Max turned his oversized dome toward Robert and gave the boy a look that said, "Can I help you?"

Robert was two and a half, and Max was a fraction of that, so he had no real memory of the details unfolding before his eyes. Other than what had been retrospectively assimilated through photographs and stories, the childhood events now taking place were nowhere to be found in his consciousness. His infant surroundings were a living intensification of the many grainy Polaroid's once taken and left to wither in photo albums yellowing at the corners.

"Mas taka twip," said Robert, in a pre-Mouseketeer voice.

The staring and the cryptic talk scared the bejesus out of Max. He tried to ask Robert a clarifying question, but he only sprayed his brother with spittle in his effort to be understood.

"Skeezure, Mas taka twip fo skeezure," said Robert in the same infantile cadence.

Christ, thought Max. He tried one more time to speak but it was articulated with toothless drool.

He began to cry.

He wailed and carried on until Jill scooped him up. She was sixteen and wearing a low cut top. His face fell between her boobs and he unwittingly slobbered on the softness of her chest.

She held him at a frightening height and assumed he'd take comfort in being bounced and cooed. It felt like climbing Half Dome in an earthquake. He looked down from the precipice of Jill's clavicles and prayed that her hands wouldn't fail him. As he clung to the ledge of her shoulder, he recalled the time he and

Reinhold lost their ropes and pitons ascending the final pitch on the Tsaranoro massif.

His fear of free falling was immediately displaced by the damp rubber nipple of a warm plastic bottle. Jill pushed the slippery object into his denture dormant mouth. He swallowed, but it was nauseating to know that the tangy cream came from his mom's mammaries. Jill gave him another bounce, and then they noticed the smell. He felt like he was sitting in warm putty with a damp towel wound round him. The strong stench of his powerful evacuation was like blunt force trauma to the olfactory, and it hit them in the nose with an unforgiving impact.

"Stinky, stinky," said Robert. He was holding a razor sharp filleting knife that his father had cleaned fish with only hours earlier. He stabbed without mercy at a crayon face he'd drawn on the kitchen cabinet.

Bones appeared dangerous as he thrust his miniature sword into the wood, defacing the ornamentation on the doors. Max looked to the baby sitter to control his brother, but she paid Robert no attention as she focused with single minded alignment on getting Max cleaned and powdered and sucking his pacifier.

She fastened a fresh diaper to him and placed him on his back in the crib. He hated being positioned in such a way. It made it impossible to observe what was taking place around him. On occasion, he would roll onto his belly and push himself upright, and the thrill was not unlike reaching a Cascadian summit. Eventually, the exertion would prove more than his muscles could bear, however, and he would find himself nauseous and depleted from his attempt to maintain such a vertiginous position.

For Max, the entire infant experience was like recovering from an injury or an illness, but without the sympathy of others. After all, he discovered, no one had reason to feel sorry for you because there wasn't anything wrong with you, other than for the fact you were a tiny and impossibly helpless creature with drastically limited modes of communication and expression.

It gave him marginal comfort to know that his condition would improve, if only slightly, as each day went by. And, if truth be told, there was a certain amount of inspiration to be found in the prospect of outgrowing your affliction, as there weren't many maladies one could say that about.

Despite the safety pins tethering him to the weight and scent of a massive and odorous cloth, his first birthday was a developmental watershed of sorts. After blowing out a candle he wasn't allowed to touch, and slobbering over a cake he wasn't allowed to eat, he miraculously moved himself from a crawl to a Cro-Magnon crouch. It seemed that his vestibular system had finally blossomed and given him the flower of balance. His struggles through pooping and mewling had been rewarded with a walk. He felt like he was balancing on a board that was resting on an inner tube that was floating on a lake as he finessed his first steps like an acrobat in a travelling carnival moving to the crowd's approval.

From the beginning, his level of awareness made the entire infantile endeavor more than mildly outrageous. Here he was, damn near forty years old, he thought, with his mom wiping his bung hole and powdering his gonads. He knew beyond all doubt that he was the quintessential polymorphous perverse, in awe of his mother's staggering beauty as she fondled his fingers and folded his toes.

He'd never remembered her so objectively, she had always been his mom, but now she was Grace. She was gorgeous and sensual and overflowing with sexuality. His current AUE would have given Dr. Freud enough empirical evidence to write a second treatise on the interpretation of dreams. He felt himself enter the dark halls of Oedipus as he fumbled to get his mouth around his mother's nipples. She spoke softly, and he listened as the *enfant terrible* of an unknowable dimension.

Although his parents were somewhat guarded about what they said in front of Robert, they spoke candidly in Max's presence on the assumption that he understood absolutely nothing. They were good conversationalists, and he heard plenty. There was talk about the conflict in Southeast Asia. They had friends who were soldiers in Vietnam and reporters in Cambodia; there was talk about who had been killed and who had been wounded and who continued to protest. They bitched about Nixon and sang the praises of Trudeau. They spoke about family grievances and money problems, and the real possibility they'd remain in Canada for years to come.

His parents were frank with one another, and it was real, because his father – not prone to tears - cried on some occasions. Max felt guilty for his auditory trespasses in moments so intimate. In spite of all his eavesdropping, however, he still had no idea what was coming his way.

He'd been experiencing the world from the perspective of an infant for close to ten months when his parents took a road trip to Toronto. There was a plan, for some reason or another, to meet up with his paternal aunt, Phoebe [21]. Even in his limited and tightly bundled state, however, he could decipher that the reunion would be a tense occasion.

When they arrived at Woodbine Beach just east of the city, there were no sentiments of endearment between Phoebe and Glenn. Their displeasure with one another was obvious and palpable in the dry

---

[21]**#9** on the Billboard Year-End Hot 100 singles of 1974. **"Bennie and the Jets"** by Elton John from the album *Goodbye Yellow Brick Road*. MCA, 1974. While frequently on the turn table at the house, the song waylaid Max as it came over the Plymouth's intermittent and static afflicted radio on the way to Toronto. Glenn was going 75 or 80 miles per hour, and Grace was holding Max so that he could see out of the window and into the passing prairie. There was something about a fatted calf, a mohair suit, and a magazine that fit with his dad's plaid pants and his mom's oversized sun glasses. Robert had spilled a bag of Old Dutch chips onto the back seat and he was eating them off the upholstery like a Hoover. Max was the member of a free and counter-cultural family headed for a destination beyond anyone's reckoning.

exchange of sarcasm and sighs. To Max, the whole endeavor felt transactional, like a vague debt owed between siblings or something. And then, the following morning, minus Robert, he and his parents packed themselves onto a plane and flew to Cuba.

He figured that he'd died and gone to hell until the plane came to a halt on the tarmac at Jose Marti and the Pratt and Whitney engines ground to a silent finish. It would be unequivocally fair to say that babies have every right to cry on airplanes, he thought. The jet's pressure intense cabin was not unlike descending a dive line with un-equalized ear drums, and the seats vibrated at a frequency that blended his organs into one. There were moments of turbulence over Florida that made the thought of breast milk prohibitive, and no matter what he did he could not convey to anyone onboard that his headache was verging on a migraine. He was positively mortified at the prospect of a return trip.

* * *

Grace once insisted on mastering the Paso-Doble at the community dance class in Nipawin, and Glenn had a treasury of *Cohibas* hiding in a humidor up in the loft. But these had never been important facts to Max; they seemed only aspects of his parent's personalities rather than vestiges of their actual past. To him they were examples of parental eccentricities that were accepted and never questioned, as were so many things that could never be accounted for; like the collection of Julio Gutierrez LP's that sat under the turntable in the front room for years.

Before he traveled back in time to 1974, he would never have guessed that his parents had been part of Castro's Cuba. They spoke with the vigorous rhetoric of committed communists as they ate communally cooked cabbage at a 'workers paradise' in *Pinar del Rio*. Max, on the other hand, ate applesauce while mumbling incoherent sentences. But that's not to say he didn't feel privileged to be a part of history's larger narrative as it unfolded with fascinating results. It was an incredible stroke of luck that his mother chose to take him through the crowds in a MacLaren folding-push-chair or carry him from place to place in an Iroquois papoose. He arrived everywhere with a seat or a perch. He was experiencing the life his parents had lived as Marxists in the fine margin of time that existed between their fervent ideology and his emergent memory.

Every day there was smoking and rum and talk of Bolshevism and shipments from the Kremlin. He acquired so much insight into his parents that he almost considered them treasonous. Their political idealism and measured attempts to take the world in a different direction, however, made him think that his own generation - raised in the bosom of corporatism and television – might be lost and without a choice at the end of history; and with only the imperative 'buy or die' left to cling to.

The most disappointing part of his day was the evening, of which, according to his calculations, there were few remaining. His mom would carry him off to a dormitory style room where he would wee away his hours with the other diaper fillers in an orphanage-like arrangement. If the evening went right, however, and the conversations were particularly heated and fierce, he would squawk and fuss in an attempt to buy more minutes in the comfort of his mother's arms, as she sat amongst her comrades in the fading ambiance of a tropical Finland Station.

It was far from perfect, of course, and the lush beauty of Cuba tended to hide and romanticize the inflexible and mechanical system that the leaders running the show exhibited. Privately, Max heard his parents express grave misgivings about the social/economic experiment being conducted. And he could tell that it wasn't working out in other ways, as well. His mom found the weather disagreeable, which confirmed his suspicion that she would always require a distinctly four-season year. And his dad found the outside world hideously censured as evidenced by his longing to read the editorials and reviews from the *Globe and Mail*.

In a crib beside a concrete wall painted with the visage of Che Guevara, Max was supposed to be taking part in a general siesta. He gave thought to the substance that was injected into his brain earlier in the day, and the possible health reasons that might have prompted such a drastic procedure. He never again saw the mysterious sexagenarian doctors, nor did he overhear his parents discuss the matter further. He would, however, remain puzzled over the details of his medical transformation for many days forward.

There was a breeze easing its way through the window next to his sleeping quarters. It wasn't especially cool, but it carried the relaxing scent of gardenias. The air in his diaphragm stretched the spaces between his tiny ribs, and his breath went out through his runny nose. There had never lived a toddler with so much on his mind, he thought, as his eyes grew heavy. He fell asleep as an infant in *Pinar del Rio* with the hope of waking up as an adult in Winnipeg, Manitoba.

2012

-Autumn-

"Everybody's gettin' low in them
Apple Bottom jeans"

When Max returned from Winnipeg, he seemed quiet and a little, what was the word, thought Rachel, pensive?

As they stood in the kitchen washing dishes, he told her that he needed to go see his mom. She couldn't argue with that. It had been a long time, almost five months since they were last at the farm.

She told him to go.

He headed to Nipawin the following week.

Max was healthy again, and he looked strong. Rachel was surprised at how fast he bounced back after his careless camping trip to Flin Flon in October. She didn't exactly know what happened to him up there, but she felt it was more than just food poisoning. When he arrived home, he was water logged and thin. He was scratched and mangy the way hibernating animals appear when they emerge in the spring and start combing the woods for food.

She remembered him pulling up in the driveway and climbing out of the Toyota. She was hit with the unshakable sense that her husband, whether he intended to or not, had gone on a vision quest. Although his body was starved and depleted, she noticed that his spirit was enlarged, and that his soul had become seasoned like something that grows intoxicating in a cask. If he insisted on camping at Flin Flon again next year, she thought, he would have to take better food and less ambition.

She and the boys wanted to go to Flin Flon, as well. They, too, wanted to camp in the bush and fish in the streams and eat beans from a can. But Max was adamant that he needed time for himself. He told them that he planned to read anatomy books and dissect frogs. He was so oddly focused sometimes that it made them all wonder if he was mentally unsound or just attractively eccentric. Rachel told him to bring back a few trout, but naturally, he forgot.

She noticed that he purchased a lot of supplies for his trip, as though he were going for longer than two weeks. He told her that everything was necessary, and while she doubted the truth of that, she let him go crazy with the credit card anyway. If Max was tired of crouching in a mountaineer tent, she thought, and he needed something taller with walls to pull on his pants in the morning, then so be it. He packed every bit of gear into the Toyota and drove off to Flin Flon. As she watched him disappear down the street, she recalled how the Toyota had arrived in their lives five years earlier.

The FJ came on a ship to Canada from Down Under. It travelled across the prairies for three days on a freight train out of Vancouver. One morning a steel container from a cargo vessel was sitting in the street blocking the driveway. It seemed out of place. The neighbors stopped to inquire, and it made Rachel feel uncomfortable. She didn't know what it was or where it came from, and she was irritated by the fuss.

Max had recently moved back into the house, and the two of them were finding the old comforts and adjusting to new discoveries. He'd mentioned nothing about a delivery of such proportion and she assumed it was a shipment for GROWERS that had mistakenly missed the warehouse. She called him at work to tell him about it, and he came home immediately.

She was standing beside him when he opened the container, and as they looked inside it was obvious the thing wasn't filled with grapefruits and cabbages. Instead, there were crates full of vehicle parts stacked up on one another like you might find in a humungous and directionless model kit. It didn't make any sense, but Max stood there smiling.

"What in god's name is this?" said Rachel.

"This is what the Australian's call a 'Troopy'," he said.

"Is that a truck, Dad?" said Joshua, who had emerged from the house to partake in the inspection.

"It sure is, Josh, and we're going to put it together just like the mechanics on Toyota's assembly line."

"Where?"

"I've rented some space over at Lionel's garage."

For Rachel, there was something unsettling about the sight of the container sitting there before them. It felt like an alien visitation. It ominously rested in the driveway, almost humming with its predictions. It seemed a Trojan horse full of microparticles carried across the ocean from a land dominated by kangaroos and snakes. She couldn't help but sense that something escaped from the container and dissipated into the air that day as Max pulled out gear shifts and drive shafts to inspect them in the sunlight.

Max slowly and meticulously assembled the truck, mostly with the help of the boys, who learned a great deal from their father concerning valve seats and piston sleeves and limited slip differentials. When the following summer arrived, they were all riding around in the 'troopy.'

After months in the making, the Toyota claimed a spot on the lane to the left of the house as though it had been parked there for years. Rachel couldn't help but grow fond of the vehicle that eventually became more than the sum of its parts. The steely power of the engine and the metallic rattle of the doors never ceased to remind her of the iron permanence that was her history with Max.

* * *

Daryl had a ten-a.m. shift at the Ag Centre on Saturdays; he'd been doing it for years; so, it wasn't uncommon for him to stop by the McVista house for a coffee on the way in to work. When he woke Rachel and Max at six, though, they knew it wasn't good.

"Did you guys hear the news?" said Daryl, "Beaver McLennan got paroled from Stony yesterday."

"Will you remind me who Beaver is again," said Max, rubbing his eyes.

"Jesus, Max, he's the guy who cut a deal with the Crown prosecutor in exchange for a reduced sentence if he agreed to testify against Darcy," said Daryl looking at Max like he shouldn't have to explain such a thing.

"You know, with what happened to Aubrey-" he tried to continue.

"Yes, I know, I know. I blanked for a minute there," said Max interrupting his friend.

The two men looked at one another and Rachel started a pot of coffee.

"I thought he was released ages ago?" said Max.

"He was, but he got sent back."

"Don't tell me," said Rachel, "My brother's looking for him; wants to teach him a lesson about what happens to snitches, or something like that."

"Something like that," said Daryl. "He's hired two hoodlums and a nut-job from the Airborne Regiment. That's what the guys over at the Base told me."

"What a bunch of nimrods," said Max.

"Yeah, but vengeful nimrods," said Daryl. "Remember what he did to that parolee from the Brotherhood who fucked up his leg in solitary?"

"Yeah, and nobody saw anything. The fucker should have gone back to prison for that."

"Max, please," interjected Rachel.

"I'm just saying…"

Rachel let out a long sigh and asked if the police were doing anything. Daryl said he doubted the

RCMP was even aware of Darcy's half-baked plan. He said the Mounties had better things to do than protect a drug dealer ex-con like Beaver.

"I have to find Darcy and talk to him," she said.

"Maybe you should call Gary?" said Max.

"He's in Fort McMurray building camps," she said. "What the hell can he do from up there?" Her feathers were standing up.

"Fuck," said Max, "Darcy wouldn't even speak to you at your Mom's funeral in the spring."

"Yes, I'm aware of that," she said with irritation, "But I have to try, don't I?"

Max shook his head and looked out the window.

"Well," said Daryl, "I see Darcy all the time at the parts counter at Northern Mac, and I can tell you for a fact, Rachel, that your brother is one disturbed mother-fucker, no offense intended. The only reason they haven't fired his ass is because his manager is scared shitless of him, so that must tell you something right there."

Rachel got up and put her coat on. "I'm leaving," she said.

When she got to her brother's workplace, the floor manager informed her that Darcy had taken the day off. She spoke with a couple of the other workers. They had the same distressed appearance she'd seen on the faces of kiddos rescued by child protective services. The silenced voices and darting eyes of his co-workers re-confirmed the menace that he was.

Darcy ended up killing Beaver McLennan in a strip club in Winnipeg two days later. His half-hitched goon squad nabbed Beaver in the men's room of the Larchmont Hotel and brought him out to the pool table in a double arm bar. That's when Darcy walked into the joint with his limping gait and cocked pistol. He shot Beaver through the heart in front of everyone. Before patrons or police could stop him, he turned the gun on himself, and that was the end of it.

A week later, Rachel received a postcard from Winnipeg. On the front was a picture of The Forks National Historic Site and on the back was a sloppily penned note that flatly stated: *It's all square now, Sis, misery loves company, your Bro, Darce.* She felt her brother's cold hands touch her from beyond the grave and she dropped the postcard in the street. When she picked it up again, she understood that he was letting her know that the limits of his vengeance had finally been reached. She was profoundly saddened that her brother's forgiveness hadn't found her while he was still alive. She went into the house, lit a match, and burned the postcard over the sink.

The Larchmont Hotel shooting on Notre Dame Avenue made national news and brought Rachel and Max into the spot light for a spell. She worried how Max would react to the Aubrey Fender story resurfacing after so many years in dormancy. But he was sage-like through the whole media spectacle. He seemed to have made peace with the original events to an extent that resembled forgetfulness; like an elderly man recalling the details of something that took place sixty-years prior.

Rachel felt guilty, though; and she struggled with Darcy's legacy as a murderer and a thief, and a man who inflicted such a dark and scarring wound on her hometown. His suicide, however, caused her older brother, Gary, to move back to Brandon, and that was a good thing.

Gary was single again and worked as a carpenter on the east side of the city. Sometimes he travelled as far as Calgary to frame houses or put up foundation forms on commercial sites. Whenever he was in town, though, he would drive over to see his sister. They would talk about the family and try to make sense of the things that had fallen apart or understand why they were never in one piece to begin with. Familial disintegration and generational loss drifted on tears if they drifted at all.

Max helped Gary for a few weekends during the summer after Gary's apprentice cut off his finger in a table saw accident. Gary enjoyed working with Max, but he couldn't get it square in his head how his sister's husband had acquired such nuanced carpentry skills. And so, like teaching a child geometry, Rachel would sit close to her brother and talk him through Max's unusual condition. 'No shit,' and, 'I'll be damned', were Gary's typical refrains. Rachel would smile and nod; it felt good to have the bond of blood back in town.

October was unseasonably chilly and the cold was chasing the green out of every leaf. When Max called to say that he was bringing a special guest for dinner,

Rachel assumed he was referring to the Border collie they'd decided to adopt from the local pound during the agency's fall fund drive. She and the boys waited with excitement for the new addition to their family to come bounding across the porch.

But when Max opened the door, there was no dog.

Instead, he stood there with a hobo. The man's hair was long, and his beard was thick, and he was coated with the grime of accumulated miles. It took only seconds, though, for Rachel to recognize who was buried under the disguise. She gave him a big hug – it was like throwing your arms around the king of pain.

Bones wasn't prone to an excess of words, but on this occasion, he was particularly taciturn, and obviously AWOL. He said that he'd left his second wife at Fort Carson back in the spring and that he'd been up in Alaska running heavy equipment on a bridge project ever since.

Over the years Rachel had seen him here and there; a wedding here, a funeral there, the occasional holiday. The sight of him on their wedding day haunted her in ways she didn't like to reflect on. He was supposed to be the best man, but the best of him seemed to be gone. He'd returned from the Balkans with something black and grim caged behind his eyes and the visceral effect left her freighted. Once wild and free, he had been hollowed of his better substance. Much of Grace and Glenn's feral nurturing seemed wasted and sadly amputated.

At Glenn's funeral, he'd changed again, but this time it wasn't all bad. He showed vulnerability and a reluctant willingness to accept help. He alluded to what he'd done and the shit that he'd seen. But the clockwork order of his thoughts was coming unwound; the rotors and the movements and the jewels no longer fit neatly into their casement. He told them about Mosul and Kandahar and working with the SAS in Mozambique. He confessed his addiction to the adrenalin of AK47's and night flights and black sites. But he never got into the deep with them, into the things only known to the brotherhood of his unit; one whose confessors had been decimated by road side bombs and roof top crack shots. Whatever was chasing him, thought Rachel, was more fundamental to his being than covert operations and confidential interrogations.

The tribe knows the warrior's face when it's painted in red and black, but after war the colors can be hard to see. Spilled blood is often forgotten, and what was once uncovered is covered again. Everyone knew that Bones had captured 'high value targets' and killed 'enemy combatants'. But it was the ones he'd killed off the battle field that worried Rachel; like state sponsored murder, strategic and premeditated. He'd been a part of various 'Agency' operations; cold and clandestine affairs that involved assassinations outside the usual theaters, like Uzbekistan and Buenos Aires. It was a primitive and feverish world that kept score with scalps. From one deployment to the next,

Bones was running along a razor's edge, a sparkling silver edge, that those who cross breath no more.

When he showed up in Brandon, Rachel had no qualms about aiding and abetting her brother-in-law's absence without leave, she would do anything she could to assist his departure from sword and arrow. She gave him space around the house and made little in the way of domestic demands. He ate their potatoes and rice and got high on their aging stash of pot. He watched a lot of movies and shaved off his beard. There were moments when it seemed like he was about to say something important, but then nothing was revealed.

He worked for Max at GROWERS until Lionel hired him as a mechanic's apprentice. He worked on cars and made his own sandwiches for lunch. He got on well with the guys at the garage who were drawn to him as men always were. Some of them would go out for beers on Friday nights and coax him into telling war stories, but he only ever said enough to leave them satisfied, and never so much as to make them feel uneasy about the assassin they were working within a wrenches length of.

One holiday Monday when the sun was out, and Max was at work, Kevin and Josh were given permission to help their uncle fall a tree in the backyard. The Northern Flickers that nested in the dying pine had not been back for two seasons, so Rachel said it was okay for the snag to finally come down. Inside the house, she was smudging the living room. Outside, she could hear the whine of the chainsaw, the smash of axes, and voices shouting in fun bravado.[22]

Then suddenly everything went deathly quiet.

Anxiety gripped her chest in the noiseless vacuum.

She rushed to the kitchen window and silently froze behind the pane. Over at the woodshed, sitting on a chopping block, was Robert with his shirt off and his back to her. The boys also had their shirts off, standing on either side of their uncle; thin tan shoulders exposed. She turned her ear to the crack between the glass and the screen and listened.

"Do you think the birds found another place to live," asked Kevin, "Mom says this tree was their home?"

"Dad said the Flickers moved, do you think they did?"

"Sure," said Robert, "Birds are pretty smart. They probably stopped living in this tree because they didn't want their home to get blown down in a wind

---

[22]**#1** on the Billboard Year-End Hot 100 singles of 2007. **"Low"** by Flo Rida featuring T-Pain from the album *Mail on Sunday*. Atlantic, 2007. Bones turned up KISS 106.0 so he and the boys could listen to the music while they worked. Rachel wasn't sure how she felt about the boys tuning into 106.0 – she thought they were a little young for some of the stuff that was getting airplay. There was a lot of sexual innuendo and the D. J's on the morning show could be pretty raunchy sometimes. Personally, though, she liked the song, and she found humor in three Saskatchewan lumberjacks stacking limbs and splitting stumps to electro-pop at one in the afternoon on a Monday.

storm. I bet if we made them a new house they'd come back."

"Can we?" said Kevin.

"Sure, we'll build a good one, and we'll put it over there on that post," said Robert.

"Cool," said Josh.

"Are these from bullets?" said Kevin, as he looked closely at the scars on Robert's back and chest?"

"Some are, like this one here and these two over here," said Robert, as he allowed his nephews to inspect the wound sites.

"Did it hurt when you got shot?"

"Yeah, it hurt, it hurt like hell," he said, and the boys laughed at his emphasis on the word 'hell.'

Robert's simple answer covered not just the injuries in question, but the universal injury inflicted by gun powder pushing peace and the devil in men.

"Can I touch it?" said Kevin.

Robert nodded.

"Does it still hurt?"

"Not any more, it's mostly numb."

Little dead zones across the acreage of his body, fractions of the flesh already waiting for you in the afterlife, he thought. If the bullets didn't kill you something else would; depleted uranium, the toxic smoke from those burning pits of shit, stubbornness.

"Why does everybody call you 'Bones'?" asked Kevin.

"You want to know?"

"Yes."

"Well then, come close, boys, and I'll tell you."

Robert crouched next to his nephews. The three were huddled together in a tripartite rugby scrum. The distance from the shed to the window, however, did not allow Rachel to hear the story that Bones told the boys. But she could see they were fascinated by his words as the inaudible sentences danced in their heads. As she walked away from the window, she wondered how the sharing of such a secret might impact their lives.

After winter and spring had come and gone, Bones made the decision to go visit his mother.

In Nipawin, he hunted deer and caught trout and told Grace where he'd been hiding for the last three seasons. There was a good chance that he also told her why he was hiding. By late August she'd brought him to his senses and he was planning to return to Colorado. He wrote Rachel and Max to say that the sway of the Jack pine and the barn swallows and the oat fields had settled him a bit, or at least leveled his head some.

The brass at Fort Carson wanted Article 15 punishment or possibly trial by court-marshal. But Robert's chain of command was given other instructions by Langley, and he was sent to Virginia to speak with a couple of congressmen and a senator. He might have been damaged, but he was distinguished in ways that could never be publicized. Soon he was back in the fold again. But his days as an operator were numbered and mostly fastened to a desk; eventually he was honorably discharged. He travelled and sent postcards from places like Cairo and Damascus before falling off the radar completely.

As Rachel read his note, she recalled a letter he'd once sent to Max during college when they were living in the Victorian on Peel Street. It came postmarked from Fort Bragg. Robert informed Max that he had survived something known as, 'Robin Sage,' a damp and meandering war game throughout several Appalachian counties won by those able to orientate themselves to an end point. It never occurred to Rachel - or probably Max for that matter - that Bones would ever have trouble finding his way from one place to another.

The letter's calligraphy was so beautiful that she had to ask Max if it was actually Robert's. Max smiled and said that it was. She contemplated the penmanship and the hand that created it, the same fingers that pulled triggers and gouged out eyes. The terrain between the civil and the savage could never be passed over without noticing a border, but the same could not be said when traveling between the heart and the heart's desire. She understood then, as she always would, that the immaculate nature of Robert's script was preserving something about the good and the gentle that god had not forgotten.

* * *

The scarecrow looked lonely waiting for the harvest party. The wheat and barley dust that once orbited the fields outside the city drifted lost down the alleys and lanes, hovering invisibly over the parks and gardens of Brandon.

The cabbages needed to be cut and the potatoes needed to be sacked. The cabbage would become sauerkraut, and the spuds would go into the root-cellar. Kevin, who looked more like his dad every day, was helping his mother put the storm windows on the house.

"Mom, do you think Dad's okay?"

"Yeah, Kevin, I think he's doing pretty good; why, what's up?"

"I don't know, he just seems kind of, you know, different."

"Well, Kev, you know he's got a lot on his mind with everything at work right now."

"Yeah, I know, but that camping trip last month went really bad, and it's kind of weird that he didn't want us to go with him, isn't it?" said Kevin, "What do you think he does up there?"

"I don't know, Kev. Maybe he just sits and plays his guitar or meditates in the silence. We know he reads and fishes, right? Maybe you should ask him yourself."

"I did ask him, and he said the same thing as you. But I just don't get why he can't do all those things with us around? I think he has a secret."

"A secret?" said Rachel. "What kind of secret?"

"I don't know, maybe he's like making drugs, like meth or something."

"Come on, Kev, why would you say something like that? You don't honestly think your father is a drug manufacturer, do you?"

"I don't know, Mom, he could be. You know how he knows everything, it's like crazy. And those business trips he takes, maybe that's when he sells the stuff."

"Oh my god, I can't believe what I'm hearing. Are the kids at school talking like this?"

"Yeah, some of them, like Davis Campbell and Blaine Fisher. They say that Dad's a weirdo and that he's going to get caught for something bad."

Rachel could see anxious tears starting to build in her son's eyes.

"Kevin, your father cares about us all very much. I can't begin to tell you how much he loves you and Josh. Your dad's behavior might be a little outrageous sometimes because of his syndrome, but I can assure you that he's not doing anything bad or illegal behind our backs, okay?"

"But how can you be so sure, Mom?"

"Because I know your father better than anyone else, that's how," she said.

"Okay, if you say so," said Kevin. "But I don't like it when people talk about Dad like he's some sort of freak. I just want him to be normal. I don't want him to go to jail like Mr. Bentley or Teagan's dad."

"Oh, Honey, don't worry about your father, he's not going to jail, I can promise you that."

Rachel wanted to believe that her words had reassured her son, but as the two went back to installing the storm windows, she knew she hadn't eliminated his doubt as much as she hoped.

Max was a hard man to explain.

From the moment he came back into her life, she could tell that he'd struggled with himself in a pronounced way. She knew that something of magnitude had shaken the very fibers of his being, but it also gave him the ability to get his life back on track. During the eighteen months he was missing in 2004, he'd found what he needed to find; and whatever it was he'd discovered, it now held him together in ways his previous life never could.

He found courage and certainty in himself, and the fortitude to overcome his addictions, and it brought him back to his children. His confidence drove his business and pushed him to do things he wouldn't ordinarily attempt. But Rachel knew that none of his feats had been superhuman. Heroic and selfless at times, yes; but mostly in ways that made others want to try harder and be better than they were the day before.

Although she had no actual premonitions about her husband, she had strong intuitive insights as to what might be going on, and this allowed her to know what he did on his business trips and camping adventures. After all, she wasn't a fool, and in the white light of clarity she always saw him resting and resetting himself in a place that even dreams could not reach; deep and profound like the preserved immortality of honey in the comb of some long abandoned hive; its clock set to a time not measured in minutes, or even in years.

2013/14

-Winter-

"This is the place I love; it takes me all the way"

When Grace flew to Cuba, she stayed at the *Habana Libre*. She had no idea the risks involved for Duncan to come see her.

He traveled over from the quiet side, the south-central side, to reach Havana. The capital was always restless with political murmurings and stirrings and investigations into government corruption. But this time the authorities had cast a wider net than usual with the hopes of catching other fish, as well. Duncan was getting the impression that the police were hunting for someone certain. As a precaution, he put on a beard and donned a Panama hat. He wore sunglasses during the day and heavy rimmed spectacles at night.

He'd led Grace to believe that he was on the island because a European think tank had placed him there, but then he kicked himself for telling her that, as it was part of the reason she'd come to see him. Initially, he tried to dissuade her from visiting. He toyed with the idea of telling her that the place was too dangerous and that the flagship office was calling him back to Madrid. But that was obviously too contrived.

Her visit would occur and there was nothing he could do.

When he learned that Pierre's flight from France was to show up at roughly the same time as hers the situation seemed almost negotiable. Pierre would be effective in bolstering his image. He would play up the false credentials and corroborate the necessary deceptions to make everything seem plausible.

When her plane touched down on the tarmac, the two men were standing at the luggage carousel as the jet taxied in. Though Duncan and Pierre had grown intensely close over the years, and Pierre had known of Grace's existence for some time, in one small point of fact Pierre remained utterly clueless – the fact that Grace was Max's mother.

As the three travelled from the airport to the hotel, Duncan made two decisions, the first of which was to tell Pierre who Grace really was. The second, was to refrain from telling her who he'd recently seen.

The week prior, in *Cienfuegos*, he'd seen Robert, walking arm in arm with the unforgettable and mercurial Barbara. They both looked directly into his face as their paths crossed on the street, but neither of them recognized him. He felt satisfied and saddened by the impenetrability of his inexpensive yet effective disguise. As he followed his two estranged friends through the alleys and the crowds, he felt a powerful need to reveal himself, an identity urge that kept reasserting itself in waves.

There was something improbable yet poetic about Robert and Barbara partnering, but Duncan was unable to determine why they would be in Cuba together. Were they selling drugs? Were they dealing arms? Were they lovers on vacation? It was hard not to watch them as they moved through town on their own private assignment; he wanted to reach out and touch them. He wanted to put his arms around their shoulders and sit close and drink margaritas. He wanted to retrieve the pieces of their lives that had fallen into the void of time.

Other than her closely cropped hair, Barbara looked the same as she did on the afternoon Sarah introduced them in Tel Aviv. Her spy novel flesh was from a *Bond* fantasy, and she glistened radiantly under the *El Vidao* lights. He could tell by the purse of her lips that she was speaking to Robert in Spanish. The two were so intimate it was hard not to imagine them sleeping together. Bones appeared languid and content with extra weight around his midriff. They were smoking by the curb in front of a nightclub when a flash on the horizon made everyone look skyward. Someone lit a firecracker on a rooftop. When Duncan's eyes returned to the street, the two had vanished.

"I can't be seen on the street this evening," said Duncan. "It was bad enough at the airport."

He and Pierre stood on the balcony of the twenty-first floor of the Habana Libre. "You'll have to show her around by yourself tonight."

"Duncan, this isn't my place, I don't know where…"

"Pierre, come on, how many times have you been here? You know the scene. Take her dancing and gambling somewhere along the *Malecon*; it'll be fine."

"She's absolutely captivating, don't get me wrong, it will be my pleasure, no doubt, but we don't know each other from Adam, are you sure you can't make it?"

"Look, I'll try, but Havana's not a good place to be right now, the fucking Russians are getting close."

"How did you say you know this woman, again; she's an old professor of yours from Queens, no?"

"She's Max's mother, Pierre."

* * *

Way back when Duncan should've bonded with his mother, he didn't. And he never connected with his father either. To his mind, his mother and father were always completely consumed with themselves, and as a result, they managed to leave consistently unfavorable impressions. They took themselves too seriously and had the self-absorbed custom of projecting arrogance onto everyone they met and everything they touched. He supposed that they wanted to raise him correctly – whatever that meant - but he never escaped the feeling that, for his parents, he was more like a project than a child. Their aspirations for him, however, were doomed before they began.

From the time he was old enough to understand his situation he knew he was different from others, and not just in appearance. He was able to easily learn things that took his peers a great deal of effort to acquire. And whether he tried to or not, he attracted attention, especially the female variety, which only became more pronounced as he got older. The words *precocious* and *magnetic* were thrown around freely from grade one to whenever. He often overheard his parents bragging to competitive neighbors about his cognitive gifts and precocious social astuteness. They said he would become a physician or an architect with all his intellectual bestowments and physical qualities.

Interestingly though, his most common complaint, and the problem that no parent or teacher seemed prepared to address, wasn't the demands and expectations connected to giftedness, or even the solitary oddness of being black in a white affluent section of Toronto, but rather the incessant boredom of being a kid in the first place. The childhood sense of wonder was pretty much lost on someone like Duncan; someone so equipped to being an adult straight away. When he was eleven he was twenty-two in his tastes; he read Vonnegut, listened to Funkadelic, and took his coffee without sugar.

When his parents sent him to Trinity College, he was forced to conduct an ongoing war against the slowness of others. At Trinity he received an education of sorts; a certain humorless refinement that played splendidly at sophisticated soirees attended by lawyers and investment bankers and others of that ilk to which his parents were constantly ingratiating themselves. For Duncan, the false refinement and social climbing were cause for rebellion. It was a rebellion that led him away from the sanctioned and permitted outlets of his parents and pushed him into the darker leisures.

At some point, the headmaster at Trinity decided that Duncan's bad behavior and negative influence on the other students could no longer be tolerated. Although no specific crime or corruption could be identified as such, it was the school's strong position that the boy had anti-social predilections. Not even his parent's money or influence could salvage the situation. So, he was moved to Northern Secondary. It was a deflating new reality for his parents to have a child who wasn't measuring up to their expectations; he knew this, and he relished his underachievement. He also enjoyed the bus line that ran past Northern Secondary and conveniently connected to the heart of the city. The unmonitored freedom of public school, as opposed to the private and cloistered atmosphere of Trinity, was liberating, and his weeknights and weekends were spent participating in various forms of clever and unlawful debauchery.

When the vice-principal at his junior high tried to expel him for an alleged theft, his ridiculously high GPA combined with his racial status encouraged the balance of the school board trustees to give him a second chance. Teachers and educational psychologists told his parents that his elevated intelligence made him lazy and troublesome and that he suffered from a lack of focus.

But Duncan had ideas.

Because of his complex love affair with the electric guitar, as well as a galvanized relationship with the base, it was decided that music might be his path. Although his parents wanted to see him in a jazz ensemble or a symphony, he took it upon himself to put together a punk band *a la Black Flag* with some guys from Downsville.

The teenagers started making noise in a double garage off Fourthbridge Crescent, but soon their tunes got listenable and then they got noticed. The drummer had an uncle with a connection to the Grim Reapers or the Coffin Cheaters or some other one percent Harley riding gang, and he found the boys a couple of musical gigs. But the promise never lived up to the billing, and the band just ended up smoking a lot of hashish and covering Motley Crue night after night in a biker clubhouse that smelled like a whore's thong. It became a drag, and Duncan was constantly stymied by his inability to uncover an original sound. Eventually, he lost patience with the other members, who simply saw the group as a vehicle for getting laid; which, in the end, of course, it was.

But his life was soon to change.

Following his sixteenth birthday, his parents went missing. He told the investigating officers that his mom and dad had gone out for the evening and failed to come home. The search went on for months, and many people were questioned, but his mother and father were never located. To the best of his knowledge, the Metro Toronto Police Service did all they could to ascertain the whereabouts of his parents, but it was never enough to bring them back, and the case eventually went cold.

In the wake of their unexplained vanishing, several unknown and intrusive relatives washed up on the shores of his pending orphan-hood and competed to fill in for his mom and dad. They attempted to bestow religious comfort or share creepy speculation as to the fate of his parents – mostly based on mystery shows and crime novel plots. But the nosey cash strapped relations never lasted long in the house because the place made their skin crawl. They were consistently freaked out by haunting sights and prowling sounds. They advised him to move out immediately when they heard submerged cries coming from the pipes under the bathtub or imagined chilling scenes of a stabbing under the stairs. But he sloughed off the horror film melodrama and slept like a baby. He had to constantly remind everyone that his parents were not dead, only disappeared; and that they'd come back.

He was the sole beneficiary of their estate, and with a legally emancipated status, he decided to rent the house to a professional couple from Windsor and move across the Atlantic. Free from meddling family and material constraints, he planned to travel Europe, but never got further than the Netherlands. He spent the next two years finishing high school through correspondence and receiving rent payments at a studio near Waterkeringpad in Hoorn.

He took eager and exuberant bicycle rides to Zaandam as many as three times a week so that he could participate in vigorous sexual intercourse with a lingerie model in the Prins Hendrickkade district. Her orgasms were wall shaking, cock clenching fireballs of desire, and he took satisfaction in his ability to liberate the curvaceous nympho in such a pleasurable manner. But he showed up early one day and discovered her shaking the walls with another man, and after that everything sort of shriveled. It didn't exactly break his heart, but it certainly bruised his ego. Later, after he'd liberated her a time or two more, she told him to go back to school, as she said that a man was nothing with nothing in his head.

He wanted college to be an extension of his time in Holland. He wanted the European party to continue at all hours. He knew he'd get his degree, but what he didn't know were the people that he'd meet on his way to the podium, the first of whom was Maximilian.

Duncan literally bumped into Max on the grounds of Old Fort Henry while dancing to The Tragically Hip. Max was moving to his own beat-less groove wearing a dreadfully worn concert shirt from a Dead show his brother once attended near Angel Camp - the weathered garment was signed by Hunter Thompson and looked as though it might have been worn through a protest.

Duncan was terribly arrogant in those days, but he was fascinated by Max in a weird sort of way. It often surprised him that his attitude didn't drive Max away. They'd been assigned as roommates, and he figured that the stubble jumper felt compelled to put up with his attitude out of Saskatchewan kindness or something; but their relationship quickly became more than mere tolerance. Max's free and accepting nature was reassurance in the genuineness of others, and that unwavering authenticity became part of his lasting signature. Duncan was attempting to make a new start and here was Max behaving like a brother.

It wasn't long after meeting Max that Duncan met Rachel. She was beautiful in the autumn sun; certifiably stunning. She had a certain *je ne sais quoi* that most of the other girls lacked or tried to imitate with a false and frightening effect. She had so much soul inside her gorgeous willowy figure that she almost glowed. She was also endowed with a thoughtful and clever tongue, and Duncan enjoyed her dry repartee. Her claws could be sharp, though they seldom came out, and when they did, she became stubborn rather than vindictive. In the beginning, he wanted nothing more than to sleep with her, and she was totally susceptible to his sexual magnetism. But she was also guided in equal measure by something that kept her away from him, something atavistic and tribal and not well understood; and, of course, her love for Max.

He wasn't surprised at the number of months it took her to hook up with Max. They might have been in love from the start, but his two friends were virgins, and it often took those who waited until college a lot longer to get over the initial hump. When their lust was finally consummated, though, it made him jealous; but then again, the entire historical thrust of Eros made him jealous for unconscious and repressed reasons he could not begin to fathom.

In late summer, before beginning their second year at Queens, the three embarked on a road trip to see Max's family in Saskatchewan. The drive was the polar opposite of a roller coaster, and its contour-less monotony made Duncan sick to his stomach. When they finally arrived, he swore he'd never do it again.

As they climbed from his car, they were met by a bouncing Blue Healer that was completely untrained. The dog was scolded by Max's father as he walked over to greet the wary travelers.

"Jesus Lady, down, down," he said to the dog. "Go on now, lay down."

Max's mother was vivacious and attractive, and she ran from the porch with her arms stretched out in anticipation of a hug.

"Rachel and Duncan," said Max, "This is my mom and dad, Grace and Glenn."

"Well, you certainly are a pretty thing," said Grace to Rachel with instant affection. "Isn't she pretty, Glenn?"

Max's father gave Rachel a wink to confirm his wife's assessment, and then he smiled at Duncan and asked how fast the young man had driven on Saskatchewan's poorly maintained pavement.

"I've heard these BMW's aren't too bad on mileage?" he said, as though he weren't completely convinced that the car was Duncan's.

Before Duncan could answer, Grace interrupted.

"You remind me of someone, Duncan. Doesn't he remind you of someone we used to know, Glenn?"

"Nope," said Glenn, "I can't say that he does."

But there was something about Glenn's reply to Grace that told his wife not to search her memories with too much diligence as it would only end in pain.

At that point, the winds changed, and another person arrived to join the welcoming party.

"You must be Bones," said Duncan to the understated force of nature that came to stand beside him.

"Nice boots," was the first thing Robert said as he looked down at Duncan's army surplus footwear with a grin.

"Yeah, I know," said Duncan, "I wear them when I think I might end up butchering chickens or milking cows."

"It could happen," said Robert with a chuckle, "But then again, anything could happen here, eh Max?"

The family held Duncan and Rachel in their warm embrace for two weeks. They talked politics and chased cattle and watched the weather come and go. Glenn taught Duncan how to use a chainsaw and mend a barbed wire fence. And Robert instructed him on how to clean a rifle and gut a fish. But it was Grace who showed him how to appreciate the beauty of the place, and that beauty had its focal point in the garden. He shelled peas and dug potatoes and ate the biggest onions and carrots he'd ever seen, all in an attempt to get closer to Grace.

She was marvelous and enchanting. She had silver blue eyes that were able to face or resist the sort of things that others simply couldn't. He could sense that she was offering him something from behind her smile, and he had trouble deciding if he should be aroused or frightened by what it might be.

Like Rachel, and hundreds of other women, Grace was magnetically attracted to Duncan for reasons that defied emotional explanation or rational calculation. It was an elemental allure that tended to the baser aspects. But nothing in life is ever all one way, and on this particular occasion, it was Duncan who was pulled to Grace more than she to him.

After they'd left the farm, he couldn't get her out of his thoughts. She occupied his dreams and captured his longings to an extent he'd never known.

Once they got back to Kingston, he convinced himself that he needed to go see her again. So, midway through September he skipped class and drove nonstop to Nipawin. He tried not to reflect on the reproachful liberty he was set on taking with his best friend's mother. His life was about impulse and attraction, he told himself, and that was how it was. He was a lodestone pulling in women like iron filings, and Grace was as metallic as any. In his questionable urges and magical complications, he assumed his impending tryst with Max's mother was *fait accompli*.

He pulled into the McVista driveway with a coasting roll and shut the engine off beneath a stand of pines that was sturdy and perfect. He was taken aback by the uncommon stillness of the afternoon and thought he could smell snow falling somewhere in the north.

"Duncan?" said Grace, apprehensive but intrigued, "What on earth are you doing here?"

"I'm not sure," he said, as he watched her emerge from behind the house with her gardening gloves.

"Did you drive all the way from Kingston by yourself?"

"Yes."

"That's crazy, what are you doing?"

"I had this powerful sense that I needed to get out of the city; that I needed to come back here for some reason."

Grace looked at Duncan as though she understood him in some unparelleled way; as if she was unexpectedly appreciating the sight of someone she hadn't seen in ages.

"You must be exhausted?" she said, "Come inside and let me make you a coffee."

"No, not yet," he said. "If it's okay with you I think I need to lay here in the grass for a minute before the sun goes down if you don't mind."

She started to laugh lightly as he stretched in the sun with exhaustion and nonchalance, but her laugh ended in sobs.

"I'm sorry for crying," she said, as she sat down beside him in the grass, "But I've suddenly remembered who you remind me of; it's my brother Nick. Just now, as you sprawled out here; that's exactly what he always did when he got home. He was unpredictable and charming and ...."

"Black?" kidded Duncan.

Grace smiled.

"No, he wasn't black, but what animates us is deeper than the skin, and you remind me of him."

"Where is he now?"

"He was killed in Vietnam," she said. "He was with the Marines at Khe Sanh."

She never forgot the news reels she'd seen. Handsome silver canisters tumbling from planes end over end into the watery jungle and exploding, pasting flames onto every thing.

"I'm sorry," said Duncan.

"So am I. When I was growing up I loved him more than anything. There's just my sisters and me now; he was our only brother."

She sat there with the weight of life and death once removed. She thought of her brother's flag and his posthumous metals resting in the attic, and his brilliant smile in the warm Connecticut sun.

"Where's Glenn?" said Duncan, suddenly feeling as though it mattered a great deal.

"Up at *Lac La Ronge* fishing with a friend from town, he'll be back late Sunday."

"Sorry Grace, I don't even know why I'm here, I should probably go."

He was making his play.

"Don't be ridiculous. At least get some rest. Go back tomorrow if you must. You can keep me company for one night, at least."

They were resisting one another with futility; they were like snow sliding off a steep tin roof. Her face was flushed, and her libido made her cheeks hot and her voice breathless.

"Look, you must be exhausted," she said, "Come inside, and I'll get you fixed up."

Her body was making predictions, and he knew that it was on.

But then something unexpected occurred.

Like an index finger accidently slammed in the door of a car or a cedar sliver driven into the wrist. She placed her hands on his face, and it was a contact different from all others; not sexual, hypothetical, or chronological. When their flesh connected he saw misplaced theories come alive behind her eyes, and her energy reached deep into his being. He was totally arrested by a touch that could only be called maternal. He became an orphan drifting home.

She made him Bengal tea and fed him melon with cardamom.

He told her that he'd been adopted at birth.

He didn't lie.

He told her that he was found in a dumpster by the garbage collector buried under egg cartons and condoms. He'd been discarded, thrown out with the newspapers and the plastic wrappers. He was quietly abused in foster care until seven months of age, and then he was adopted by a wealthy white couple who were childless and questionably intentioned. They raised him in a home where he wanted for no material thing, but he said that he struggled with expectations and racial bias, and rebelled against his parent's attempts to shape him like clay. He said that he blamed himself when they disappeared. He wanted to find them and apologize for whatever it was that made them go missing. He believed that because he was motherless, perhaps he was soulless as well – and who could ever love someone like that?

"Your life has been what it is," said Grace, "But you can begin again, you know, from here. Your secret is safe with me, so consider yourself emancipated."

To continue in darkness or to fall into the fold of love, there was a sharp edge and a hard attraction to Grace's proposal. She didn't want Duncan to mistake the considerable weight of his decision for something soft and inconsequential. The two of them were briefly conscious of one another in a way most people never experience as they quietly prepared supper. An umbilical connection was forged as they listened in silence to the steel weathervane rooster rotating on the barn roof across the yard.

"You know, Robert is adopted, too, kind of similar to you."

"You're kidding?" said Duncan, somewhat surprised, yet in some way not at all.

"Yes, and we've never told him to this day," she said.

"In early '71, Glenn and I were living on a commune in Connecticut, and one evening a young woman with a newborn was dropped off by a biker on his way to Albany. She spent the night, but the next morning she was nowhere to be found. We heard Robert's cries from the barn where he'd been left among the sheep and the goats. No one knew what to do with him, so Glen and I took it upon ourselves to be temporary caregivers. Naturally, it didn't take long for us to become inseparable from him. Soon we were passing him off as our own while those around us drifted on and off the commune. Eventually, everyone assumed he was ours. And then we fled to Canada shortly after."

He passed her the salt as she continued to talk.

"Robert never seemed to need us. Sometimes I think we could have left him nestled among the straw bales and he would have fended for himself just fine. He would have grown up with the animals like Tarzan or something.

"Max, on the other hand, needed more care. He had seizures when he was an infant, and though you wouldn't know it now, it left him fragile. Robert always looked out for him, but I worried. I'm glad he met you and Rachel."

"Max feels like the brother I never had." said Duncan.

The statement made Grace smile.

She told Duncan she would do what she always did when Glenn was away fishing; drink fine wine, eat imported cheese, and watch foreign films until three in the morning. She told him he was welcome to join her as long as he could tolerate subtitles.

They watched *La Regle Du Jeu* and *Les Enfants du Paradis* before dosing off with popcorn on their laps. Somewhere in the middle of nowhere, Duncan had been seduced into the bosom of a woman with a maternal quality so extensive that it completely swallowed him in its embrace.

The following morning, she prepared a hearty breakfast of pancakes and eggs and bestowed him with a sensuous and lasting hug. He inhaled her scent and wanted to keep it inside him for as long as time would allow. As he began his journey back to Kingston, however, her lingering magic slowly began to evaporate, but it never disappeared altogether. It was an ephemeral moment, but she had exposed him to the unconditional love of a mother. A spiritual adoption had occurred that he would never be able to explain, nor would he ever need to.[23]

---

[23]#8 on the Billboard Year-End Hot 100 singles of 1992. **"Under the Bridge"** by Red Hot Chilli Peppers from the album *Blood Sugar Sex Magik.* Warner Bros, 1991. Duncan was an orphan reclaimed. But under the bridge is where he'd give his life away. Grace was so much better than anybody he'd ever met. But under the bridge is where he'd give his life away. He needed mother's milk, and she became his de facto. But under the bridge is where he'd give his life away. He couldn't explain it, but somehow she had let him in on his birthright and introduced him to himself. But under the bridge is where he'd give his life away.

* * *

He ordered the wontons and chow mien, and it was delivered to the suite just before Grace got back from the esplanade. She told him that Pierre had gone for soda, so the two shared a cold lager while they waited for his return. Their mouths watered from the smell of the Cantonese flavors that had been simmering in a wok on a junk in the harbor.

"I told Max about us," she said.

Duncan gave her a surprised and uncertain look.

"I told him how we've stayed in touch over the years, and that it was me who requested your help when he was so low back in '04," she said.

Duncan would never forget the day she called him in Arcata. He remembered how concerned she was. She could have called anyone, but she chose him. He knew she considered him like a son, sort of estranged and mercurial, but not so different than Robert, he thought. Naturally, he told her that he'd do what he could.

"Max has done well since you helped him, but he has me worried."

"What do you mean?" said Duncan.

"Well, at first it was just parlor tricks, you know, all the music he could suddenly play and the languages he could speak. Then he saved some lives, and he got in the papers and on television. Of course, people are brave every day, but I was proud of him just the same."

"What's the problem then?"

"I think he's going too far," she said. "It's like the size of his mind is eclipsing his common sense. Are you aware that he flies airplanes without ever having taken a lesson?"

"Really?" said Duncan, both humored and shocked at the thought of Max flying.

"He knows things as well, and it scares me."

"What sort of things?"

"Well, like the fact that Glenn and I once lived here," she said.

"What, here in Cuba, you're kidding me?" said Duncan. "You never mentioned that before."

"I had no reason to. I suppose I always wanted it to stay between Glenn and me. We were Trotskyites trying to move the world in a better direction, or so we thought at the time. We left Robert with Glenn's sister and parents, but we brought Max along; he was only a baby, still breast feeding.

"The boys never knew anything about it," she continued, "and the rest of our family thought we were in Mexico working with missionaries."

"So, he figured out that you lived here at one time, that's not a big deal, is it?"

Grace looked at him sheepishly.

"It's not that simple," she said. "He mentioned something else, as well; a vaccination."

Duncan looked at her with no idea where the conversation was headed.

"I blame myself for not getting a list of the active ingredients given to my son," she said, "but now he's convinced that whatever was given to him is responsible for his cerebral anomalies."

"What was the shot for?" said Duncan, now immensely intrigued with her story.

"The doctor said it would remedy his seizures."

"Where's the doctor now, there must be some records?" said Duncan.

"The doctors would have long since passed on by now," she said. "Besides, they weren't your typical doctors; I guess you might call them witch doctors."

"What? Like indigenous healers?" said Duncan.

"No, no, they were European and quite sophisticated," she said. "I'll never forget them; Felix and Aloysius, they cut a very striking presence."

Duncan's breath left his chest.

He sat on the edge of his chair and attempted to keep his head about him, but he felt like he was losing his shit. He was nauseous and clammy.

Grace noticed nothing.

Suddenly the door to the suite swung open, and Pierre walked in carrying two bottles of *Canada Dry* ginger ale.

"Hey, look what I found," he said, "we can drink it with our egg rolls?"

2013/14

-Winter-

*"I pretty much buy everything at thrift
shops these days"*

It was happening more than he cared to admit.
He'd doze off somewhere for a minute – in an arm
chair, at the beach, while reading the paper - and then
he'd wakeup and have no idea where he was. It could
be startling, especially when the identity of the
country or the year was in question. The world had
changed more than one might expect between 1991
and the present. It wasn't always obvious at the end of
a slumber where exactly you were on the spectrum of
time[24].

---

[24]**#1** on the Billboard Year-End Hot 100 singles of 2013. **"Thrift
Shop"** by <u>Macklemore and Ryan Lewis featuring Wanz</u> from the
album *The Heist*. Macklemore, 2012. Max usually looked for a
prevalence of smart phones or people completely pre-occupied
with their palms to know if he was current in the stream of time.
Often, however, he'd wake up to the sound of a song from the
Nineties and find himself clueless as to his whereabouts. And of
course fashion and architecture offered only meager clues as to
the date. His blood pressure would spike as he sat up and looked
around. He wondered how panicked he appeared as his eyes
darted here and there. Though music wasn't always

Earlier in the morning, while resting in a wicker lounger, he had taken a catnap, and when he opened his eyes, he was once again overcome by the dreadful sensation of being irretrievably lost. He glanced at the pool in front of him and the palm trees over the wall behind him, their fronds swaying whimsically to a breeze he couldn't feel. He heard the abandoned and joyful shouts of children playing in the absence of adult supervision. The weather was hot.

He was in Cuba.

He was in the now.

He recalled the ride from the airport in a well maintained '52 Oldsmobile, and the pretty check-in concierge at the *Hotel Nacional*. He remembered arriving with Rachel, and the Rembrandt hung on the wall. His heart rate slowed to the pace of a jog and the sun settled on his stricken face like a compress.

He'd wanted to come here the year before, to search for the clues to his past, but Rachel was still reluctant to travel overseas. He told himself that he could simply visit the place in an AUE (several times if he needed), but the voice in the back of his head counseled him to look for clues in real time. In the end, it probably didn't matter much, he told himself, given that the information he was hunting for had been only orally transmitted and that the breath behind such knowledge was now as faint as a radio wave on Mars.

---

representative of the year, this time it was. "Thrift Shop" clearly placed him in the now.

Then, two months ago, out of nowhere, Rachel told him she was ready to leave Canada for the first time in her life, it was like a religious conversion. He didn't know what to say, and he didn't know who was happier, himself or his wife. Soon they were booking tickets and boarding planes.

They wore their flip-flops on the tarmac at Jose Marti, and Rachel strode into the Cuban morning with an aggressive focus on her new permission toward life. She told Max that she wanted to swim with dolphins and get a tropical tan. She was over her fear of flying, and they were both about to enjoy the results of such a change.

She became a bird of paradise in Cuba, and Max was a bumble bee. The couple explored the old city and made love on the beach. She adopted a Latin flare in her clothing and her tastes, and Max found himself staring at her when she moved through the streets in a speckled sun dress or crossed over the sand in a polka dot bikini.

Her flesh grew more intoxicating with each setting sun, while his, on the other hand, received a series of blistering sunburns as a result of falling asleep in the midday rays, fully exposed and unattended. He was forced to bathe in aloe and contemplate the onset of melanoma.

They took part in sunrise hikes and midday surfs that resulted in voracious salt water appetites, one of which ended in a feast where Max binged on a plate of Chiles Rellenos and then wound up with a dreadful pressure in the bends of his transverse colon.

When he woke at midnight and began hunting for an Alka-Seltzer tablet, he discovered that Rachel had stepped out for the evening. He imagined her moving through the steamy *ciudad* with her hair caressing her back in a shoulder exposed top. He wanted to go out and find her. He wanted to bump into her in the night, to surprise her, to be seduced all over again by her disarming aura. But, unfortunately, his gas embalmed sphincter shackled him to the porcelain in a physical state the opposite of comfort.

As he slowly came to life the following day, he realized Rachel was still gone. He vaguely remembered her mentioning a trip to *Nueva Gerona* where they were to join an introductory dive tour on *Juventud*. She'd obviously departed early in the morning, assuming he was in no condition to go with her.

He would be alone in Havana for two days.

It wasn't long before he found himself daydreaming at a coffee bar on *Parque Coppelia*. He could see Rachel moving in firm silky strokes under the Cuban water near *Juvendud*. Her skin was salty, and her hair smelled like coconut and kelp. She'd followed turtles off coral walls and used a spear gun to catch Snook. She echoed the day's adventures to the friends she'd made, and her enthusiasm splashed everyone with the rhapsody of the sea. They would all be lounging on the beach as they ate guava *empanadas* before a flickering flame ignited from Caribbean fig branches.

He snapped out of his reverie and grabbed hold of the present. If he'd come to Cuba seeking answers, he told himself, then he wasn't getting far.

The streets were lazy from the heat, and part of him was lazy, as well; content to allow the mystery of Insynnium to remain unsolved. He sat in the shade staring at nothing in particular while at the same time vaguely sensing that someone recognizable might come wandering along. The temporary reprieve from the sun caused his head to cool and his thoughts went to his mother.

* * *

He should've confronted his mom in an AUE, where all would be forgotten at the bottom of an abyss, but he didn't. Instead, he drove hardheaded to Nipawin in real time, impulsive to solve everything in real time. When he reached the farm his brain was alive and his hair on fire in real time.

After dispatching with pleasantries, he came right out with the cross examination. Rachel would have killed him for being so insensitive and forward.

"So, Mom, you and Dad were like communists, right? I mean, at one time."

"Oh, Max, communist is such a heavy and loaded word, more like socialists, probably. Why do you ask?"

"I've been doing some regression therapy with Dr. Halley, my psychiatrist at Swedish; you know, as a part of the medical investigation into my condition," he said.

"Yes?" said Grace cautiously.

"So, but you and Dad actually went to Cuba and took part in like Marxist indoctrination and stuff, right?"

"What in god's name are you talking about?" she said.

He pushed his interrogation forward against his mother's obvious and painful resistance, and he refused to yield out of any obligation to kindness or maternal deference.

"And you took me with you," he said, "And I was given some kind of injection, some sort of vaccination or inoculation."

"I have no idea what you're talking ab-"

"-you know exactly what I'm talking about," he said, aggressively cutting her off in mid-sentence. "Why didn't you ever tell me about this?"

Grace caved to her son's magically procured evidence.

"Times changed," she said. "Your father and I became embarrassed for what we'd done. You know, being a part of Castro's movement. We decided it would be best if no one ever knew."

"Jesus, Mom, I wouldn't care if you'd stood shoulder to shoulder with Lenin, I'm not talking about communism, I'm talking about the shot, the injection, why didn't you tell me about *that*?"

"We were told it was an herbal vaccine derived from a plant that came from the Middle East. Your father and I were desperate. You were having devastating seizures, and you were so tiny, just a baby, we didn't want you permanently disabled, or worse."

"And the man who gave me the shot, his name was Felix, right?" said Max.

"Yes, that's right," said Grace, "And he had a partner who helped him-"

"-Aloysius?" said Max.

"Yes, that's right!" said Grace, startled by the information at her son's disposal.

"That vaccine may have something to do with my condition," he said. "Can you remember the name of the drug or the plant or anything at all? Did you write it down somewhere or something? What about Felix and Aloysius, do you have any information on them, maybe I could locate them?"

He looked overly fixated verging on frantic.

"Max, you can't be serious!" she said, "Felix and Aloysius were in their sixties at the time; they would be long dead by now. And the vaccination was just herbs; it was nothing pharmaceutical."

"But it helped me, right, it cured my seizures?"

"Yes, it did," said Grace, "and for that I've always remained grateful."

Max realized that his mom was right, of course, and that the drug had served its purpose, and whatever lingering side effect it still posed was nothing short of impossible to resolve.

"How do you know all this," she asked.

He thought for a second about how he knew the things he knew and simply replied, "Regression Therapy."

A boiling frustration rose in her heart, it was her turn to rend the veil. She loved Max, but she knew her son was lying. His uncanny knowledge was making him a stranger to her.

"Did your regression therapy also allow you to know that I've been in regular contact with Duncan Wisegerber over the years?" she said.

She wanted Max to know that he wasn't the only one who possessed privileged information. The distressed look on her son's face, however, gave her an unsatisfactory pleasure.

"Is that right?" said Max. "Well, where is he then?"

"Cuba," she replied.

He understood Duncan to be living in Khartoum, but that had never seemed right to him; Cuba seemed much more plausible now that he heard her say it. He felt betrayed and confused and immensely diminished by her revelation.

"I tracked him down back in '04 and asked him to help you," she said. "I was worried for your life, and things were such a mess. We've stayed in touch ever since. I know what a good friend he's been to you through the years."

"And?" said Max.

"And nothing," she said. "Except, of course, my hope that you might try and patch things up between Rachel and him, talk with her, Max, let her know that he's not what ever she thinks he is."

Max suddenly realized that his mother knew nothing of the comas. Duncan had kept his promise not to mention Insynnium or time travel or any of it. All he had done was stay in touch with her over the years, and give her updates on his whereabouts. He might have had the courtesy to disclose this, thought Max, but he didn't care, because in other ways - ways that counted - he seemed more trustworthy than ever.

"It can't be like it was, Mom, it's just not like that anymore," said Max.

"You mean you don't consider him a friend, after all he's done for you?" she said.

"Of course he's my friend, but Rachel's my wife, and she's not there yet, she might never be there."

"Have you asked her?" said Grace. "You might be surprised to know the things she has let go of."

"I know what you think, but it's not like that, it's something else, it's something more elemental, trust me."

"Well, whatever it is, I hope she can eventually forgive him. Nobody is all one way, you know."

"I certainly hope not," said Max.

After visiting with his mother, he attempted to get hold of Duncan, but to no avail. Either his mom had completely bluffed him or Duncan simply didn't want to be reached. Max also tried to contact Pierre, but that was equally futile.

Fuck it, he thought.

He saved up his months with boldness and determination, and once again ventured into the foothills of Alberta for an extended coma. This time, however, he used his medical training to assist himself.

While not apparent from the outside, the space within the walls of his tent resembled a field hospital. There was a military cot and a full range of sterilized supplies. There was also five gallons of parenteral IV solution, and infusion pumps operated by twelve-volt batteries to push nutrient rich solutions through his veins for 144 hours. There was a bladder catheter, mechanisms for post-coma enemas, and enough penicillin to knock an infection out of a Clydesdale.

He reclined on the cot and closed his eyes. Insynnium pulled him into its epicenter like a spider going down a drain full of fireworks.

In all his AUEs, Max had never been to the Sierra Nevada. He wanted to drift along its juniper shale slopes with a dog and a horse and a rifle. So the first thing he did was catch a Greyhound to Reno. Not long after arriving, he found himself in a saloon dancing with a couple of cowgirls from Dallas who told him they were going on a barn storming tour of Carson City the following day.

He joined them the next morning shortly after dawn, and they drove to a local airport. Moments later he was buckling into the open cockpit of a reconfigured float-plane. He'd been up in small planes before, but never in one with such an abundance of thrust. The robust acceleration of the engine completely hooked him. The experience felt limitless; a detachment from gravity as if riding a bullet; the steep climb, the G-force dive, the fluttering and graceful touchdown on Lake Tahoe. They'd surfed the sky with a throttle and pierced clouds at three hundred knots.

The pilot told Max that he spent his winters restoring airplanes at a hanger east of Indian Springs. He said he was looking for an apprentice with the right stuff, and he wondered if Max might be interested. Max told the pilot he had nothing but time.

The aviator/ mechanic went by the name of, Chuck, just like the one who broke the sound barrier. He was a former Marine Corp Wing Commander who'd spent numerous tours casting a Phantom's shadow over Indo-China. In peacetime, he'd worked for TWA, and then briefly owned a spray plane business in Oklahoma. He loved working on aircraft, and the smell of the high octane fuel vaporizing in the desert gave him the same rush that others got from cocaine. He instructed Max on the nuanced mechanics of several different aircraft, including two aging fighter jets. For four years Max wrenched his way around floating carburetors, ailerons, and blade torque force.

Chuck also taught him to fly.

They went up in a Cessna or a Piper Malibu almost every day. But Max received training on the Beechcraft and the de Havilland, as well. He practiced stalls and spins and flew by instrument through spiny gray canyons at night.

After hundreds of hours of takeoffs and landings – including many on turf and water - he left the nest for good and took to the air in solo form. Up in the ether, with 450 horsepower of radial air-cooled nine-cylinder hammering away in the soundless void, he found an affinity for the balsam bones that birds know. He informed Chuck that an eagle was calling from somewhere east of Anchorage.

They parted ways on the best of terms.

His airborne mentor headed south to Vegas for an eye exam and a poker game.

Max went the other way.

He flew north to the Yukon and lived out the last two years of his AUE as a Bush pilot in Whitehorse. He ferried supplies to remote Inuit settlements and took fisherman and hunters into the wilds beyond Johnson's Crossing in search of arctic grayling, caribou, and grizzly. When he closed his eyes the final time, he was bivouacked by his plane with a couple of geologists going to Big Salmon. There were two sand-hill cranes dancing with outstretched wings along the shore of a rock strewn river bank; black silhouettes on a canvass of baby blue and arched red.

After emerging from his record setting AUE, he spent three days performing self-administered ozone colonics and drinking copious amounts of blue-green algae. He also partook in generous doses of electrolyte cellular re-enhancements – supplements he was now selling at GROWERS. After his physical revitalization, he drove home to Brandon. When he walked through the door, Rachel said that he looked like a million bucks, radiant and rested. He went back to work at his grocery store the following morning.

They were finalizing their arrangements for Cuba when they received a letter from Bones. His beautiful handwriting was such a contrast to his powder-burnt life, but maybe things were changing. He'd written to inform them that he'd met a woman who'd become his fiancée. Her name was, Rivka, and she was an Israeli living in Chile. He said they had an apartment in Santiago and were working with farmers who'd been exploited by land barons and drug cartels. He also emphasized that they shouldn't mention anything to Grace until a wedding date was set.

Max read aloud to Rachel his brother's optimistic words, and their hearts grew hopeful as they entertained the notion that perhaps Bones was finally emerging from the shadows to come live with the rest of them in the light. But there was no return address on the letter, and Max thought about that, as well.

On their flight to Cuba, Rachel fell asleep following takeoff, and Max opened the Globe & Mail that was resting on his lap. A small article, halfway down the fourth page, caught his eye and made him think of Duncan.

The article reported that a construction crew in Toronto working on drainage upgrades to Blythwood Ravine near Lawrence Park had discovered the remains of a man and a woman who authorities believed to have been missing since 1987. The couple had been identified through dental records as Terrence and Beverly Fairentosh; the cause of death was not released, but foul play was suspected. Max wondered if Duncan or - perhaps more importantly - Duncan's parents, had ever known this couple in their wealthy upscale neighborhood.

He recalled the feckless streets and the sturdy oak trees that stood like sentinels before homes that, though beautiful, probably represented the least of their owner's assets. He remembered the day Duncan introduced him to Mr. and Mrs. Wisegerber. He tried to recall what they looked like and how they sounded when they spoke. He wondered if they'd been interviewed by detectives yet.

At the beginning of their third year at Queens, he and Duncan went to Toronto for its eponymous film festival. During the drive, Duncan said that he wanted to swing by his parents. Max was pleased with the sudden decision because he and Rachel had been badgering Duncan to meet them for over a year and a half. There was always an excuse: they were out of town, away on business, on a cruise, not a good weekend, and so on and so forth. Then, just like that, he was riding to the house of Wisegerber. Rachel, by circumstance, wasn't with them because she'd gone back to Brandon to see her mother following an incident involving her sister, a pickup, and a guy from Oka. He always felt it was unfortunate that she was unable to accompany them; things might have been different, he thought, or at least clearer somehow, had she been there.

The Wisegerber's were not near as uptight as their son made them out to be, but there was definitely an element of the reserved and fastidious about them. Duncan's father was Haitian with a strong Duvalier-like presence; he was midnight-black and wore large heavy rimmed glasses over flinty bloodshot eyes; he was amply handsome. His mother was Mulatto with a stern and concentrated expression that tended to obscure her beauty. It was no secret, thought Max, where Duncan's good looks had originated.

His mom and dad were more like awkward and vigilant grandparents than actual parents. He said they had him late in life. He was the only child of a dentist and a lawyer so he joked that he'd always have good teeth and the ability to argue. Max had to concede that in most respects the two were pretty much as Duncan had described them. In fact, you couldn't have found a pair of Oscar toting thespians that could've done greater justice to his description. If only Rachel could have met them, thought Max.

The Wisegerber's lived in a massive brick and marble house on Rosemary Lane. The place wasn't quite a mansion, but it came with the same prestige. In fact, the entire Forest Hill neighborhood was impressive and intimidating with its fifth-degree masonry archways and gilded address plates. Max was caught off guard, however, when he entered the house and found most of the furnishings covered in sheets with the air stagnant and unlived in. Apparently, the Wisegerber's had only recently moved from the place where Duncan grew up and were just beginning to settle into their new location.

Duncan's dad, Reginald, recounted how the family relocated from Blythwood Road because property taxes were killing them. However, when Duncan conferred with Max in private, he reported that the relocation stemmed from an ill-advised purchase of junk bonds by his father in a leveraged buyout gone south. Duncan further asserted that there existed a significant discrepancy between what his parents assumed their intelligent quotients were, and what, in fact, their IQ's amounted to.

Max felt that Duncan, to his credit, was on his best behavior around his folks, except for two unusual instances, the first of which was almost unnoticeable until the second rendered it remarkable.

Duncan's mother had asked her son an innocuous question about school, but the question she posed contained an egregious inaccuracy.

"How's school going, Devon," she said without consideration of correction.

When Max heard this, he thought it was strange, but decided to let it slide in case he might have miss-heard. Within a few minutes, however, the incorrect name became an elephant in the room.

"Devon, the Fulton's are coming over for drinks," said his mother. "Would you and Max care to stay for dinner?"

"Sorry, we can't, we've got other plans," replied Duncan absently, as he remained absorbed in *Super Mario*.

When she left the room, Max turned to Duncan.

"Your Mom just called you, 'Devon,'" he said, "and she did it earlier as well, what's up with that?"

"She did?" said Duncan, with an odd flicker in his eye.

"Yeah, she did."

Duncan set the Nintendo control on the floor and left the room in a frustrated state, but Max took over the game and managed to run up a pretty decent score on the *Donkey Kong* lineage. Twenty minutes later Duncan returned and announced to Max that they were leaving. Duncan's parents said goodbye at the door, but they both appeared emotionally rattled. His mother seemed like she'd been crying, though Max couldn't be sure.

As they travelled to Yorkville, Duncan drove the car past Lawrence Park to show Max the original Wisegerber residence, an honest to god mansion.

"They should have hung onto it," said Duncan, "Its worth about four point five now."

"Whatever," said Max, as he gazed at a house he couldn't imagine owning.

"So, *Devon*, what's the first movie we're going to see at the festival?" he said in jest.

"Fuck off," said Duncan with an edgy and complicated smile. "My mother has a brother dying of AIDS in Port Coquitlam. His name is Devon. She keeps confusing the two of us; she says that I remind her of him. I fucking hate that."

"Hey, to hell with it, man," said Max, "Let's just have fun this weekend. Your parents seem alright, I'm sure moving to another house is harder on them than you."

"They don't give a shit about me," said Duncan. "We can't all be as lucky as you. I mean, Rachel couldn't even make it today because her family is so effed up."

Duncan was expressing uncustomary jealousy and agitation. And Max, lacking the ambition to argue a losing position, decided to drop the subject. Besides, Duncan's family dynamics were of little interest to Max in the big scheme of things.

The following week, when he told Rachel about meeting Duncan's parents, she was hugely envious, and he felt a twinge of satisfaction in that. Later in the year, though, when things got strange between them all, she asked Max to go with her to Toronto to meet them. They went to the Wisegerber home more than once, but no one was ever around.

Max fumbled some facts on a couple of occasions when Rachel pressed him for details regarding Duncan's parents. This led to an odd and flippant comment by her that perhaps he'd met impostors – people only pretending to be Duncan's parents. She said that maybe it was all a ruse, though she made no attempt to explain why he would go to such lengths. Max told her she was paranoid. He said that Duncan's resemblance to his parents was obvious.

Rachel said appearances proved nothing.

* * *

He was sipping a caffeinated beverage and nibbling on biscuits when the man walked past. He immediately jumped up and ran into the street for a better look.

"Holy shit Pierre! How are you?"

"Max!" said Pierre with a smile that was a tepid surrender to lunacy.

"What are you doing here?" said Max.

"Vacationing," said Pierre, "And what about you?"

"Same."

"Are you alone?" said Pierre.

"No, I'm with my wife."

"Oh splendid," said Pierre, "I would love to meet her. Can the two of you join me for dinner tonight at the Imperial Palace?"

"No, she's on a dive trip," said Max, "She won't be back until Sunday."

"What a shame," said Pierre, "I leave tomorrow."

"Another time, I guess," said Max, grateful that he didn't have to explain someone like Pierre to his wife.

They walked into a café and ordered some food to celebrate their unexpected reunion. Pierre drank Champaign with orange juice and Max had a banana daiquiri minus rum. Pierre told Max that France was cold and that he'd come to Cuba to soak up some sun; he said he'd been in Havana for two weeks, but he didn't mention Duncan or Grace. Although Pierre's head was reeling from running into Max, he listened with customary patience as Max detailed some more of his intricate and extensive time travels.

At first, Pierre scolded Max for subjecting himself to such outrageously protracted comas. But his concern for Max's unacceptable behavior ceased when Max began telling him about a bizarre vaccination and the mysterious men who administered it. The Frenchman was completely aghast at what Max was attesting to, and he hoped that his expression of shock wasn't overly conspicuous.

"And so you feel this inoculation you were given is what's responsible for your time travel?" said Pierre.

"Exactly," said Max. "If I could get my hands on the vaccination, I could give it to others and prove what I've been telling you for years."

"Let me get this straight," said Pierre, "The theory is that Insynnium plus xyz vaccine equals time travel, is that correct?"

"Yes, more or less," said Max. "But what reason do I have to expect I'll ever find the vaccination?"

"Never say never; don't give up," said Pierre.

"You mean like Duncan?" said Max.

"What are you talking about?" said Pierre.

"I'm talking about the fact that I haven't heard from him in over a year."

"He's working in Dubai," said Pierre.

"And what?" said Max, "He can't return my emails, or give me a call?"

"I don't know," said Pierre, "It might have something to do with his security clearance."

Max was silent as he looked at Pierre.

2013/14

-Winter-

"Didn't Dolly Parton sing this song once?"

She tied her sarong around her hips and used the sunglasses to push her hair back from her face. She took a seat on a bum-polished wooden stool before a mahogany countertop and ordered a mojito at the outdoor bar. She savored the sugary intoxication of the rum as her senses came alive to the Caribbean winter. The man sitting next to her gave her a quick glance and then resumed staring at the horizon.

"Beautiful, isn't it?" said Rachel, feeling a little forward as the alcohol kicked in.

"Yes, quite," said the man seated next to her.

She noticed his accent and asked, "From France."

"Yes," he replied.

"You're having a cold spell this year," she commented.

"We are indeed, *mon cheri*. The Cuban sun is most welcome," said the man, as he eyed Rachel more carefully than casual. "And where are you from, my dear?"

"Canada."

"Is that right?" said the man, as his apprehensions lightened, "I was born and raised in Quebec City, spent most of my life there as a matter of fact. What part of the country are you from?"

"Brandon, Manitoba," said Rachel, "Have you ever been?"

"I can't say I have," said the man, but he smiled as though something in his mind had come full circle.

He was bald with a well-tanned face and small circular glasses that were almost like pince-nez. Rachel imagined him as a retired professor having a tumultuous affair with an ambitious Cuban mistress.

"I know someone from Brandon," he said, "maybe you know him too?"

"Maybe," said Rachel, "what's the name?"

The answer was about to trip off the man's tongue when suddenly his cell phone began vibrating and blasting an uncomfortably loud version of *London Calling*.

"Excuse me, miss, I need to take this," said the man distractedly, "maybe we can catch up later. I'm sorry, *bonsoir*."

Rachel watched as he trotted with barefooted haste down the beach speaking French into his phone with expressive hand gestures.

She went back to her mojito and the sinking sun, still casting its image like the embers of a drifting pyre.

Moments later, she felt someone approaching her from behind, a warm sensation began to flow through her body, and her heart opened like a flower. She waited for his embrace with her eyes focused on the sky's last reflections. When his arms reached around her she let go of all she had gathered from the sea.

"Hey good look'n," she said, as his mouth kissed her ear. "Look who's alive and kicking."

"Rum?" said Max, appearing pleased with his wife's minor indulgence.

Rachel nodded.

"Senior McVista, what is your pleasure?" asked the young Porto Rican bartender from behind the counter.

"A tonic and lime, Jeeves," said Max with a grin.

Rachel smiled. After years of asking, she'd finally acquiesced to his invitation to travel. When she turned forty, she felt something let go of her, like a balloon or a zeppelin cut loose from its moorings. At long last, free to drift. She felt a yearning to see the constellations from other perspectives and hear the wind in other countries, so why not start with Cuba, she told herself.

"See that fishing boat frozen on the horizon?" said Max as he took a seat beside her, "Beautiful, isn't it?"

"Yeah," she said, "This place feels surreal; like we've travelled back in time, you know, with the old cars and the donkey carts and general lack of amenities."

"Yeah, I know what you mean," he said.

The two of them looked at one another like carefree dreamers with simple needs. He took hold of her by the waist, and she grabbed his hand, and soon they were suspended in dance as the sounds of a street-side quartet came to life beneath the moon. Live music was everywhere, and for Rachel, it was the great signature of Cuba to indulge in such a delight.

They buried their feet in the cooling sand as the day relinquished its heat back to the stars.

Later, at their cabana, they rolled around in the dark like lovers do, re-mastering each other's longings and typography. After that, he fell asleep reading *The Ghost in the Machine* - an old Picador edition that had gone brittle along the spine. And she returned to *Fifth Business*, it was like comfort food with its library annotations and worn jacket cover. When he woke up from his nap, she begged him to come out into the nighttime of old Havana, but he was suffering from a tortured stomach. And to compound matters, he'd also acquired a sunburn.

She left him to rest, coated in aloe beneath the rotations of a wobbly ceiling fan and the lapping shadows of a dwindling patchouli candle. With the slip of a click, she closed the door behind her and headed out on the town.

She made her way through the evening markets littered with global tourists and moderately aggressive vendors until she happened upon a nightclub called, 'Neptune.' The neon trident over the entryway caught her attention, and she went inside to see some salsa. As she eased her way through the humid and dimly lit interior, her eyes came to rest on the last person she ever expected to see there.

* * *

Grace was slender with uncorrected vision and smooth, beautiful hands. She was extremely attractive by anybody's reckoning. Her eyes were a gorgeous silver-blue that seemed to want you in their gaze. She was natural with her movements and comfortable in her skin. When she hugged her for the first time, Rachel fell into a filial trance from which she never quite emerged.

Glenn was an accountant who didn't look like an accountant. He was good with numbers but you'd never have guessed it. He looked like a man more at ease around a hammer then a pencil. His hair, in its coarseness and disarray, had been passed onto Max in its entirety. Glenn impressed you as a man of good fortune and wise judgment, and his kindness rubbed off on those around him. He radiated calm warmth on every occasion Rachel was with him.

Grace and Glenn had discovered the end of the line in 1971, and it was found on fifty acres of farm land abutting the banks of the Saskatchewan River. On a run down and foreclosed piece of real estate in the middle of nowhere, the displaced couple from New Haven made a life that flowed compatibly through all four seasons.

They planted lawn the first year they arrived but it died and came back as clover for the chickens and the bees. Un-manicured paths took you among raspberry bushes and vines of sweet peas that crawled over fences mended several ways. There were mushrooms emerging by trees and toad stools growing wild in pastures where cows and horses ran with crows. Squirrels and foxes hid within wooden granaries and the dilapidated foundations of buildings that were falling back into the earth. With its dominant barn and rugged appearance, the place was an outpost to the loneliness of the north.

The McVista home was a lodge chopped from timber that resembled something the *Voyagers* or *Coureur de Bois* would have constructed as a trading post for whiskey and furs. The house smelled of spruce and pine and had a steeply pitched roof covered in weathered tin that repelled countless combinations of ice and sun.

Inside its thick log walls was a wood stove that could dry your bones to kindling on damp mornings or in the path of November winds. There was a magnificent set of moose antlers mounted to a cross beam, on the horns of which hung different things depending on the month.

The breezeway was full of fly rods and tackle and a couple of old Remington bolt action rifles. Robert was a hunter but everyone else fished. There were fish on the walls and in the freezer. There were floats and weights and lures strewn about the garage tanlged in miles of line and hook. Rachel had never caught a fish in her life, but when she did, she became infected with the same aquatic contagion that raced through the blood of the McVista family. On warm weather visits, she would rise to the crow of the rooster and make her way to silent spots along the river. Sometimes she would catch something and sometimes she wouldn't, but the sound of nibbling fish among the ripples of sunrise was an experience of peace wholly apart from all she'd ever known.

Long days drifted in hours that passed as slow as those when she was seven. Even Duncan, with his high octane urban needs, was pacified by the time spent living on old Indian land. Glenn put them to work on tasks that built calluses on their hands and created cuts on their arms. For twenty-something's raised in populated places, the remoteness of the McVista property was almost romantic. Under a strange and quiet force, they found an extraordinary contentment slopping pigs and repairing corrals. In the afternoons they'd fit the horses with bridles and ride them to fishing holes in search of rainbows and brook trout.

Rachel loved most the moments when she could join Grace on her hands and knees in the garden. She dug up weeds and captured earth worms while Grace described the difference between an azalea and a daffodil. Occasionally neighbors would stop by and whine bitterly about the aggression of the mosquitoes and the size of their bites. Rachel's skin, however, remained smooth and welt-free, the result of some rare First Nations inheritance. Tough and resilient, this was the land of her people; a land of myths and legends.

Glenn would tell stories around the campfire. Especially about how he and Grace once lived on a commune and grew their own food and built their own stuff. It sounded Walden-esque with a touch of *Easy Rider* and a pony tail or two. He said that back in the Sixties lost hippies came to the countryside searching for the things they couldn't find in the city. He said they were naïve and believed that everything would sprout if you played enough music and smoked enough grass. He said *Earth, Wind, and Fire's* tour bus broke down once at the gate on its way to a show; everyone laughed because the voracity of such a claim seemed so impossibly hard to ever verify.

One night after Max's parents had retired to bed, and the deadfall fire in the backyard had burned to a simmering glow; Rachel, Max, Duncan, and Robert sat on stumps passing a joint. The four became amateur astronomers as the psychoactive properties of the cannabis revealed Orion's Belt and The Big Dipper, as well as less obvious signs in the twinkling sky.

Bones began telling stories about his time in the army. He said he had his Ranger tab but now he was focused on the beret, whatever that meant. There was 'goat-lab' and 'interurban combat' and advisory tours in ravaged lands where his team would move through bullet pocked villages inoculating children and extracting teeth from brittle mandibles. He said it was about winning 'hearts and minds'. But it seemed awful and medieval, and Rachel had a heavy heart about it. He was on medical leave while he recovered from a combat injury in the Persian Gulf. But he was going back soon; to a reality that the others could only vaguely comprehend.

"I've heard that units like Delta don't even wear dog tags in case they're captured," said Max.

"Well, I'm not there yet, bro, but the truth is I won't know anything until I know it, if you know what I mean?" said Robert. "It's like chopping the head off a chicken or eating peyote, you just can't know what it's like until you experience it; after that, it becomes who you are, for better or for worse. I know guys in SF who've done a pile of crazy shit, but at the end of the day they drop their cocktails and trip over their shoelaces just like you and me."

"Were you scared when you got hit?" said Duncan.

"Fuck yeah," said Bones, "But I kinda knew I'd be okay, you know?"

"How did you know?" said Rachel.

"Something told me it wasn't my time yet," he said. "It all happened so fast, with the shock and the adrenaline. When I found myself breathing again, I knew."

Bones knew, thought Rachel; it was the rest of them that would never know the sensation of blast waves and fragmentary impact, god willing.

After that summer, she didn't see him for a long time. Glenn would give updates on his deployments, but it was always vague as to where he was. Later, in '94, however, there wasn't a sliver of doubt in any of them as to where Robert had ended up; it was the former Yugoslavia.

Glenn supported the U.S. effort to control Milosevic, who he said was a perpetrator of the worst kind of evil. Besides that, and a couple of other qualified exceptions, Glenn was highly skeptical of the United States government and the questionable ethics of Bill Clinton, though he thought *Bubba* would be remembered as the best 'Republican' president since *Ike*; oval office shenanigans notwithstanding.

Grace was more hesitant about U.S. intervention in the Balkans. She knew it was bad, but where was Europe, she asked. It didn't sit well with her that comparisons were being made between the Holocaust and what was taking place in Visegrad and the Lasva Valley.

She and Glenn would get into arguments, and she would tell him that people were forgetting their past and the meaning behind words. He would retort by telling her that the U.S. couldn't sit on the sidelines anymore because of what happened in Saigon. He said it was different now, and that she needed to take note of the difference. His attitude would infuriate her and she'd leave the house for long walks where she'd fret about the fate of her Green Beret son.

She had been raised by a Yiddish speaking mother who had come to the United States by way of God's grace, and thus her daughter's name. Through the benevolence and understated heroics of a Belgian chocolatier that facilitated the remarkable extraction of one hundred and fifteen Jews from Bialystok in 1940, Grace's mother made her way to Connecticut where she found a husband and raised four children.

Grace and her siblings were brought up under a kosher roof in a row of tract houses that fronted a maple checkered park along the Yantic River in Norwich. Her father was killed by a Chinese bullet at Chosin Reservoir, and her only brother, Nick, died the same way at Khe Sanh. And Grace's mother was consumed by inconsolable sadness from which she never recovered.

She honored the memory of her mother by abstaining from pork and speaking a little of the old world tongue in the shtetl-free community of Nipawin. She took immeasurable pleasure at subtly integrating Yiddish into the language arts curriculum at Crestview Junior High, where she worked as a vice principal. She also kvetched about the town's lack of Chanukah candles and matzo ball mix; all of which she ended up getting from Montreal through a mail order catalogue.

She met Glenn in 1968 at a student protest on the Yale campus. They dropped out of school together and travelled the US participating in civil disobedience against the war in Vietnam. After two rotations of the calendar, they ended up back where they began. And in 1970, while finishing their degrees at the University of Connecticut, Glenn was requested to report for military induction.

Grace said that when Robert was born in January of '71, she could tell by the look in her husband's eyes that no war was going to separate him from his son. The three chose, instead, to temporarily hide on a commune outside Ithaca.

Eventually, the McVista's loaded their belongings into a U-Haul hitched behind a Plymouth and drove to Toronto. Teachers were needed in northern Saskatchewan, so the couple was redirected to the prairies. Max was born two years later.

Although President Carter eventually pardoned the draft dodgers, the couple chose to remain for good, along with their two boys, in the land of Tommy Douglas and the Aurora Borealis.

One winter, over the solstice, after their exams had wrapped up, the daring students living in the purple Victorian on Peel Street made an epic pilgrimage through blizzards and plummeting temperatures to bestow Christmas cheer on Max's parents. After overcoming frozen fuel lines, icy highways, and sleep deprivation, the crazy young merry-makers - much to the flabbergasted amazement of the McVista's – all emerged from Duncan's reliable German sedan ready to drink eggnog and eat shortbread.

They went caroling on Christmas Eve (Glenn was a Presbyterian in his blood if not his faith), and their voices carried long on the frost. Glenn had a team of draft horses that he harnessed to a sleigh piled high with slough grass. They made their way from farm to farm singing about snowmen and chestnuts. The wind swept bitterly across the open fields and Rachel held fast to a buffer of blankets and sipping whiskey. A winter day could be dim by four, and positively black by six. The sparse and flickering yard lights of neighbors separated by miles of snow covered roads made it seem as though they were navigating the Northern Passage on an ice encrusted vessel. The kerosene lanterns and the breath of the strident Haflingers were, for Rachel, the only reassurances against sinking into the penetrating coldness of December.

There was a stand-alone sauna near the barn, a cedar creation that could warm the very marrow of your being. It had the appearance of a giant rum barrel tipped on its side. A stove pipe protruded from its snow covered roof and a hobbit sized door was its entry. It was the crowning achievement on a freezing evening to climb inside the sauna and sweat till you had to go roll in the snow. Rachel thought that her heart would stop each time her pores were sealed by the vein chilling ritual of going hot to cold. But she always came alive next to Max in the animal warmth of their combustible love.

And for her, that love wasn't limited; it was inclusive and contagious.[25]

---

[25]**#1** on the Billboard Year-End Hot 100 singles of 1993. **"I Will Always Love You"** by <u>Whitney Houston</u> from the album *The Bodyguard: Original Soundtrack Album*. Arista, 1992. Rachel always felt that if Duncan had had a sister she would have looked like Whitney. The movie with Kevin Costner was a cheesy and sappy affair, but the song reigned supreme. The girl had some serious pipes, but Rachel had an odd premonition that she would one day lose her voice, and though it wasn't certain how, or even when, this might occur, she definitely understood that the silence would represent a monumental loss. For her, there was something noble about the vocal chords and lungs of someone who could stretch their notes across such vast physical expanses and emotional plains.

She couldn't say for certain how beautiful Grace had been at Woodstock or how courageous her protests had been at Berkley. Nor could she speak to the delight Glenn had taken in wearing moccasins and raising bees and making chokecherry wine on a commune while hiding from the army. But she knew intuitively from the evidence in front of her they were the universal parents; the embodiment of what every child wants; grateful, supportive, forgiving. The two had relied on one another through the crucible of bitter parents and the loneliness of being separated from friends. The essence of their connection would forever transcend geography and grudges and the time hardened aspects of what is bred in the bone.

On the multi-hour drives back to Kingston, after spending time in a state of unconditional acceptance, Rachel would feel an emotional completeness permanently affixed to the destiny of her character. Leaving the birch and pine oasis was like listening to a Leonard Cohen song, and as their college days went by, she and Duncan came to love Max's parents in ways they didn't, or couldn't, love their own.

The last time Rachel went to the farm, they'd gone at Grace's request. She'd made a decision to sell the place, and she needed help sorting through the accumulations of her life. It was a long way to drive from Brandon, but even further from Kingston. Rachel thought that they all must have been touched by madness making the trek back when they were students.

When they arrived, she noticed in ways that had eluded her before that the house's logs were relinquishing their varnish and that the squirrels had nibbled and scratched the entire ecology down to a faded gray. For the first time, she could see decline at the home of hippie.

In a shiplap granary used for storage, she discovered a vintage collection of tied flies and reels and other fishing supplies that had once belonged to Glenn. Inside a multi-layered tackle box, bone-dry in a Ziploc, she found four photographs. The first was a snap shot of her and Max holding a northern pike caught at Tobin Lake. The second was of Robert in uniform standing beside his dad. The third was of Duncan stretched out on a small piece of lawn beside the driveway in a scene Rachel could not recall. The fourth was a faded Polaroid from the late Seventies showing Max and Robert standing between their grandparents at an unknown location by the seaside; Bones had a corn cob pipe in his mouth like Popeye, and Max was posing with his hands behind his back and his eyes crossed.

She thought about showing Grace the photos, especially the one of Duncan lying on the grass by the lane, but she put them in the pocket of her jacket instead, and then forgot about them for several weeks.

Grace was struggling with her decision to let go of the farm, and it seemed that she wasn't quite sure what she'd do when she found herself living in the gossip of another town or the anonymity of a city. Rachel wanted to tell her to stay, to remain on the farm. She wanted to tell her that they would move up there and look after everything. But that time had passed, and they all knew it. The farm was running down, and it needed more than a grocer and a social worker to shore up its crumbling foundations.

When they left Nipawin, there was a large formation of geese acting as an overhead escort under a sky that was gun metal blue. Rachel knew that a farm auction was on its way someday soon, and she knew that when the difficult day arrived it would bring tears to her eyes as a part of her heart was sold to the highest bidder.

* * *

She walked out of the Neptune and collected herself in a tropical waft of air. The breeze along the boardwalk felt spacious and oxygen abundant. She couldn't believe who she'd just seen. She asked herself what to do, but was given no easy answer. Grace McVista's presence and beauty, so mysterious and unmistakable, left her with several questions. She wanted to approach her and give her a hug. But something told her to let it slide, and leave her without intrusion.

In the end, Rachel resolved not to mention anything to Max. If he saw his mom here by happenstance, she told herself, then so be it, but she wouldn't be the harbinger of this particular news. This was Grace's business, and she would give her the space she needed to tell everyone when the time was right.

Grace almost looked as though she belonged there inside the Neptune sharing cocktails with a stranger in a snap dress, as if Cuba had been her home in another life; the same jewel in a different crown.

Rachel waited outside the club for awhile.

When Grace emerged beneath the neon trident, her head was tossed back in laughter. Rachel followed her for a couple of blocks, but she was smooth in the crowd and it seemed ridiculous to pursue someone so elusive. Soon she was absorbed by the shadows of streets long gone to sleep.

Part V

Confession or Concealment

continued...

2014

-Autumn-

"I can't actually say I've had lipstick on
my passport, but..."

One minute he was nursing a daiquiri in the darkest corner of his apartment, the next he knew he was being chased through the streets to the sea.

He should've never answered the door.

He ran until he sprained his ankle, and then he crawled under the wooden girder of a rotting pier that extended into the harbor like a nail damaged finger in a salt bath.

The foot steps of those in pursuit were soon on top of him. His grip began slipping from the rusty iron tie rod from which he was dangling. He clung in vain as the cops and dogs rested breathless above his knuckles. When he finally let go his grip, he bounced off two cross members and bruised his ribs as he plummeted downward into the water with a significant splash. He managed to anchor himself to a sharp barnacle perch as those hunting him repositioned themselves. He felt as though he's finally arrived at the very place he'd been headed to all his life; soon to be at rest forever among the crust of the crustaceans and the smell of creosote pilings as the lapping brine slowly dissolved him like a pair of Eliot's ragged claws.

His secret had eaten him alive, and he planned to take everything to the grave, but the revolver tucked into his waistband was now fireless with seawater, and the bullets intended to go into his brain rested damp and quiet in their chambers. It didn't matter, he told himself, they'd never take him alive. He would never talk, Grace would never die, and no one would ever germinate those goddamn seeds again.

Pierre had been dead for three months, leaving Duncan as the lone holder of the secret. The professor said he wouldn't allow himself to be captured, and he sure as hell wasn't kidding. He blew his entire French Villa to smithereens, taking all of Felix's formulas and correspondence along with him, not to mention the many ideas still afloat in his mind. His suicide earned him a byline on page nine of *The Globe and Mail*: <u>Canadian National Dies in House Explosion near Lyon</u>. When Duncan read the news, he thought about what Pierre told him the last time they spoke.

"I've re-created it," he said with uncustomary glee almost verging on mania.

"What's that?" replied Duncan.

"Max's vaccine," said Pierre, "You know, the one he claimed was injected into him in Cuba when he was an infant. The one he thought accounted for his time travel."

"Yes, and...," said Duncan with hesitation, not wanting to hear what might follow.

In earlier conversations, he'd learned how Pierre had run into Max in Cuba, and then he'd heard mention of Max's initials in Felix's meticulous clinical ledger – as if initials were irrefutable verification of something so unwittingly and independently bizarre.

"Max wasn't making it up," said Pierre.

"You've tried it then, have you?" said Duncan skeptically, "You've time travelled?"

"Yes," said Pierre, "I have."

Duncan was speechless. Pierre would never lie about such a thing; the Frenchman was seldom given to even mild hyperbole.

"His suspicions were correct," he continued, "the vaccination in conjunction with Insynnium caused me to travel back in my life just as he described. I was comatose for twenty-four hours but I subjectively experienced the opposite of an unconscious state. For one year I re-lived a portion of my life that was as real as this conversation we're having. It's no wonder the poor bastard had trouble articulating his experience, its 'inarticulable' – if that's even a word?. He's definitely not crazy, not at all. In fact, his life staggers my imagination."

"And what about his inability to time travel to dates past the year 2000?" said Duncan, "that always seemed odd as hell to me."

"Solved," said Pierre. "It has to do with your birth date vis-à-vis the turn of the millennium and how many days into the sign of the zodiac you were born. There's this whole astrological component that can be calculated using numerology and wave-particle duality. Basically though, Max's little hang-up with the year 2000 can be overcome using a few quantum tweaks."

Duncan heard nothing that followed the phrase, 'vis-à-vis'. Who says shit like that, he thought. Pierre sounded as crazy as Max.

"So, what now?" said Duncan, totally divided in his mind; one part completely intrigued one part utterly incredulous.

"They're closing in on me," said Pierre, "I'm mailing him the vaccination along with the secret to Insynnium."

There was a pronounced silence.

"Don't worry," said Pierre, "by the time he receives the information I'll be history. And by the logic of the curse, once I'm gone, Max could know."

Those were the last words Duncan ever remembered Pierre saying. The dialogue went on longer, of course; with Duncan questioning Pierre's choices and discretion, and making the counter assertion that things might not play out as the professor foresaw. But in point of reality, that's how it ended; with Pierre blowing himself up, Duncan remaining in hiding, and the most sought after secret on the globe travelling by post in a battered parcel from France to an address in Manitoba.

The vigilance of being on the lam for so long, in combination with the unfolding pressure of a worldwide manhunt, caused Duncan to wonder how strong his gravitational pull had become - like a white dwarf morphing into a black hole, his accelerating mass had finally pulled the entire galaxy of his life into the singularity of Insynnium.

As he huddled near the base of the pier he'd fallen from, he was suddenly seized by an acute pain in the left cheek of his ass. He toppled into the water and felt himself sinking. His eyes were wide open, but it was only the twilight of a fading rim-fall that he could see. He tried to suck in air, but his breath had been sealed off for eternity. He thrashed like a fish caught in a gill net and then went limp in a tunnel of light. An illuminating sense of relaxation began to fill his soul.

He found it an irony befitting his life that his last synopses of thought should arc toward Rachel. He wondered if the events of the last two days were the same ones she'd clairvoyantly witnessed twenty years prior: him, under a bridge refusing to be taken alive by authorities. Sinking. Sputtering. Expiring.

His last thought was that it all might have been avoided.

* * *

From the first time he met her, Rachel had uncanny powers of precognition. She simply saw things before they happened. Most of the time it was minor events like a parakeet dying or a gold fish going belly up. Other times, however, it was more momentous, like a car wreck or a furnace explosion. He recalled the days when they lived in the big house on Peel Street. She awoke in the middle of the night once to tell Ritchie that he had to drive to Centreville to save Emily from a hot air balloon accident. Duncan went with him in the early hours of the morning to find her. Richie's girlfriend required little convincing to stay out of the balloon, especially when she learned Rachel had issued the warning. He was shocked by the rest of the balloon enthusiasts who balked at the cautionary insight and went up in the air regardless; on the flight to Roblin their basket caught fire and crashed to the earth tragically killing everyone aboard. It was moments like those that gave folks pause.

Sometimes she could predict elections, and sometimes she couldn't. She never got a hit on a winning horse, or a lottery number or any kind of sports score that Duncan was ever aware of, although he did suggest to her from time to time about looking into those lucrative subjects with a little more verve and attention.

Most of the time she would let you know when things were amiss, and even when she didn't, everyone could tell when something was up because she looked sadly preoccupied, like someone for whom the doctor had given a terminal diagnosis. Duncan respected Rachel's gift, and he admired the restraint she attached to that which she revealed, it was never to be taken lightly. She also did a clinical internship at an insane asylum once, and he thought about the courage involved with that; given her proclivities, what a brave thing it was.

Though she adamantly claimed never to have received a premonition about Max, Duncan knew that she'd had insights about *him*. Sometimes she would tell Duncan not to drive to the grocery store or use a certain chair when changing a light bulb or have intimate relations with particular women. She didn't have to specify her reasons in order for him to listen, they all paid attention, that was just the way it was. There was an understanding and a trust among friends.

At first, he didn't want to admit that she was hiding something important from him. But he had a knack for collapsing facades, and the signs were impossible to miss. He started to notice her behaving oddly toward him, as though she were slyly attempting to distance herself from a part of him that no one else was able to see. Her actions were subtle in the way folks on a crowded bus rearrange themselves to avoid brushing up against someone with a dreadful smell.

There was a part of him that would always regret his decision to confront her. Perhaps his attempt to get at information that would preserve his life could have been handled differently, perhaps not.

"So, what do you know about me?" he said.

"What do you mean?"

"I mean what kind of future have you seen for me?"

"Nothing," she replied.

"We've been friends for three and a half years, and you want me to believe that you haven't had a major premonition concerning my existence?"

"I'm telling you the truth, Duncan."

"Come on, Rachel, I know what it is."

"What is it then?" she said. There was something pushing her off balance. She wanted to run away from the words he was about to say. She was scared.

"It's my death," he said. "You've seen how I'm going to die, and it's not good. I'm going to die violently or something, aren't I?"

He saw the imbalance right itself, and the tension released its grip on her, as though she were ready to make a concession. She became less guarded and suddenly seemed as though she would come clean. He'd touched on a nerve and the application of pressure would liberate everything.

But it didn't work out that way.

"What makes you think you're going to die violently," she said with some lingering trepidation.

Though generally able to remain calm in difficult conversations, he was suddenly angry for reasons not totally clear to him. He could feel his control over his own life slipping irretrievably.

"Cut the shit," he said, "seriously, don't use that psychotherapy crap on me, let's be honest."

"Why are you badgering me like this?" she said.

"Why are you being such a selfish bitch?"

"Fuck you, Duncan."

"So, that's it then; you're not going to tell me anything?"

"There's nothing to tell," she said.

Duncan realized with frustration and disappointment that from her perspective there really was nothing more to say. The case was open and closed. He suddenly understood that she had a code that was exclusively hers, a code that would never yield to anyone or anything, even the compelling powers of love and friendship. Her stubborn refusal to reveal what she knew about his death was evidence of just how psychologically fucked up she was. He knew she carried the baggage of an abusive family, and that her unresolved issues with her mother had probably transferred to him, but none of it excused what she denied him that day.

In spite of the fight, their friendship limped on for awhile. It took time for the grudge and the distrust to completely ossify their hearts and emaciate their friendship. Seemingly paralyzed by forces much larger than themselves, Duncan and Rachel stood on separate sides of a void that was growing deeper and wider with each passing week. Eventually, by the time graduation arrived, they seldom spoke to one another; it was easier to be silent than endure arguments filled with invective.

Duncan was never able to establish whether Rachel said anything to Max, but he began warning him about her, nonetheless. He told Max it was just a matter of time before she turned on him. He said that the girl wasn't what she seemed – manipulating god's plan and selfishly owning fates. But the arguments fell on deaf ears, and it was obvious that Max would never be dissuaded of his loyalty to her.

Duncan let Rachel go, and Max along with her, but not in a way that was unassailably permanent. Though they drifted to their separate ends, there was a cosmic assurance they'd meet again. When Duncan rescued Max from his miserable drunken life, Rachel's talismanic ability was still there like a grand puppeteer guiding the tides and swaying the opinions of men.

He never ceased to be amazed by the size of the spell that she cast, especially over Max. After all, Max understood the risks associated with her just as sure as he understood the risks connected with Insynnium, but he went back to them both as though they were the fountain of everything. Duncan couldn't decide if it was love or madness.

As far as he knew, Max had never said a thing to her about his comas or his time travel, although he'd certainly made up a lot of shit. He chuckled when he thought of what Rachel would make of Max's thousands of miles of AUEs fanned out over the farthest horizons of plausibility. He wondered how understanding she'd be when she discovered the father of her children routinely risking his life to achieve a strange and unfathomable fix. But more than that, he was satisfied by the prospect of her never knowing any of it. Poetically fitting, he thought, for the woman who supposedly knew everything yet withheld it like a miser.

He was once asked by Grace if he could ever reconcile with Rachel. But even if he chose to, he knew Rachel would never have it. She would never be able to suffer the unpleasant reminder of her incapacity to forgive or her inability to share. She saw herself all one way in the light, and Duncan would always remind her of a shadow that she'd just as leave forget.

* * *

The shackles on his ankles were locked like jaws, clenched iron bangles that made the bones hurt. His wrists were in handcuffs - the steel kind that might be picked with a hairpin in a dungeon. Whoever captured him meant business in an old school Stalinist way[26].

"Tell us what you know, Mr. Fairentosh," said the investigator with Gletkin-like darkness.

"Who the fuck *are* you guys?" said Duncan.

"I'm with the Canadian Security Intelligence Service," said the interrogator, "And behind that glass are two members of the Toronto Police Department, one FBI agent, and three Revolutionary Police Force officials."

"Well, I'm not saying a goddamn thing until I see a lawyer."

---

[26]**#6** on the Billboard Year-End Hot 100 singles of 2014. **"Talk Dirty"** by Jason Derulo featuring 2 Chainz from the album *Talk Dirty*. Beluga Heights, Atlantic, 2014. Duncan was further along the song, but still, he didn't want to succumb. The cops were acting like they'd caught the Haitian Yeti. He was sitting with a full beard and sweating. His interlocutors wanted to know things that he didn't know himself. It was getting far out, he thought; maybe Rachel hadn't seen his death after all; maybe she'd seen something worse, something too disturbing to be shared. "The mind is a large and curious monster kept in captivity." Who said that, he asked himself. Then he realized the answer.

"As you please, but you *are* aware of why you're being held?"

"Yeah, I think so," said Duncan, slightly unsure. "But tell me, where am I, and how did I get here?"

"You were shot by the police with a tranquilizer dart," said a thick-looking officer with his back against the door. "You're lucky you didn't drown when you fell off that pier. We've had you here for about an hour waiting for you to come around."

Duncan didn't need an attorney to tell him there was something drastically unlawful with the manner in which he'd been shot and detained: the naked and undivided heat of a bare light bulb hung above him, the stripped torso, and the complete lack of medical attention at an undisclosed site. What the fuck, he said to himself, was he going to be waterboarded for information on Insynnium?

A short powerful man with sunken beady eyes and hairy muscular forearms came close to Duncan's face and said, "We know who you are, Vincent, and we know what you've done."

There was that name again, he thought; he was thoroughly confused. In his disorientated state, these men, these operatives, were attempting to pull information from his brain as though the recalcitrant facts were simply decayed teeth that would release from their roots with enough applied force.

"You know what, guys," he said, "On second thought I think I need to be reminded as to why I'm being held."

"Ok, smart ass," said the large pear shaped guard by the door as he walked over to the intercom wired into the wall of the holding cell.

He pushed the button and spoke.

"Hey, Garston, you want to bring in the file we've been collecting on this asshole, he needs to have his memory refreshed."

2014

-Autumn-

"It sounds like Happy, so shouldn't I be smiling?"

-

Max walked up to the driver side door of his FJ.

"Where you headed?" said the owner of the vehicle parked next to his.

He recognized the man; he was the adult son of the overprotective and thin-haired woman with a yappy service dog who'd entered the restaurant earlier. The man seemed disabled, but Max couldn't exactly put his finger on what the disability was. Perhaps it was an accumulation of things; a lack of affection, too many sweets, a chronic infection, something congenital. Just behind the man was a rusty Chevy Valiant with the dents of several collisions and a number of boxes stacked in the backseat; clutter and dog hair were present.

"Nordegg," replied Max.

"Hunting?" said the man.

"Maybe," said Max.

"I've heard that the Sunchild & O'Chiese Indians are getting some big animals this year, pretty decent sized racks," said the man. "My brother shot an eight pointer up there once."

"Is that right?" said Max.

"Yeah, he was a crack shot," said the man, as he fidgeted with his keys.

The two looked at each other for a moment as though observing some once removed kinship.

"Is it hard to drive with the steering wheel on the wrong side like that?" said the man, as he motioned toward Max's jeep.

"A little at first, but you get used to it," said Max, realizing again that he still underestimated people's observational faculties.

"Were you ever in the Canadian Forces?" said the man.

"No," said Max, "why do you ask?"

"No reason, I guess," said the man. "You just remind me of my brother; he was with the Patricia's."

Max thought about Robert, and how he'd once told him that the understated Canadians were some of the best battlers in the field.

"Is your brother still in the army," asked Max.

"No, he's dead now," said the man, "He was killed in the *Shah-i-kot* Valley; you know, Afghanistan."

"Sorry," said Max, he wanted to look away.

"It's okay," said the man.

But Max could tell that it wasn't okay, nor would it ever be.

"Here comes my mom," said the man, "I better help her get back to the car, you know moms. Have a safe trip out there."

"Thanks," said Max, "Take care of yourself."

He watched as the man dutifully assisted his struggling mother across the cold parking lot. He thought about the many risks taken with hearts and lives.

While backing out of the parking stall, he rolled down the window and said goodbye to the man one more time, almost as if apologizing for something that was beyond his control. The same tune was blasting from the vehicle again like there was only one song left in the world[27].

Back on the highway, he passed by fields of brittle straw bails and sturdy horses growing in winter hair and waiting for coyotes and waterfowl. He thought about Kevin's hockey camp and GROWERS and his mother's farm auction. Then he thought about Insynnium and AUEs and Rachel's smile at the end of a Manitoba rainbow.

---

[27]#1 on the Billboard Year-End Hot 100 singles of 2014. **"Happy"** by Pharrell Williams from the album Despicable Me 2: Original Motion Picture Soundtrack. Back Lot Music, 2013. Maybe there was only one song left in the world, but who could say for sure whether this was it. The song remained in Max's ears long after he drove out of town. Music was like that; it opened up vistas in your mind and allowed them to flower in the light of your daydreams. He knew that for the rest of his life every time the tune emerged from a speaker or a headphone he would always think of the indescribably disabled man and his mother and their clinically loud dog stumbling around a rickety Valiant. He would also, of course, recall with clarity how his cell phone was once destroyed by a Coke and a clumsy girl in flip flops.

He imagined himself travelling further than he'd ever travelled before. He began to wonder if his ambition for longer and longer AUEs was the product of arrogance or perhaps something worse. At some point a line would need to be drawn in the sand and he firmly planted on one side of it. He told himself he would tell her everything when he got home.

* * *

After they got back from Cuba, he received a phone call from Duncan. He was tempted to hang up on him, but he couldn't resist hearing what he had to say for himself. He also couldn't remember the last time he'd spoken with his friend.

Duncan told him that he'd been reassigned to Riyadh for a two-year contract doing statistical analysis for the Kingdom. Of course, he apologized for being manipulative and disingenuous about his relationship with Grace. He told Max that he was lucky to have such a remarkable mother, and Max certainly couldn't find fault with him on that point.

"Pierre told me that he ran into you in Cuba," said Duncan.

Max was silent.

"What are the chances?" said Duncan. He told Max that Pierre was back in Lyon, but that he hadn't spoken to him in weeks.

There was another pause, and it was heavy.

"I can't say when I'll speak with you again," said Duncan.

Max said nothing and let his silence hold a charge, an indictment.

"I believe you," said Duncan, "You know, about the time travel and all."

"I don't care anymore," said Max. "It makes no difference to me what you believe."

"Just know that I believe you," said Duncan.

Max thought his friend sounded lonesome and exasperated, as if the foreign assignments and assorted security clearances were taking their toll.

"I'm going to tell Rachel everything," he said. "I'm going to tell her about you and how you saved my life; about Insynnium and Pierre and the comas and the time travel, all of it."

It was Duncan's turn to be silent.

When he spoke again it was the last words Max ever hear from him.

"Just consider the cost of trading one truth for another," said Duncan.

Max sent several emails to follow up on their phone conversation, but he never received a reply. It was as if Duncan had absolutely vanished. He thought that perhaps his friend's impulsive and libidinous nature had finally led to imprisonment or, god forbid, a beheading.

In late June, however, he received a call from Pierre, who told him that Duncan was on a sabbatical at a temple in Bhutan. The professor also said he was about to post Max a package from France and that he should keep an eye out for its arrival. When Max asked him what he was sending, Pierre said the item would explain itself.

He waited with anticipation for fine wine from *Vosne Romanee* or cheese made in *Auvergne* to land on his doorstep, but he received neither, nor anything else for that matter. He emailed Pierre several times to let him know that the parcel had failed to turn up; but, as with Duncan, he got no reply. What could you expect, he thought, when you have friends living half way around the globe?

In mid-August he went to see his mom.

"Max! Oh my god!" said Grace, as she ran out the door to give her son a hug, "It's so good to see you! I didn't even realize..."

"I got dropped off at the road," he said.

"Dropped off?" said Grace in puzzlement.

"Yeah, Keith Tensbee was fishing at Tobin Lake today, and he offered me a lift."

"I don't understand," said Grace, "What were you doing at the lake?"

"It's where I landed the plane," he said with a smile.

"That's not even funny," said his mother.

"Come on, don't look at me like that," he said, "I've become a pretty good pilot."

"When?" she said, "You're not a pilot! You don't even own a plane! And I don't want to know what sort of a fool lets you borrow his."

He could see her blood pressure begin to spike.

"It's all right, Mom, I know what I'm doing."

"Jesus, Max, you have to stop this shit, it's getting out of control," she said. "It's one thing to play the guitar and speak Pashtu, but flying an airplane is a whole other matter. Think about Rachel and the boys for god's sake."

"They know, and they're cool with it," he lied.

"They know you flew up here by yourself?" she said incredulously.

He could feel her eyes bore into his falsehood.

"I don't believe you," she said, "Rachel has never mentioned you flying solo, she thinks that friend of yours, Barry, or whatever his name is, does the flying."

It felt like an odd conversation for him to be having with his mother given everything else that he was hiding from her. Flying an airplane without a license seemed a rather minor transgression.

"Ok, so they don't know," he confessed. "I'll tell them when I get home."

"If you make it that far," she said. She knew that her son's track record in the truth department wasn't good. He'd made the same promise several times before.

Max rolled his eyes. "Have you heard from Duncan?" he said, attempting to change the subject.

"Not since spring," she said, "I think he was transferred to Dubai."

"Riyadh," said Max.

"What about Robert?"

"Just the letter," said Max. "I guess he's still in Valparaiso."

He paused for a moment and looked at his mother. She'd endured so much, he thought, she should know.

"Look Mom," he said in a confidential tone, "Robert didn't want me to say anything to you, but he's met a woman, and he plans to marry her."

"Oh my god," said Grace, she was transformed by the news.

"He told us in the letter, but he didn't want us to… well, he wanted it to be a surprise."

"I won't let on," she said.

"I think he wants to buy the farm, too," said Max.

"Really?!"

"Yeah, he's flying to Winnipeg in December," said Max, "And he's bringing his fiancée to tell you the news."

"Oh, this is so wonderful, I can't wait to see him," she said, as tears formed in her eyes. "It's been so long."

For Max, his mother's joy seemed to remedy the many overarching concerns that had been building between them. She was making lunch with a smile, he thought, and holding onto that old light they called hope. He spent the remainder of the weekend trimming trees and fixing a couple of bird houses. He flew back to Brandon after several reassurances that he would never take to the sky again without a license and proper instruction.

From the window of the de Havilland he watched as the wings cast their shadow across the land. He admired the miles of standing hay and grain blanketing the earth. Perfect squares of property as far as the eye could see rapidly sweeping beneath him. Only the creeks and streams smeared the flawless grid like a divine scar on man's order. He banked slightly left above Yorkton and made a heading for Rivers. By late afternoon, Barry was fetching him from the banks of Lake Wahtopanah.

In October, Thanksgiving arrived, and again he asked himself: confession or concealment?

He knew that if his tongue started to run there would be no arresting the narrative.

Hey, Rachel, I just wanted to let you know that our life together over the last decade has been based on a clever manipulation of the truth. Yes, that's sort of like a lie, I suppose. Anyway, you know all the hidden talents I have, well I got them by time traveling. Yes, that's right. I take Insynnium... yes, you heard correctly, Insynnium the sleep aid. Well, anyway, I take it once a month, and it puts me in a ridiculously deep coma that no one is capable of explaining. What? Well, yes, I suppose you could say that the coma is dangerous. But the good news is that I'm time traveling. Ok, Ok, just hear me out. Some months I don't take the drug at all. In fact, sometimes I save up six or seven months and then swallow a whole bunch of capsules at once and have a coma for like seven days. What? You don't understand what I'm saying. Ok, well, you'll love this part then. You know, Duncan Wisegerber, our old friend from college? Yes, I know you had a bitter falling out with him. Well, guess what? He's the one who introduced me to Insynnium back in

2004. Yes, I know I was a drunk, but the drug saved me from myself. Yes, I know, that's another story. Anyhow, Duncan and I have been in regular contact over the years. What? You'd like to talk with him? Well, I'm sorry to say that I've recently lost contact with him. The last I heard he was moving to Azerbaijan. Yes, that's right, north of Iran. Oh, and finally, I fly Barry's float plane on a regular basis to keep up my piloting skills. Yes, that's right... I learned how to fly while in one of my AUEs. An AUE? Oh yeah, it means Alternative Universe Experience, my special way of saying time travel. So, Rachel, when should we tell the boys and our friends about this exciting new development?"

In such a scenario, he saw his life unraveling before his eyes. He told himself Duncan was right; it was better to keep his mouth shut and live with the reality that he'd created rather than exhuming the one he'd buried. But his fingers itched with the urge to articulate a letter tender and compelling; a confession that would be impossible for her to resist, one that would ease her into his world.

* * *

He pulled off the David Thompson Highway and bounced the jeep down an abandoned right-of-way. He should have been more concerned with the dryness of the woods. The natural signs were present everywhere: low to non-existent creek flow, yellowing needles on the conifer tees, and most of the deciduous ones already missing leaves. He could have been driving through a kiln.

When he found the spot that he went to every year, he noticed the stream beside the campsite to be nothing more than a bed of rocks from which all trace of water had long since evaporated. He walked through the area and gazed into the northern sky. There was a group of thunder heads brewing above the peaks. He told himself rain was on the way and that when he awoke in a week's time the creek next to his tent would be flowing.

He unpacked the jeep and staked out everything in seclusion. The entire setup resembled a mobile surgical hospital. The outside was camouflaged in brown and green and blended in with remarkable effect. The inside was sterile and faintly vascular.

He pulled on a hospital gown and washed his hands. He catheterized himself, and inserted an intravenous needle into his median cubital vein. He connected himself to a saline drip run by an infusion pump. The procedures were difficult and uncomfortable, especially when performed on oneself, but necessity if he expected a swift and painless recovery.

He'd been saving time since April, and there were 168 hours of sleep coming his way. He ingested twenty-one capsules of Insynnium by swallowing them three and four at a time with copious amounts of water. It was a feast of spice that would sustain him for seven years. His body sunk into the cot and his head went heavy, and the next thing he saw was…

...the chestnut color ceiling of the living room in the old Victorian on Peel Street as he looked up from the sofa he was stretched out on. Rachel walked into the room and sat beside him. They were at the peak of their youth, and he sat up and kissed her on the lips.

"You dozed off," she said, "Are you ready?"

"Ready for what?" he said.

She laughed.

"You crack me up," she said, "We're going out for Marti Gras tonight, did you already forget?"

"Oh yeah, that," he said, with a grin that masked his disorientation.

Duncan walked into the room.

"You guys wanna get high before we go out?"

"Yeah, why not," said Max.

The three of them passed around a joint.

There were never better friends.

2014
-Autumn-

"Did you ever find those waterfalls you were searching for?"

Rachel had prepared an early dinner for Kevin and Josh. The plan was for the boys to get home from school and have a quick bite to eat before she took them to lacrosse on her way over to Marilyn's. She was in the midst of setting the table when the doorbell rang. The next thing she knew she was standing face to face with a postal worker holding a small cardboard box covered with air mail markings and Eiffel Tower stamps.

"Can you please sign for this, ma'am?" said an official yet apologetic-looking young postman.

"What is it?" she said.

"It's a delivery for a Mr. Max McVista," said the postman, "He does live here, doesn't he?"

"Yes, of course," said Rachel, as she signed the slip.

"Ma'am, on behalf of Canada Post, I would like to apologize for the late delivery of this item. According to our records, Mr. McVista's parcel came into our possession roughly three months ago, but somehow it was misplaced at one of our turnaround warehouses.

I'm very sorry for any inconvenience or distress this may have caused."

"It's all right," she said dismissively.

She studied the nameless return address in the top margin: *Lyon, France*. She felt as though she were having a moment of déjà vu before she realized the similarity between the package in her hands and the jeep that had arrived in their driveway years before. She laughed to herself and wondered what on earth Max had ordered for himself this time.

"Please give our apologies to Mr. McVista, will you?" said the postman.

"I'll be sure to tell him," she said, "He's on a camping trip, but he'll be back next week."

"Not in Alberta, I hope," said the postman, grinning as if he'd made a joke.

"No, he's up in Flin Flon," she said, "Why, what's going on in Alberta?"

"Deadly wild fires in the West Country out there," said the postman. "My sister was working near a town called Nordegg. Their whole crew had to be evacuated last night. She said multiple lightning strikes and dry, windy conditions made the place an inferno."

"My god, that's awful," said Rachel. "Is she okay?"

"Oh yeah, she's fine," said the postman with a relaxed smile. "Well, I'd better get going, ma'am; once again, very sorry about the misplaced mail."

The package felt light and mysterious in Rachel's hands as she watched the postal van continue down the street with the rest of its deliveries. She wanted to open the parcel and see what was inside. Who did Max know in France? He hadn't mentioned expecting a delivery. He'd probably forgotten to tell her; but still, she was deeply curious. There was something in the way of the package that indicated it had been put together by hands that cared. She sensed that a person of heavy intellect and sophisticated taste had meticulously prepared whatever was inside, but who could say for sure without opening it. In the end, she told herself she was simply over thinking the matter and that the package was nothing more than unsolicited samples of organically sourced, fair trade skin cream or intestinal enzymes vying for space on the shelves of Max's crowded health food store.

She'd ordered stuff online over the years, and it drove her crazy whenever Max opened her purchases before she got her hands on them; it always felt like he'd unwrapped her birthday present or something. She didn't want to reduce herself to the same discourtesy, so she let the package be. She put the odd-looking parcel on a shelf high above the washing machine where it would become unnoticeable and less tempting. She suspected that in a few days she'd forget all about it in the same manner that the mail service had.

When her mind returned to the postman's comments about the fires in Alberta, she thought about Max camping at Flin Flon. She could see him unwinding among the stands of leafless poplar, their stark and naked limbs in bare contrast to their evergreen brethren with needles hard against the wind.

All around him the fallen and dust covered foliage, dampened by misty drizzle, would provide a soft floor for his cot. Quiet porcupines and dry grass voles awakened by dusk would rummage under his truck. The fat and clever creatures of the forest preparing their homes for the cold blanket of white that would seal them into their semi-hibernation and slow winter ways.

He would catch fish in the twilight, and recline on his back to gaze at the stars. His yearly getaways to Flin Flon had proven salubrious for them both. When they were apart, he got plenty of rest and recovered from the long hours committed to GROWERS. She, on the other hand, stretched her lungs in the space of his absence - that is to say she went on runs and did yoga and treated herself to a spa or two. It wasn't like she was prohibited from doing these things when he was around, but when he was away the minor liberties and micro indulgences felt freer and less noticed, and that, for her, was the difference.

At Thanksgiving, she got the sense that he wanted to tell her something. He seemed conflicted about his camping trip. He told her that he'd made up his mind not to go. She encouraged him to reconsider. She reminded him how refreshed he would feel when he returned, like a man just off a three-month vacation, she said, and he groaned. In the end, he reluctantly accepted her loving shove and went into the wilderness once more.

There were things that she still needed to speak with him about, though.

She wanted to talk about Kevin failing science and the tattoo on Josh's arm - who tattoos children? She also had some questions for him about the aggressive young female reporter from the Winnipeg Free Press who seemed overly zealous about 'interviewing' him again. But more than all this, she wanted to confess how she had used his talents and skills to advance her psychic agenda, something for which she carried a great deal of guilt. There was also the matter of his mother. The longer she went without mentioning that she'd seen her in Cuba, the more difficult it became to broach. She feared that if she waited too long to tell him, the information would make her an accomplice to something of which she knew nothing.

She thought about Grace.

They'd spoken recently on the phone. But it was a conversation that made her sick to her stomach.

"Was your Thanksgiving good," she asked.

"Yes," said Grace, "the Knights of Columbus had a community dinner that was well attended."

"Did you do anything else over the weekend?" said Rachel.

"Not really," said Grace. "It rained quite a bit, so I stayed inside and watched movies."

"What did you see?"

"A silent film called, *Dr. Mabuse*," she said. "I'd been wanting to see it for years, and it didn't disappoint."

"I know the one," said Rachel, "I saw it on the CBC when I was a kid, can you believe it? I was expecting Charlie Chaplin or The Three Stooges, it kinda freaked me out."

Grace laughed. "I saw a film by Pasolini, as well," she said, "called, *Oedipus Rex* – it wasn't that good, but I'm a sucker for Greek tragedies."

Rachel had seen that one too, or one awfully similar in a film studies class at Queens. A series of disturbing images unexpectedly flickered through her brain, and she was immediately overcome by a wave of nausea, the source of which was unknown to her consciousness.

"Hey, Mom, sorry, but I need to run," she said, "I just remembered I have to pick Kevin up from hockey, I totally forgot."

"Ok, Hun, give my love to the boys, and say hi to Max when you talk with him next."

"I will, Mom, bye now."

She dropped the phone and ran to the toilet where she retched up her lunch. She was dizzy and felt like she had morning sickness. She retrieved the electric heating pad from the linen closet and placed it over her belly. She closed the blinds in the bedroom and tried to let the symptoms fade away.

There was an embedded trauma in the folds of her mind and, on occasion, it would rapidly make its way to the surface of her awareness to be identified in the light of conscious thought. She'd been trying to deal with the issue for years, but her fear of what the ultimate truth of the matter might be caused her memories to separate into particles of darkness.

* * *

She visited some cousins once at Churchill when she was a child. They travelled for two days by rail to get there, and when they arrived, they watched a polar bear devour a man near a light standard across from Gypsy's Tavern. The man was drunk, and he was throwing fish at the bear like an idiot. The snow was packed hard on the surface of Thompson Street, and the fool slipped in the middle of the road as fools do. The animal of reckoning was as large and as white as the North and unspoiled by the stains of civilization. It ran toward its prey with ripping teeth and swooping claws. The heavy winter parka bundled around the inebriated victim offered no protection to his major organs. By the time local intuits fired their large caliber weapons into the bear's hide, the drunk resembled a ravaged and punctured seal bleeding rye onto the ice.

Rachel learned then that the beast was not a friend, and that it could never be truly tamed. The bear didn't choose to tap the unconscious; it was the unconscious; the owner of predatory instincts foreign to humans. For years the incident at Churchill remained the most unnerving thing she had ever seen. And it pretty much stayed that way until her final year at college, when she witnessed the horrific acts of Duncan Wisegerber.

Duncan was quietly captivating at the beginning of her dream, and she followed him along the neighborhood streets. He was about fifteen or sixteen, she would guess. At first, it struck her as odd that he was so young. It was always the future to which her inner eye was focused, and except for occasions she could count on one hand, she typically didn't dream about someone's past. But in this particular sequence, it was evidently the late '80's; the men were sporting feathered hair, and the women were in high pocket acid-wash denim.

They were walking through a wealthy district of what appeared to be Toronto. They approached a large brick house covered with English ivy and another kind of crawling vine. There was a Bentley parked on nouveau cobblestone. Duncan strode past the car and up to the entrance with aplomb. The door opened, and Rachel went in behind him. The interior was large and opulent. At the far end of a regal living room was a baby grand piano sitting in front of an open glass door.

Rachel noticed a woman with summoning lips and unforgiving eyes appear at the edge of the room. As the woman met Duncan mid-floor, her body was engorged with sexual anticipation that was palpable in the air. She was clad merely in a negligee and Rachel could see suggestive parts of her flesh clinging to the transparency of the silk. Duncan embraced her and they began to share tongues. The two were familiar with one another on an orgasmic level, as though it were an ordinary after-school rendezvous for him to be pleasuring chesty trophy wives for extracurricular credit.

The dream made her a prisoner in its libidinous chamber. There was an uneasy and prurient force as her entire sensorium was penetrated by the living image before her. It was as though she had become a willing participant in the carnally charged landscape. She was certain that she could feel Duncan every bit as much as the other woman. She fellated him in a brazen and shameless three way as the mystery woman moaned with audible pleasure. She climaxed twice as his tongue smoothed out those parts of her that were hard to untangle. She pushed aggressively into his sturdy movements in ways Grecian and Roman and Chinese too. She was letting go of something, but gaining something as well; like an unwanted appendage such as a tail – both special and hideous at once. She was on the verge of surrendering to another momentous sensation when suddenly there was an ear shattering blast and the oxygen evaporated from the room.

It sounded like the world had disintegrated in a fragmentary explosion. In a flash, she realized everything was different. She saw blood strewn across the walls, and pieces of skin and bone freckled over the bed. The pleasure dome of gratification had collapsed into a murderous nightmare, and she found herself holding her breath in the corner.

At the door of the bedroom was a man with a shotgun, blue smoke rising from its orifice.

Duncan was naked on the bed and covered in his lover's blood.

"She deserved what she got, and you're next, Son," said the man, as he massaged his weapon with trembling hands. "Did you really think you could keep fucking your mother behind my back?"

He reached into his pocket and pulled out two more shells and they tumbled into a Freudian abyss.

The break action of the gun barrel exposed its jammed breach, and the man fumbled while reloading. Duncan leapt from the bed and ran at him in a flying tackle that took them both to the ground in an ancient scene of patricide. Duncan's hands encircled the man's neck in an effort to choke the life from his limbs. The man/father was handsome, but his features began to distort and turn purple, and his tongue came out of his mouth like a slice of spoiled liver; his legs thrashed violently beneath Duncan's sanguine form. It was the adrenalin of an Aztec avenging himself on a conquistador in blood-red archetypes.

Rachel's silent screaming echoed down hollow walls that found no reply or call of rescue from the dream. She bore witness to events beyond her comprehension. Her horror grew exponentially, however, when she realized that Duncan, in his self-defense, had become something else altogether. The teenage lover had metamorphosed into a corrupted version of Prince Oedipus whose fiery eyes climbed from an inferno of vengeance. He moved in cold and appraising calculation, with motives both apparent and concealed to the reach of anyone's powers. Events that should have reduced him to a quivering basket-case brought out an alter-ego instead.

At an improbably controlled heart rate, he dragged the bodies of the victims into a spacious and well lit kitchen. Something serial and Patrick-Bateman-ish took over as he dismembered their flesh with cleavers and bone saws. He slid the pieces of severed anatomy into canvas bags and placed them in the trunk of a Mercedes parked in the garage.

Closing her eyes could not obliterate the fatal vision; she saw everything she tried not to. In the random and scattered chronology of a dream, she found herself in a forest on a trail blackened by night and covered in leaves. She was following him again, but less as a canine and more like a serpent. He dug a hole in the woods, and it was deep and full of roots and way above his head by the time he'd finished. He threw the remains of the bodies into the ground and covered them with earth and lye.

When she awoke from the nightmare, her pajamas were damp with sweat and she was chilled to the edge of nausea. Max didn't budge as she climbed from their bed. The hardwood floors of the Victorian were cold as ice as she made her way to the bathroom on bare feet. The house scarcely made a creak. Outside, dogs were barking in an alley. She sat in the living room with a blanket around her trying to budge her mind from what she'd witnessed.

She watched re-runs of Gunsmoke and MASH until four a.m.

The next day the snow came.

She remembered it well because they all celebrated Marti Gras in the evening under street lamps occluded by tiny grains of whiteness. They got high and danced with beads around their necks, and she made an effort to see things through a normal lens, though it was impossible. She slipped into prolonged hypnotic stares and watched Duncan with more concentration than she should have. She knew he could feel her gaze and her pendulum-like fascination oscillating in his direction, but she was powerless to stop herself.

An odd tension began to accumulate, and she found that she could no longer touch him as she once had due to a rare and indefinable static charge.

When he went off to Quebec City with some Dutch friends who'd come to visit, she was relieved by his ten-day absence.

"Max, you said that you met Duncan's parents, right?"

"Yeah, we swung by their place that time we went to the film festival," said Max, "Why?"

"Do you think you could find their home again," she said, "Like if we drove there this weekend?"

"Yeah, probably," he said, "but shouldn't we wait for Duncan?"

"I'd just as leave he didn't know," she said, "I mean, if that's cool with you?"

"You've seen something?"

"No, I don't know... maybe," she said, "I don't feel like I can talk about it yet. I need to meet his parents to make sense of it."

"Okay," said Max, "let's go this weekend."

"You said his parents were Haitian, right?"

"Well his dad is for sure," said Max, "but his mom's Mulatto with Dutch blood. I think he looks more like her."

"I see," said Rachel absently.

The two people murdered in her nightmare were white, but she couldn't shake the sense that they were his parents. She needed to meet whoever Max had met and ask them some fundamental questions. If Duncan's parents were really the ones Max had seen, then who the hell was the couple in her dream? Both possibilities filled her with equal aversion.

Any way you sliced it, he'd chopped up two individuals in a grim and violent act and buried them in the woods.

It didn't help that *The Silence of the Lambs* was playing in damn near every theater.

She and Max drove to Toronto and he was able to locate the house to which Duncan had taken him. They rang the doorbell and waited, but no one ever answered. They inquired with the neighbors, who verified that the couple was Haitian, but the last name wasn't Wisegerber, it was Baptiste or Baptisne. Evidently, they were always traveling and seldom at home. Also, the house wasn't the one Rachel had seen in her dream. She asked Max if they might be able to find the other one, the house Duncan said he'd grown up in. Max was irritable that day, and said Duncan's parents obviously wouldn't be living there, but he took her over to the address nonetheless. She recognized it immediately and was seized by a paralyzing post-traumatic jolt.

She couldn't so much as bring herself to approach the door. She told Max to forget about it and they drove home.

Back in Kingston she tried hard to control her emotions, but it was obvious that she was distressed and uneasy around Duncan. Her attempts to stay cool and conceal her thoughts suffered a reverse effect. Duncan's presence was a hair shirt she was unable to shed. A heavy wedge began to set itself between them; it was only a matter of time before he approached her, and it wasn't easy.

"I know what you've seen," he said.

Her throat tightened, and her skin went clammy; she knew what he was capable of.

"What are you talking about?" she said apprehensively.

He stepped close and took her hands in his, "Why so nervous, Rachel," he said with smooth charm, "What are you hiding from me?"

His body and seductive presence, once so alluring, began to feel menacing and creepy. She felt a shiver of panic and wanted to run.

"My death," he said, catching her completely left footed, "Please tell me about it."

There was no irony in his eyes or veiled distaste in his words. He meant exactly what he said without any slight of hand. She realized his thoughts were innocent of all but a concern for his future. At that moment, she knew beyond a reasonable doubt he hadn't the slightest awareness of what he'd done.

Terms such as repressed memory and dissociative amnesia sprang into her mind.

"Duncan, I have no sense about your death," she said with honesty, reeling from an almost euphoric release now that she realized the beast was caged.

"I know you never tell anyone about things they can't change," he said undeterred, "But you can tell me about my death, can't you; even a clue?"

"I've seen nothing of your death," she replied. She *did*, however, think for weeks about the massive Freudian dimensions of his actual dilemma.

He didn't believe a word she told him that afternoon or any of the days that followed. He began drifting away from her in anger and resentment. She never resolved the fate of his parents or the true magnitude of the events she'd witnessed; instead she closed herself off to the whole thing entirely. There would always be a dark star animating Duncan's life, something controlling his destiny of which he wasn't aware; a primal ritual of sex and death so entombed in his subconscious that he could live out the rest of his days without ever being privy to it.

Although they managed to get along well enough to drive up to the farm one final time before graduation, it was a trip made in a state of sober awareness and holding onto fractured plans. Though neither of them wanted to try and articulate what they were feeling, the lingering sentiment was that they were occupying each another's presence for what was probably the last time.

She rolled down the car window as they approached the farm and she was hit by the scent of budding bam and juniper blooms. She allowed her anxieties about the future to thaw with the transforming northern landscape as it marched its green resistance over the penetrating frost.

One evening before dark, under light scattered clouds, she saw Duncan standing solitarily at the road. The sky appeared unknown and infinite. As she walked toward his silhouette, she tried to find solace in her choice not to tell him anything. She wanted his forgiveness for a trespass she couldn't reveal. When his easy gaze landed on her, she was fooled into thinking the path to redemption would be simple.

"I don't know what you've told Max," he said with bitterness, "And I'm not sure I care. But don't you dare leave him blowing in the wind like you did me. He loves you too much, and he trusts you completely. If you ever have a premonition about him, have the decency to tell him, no matter what."

"I don't want it to end like this," she said. "Believe me when I tell you that I don't know what your future holds."

"Save it," he said, almost in resignation. "Next month we go our seperate ways."

He turned and walked off, and she didn't try to stop him. She didn't want him to leave, but she couldn't run to him and he couldn't remain. She watched him disappear into the half-lit darkness that borders camp fires and lights temples. After that, he vanished from her life in ways that were more than just physical. He didn't go all at once, of course, but in bits and pieces until eventually her thoughts of him became occasional like a shadow.

As they moved out of the house on Peel Street and divided up the chairs and the plates, she could already see ghosts taking up residence where so many memories had had their genesis. She hoped that the gray emotions of everyone departing the post-secondary address didn't predict the end of happiness; but still, she couldn't help thinking that it had to be the end of something or other. She missed Kingston even before she left, and she missed it for years afterward in ways that couldn't be satisfied by merely visiting. Her college days eventually entered another universe, accessible through photographs and moments of sentimentality.[28]

She never had another dream, or even the slightest premonition, regarding Duncan ever again. For a year

---

[28] **#2** on the Billboard Year-End Hot 100 singles of 1995. **"Waterfalls"** by TLC from the album *CrazySexyCool*. LaFace/Arista, 1995. The Nineties were a time of great beginnings, in between Ronald Reagan and Dot-commerce existed Pearl Jam and plaid and skit comedy featuring Chris Farley. No one in their right mind wanted to be caught dead in a three piece suite, nor did anybody know what the hell 'monetizing your app' meant. It was like folks had finally realized that their standard of living had plateaued and yet no one really gave a shit. It was good to be young in the decade before everyone gave up their privacy and started staring at their palms. Not even Rachel could've foreseen the changes coming to her generation as she lounged in a hammock on the porch listening to her new compact disc.

or two, she secretly harbored the ambiguous hope that he would find his way back into their lives, but she couldn't possibly imagine in a realistic sense what that would mean for her, or how such a scenario would play out.

For a long time, she questioned whether she'd done the right thing by him. Perhaps she should have listened to her heart, and assisted him into some kind of therapy or psychoanalysis to reclaim his past. But she listened to the Great Spirit instead, as she always did; and it told her that his fate was not hers to interfere with or control. The dormant nature of his past would either breathe again or it wouldn't.

Whenever she thought of him, she thought of the sweet peas that bloomed by the edge of the flowerbed, or the polar bear at Churchill gone north to fish from floating ice, or the day's end rays of the sun as they landed among the birch trees with a violet result; displays as natural as gravity and as rare as comets.

* * *

It was early Sunday morning, and she was at GROWERS grabbing a few things when she saw the front page of *The Globe and Mail*.

"Good morning!" said Marilyn, who was working at the check-out.

"…"

"You okay?" she said, as she touched Rachel on the shoulder to bring her into the now, "You look as though you've seen a ghost, girl, is everything alright?"

Rachel snapped out of her fixation on the paper.

"Yeah, I'm alright, thanks," she said, "Just thought I forgot my wallet in the car for a minute, that's all."

"Do you want the 'Globe' as well, Hun?" said Marilyn, as she motioned to the newspaper Rachel was clutching in her grip.

"Uh-huh," said Rachel, as she found herself absorbed once more by the picture on the front page.

"You sure you're okay, Rach?"

"Thanks Marilyn, I'll be fine."

When she got to her car, she read the headlines in earnest. She would recognize Duncan Wisegerber's handsome face and smug aplomb anywhere in this world or the next. The picture was clearly of him, and she let out an audible sigh as she realized how much he still looked like Lenny Kravitz. She couldn't find any mention of his name in the article, though; he'd been identified as, 'Vincent Fairentosh' – a name that meant nothing to her. He was being held in a Cuban jail on charges of murder.

Apparently a joint task force from the RCMP and Toronto Police had been working with Cuban officials to locate and apprehend the suspect. Duncan (or Fairentosh as he was referred to), had been a person of interest for more than a year following the grizzly discovery of human remains buried in a Toronto park.

Rachel tried to reach Max on his phone several times, but the call was unable to connect. The cell reception in Flin Flon was notoriously poor. She desperately wanted to leave a message for him; she could only imagine the look on his face when he finally received her text.

She also found it odd that Grace hadn't called; she'd surely seen the story by now. Rachel emailed and texted, but got no reply.

Later in the morning, she checked online for updates.

At night she watched *The* National on CBC for further information. The authorities were revealing little until the suspect could be extradited back to Canada for further questioning. It wasn't even gripping news by the end of the day, long since eclipsed by the voices of politicians and the actions of celebrities.

The remaining headlines touched on by the anchor hit Rachel with less velocity. It was mostly stuff she was already tangentially aware of: the wild fires in Alberta that had claimed the life of a camper near Nordegg; former U.S Vice-President Al Gore's ongoing 'dollars for solar' scandal; and a funny bit about the Prime Minister sharing a vape-pen with members of the Nordic Counsel.

When she went upstairs to take a shower she missed a report concerning an armed skirmish on the Chilean boarder between the Argentine Army and a group of militant farm workers, rumored to be led by a former US Special Forces operative. When she returned to the television, however, she caught an investigative piece on the Fifth Estate that gave her pause. It was about a doctor from the U.K. who was conducting a study on the growing number of people now suffering from memory loss associated with the over-use of Insynnium.

Sometimes there really was nothing left to say, she thought.

Just beyond the kitchen window, she heard the Northern Flicker again, long past its leave date. She was worried that it might be trapped by a disorder in its instincts or the death of a mate. It occurred to her that maybe its warbling song was giving her a message, a lingering and long overdue reminder to be careful what you ask for, because the wind can blow in unexpected ways.

She went outside onto the patio with her ceremonial pipe. She pulled the smoke into her lungs with gratitude, and then watched as the sweet smelling herb was released. Her native prayer drifted up into the night sky on a cloud of warm breath and floated with weightlessness beneath the stars. The trees were bare and dark and she could smell winter forcing its way across the plains. She listened as the Northern Flicker make its familiar call – wik-wik-wik-wik, wick-er wick-er.

THE END

Acknowledgments

The author would like to thank those who were so kind as to read past drafts of this novel and offer their feedback – it's been a labor of love. To those family, friends, and editors - Norma, Charles, Linda, Tasha, Scott, Patty, Carol, Janice, Michelle, Sage, Dari, Helly, Sonya, Flower, and all other inquisitive folks who discussed plot and character with me – I say thank you. Particular thanks to my mother, Phyllis, and above all, my wife, Heather.

CPSIA information can be obtained
at www.ICGtesting.com
Printed in the USA
BVHW071015171218
535790BV00002B/48/P

9 781644 383582